AUTHOR'S NOTE

...originally wrote this book in the late 1970s. It was the era of the 'Romantic' superstars, like Rosemary Rogers and Katheen Woodiwiss. After many frustrated attempts to sell the book to various publishers, I finally (with the help of my agent, Christine Tomasino) sold *Love Once In Passing* to Avon Books in late 1979. It was first published by them in November 1981.

I had a tremendous amount of belief in *Love Once in Passing*, even though it bucked the trend and was not a traditional romance, but a time-travel romance. I didn't expect miracles, yet, to my delight, the book hit best seller lists, created a tremendous amount of talk in the romance writing industry and encouraged hundreds of readers to write to me with their thoughts about the book.

I'm thrilled at this republication of the book by ImaJinn, who will also soon be republishing its sequel, *Love Once Again*, along with another, not-previously-published novel, *Night and Day*. I'm grateful for independent publishers, like ImaJinn, who have the courage to promote and publish good books that would be ignored by the homogenized corporate conglomerates who now rule our once independent publishing houses. And I give special thanks and plaudits to Linda Kichline, who is the creative power behind ImaJinn Books.

I would remind you how much technology has changed in the past twenty years since *Love Once In Passing* was first written and published. I wrote this book and typed three revised drafts of it on an electric typewriter—word processors and home computers didn't exist when this book and my next few books were written—but the interactions of people haven't changed much at all; we still feel anger, jealousy, love, friendship, caring and other emotions that we have carried with us since a human first cracked one rock against another to make a tool.

I sincerely hope you, the readers, who are the most important component of the writing equation, will enjoy.

Jo Ann Simon
April, 2002
Camden, Maine

D0067857

Other Books by Jo Ann Simon

Love Once Again

Love Once in
Passing

***

Jo Ann Simon

LOVE ONCE IN PASSING
Published by ImaJinn Books, a division of ImaJinn

Copyright ©1981 by JO ANN SIMON
Published in arrangement with the author
Library of Congress Catalog Card Number: 80-69912

ISBN: 1-893896-67-6
(Previously published under ISBN: 0-380-78154-9 by Avon Books)

10 9 8 7 6 5 4 3 2 1

PUBLISHER'S NOTE:
This book is a work of fiction. Names, characters, places and incidents are products of the author's imagination or are used fictitiously. Any resemblance to actual events or locales or persons, living or dead, is entirely coincidental.

Books are available at quantity discounts when used to promote products or services. For information please write to: Marketing Division, ImaJinn Books, P.O. Box 162, Hickory Corners, MI 49060-0162, or call toll free 1-877-625-3592.

Cover design by Rickey Mallory

ImaJinn Books, a division of ImaJinn
P.O. Box 162, Hickory Corners, MI 49060-0162
Toll Free: 1-877-625-3592
http://www.imajinnbooks.com

ONE

An extremely handsome man was sitting next to me, but I didn't know him.

Moments before I'd been alone in my car, rounding a corner on a narrow country road on my way home from work. Beyond the windows, the spring landscape was displaying its full beauty. I glanced to the right, and I saw him, there in the passenger seat beside me where nothing had been a moment before. Real. Alive. As if he'd materialized from thin air!

I gasped in surprise, slammed on the brakes and screeched to a stop on the narrow shoulder along the road. Damn, but he was sitting not three feet away, as real and substantial as the leather of the seat cover beneath my fingers. He was staring at me in equal confusion.

Had he been hiding in the back seat of my notoriously unlocked car? But I remembered checking the back seat before I left the office parking lot.

As we stared at each other, both in disbelief, I noticed at first his eyes, a brilliant blue that bordered on ice and sky; I noted the strong bone structure of his face, his broad-shouldered body. Square, finely shaped hands, muscular thighs, and long legs. The ruffled front of his white shirt rose and fell evenly with his regular breathing. I saw, and felt, the total masculinity of him, the aura of health and strength that his eccentric clothing couldn't disguise.

But his clothing confused me even more. He was dressed like a man from another century. Besides his blue jacket and frilled shirt, he wore a vest of patterned satin, beige pants that clung like second skin, and knee-high leather boots polished to a military shine. He looked like a participant in the historical re-enactments that were taking place in so many local areas, except that he looked more authentic.

But how did a reenactment guy suddenly jump into my car? What the heck was going on?

This man was real. I was awake, and I did have lungs to force out a scream, yet I sat like a rock, inert and staring and giving him extra seconds to take action.

Part of me wanted to run; the other part was fascinated, and I hesitated on the brink of danger.

Why didn't he move? His silence and boldly staring eyes

were debilitating me. Finally I found my voice. "What are you doing here? What do you want?"

The voice that lashed back at me was deep and melodious, with a cultured intonation of Queen's English, but the tone was as cold as a January morning. "You ask what I want? Wouldn't it be more logical for me to ask you that question, madam?"

"Who are you?"

"You must be as well aware of my identity as I," he snapped. "Why the charade?"

"I've never seen you before in my life!"

"I think you are lying."

"Lying! What is this, some kind of a joke?"

"If it is, I certainly was not a party to its instigation, madam."

"Then what are you doing here? How did you get here, and who *ARE* you?"

His hand slammed down on the seat between us. "Would you kindly cease with this act of innocence! You brought me here for some purpose, and I would like to know what it is. Were you planning to rob me?"

"Me?"

"Yes, you, madam. Although you obviously were not successful. Did I waken too soon and spoil it for you?" He paused and continued to look around in disbelief. "And what has become of your accomplice? Since you surely do not have the strength to have knocked the daylights out of me, I can only surmise that he turned tail and ran when I began to come to. Nice gentleman, he, to leave you to face my wrath unaided."

"What are you talking about?"

"I know something peculiar is going on," he sneered, "when one moment I am riding down the Kent Road with a horse between my legs, and the next I am seated in a vehicle whose interiors bog my imagination, beside a brazen woman whose skirts only reach her knees. Pity you let me come to my senses before quitting this spot yourself. I can easily overpower you, and if that thought has not occurred to you on its own in the preceding minutes, I suggest you consider it seriously now."

"Nothing's occurred to me," I said, drawn between fear and anger. "I don't know what's going on! And why are you laying this Queen's English on me? Are you trying to distract me, impress me, or what? You sound like someone auditioning for a Broadway play, or a movie. This is a stunt, right?"

"Stunt?" he asked, truly bewildered.

"Yes. You're an actor...right?"

His eyes flashed in anger as my words sank in. "An actor! You *DARE* to include me in that low life group? Oh, you do possess the barbed tongue of insult."

All I could think was that the man, incredibly handsome though he was, had to be insane. I slithered away from him and put my hand in reach of the door handle.

"I am not a fool, madam, so do not expect me to believe you are as innocent as that gaping jaw of yours suggests. Try that pose on the stage from which it undoubtedly sprang. For the present, direct your talents toward more serious channels and give me the answers I want before I am tempted to jog your memory."

"It seems to me you're the one who owes me an explanation," I said as reasonably as I could, waiting for the moment when his attention was distracted, and I could unclip my seat belt, open the car door and run. I knew too well that beauty was only skin deep, and that some of the worst criminals in our world's history were physically attractive.

"Is that so?" His face reddened as he reached out to grab me. I immediately drew away, shriveling into the corner of the seat, but he managed to take hold of my wrist, tightening his fingers painfully in an iron grip.

I saw his eyes narrow and a muscle twitch in his cheek above his gritted jaw. "You're a fool to deceive me."

"I'm not deceiving you!"

"You are," he roared. But suddenly his expression changed; his eyes brightened as he leaned back in the seat, more relaxed. I saw flickers of humor dancing in his eyes and didn't know what to make of it. I watched him numbly as he began to chuckle, then drawled slowly, "Or might I be misconstruing the situation altogether? Robbery does seem to make little sense when one considers the circumstances. You are not the perpetrator, but only the pawn. How ingenious of my friends to devise this tableau...simulate an abduction, carry me off to a lonely spot, then furnish a lovely lady in distress as the bait. And when I proceed to do as is expected of me and ravish her, the talk will be all over London that I have lived up to my black reputation. Of course you could not speak up when your part in this plot is to appear the innocent victim, blind to the ways of the world and dumb to this gentleman's intentions." He burst out laughing. "Ingenious, ingenious. I'll have to congratulate them myself when I return to London. I didn't know they had it in them!"

This guy really is nuts, I thought I tried ineffectively to free my wrist from his grip.

He felt the pressure, and his brows flicked up. "You are not drawing away, are you? I thought this was the moment you had been waiting for...what you were sent here to achieve." He moved toward me. "Never let it be said I am one to pass up so inviting an opportunity."

The quick laugh was derisive as his shoulders squared against me. The hand that held my wrist pulled me resolutely toward him. The other reached out to drag me against him. I felt his warmth as our bodies connected. His arms slid around me, pinning my hands to my sides, then they slid down my back, tightening their hold. His face was directly above mine. I felt his breath in warm gusts on my cheeks and my neck. His eyes flickered with wild lights.

The palms of his hands pressed against the thin material of my dress, pulled the fabric, burned through to my skin. His head dropped, and his mouth was a sensuous blur as it neared. His lips moved softly, then hesitated not a hairsbreadth from my own. He was so close I could smell the spiciness of him, as well as his sweat, and could see the barely evident new growth of beard on his clean-shaven cheeks.

Then suddenly he released me. I fell in a heap against the car door. I didn't know whether to laugh or cry. I stared open-mouthed at his receding face.

He was chuckling. "You can close your mouth now. I was testing my theory, but your reaction puzzles me."

"What did you expect?"

"Cold feet, my dear?"

"You're actually enjoying this!"

"I have not found it particularly enjoyable to this point," he retorted.

"Then what do you want from me?"

He studied me critically. "Outward appearances aside, you do seem too ladylike to be involved in this prank. I'm guessing you're in way over your head. I am just wondering which of my cohorts enlisted you—what methods of persuasion they used to get you here. I immediately think of Overton, but doubt he has the courage to run into a dark alley by himself, so it must have been Gresham." I stared at him dumbly. "Oh, I realize you're not going to give them away, but your naivete amazes me. What did you think was in store for you when you agreed to play this part?"

"I repeat, I don't know what you're talking about!"

"Really I'm not such a brute that you can't make an honest, if somewhat tardy, confession to me without fear of retribution." His eyes glanced beyond the car windows into the deepening dusk. "By the way, what have you done with my horse? Not that I think for a moment you will tell me, but I'd hate like the devil to lose him. Damned valuable piece of horseflesh."

I shrugged dumbly.

"You don't appear to know a great deal about anything, do you?" he flashed out bitingly.

"What do you want me to tell you?"

"I didn't ask to come here, my dear. Nor did I ask to be placed in these circumstances. If I had the vaguest notion of my whereabouts, I myself would be only too happy to leave."

"Then why don't you?" I felt so Goddamned impotent and frustrated. "What do you want me to say? Tell me the words you want to hear and I'll say them. Just so you'll let me go..."

His blue eyes were puzzled. He squinted. "There is obviously a misunderstanding here. But damned if I know what it is. Listen to me," he shouted at my white face. "Hear me out, for God's sake! I do not intend to harm you."

"I don't believe you."

"Why, may I ask?"

"Why?" I was flabbergasted. "You ask me why— after you break into my car, come at me like a maniac, accuse me of things that make no sense. And look at you! Dressed up like someone out of a history book." I noticed his eyes dropping over his clothing as if he couldn't help himself. "And the way you talk, with that high-sounding English accent—I feel like I'm listening to the sound track of an old movie with m'lord and m'lady and the knights in shining armor."

He held my forearm tightly. From the expression on his face, I gathered he wasn't pleased with my last remarks. "If it is any consolation to you, I find your actions and your behavior and your dress and speech just as shocking. Are you prepared to listen to me?"

I nodded, but my jaw was set, and if it weren't for his fingers gripping me, I would have put as much distance between us as possible.

His brow was furrowed in a dark frown. "When I left London shortly after dusk this evening, I was intent on arriving at my home in Kent before midnight." He shot me a quizzical look. "Although since it is now twilight, I suppose I should correct that to last evening?" I made no comment, and after a short pause, he continued. "At any rate, I was setting a good pace. I was ten miles short of Cavenly when I recall my horse became a bit edgy. I remember checking him with the reins in an effort to keep him to the center of the track, out in the moonlight. I suspected that there might be some culprit hidden in the hedges waiting to waylay me." He threw a dampening look in my direction. "My next clear thought is of looking out this window over here, seeing the unfamiliar scenery and suddenly waking up to the fact that my horse was no longer beneath me. I glance over to be greeted by a most unwelcoming pair of eyes—yours, madam—and what am I to think but that I've been knocked senseless, probably robbed and, for some unknown reason, carried off to this spot where I am being held captive by a very defenseless looking woman. Either that, or I have gone stark raving mad!"

I tended to agree with his last supposition, though I didn't say anything. What an imagination the man had. I smiled at him, sitting there so complacently, as if his story would settle everything. "You're crazy. You must know as well as I do that you're not making any sense. How could you be riding down a lane on horseback one minute, and the next be sitting in my car? And you're talking about England, I presume. But that's impossible, too, unless you're trying to tell me it's plausible now to make a transoceanic flight in the blink of an eyelash—without benefit of a plane! And that still doesn't explain how you managed to appear out of nowhere. If that isn't enough, you physically threaten me, try to rape me, insult me, scare me so much I don't know if I'm coming or going while all the while it's you who found a way to sneak in here and scare the shit out of me for some reason I've yet to figure out. I don't know where you came from, and I don't accept a word of your cock-and bull story."

He was laughing a deep rumbling sound that shook his shoulders. Nothing I'd said seemed to have fazed him. "You have a way with words, my dear. I foresee great success for your future on the stage."

"God damn you!" That was the last straw, and in fury I spit in his face.

He laughed all the harder, wiping off the spittle on his cheek with the back of his hand. "Then pray give me an argument I can swallow without choking on it."

"And I shouldn't be choking on your story? Here I was,

driving peacefully home from work, alone, when you drop in to scare the hell out of me!"

He glanced quickly out through the front windshield.

"You might be good enough to explain to me how you drove here with no horses in the shafts, when I can look out and see with my own eyes that none are there. Or am I to surmise they are invisible—just as I appeared out of nothingness?"

"Since when do you need horses to drive a car?" I asked in disbelief.

"I suppose this extraordinary vehicle of yours is self-propelled?"

"Isn't yours? Oh, no, I forgot—you ride a horse."

"On occasion, but this is not a horse."

"This is an automobile, kind sir. You have heard of them, I presume?"

"I have not."

"Well, I hate to disillusion you, but we're not living back in the days of the horse and buggy."

"It has not occurred to me I am living anywhere but where I was before I lost consciousness." He was furious.

I thought it was becoming rather amusing. "You said that was Kent?"

"Yes!" His eyes were hard. The glittering blue was barely visible.

"Kent, England?"

"Where else, woman?"

"Well, you're a hell of a long way from home."

"Is that so," he sneered. "Suppose you tell me exactly where I am."

"In the United States, of course—where you've been all along except for this fish story you've made up. If you're so intent on reenacting a drama from the pages of history, you should have chosen a spot closer to your supposed home!"

"That is impossible! You are lying."

"Why should I lie? This is Eastport, Connecticut. If you think you're somewhere else, you must be living in a fantasy. Which doesn't say too much for your story, does it?"

"Nor yours, since I am telling the truth!"

"And so am I." I saw his obvious signs of fury, the veins standing out in his neck. But now I was intent on the crazy game we were playing. "All right, I won't argue with you," I continued. "But what's the date today?"

"I am sure you know as well as I it is the fifth of May...the fifth of May, 1812."

I shouldn't have been surprised. His period costume and speech fit in very well with the year he had stated.

"So you're a man from 1812. I suppose the next thing you're going to tell me is that you're some English lord or other?"

"That is precisely who I am, dear woman, and I'll thank you not to take that tone of voice with me."

"Oh, a lord! No doubt with fabulous estates, a London house, prominence that will boggle my mind?"

He glowered at me. "I wouldn't have chosen exactly those words to describe myself, but since you have, yes!"

"You even believe it yourself."

"Damn! Of course I do. It is the truth. My birth and precedents are evident, which is far more than I can say for yours. Though I suppose I should take into account the fact that you are obviously not an Englishwoman."

"I'm not. And I'm proud of it if the way you're behaving is any example of an English gentleman."

"And whom," he drawled, "have I had the dubious honor of addressing?"

"If you're asking my name, I'm Jessica Lund—Ms. Lund to you—but why I should even tell you is beyond me."

"Delighted, I'm sure. Westerham—the earl of Westerham."

"Oh! Pardon me, I'm addressing an earl."

"You are, woman. Be good enough to remember that fact."

"Shall I kiss your feet now or later?"

"Enough of that sharp tongue, or I'll be more than happy to make it temporarily useless to you!"

"What are you planning to do? Cut it out? Is force the only means you know to make your point, Your Lordship? Well, I have a few plain facts to lay before your feet." I glared at his handsomely stubborn face. "First, let me tell you on good authority that this is not 1812. This is 1981, and whether you like living in this age or not, whether you think the past had far more romance and adventure than our current age, you are here. Second, this is Connecticut, and I'm sorry if you thought you were still in England—you're not. Third, whether you're a lord in fact or not, which I seriously doubt, you are on democratic soil, and don't you dare be condescending to me. Last, this is my world and my car, and you were not invited into either. You are interrupting the peaceful functioning of my life, and if either of us is to continue functioning happily, one of us has to go. Be it you or me, I'm not going to sit here and play this silly game a second longer." I reached down and unclipped my seat belt.

"Why you little vixen," he roared. "How dare you?" He had me with both hands now, shaking me so my teeth fairly rattled in my head. "Never have I had a woman speak to me like this."

"Maybe it's time one did! Why don't you wake up? Look around you. It's time someone shook you loose from your delusions before you're beyond help. This is the twentieth century, and I don't think you're as crazy as you'd like me to think with this eighteen-hundreds act of yours."

"You think I am mad!"

"What else do you expect me to think?" I didn't like the look on his face. I tried to temper it a little. "Maybe you've had a nervous breakdown or something. Look, maybe if I drove you around, down some of the streets, through town, you might see something familiar. What harm would there be in that? It might help you get your bearings. All right?" I pushed my point further as I saw a tiny hint of receptiveness or, just as likely, confusion, in his eyes. "If you'll just let go of my hands for a minute. I'm not trying to run away."

His fingers loosened their pinching hold, and I took that second to pull free and whirl around in my seat. I turned the keys in the ignition, stabbed the gas pedal and heard the engine roar to life. He heard it, too, and stared in astonishment. I threw the car into gear and skidded off down the road.

He sat frozen in amazement. The only movement he made was to drop his hands to the seat and turn his head to have full view of the scene flashing by the window. I heard him mutter a startled expletive under his breath as I raced the car away from the isolated residential districts toward people, toward help. We whizzed past a small neighborhood shopping center. A motorcycle flew by at breakneck speed. We passed the overpass to the parkway. It was only about two more miles to town.

The bewilderment etched on his tanned features was complete. Could he really think he was from another age? Or, inadmissible as the thought seemed, could he be telling me the truth...or at least what he thought to be the truth? I hadn't seen anyone hiding in the car when I left work, but then how had he gotten there? I'd made no stops. Was *I* going crazy?

Suddenly, he grabbed the steering wheel and pulled it from my fingers. The car veered to the right and up on the shoulder of the road, where it promptly stalled before my foot could get to the clutch.

"What are you doing?" I cried.

His hand still gripped the wheel. When I turned my head, he was facing me, a mystified yet excited look in the terribly blue eyes. His voice held the urgency of sudden discovery. "By God, it's beginning to make sense! All the pieces fit like the parts of a puzzle. I don't believe it! That is why I don't remember being attacked. Why one moment I was on horseback and the next beside you. Why, when last I remember it was late evening and pitch black were it not for the light of the moon." His eyes searched mine penetratingly. "Do you realize what has happened?" He shook his head quickly, "No, of course you do not. You have not believed a word I've said thus far. But it is clear as day to me now. Everything falls so perfectly into place, I have trouble believing it myself. Do you realize I have just jumped into my future, with no more difficulty than a snap of a finger? I have just made a journey of nearly two hundred years, and I'm here to talk about it." He slapped his hands against his legs and his arms as if to assure himself he was all there. "I'm here! I'm alive! I'm well! It is completely and utterly extraordinary!"

"I don't think you've got it quite right—"

His eyes cast about hungrily. He didn't wait for confirmation from me. "And all these inventions! Just this fantastic vehicle alone, and did you see that machine flying by us before? Look at us, tearing along the highway at speeds I never in my wildest imagination thought I'd live to experience. What is it that powers this vehicle? An engine no doubt, but steam? Or something more modern?"

He was firing questions at me so quickly I couldn't answer them.

"What else can you show me? These pavements alone are marvelous." I raised my eyebrows when I thought of the potholes I'd just skirted. "To think of never getting mired in the mud and ruts. And what are these poles and wires up in the sky? What purpose do they serve? And those boxes hanging over the roadway with the colored lights? Could they possibly be signals of some kind?"

He would have continued further, but I motioned him to be quiet. "Wait a minute. Just wait and let me think. What are you trying to tell me?" I scowled. "You don't really expect me to believe you just jumped out of the past?"

"But of course I do." He was grinning, a childlike grin of wonderment. "Do you not see what has happened?"

"No! I don't see anything at all. All I see is a man who was very confused a few minutes ago, who now thinks he knows what has happened. But you've got it all wrong. You couldn't have jumped from the past— you only think you did." I wagged my head in defeat at the unrelenting and unprecedented things happening to me. "Oh, God, I don't know what to think anymore. I don't know what's going on. Why don't you just leave me alone?" I closed my eyes wearily for a second.

"You still think me insane, do you not?" he asked. "You do not have to deny it. I can see it in your eyes." His bored into me. "Whatever you may think of me," he continued in an entirely sane-sounding voice, "I am not a fool, nor did I leave my faculties behind me. I am not a dreamer and not inclined to wild fantasies. I am normally a level-headed man who sees and believes only what is in front of his eyes, and I am not imagining what I am seeing at this moment. I see a greenish-eyed young woman clothed in a dotted dress that is far too short, with hair falling about her eyes when it should be atop her head. I see houses and scenery around me I have never seen before. I see self-propelled machines flying by the windows and am seated in one myself. I see all manner of things that are new to me. Yet, from the accusations you have thrown at me, you seem to think me a modern man deluding myself that I have just sprung from the past. I can't tell you how wrong you are. It is a complete riddle to me to find myself in a place and time I'd no inclination to ever be. Yet it is real. I am not lying to you. Believe me, I have nothing to gain by telling you I am someone I am not, though I do have a great deal to lose in my own world by being here. I am the earl of Westerham, Miss Lund, and I have just walked out of the pages of history to pay you a call."

I took the opportunity once again to give him careful scrutiny. His clothing was expensive, as was obvious by the texture of the cloth and the fine tailoring, and it did look like the pictures I'd seen of clothing men had worn during the early nineteenth century. His dark hair was cut in a shaggy, longish style that hung to his earlobes and encouraged natural curling. A very attractive style, I thought. Still, it could all be a costume. "You'll have to give me a lot more proof than you have," I said finally. "I could put you in jeans, and no one could tell the difference between you and any other guy walking down the street."

"Jeans? What are they? I've never heard that term before."

"Blue jeans," I said. "Don't tell me you've never heard of them before? Blue died denir work pants that first became popular during the California gold rush? Please, give me a break!"

He chuckled, "I fear my tailor would be highly insulted by your comparisons. You have heard of Weston?"

"I've read about him, but you could have, too. Who's to say he made that jacket?"

With a self-assured gesture, he pulled open his coat to show me the tailor's label stitched neatly to the silk.

I wasn't convinced, much as I was taken aback. "So it's your great-great-great grandfather's jacket that you dug up out of a trunk in the attic."

He took a deep breath. "I see I shall have to provide you with indisputable evidence."

"Yes!" I never thought for a moment he could. As I watched, he reached into his pocket and pulled out a leather purse, from which he poured a handful of coins. He took my hand, turned it upward, and slowly dropped them into my palm. For a moment I was too startled to do more than stare at the glowing discs. I'd never seen gold money in my life, but I knew enough to realize these were the genuine article and worth a small fortune.

I gaped at him.

"Well, go ahead," he said, eyes twinkling. "Examine them. You wanted more proof."

I switched on the car light and, gingerly at first, then more eagerly, turned them over one by one in my fingers. My stupefaction increased at the coinage dates flashing before my eyes: 1798, 1802, 1811, 1795. All bore the likeness of His Majesty George III. Any collector would have given his eyeteeth to own two or three, let alone the dozen or so that were now in my hand.

"You observed the dates?' he drawled. I nodded. "They appear authentic to you, do they not?" Again I nodded. "Now you might tell me how I came to be in possession of these coins if the story I am telling you is not the truth."

"Out of the same trunk."

"By God is there no end to your skepticism? Does it seem probable to you that anyone would be fool enough to stash this much gold coin in an attic trunk?" He sighed in exasperation and began digging once more through his inside pockets.

This time he produced a packet of folded papers of various sizes. He slapped them into my free hand, collecting the coins from my other and returning them to his purse.

"What are these?"

"Letters written to me in the past several days. One I began writing myself before I left London today. Read them," he insisted.

I unfolded the first one in the stack and began scanning the page. It was of vellum and crinkled under my touch. The letter was dated 3rd May, no year, and was addressed to the Hon. Earl of Westerham, St. James Square, London. The writer was a member of a law firm, and the letter laid out the expenses for the first quarter on some property in Sheeps Street, London. The paper was new, the ink fresh, the handwriting florid but not too difficult to read. I unfolded the next eagerly, reading it quickly, then going on to the remaining letters. I was fascinated. The subjects were varied, although they all seemed to refer to political and business matters. The letter addressed simply "Westerham" was a plea for support on a trade bill up before Parliament and was signed so illegibly I couldn't make out the signature. Another, written by a partner in the firm of Cooke & Sons, went into a huge amount of detail on the advisability of the earl's further investing in a newly formed shipping company due to the unstable relations with the American states and the possible embargo on shipments to that country. One other mentioned some relative's gambling debts with a very careful question about whether the earl would stand to make them good. Postage franks appeared on the back of two letters. The others had only the earl's address and broken wax seals.

I looked last at the letter he had written. I was struck by the bold, forceful handwriting that swept impatiently across the page. It was dated 5th May 1812 and addressed to George Pembrick, Esq., Pembrick & Sayers, Fleet Street, London. It wasn't finished, stopping abruptly in the middle of the second page with a half finished sentence, but the crest at the head of the ivory sheets left no doubt as to the identity of the writer. "As regards the Downshead property in Surrey, I am putting five hundred pounds at your disposal to make whatever repairs you deem..." I read no further, feeling like I was prying into things that were none of my business.

I rested my eyes blindly on the unfinished letter and had the very definite feeling that these were genuine. The paper was too new, the ink too fresh to allow for their having been stored in a dusty trunk for the last hundred and eighty years.

"This is absolutely unreal." I shook my head slowly. "I can't believe it."

"But what more could you want? You have already told me I look, act, and dress the part. You have seen my letters, the contents of my purse. Unfortunately, I am not in the habit of carrying about my birth documents in order to prove my identity to disbelieving women. Would you like me instead to recite the birth dates of George III and his numerous family? Or perhaps you would care for a description of the bills presented before the House of Lords this past session. I am a member, you know. I was in the House this afternoon, by the way, before embarking on this fantastic journey. Or perhaps you would prefer a recitation of the attendees at the last Almacks ball, or better yet, Sally Jersey's soiree last evening?"

I knew enough history and had read enough Regency novels to know what he was talking about when he mentioned Almacks, those select assembly rooms where admission was by voucher only to the choicest of society's young ladies, and where Lady Sally Jersey, the reigning queen of London society at the time and, supposedly, onetime mistress to the Prince of Wales ruled. It didn't seem likely that even a maniacal genius could come up with so many points of evidence so quickly. I was dizzy just considering it.

"But it's impossible," I argued. "Just utterly impossible!"

"You think I don't realize the impossibilities of the situation?" His voice was firm, as emphatic as my own.

"'There must be another explanation."

"What do you suggest?"

"I don't know." I buried my face in my hands for a moment. "But you can't just have jumped here like magic from 1812."

"If you are suggesting I came by normal means, living through each individual year, you will have to admit I have aged remarkably little for a man of approximately two hundred years." His lips curled teasingly, although I knew he was deadly serious.

"That's not what I'm suggesting at all. I'm suggesting that you're a bold-faced liar with a more than working knowledge of English history."

"I admit you have had a stranger thrust upon you—one who could be telling a well-oiled lie about his identity—but that hardly explains how I arrived here this afternoon. How I seemed to have appeared out of nowhere, as you described it. I am not sure myself how I could perform that stunt unless I was telling the truth."

"You could be a liar with skilled acting abilities."

He sighed, his eyes looking heavenward for support. "Even liars and actors have their limitations."

There was merit to what he was saying. I couldn't explain

his sudden appearance any more than he claimed he could. I was silent as my mind searched for any theory that might be remotely plausible. Could he, in some incredible way, have been picked up intact out of the stream of life back in 1812 and held in a suspended state by a force or power neither of us had the knowledge to understand? Could his essence have been held until today, when he'd suddenly been reinjected into life's stream? It seemed to me that Einstein had a theory about time being a river and people moving, like logs floating on the surface, from one point to another...but I wasn't sure. Today was May 5th and in the same month, the same day as he described — nearly two hundred years later. But why was he here in Connecticut and not in his own home?

"Are you still with me?" His deep voice interrupted my contemplations. I looked up to give him a blank stare.

"You are reasoning it out, I presume?"

I nodded.

"And have you decided my fate?" He smiled, knowing perfectly well I hadn't the power to decide that.

"No, I was only thinking, trying to figure out what's happened—whether you are a liar, or I'm just being thickheaded."

Surprisingly, he reached out and laid a gentle hand on my shoulder. There was understanding in his voice. "Would you believe me," he asked, "if I told you I have a very good idea what is going through your mind, and I sympathize? I fear that there is no easy explanation, but couldn't we for now, instead of pondering the unanswerable, accept it for what it is? I am tired of arguing with you. I am tired of trying to untangle the mystery. I only know one thing for certain—and that is I am here, explainable or not. Until and unless I fade out of your life, much as I entered it, I'm afraid I'm in your hands."

Two

I don't know what it was about him—maybe the sincerity in his eyes, the firmness of his convictions, or the evidence he'd shown me—that changed my feelings about him in midstream from cynicism to trust—that made me look into his pensive and unsettling blue eyes and tell him I would try to accept the incredible—that he'd been jettisoned here from another age. I offered to bring him to my home and give him any help I could until the mystery was solved.

It was hardly the cautious, practical part of me that offered. It was the adventuress, the prober, the spirited half that was unwilling to listen to convention and sensibility.

Before starting the engine, I studied him carefully, hoping that I was right in trusting these hastily made impressions, that I wasn't bringing a rapist home to my bed. He took in my stare without comment, and after a moment I returned my gaze to the road before me and started the car.

"I suppose we should come to some agreement on what to call each other," I mused. "Or do you insist on Your Lordship?"

"No. Let us dispense with formalities. My name is Christopher."

"Christopher...Westerham, was it?"

"Dunlap. I am the earl of Westerham, but Christopher Dunlap."

"To me you'll be Christopher Dunlap. Perhaps it's none of my business, but are you married?"

His eyes swung to me for a moment before he answered. "No."

"I was curious."

"A logical question under the circumstances. Are you?"

"Married? No."

"And did I hear you correctly when you said you were bringing me to your home?"

"I wouldn't know where else to take you, unless you'd rather I took you to the authorities so you could explain your situation to them."

"Hardly! However I cannot quite summon the image of your family welcoming me with open arms—a perfect stranger you have picked up more or less," he chuckled, "off the side of the road."

"There'll be no one to question me. I don't live with my family." The thought crossed my mind that I was being too frank. The wise thing to do would be to proceed with caution until I was sure of the truth of his story. Still, something about him provoked an honesty in me that went beyond the bounds of common sense. I felt an intrinsic truthfulness about him, and I didn't think it was my own heedless desire for adventure that told me that. Of course I tried not to discredit that he was one of the most handsome men I'd ever met in my life. Yet there was more to him than just that perfect appearance. He had an air of intelligence and perceptiveness, and it seemed, an underlying warm sensitivity that didn't speak of a selfish, egotistical mind.

His expression was puzzled. "You live alone?"

"I have a small house outside of town. It's not much, but you'll have a roof over your head for tonight anyway."

"This is customary? An unattached woman living by herself?"

"Very common and perfectly acceptable, though I know it wasn't the thing to do in your day."

"No, it definitely is not—was not! Especially for a lady with the qualities you seem to possess. I will say, though, that from the conversations we have had thus far, you appear capable of handling yourself."

"If that's a compliment, thank you."

"I am only being truthful. So there is no family to concern ourselves with, and you don't think your servants will find my sudden arrival a bit peculiar?"

"If I had any, that would be an excellent point."

"Have they gone out of fashion as well?"

"Except for the very wealthy, I am afraid so. I can only scrape up enough from my job to keep myself and the house in the black."

"You are employed. What sort of job do you have?"

"An office job. I'm an assistant copywriter. It's my job to help manufacturers sell their products."

"You have been at it long?"

"About six years."

He frowned. "How old are you? I realize that's an impertinent question to ask, but you seem too young to have been employed for that length of time."

"I'm twenty-eight. How old are you?"

"Thirty-two on my last birthday."

"And you've never been married?"

"No."

"I thought it was almost obligatory for a man in your position to marry and produce an heir."

He smiled then, his eyes glinting with mischief. "You fear I am in some immediate danger of impotence?"

My face reddened. I riveted my eyes out the windshield, thinking again how incredible his appearance in my life was.

We arrived at my house, and I pulled into the long gravel drive. I lived on the outskirts of Eastport in a countrified area near the coast of Long Island Sound, where the feel of Old New England remained. The house was a small colonial built in the early 1800s. It wasn't imposing. But the setting, at least in my eyes, was lovely. The house meant a lot to me and was about all I'd been able to salvage from a disastrous marriage that had ended in divorce two years earlier. I parked in the drive and turned off the engine.

I turned to him. "To get out, just pull up on that handle on the door." I opened my own door, got out and walked around the car. I had my first unhampered view of him when he slid from the passenger seat and stood. I'd been expecting a tall man, although I'd always had the impression our ancestors were a shorter race, but I was not prepared for the six feet of broad-shouldered elegance that faced me.

I started up the path to the back door. He followed close behind and waited while I turned the key in the lock. I glanced over my shoulder to find his piercing eyes upon me. A chill ran down my spine, but a pleasurable one—a chill that left me warm as though a gentle hand had caressed me.

"I must say your home appears as lovely as its owner."

I was surprised by his subtle compliment. I was aware of some of my attributes. A decent face with high cheekbones and a straight nose, hazel eyes flecked with green, and a nice smile. My hair was long and dark and my figure more than passable. Yet with all the positive qualities I could check off, I couldn't see that my looks would seem special to him. Compared to the women of his acquaintance—pampered, richly dressed, gracious, and elegant as only high birth and money can make you—I felt like a pale shadow.

Though it was small to me, the house's warmth and charm more than made up for the lack of spaciousness. The floor plan was simple: a large fireplace and the stairwell were located in the center of the house and divided the space into two equal-sized rooms—living room to the left and dining room to the right. The living room was enhanced by a large old fireplace restored to its original beauty. The kitchen ran behind these two rooms, stretching the width of the house. The ceilings were low, and the floors not precisely straight. The floors were natural wood in both rooms, and there were two small, brightly colored oriental rugs scattered over the wood. Dark-stained beams framed the open entrance to the living room, accenting its white plaster walls. Deep red draperies hung at the windows, and the furnishings were in natural tones. All told, the rooms had an atmosphere I was always glad to come home to.

Upstairs the floor plan was the same except for the bathroom tucked in behind one of the two bedrooms. The ceilings were low here, too, and I'd covered the wide-board floors with room-sized patterned carpets I'd picked up at a tag sale. I used the larger bedroom myself and had the smaller one equipped with a single bed, a desk, and a bookcase. It was used as either a guestroom or a study.

We finished the tour, coming back to the hall at the foot of the stairs. He was standing in the doorway to the dining room, his dark-waved head nearly brushing the top of the doorsill. He eyed me speculatively, the soft smile on his lips seeming sincere. "My compliments, Jessica."

I nodded in thanks and, not allowing my gaze to rest too long in his, turned and walked determinedly toward the bar cabinet at the far side of the room. "Can I get you a drink?"

"Brandy, if you have it."

It wasn't a usual item in my bar stock, but someone had given me a bottle of good French brandy for Christmas that year. I poured a little of it into a snifter and handed it to him. While I made a Scotch-and-water for myself, he crossed to the rustic dining room table and seated himself in one of the chairs. His eyes watched my every movement, and I was beginning to realize that just by that look alone the man had the power to make me exceedingly self-conscious. I set my glass on the table beside his.

He eyed it critically. "You drink spirits?"

"One of the several disgusting male habits women have adopted in the last hundred years."

"You'll permit me to reserve judgment on that for the time

being?"

Grinning, I lifted my glass toward him.

"Cheers," he toasted.

I took a much-needed gulp, but noticed he only took he smallest sip from his own drink, quickly lowering it and rolling the bulb-shaped glass in his large hands. Why did he have to stare at me? He made me feel so awkward, so gauche in comparison to his sophistication. I turned my head quickly and spotted the stereo. Hoping to shake him off balance as much as he was shaking me, I clicked on the tape deck and looked back to him as the chords of a modern rock ballad reverberated around the room.

His reaction was immediate. Startled as if pricked by a pin, he swung around and searched into every corner of the room. His eyes were wide, puzzled. He was taken completely off guard. Seeing his suave, cool self fall victim to confusion made laughter bubble up in my throat. When he saw my expression, his eyes slowly narrowed. "Music with no musicians, madam?"

"I know you're surprised."

"Obviously! But if you will recall, I experienced several similarly remarkable surprises before we reached this house." He was listening intently to the music even as he spoke.

"What do you think?" The tape was a collection of one of the more popular rock groups, certainly strange music to his ears if he'd just sprung from the early nineteenth-century ballroom.

"I think I like it—quite an unusual rhythm, though."

"Maybe you're used to chamber music and the concertos of Mozart and Beethoven?" I removed the tape and replaced it with Chopin, although Chopin would be new to him, too. The notes of a beautiful nocturne drifted into the room, tingeing the atmosphere with reminders of an earlier, more romantic age.

He lazed back in his chair, listening. "Amazing bit of extravagance. How does it work?"

Not that knowledgeable about its operation myself, I didn't know how to explain the technology to him. I tried my best, and at the end of my dialogue it seemed he'd gleaned the basics, because he nodded and commented, "Quite a simple principle, really, once you have the technical skill to achieve it." He rose and went round to examine the equipment at close hand.

When he returned to his chair and sat down, he gave me a warm smile. "Well, I certainly won't be lacking for occupation while I am here."

I'd been considering his reactions, rethinking the incidents from the time of his appearance to the present moment. He was lost in thought, too, the soothing music providing a perfect background accompaniment. It was several minutes before he suddenly smiled, flashing white teeth, and laughed shortly. "I am just recalling the expression of loathing on your face after we met...the odd epithets you rained on me. You seemed to think me the son of Satan."

"I think bastard was the word I had in mind."

"So I am a bastard? It gets better all the time. I believe I know a few others who share your opinion."

"I didn't say I think that now."

"What do you think now?"

"I'm beginning to think you're telling me the truth. I'm fighting it, but it does seem to add up to what you say it is. It's just that I'm so damn gullible I'm afraid to trust myself. I keep thinking there's still a very good chance you're pulling a fast one on me. But it's fun—so far."

"I'm delighted to hear that. You realize, I hope, that I am not in the habit of molesting undefended women."

If his actions shortly after meeting me in the car were any indication, he certainly couldn't prove it by me. But, of course, his own perceptions had been different then. I held my glass to my lips. "I'll soon find out, won't I?"

"I can leave."

"No," I answered, too quickly. "I mean it's only natural that something in the back of my mind refuses to believe what's occurred this afternoon."

"Something in the back of my mind shares your sentiment, but shall we come down to the basic facts again? We are forced to accept what neither of us wants to believe, simply because it is happening. Do I need to stress that point any further?"

"No."

"Good, because beyond what I've already told you and shown you, my points of evidence are wearing thin —you'll have to accede to the fact that I am who I say I am."

The clear tones of a Chopin waltz lilted through the room as he set down his glass and concentrated instead on the music. "Modern?" he asked.

"Not that modern. Chopin. Composed in the mid-1800s. Do you like it?"

He nodded. "Very much."

"This is his waltz dedicated to Madame de Rothschild. If you'd spent a few more years in your own time, you might have heard him firsthand."

He was staring at the opposite wall and suddenly seemed very far away. There was so much about him I didn't know, yet the longer he was in my presence, the more firmly convinced I was that he was telling the truth. I felt strangely in awe of him—the fact that a man like himself, so different from the men of my own acquaintance, could so unexpectedly have entered my life.

"Tell me about yourself."

He broke away from his study of the wall, curious. "What would you like to know?"

"How you lived, what it's like to be a nobleman and have wealth, estates and prestige. It's an entirely different world to me."

His eyes were on my face, although I don't think he was actually seeing me. "You know," he answered thoughtfully, "I've never really stopped to think of my life...at least not in terms of describing it to anyone. I am afraid in comparison to what I expect you are anticipating, it is rather dull." He paused, considered a moment, and continued in a quiet voice. "Generally, I begin the day by taking my stallion out for a ride about the estate...return about nine for breakfast...spend the rest of the morning at the stables checking the horses, inspecting the feed supplies, pastures, supervising the training. I have an overseer, of course, but I keep a personal eye on things—the breeding and training that no outsider could have as deep an interest in as myself. My afternoons are spent on estate matters, tenant problems, and the like, or in going over accounts. After a fairly early dinner, I relax in the library or my study. Occasionally I have guests over or a hunting party in, in which case we might play a few hands of cards or a game of billiards. I usually retire before midnight." He sipped from his glass.

"Of course, when I'm in London, it's a little different. I still rise early for my morning ride in the park, but the balance of my day is divided between business, solicitors, the House, one of my clubs for a few hours, perhaps an hour's workout sparring at Gentleman Jack's, then back to my house at St. James. From there it depends upon what invitations await me on my desk, and my mood for the evening. There is rarely a night without a rout or party of some sort, but sometimes I go to White's for a few hours, or spend a much more pleasant evening in the boudoir of one of my amiable lady friends...which confession does not offend your proprieties, I have a feeling." His lips turned in a half smile. His eyes taunted me.

"No."

"Intelligent woman. But enough of me. I want to know more about you."

In my eyes, my life seemed positively boring—the dream of how I wanted my life to go and the reality of how it went were poles apart. It was difficult for me to force any excitement into my voice. "I work in an office Monday through Friday, nine to five. It's an advertising agency, if that means anything to you."

"I know what an advertisement is. I presume you write them or place them for merchants and whatnot." He pronounced it ad-ver-tis-ment. I smiled.

"I only do some of the writing myself, but when I do, the man I work for gets the credit."

"You do not sound very happy about that."

"I'm not. I guess in your day it was close to impossible, if not unheard of, for a woman to get ahead in business. As much as that situation's been improving in the last few years, it's still rough. There seem to be quite a few men around who'd prefer thinking a woman's best talents by nature lie in clerking chores in an office or housekeeping and mothering at home. Not all men, of course, and it might even be I'm stuck in the wrong company—though I suppose I shouldn't say too much on the subject, since you probably share the old-fashioned views?"

"I admit I have in the past been of that opinion."

I noticed the quizzical turn of his eyebrows and laughed. "Well, anyway, once I'm home from work I cook myself dinner, relax for a while, do laundry or straighten up the house. Sometimes I play the piano for an hour or two, read, go out to dinner or for drinks with a friend. When I can afford it, I entertain here, though on a modest scale. The height of excitement and adventure, wouldn't you say?"

"I find what you are doing admirable—certainly more than any woman of my acquaintance would attempt."

"I don't mean to sound so cynical," I clarified, "but sometimes it seems I'm working so hard for so little. Spinning my wheels."

"Surely you realize there are a great many things in life that are not fair."

"Of course. But I'd like to try to do something about those that annoy me the most."

"And if you succeed in having equal footing with a man and more money in your purse, then will you be happy?" All the while he'd been listening to my words with concentrated attention, and now his eyes caught and held mine tenaciously.

I turned and looked out the window. "I'm happy enough, except that my life is so unstimulating, and at times I feel powerless to do anything about it. I've been told I'm the type of person who'll never be content. What about you? Are you happy?"

"I keep myself busy enough to avoid that type of contemplation. I have my health, my friends, and wealth enough to suffice my needs."

"But that's just what I'm talking about. You have so much, you don't realize what it's like to live on the other side of the fence. How can you really sympathize with me when you've had everything handed to you on a silver platter?"

"You are wrong, you know. My life may seem gilded in your eyes, but it has had its difficult moments...enough of them so that I can understand the point you are trying to make. You are an intelligent woman and sensitive enough to be troubled by what you face in competing in a man's world. I can see that, although I have to be honest in saying I don't necessarily agree that women should be on equal footing with men."

I wasn't sure whether I was more gratified by his sympathy or angry at his presumption of his male superiority, but at that point I didn't care to carry the discussion further. I shrugged my shoulders. "Forget it. Let's change the subject. Tell me more about the lavish parties and beautiful men and women. I've read about them, but I often wondered if the stories were true."

"True? I suppose some of it is. The extravagance is there, and the balls and assemblies can be vastly entertaining, but it is like anything else—once you have too much of it, you cease to appreciate it for what it is. You no doubt would enjoy yourself tremendously in London. At Almacks, for instance—God, the women are extraordinary—the matrons with their oversized turbans and pompous ways; the society misses so shy and unsophisticated in white muslin. And then there are the dandies in their rainbow assorted apparel with collars so ridiculously high they often can't turn their heads. Of course, one must not forget the social climbers and hangers-on and the opportunists."

I could see his mind whirling back to his memories.

"Since I am not in the marriage line, Almacks has never held the attraction for me that it does for others. It is more my habit when obligated to attend to stand on the sidelines with a few of my four-in-hand friends - keeping a running tally of just how many of the primping society mamas approach within an hour with their milk-water daughters in tow. They should know better than to think that after thirty-two years of defending my bachelorhood, I would be baited into the marriage bed by a simpering girl just out of the schoolroom. Aside from which, I am as well aware as they, that if it were not for my bank account and title, they would not be tripping over their proprieties to get to me. I make my polite excuses for not taking the little misses for a turn about the floor, then later in the evening stand for two or thee dances with one of the more seasoned beauties in the room whose thoughts I know to be far more in tune with my own line of thinking. Then you should see the mamas blowing out hot air behind their fans in those little gilt chairs at the side of the room." He paused, then smiled.

"Generally I depart for more exciting environs well before the dancing is over, giving them more to gossip about—this time without the aid of their fans—and friends who are waylaid longer than I tell me about the stir the next day. It has gotten to the point where they are placing wagers on the books at the clubs as to how long it will be before I am banished from the white list at Almacks. Now I admit my reputation in the petticoat line is far from spotless—a condition I have done nothing to alleviate—but no patroness in her right mind is going to blacklist an earl on the grounds of a few snubs and flying rumors." He smiled to himself at his reminiscences. "Needless to say, the next time I make an appearance, the same matrons and daughters are all there waiting, the mamas pushing their daughters forward, hoping for a sign of interest from my corner."

I watched his eyes drift in a blind stare as he remained with his thoughts. His profile was silhouetted in the lamplight. In his relaxation, tired lines were evident on his face, but the nose and square cleft chin were elegant—the features you'd expect to see in an aristocrat. His forearms rested on his knees as he held his drink loosely in his hands. A stray lock of dark hair had fallen across his scowling brow as he took occasional sips from his glass, still pondering. He brought his eyes slowly back toward me and blinked for an instant.

"Forgive me. I have been off in my own world and neglecting you."

"You have good reason."

"I was thinking of this country of yours. You know, we never quite knew what to make of this experiment with democracy...whether it would last or succumb to the storms of time."

"If two hundred years is any measure, I'd say we'd weathered well."

He frowned. "You will forgive me if it seems much less to me. You probably remember reading in my letters that I have been considering a shipping venture to these coasts and have been warned against it. My advisors seem to think current relations are too great a threat to a new operation with the embargo and all, much as I am not of an inclination to follow their counsel. This country fascinates me—a land bursting with opportunity, fortunes begging to be made by anyone with enough ingenuity and intelligence." His hands were busy again, swirling his glass as he stared into the funnel the motion made in the dark liquid.

"You'd be wise to listen. The embargo ended in war, in 1812."

"So, the hawks had their way. Damnable fools, most of them, without the foresight to see beyond their noses! As a matter of fact, in the House today several of them pulled me aside trying to persuade me into their corner. But I cannot see their argument—not only because of what it will do to my personal interests..." He shrugged. "Well, it is done now."

"And there've been worse wars since—although fortunately not between our two countries—but they don't make for pleasant conversation. You said you were in the House of Lords today. What else did you do?"

"The usual round—first to my solicitors, then on to George Pembrick's office in Fleet Street, and from there we went together to have luncheon at White's, my club."

"Do you know it's still in existence?"

"White's? Is it?" He laughed with fleeting excitement. "So I could still pay a visit to my old haunt. How interesting. I wonder if it has changed greatly."

"I would imagine it has."

"Yes, and then none of my old friends would be around any longer...it would not be the same. In any event, on that last day, after I left White's, I went to the House, spent a few hours in futile debate, and returned home to St. James. It was right after dinner that I began to grow restless and decided to start out for my estate in Kent."

"You called it by name before."

"Cavenly."

"Yes."

"I believe the origins go back to a hamlet that stood on the land now occupied by the manor house. The name was probably altered from its original form in the passing centuries. You know, I actually had not planned on leaving London until morning, but I had this unreasonable desire to return home. I left shortly after dusk." He paused, his eyes on my face. "Have you stopped to consider that if I had curbed my impatience to be home last evening, none of this might be happening?"

It was getting late. We hadn't eaten, and perhaps he wanted another drink. I motioned to his empty glass. "Would you like a refill?"

He glanced down, shook his head. "No, actually I was thinking more of getting washed up a bit."

"I'll show you the bathroom, and while you wash up, I'll get some dinner."

I led him up the stairs to the back of the hall and my newly remodeled bathroom. "You'd better let me show you the lights and water and give you some towels before I leave you on your own."

He watched in fascination as I operated the taps at the sink and tub, then the shower, careful not to send the spray onto either of us or the carpeted floor. "Remarkable," he stated. "And you think I have lived a life of convenience."

He glanced at the toilet, which I'd deliberately overlooked explaining, but from the expression on his face, I thought he guessed its purpose.

"There's also electric light," I continued as I flicked the switch by the side of the door. "All the lighting is electric, and you'll find a switch plate just inside the doorways of most of the rooms in the house." I returned to the hallway and gestured to the smaller bedroom. "You can use this room if you like."

His attention was now caught by the hot water steaming

forth from the sink tap. I left him to experiment and went to the linen closet to gather up some towels, in the process coming across a bottle of cologne left behind by my ex-husband. I didn't know whether Christopher used cologne, or if he'd even recognize the toothbrush I added to the heap, but although I'd read that dental hygiene in his century left much to be desired, he must have used something to maintain the strong set of white teeth he possessed.

When I returned to the bath, he was fingering some containers standing on a glass shelf along one wall. I watched as he lifted a stick of deodorant and read the back label. I saw a smile playing at the corners of his mouth as he put two and two together, removed the top, and spread the deodorant across the back of his hand. He took a whiff and grinned boyishly at me. "Interesting invention, if I'm guessing correctly at its use."

He replaced the deodorant and turned his attention to the things I'd just deposited on the vanity. His eyes immediately hit on the cologne and the blatantly masculine label glued to the tinted glass. "Are you always so well prepared for unexpected male visitors?"

"That was my husband's."

"Husband!" He jerked back as if I'd slapped him. "I was under the impression..."

"I should have said ex-husband. I'm divorced."

The expression that suddenly rippled across his face wasn't quite readable, but the squint of his eyes, as if he was now considering me in a very different light, spoke volumes. "So, you are divorced...I see."

"My being divorced has nothing whatsoever to do with the state of my morals. That is the subject you're speculating about, isn't it?"

He laughed.

"Or, to speak more bluntly, I am not fast, nor do I wish to be taken advantage of. Divorce is not the scandal it was in your day."

"I think we understand each other, my dear."

"It's to your disappointment if we don't."

"Yes." Still smiling, he took a towel from the fluffy pile I'd left. "Well, you have certainly seen to my comforts nicely."

"Then if you don't need anything else, I'll start dinner." I shut the door behind me and descended the narrow stairs.

A few minutes later, as I was checking the steak for the

last time, I heard his warm baritone behind me.

"A woman of many talents, I see." He crossed the kitchen toward me. The dark waves of his hair were damp and glistening, and as he approached, I caught a whiff of cologne.

"Feel better?"

"Like a new man."

"Good. Dinner's almost ready." I forked the steak onto a platter and filled the other dishes, then motioned him to the other room, "If you'll pour the wine, m'lord, we can start."

He filled the glasses, waited behind my chair to help me as I brought in the food. When we were finally seated, facing each other across the table, he lifted his glass and held it toward me. The rims met and tinkled melodically, and as if in silent agreement, our eyes, too, met and held for an instant. In that second I felt myself drawn to him like a needle to a magnet. I saw the glow of the candle flame reflected blue in the eyes that were now restful pools, and I almost saw beyond that to the days that might lie ahead for us together. I looked away quickly. When I glanced up again, he was concentrating on his food. Considering it was his second dinner that evening, his appetite was impressive. We didn't speak until the plates were nearly empty.

"For two people who should have so much to talk about," he spoke up, "we have certainly been silent."

"I thought you might be tired."

"I am a bit, but it is early yet for you."

"It's been a long day. There's no reason for you to stay awake on my behalf. Besides, I'll have some cleaning up to do before I go to bed."

He hesitated. "Actually, I've been giving myself and the matter some honest thought. I really do not think I should spend the night under your roof."

"Why not?"

"If you have not ascertained that for yourself, you're not the sophisticated woman I took you to be."

"I thought we had an understanding."

"We do, if we are both following the same thought patterns."

"Then as long as you're a gentleman..."

"You are not at all concerned what others will say or surmise?" He lifted his expressive brows.

"There is no one to say or surmise. I doubt anyone will even notice you're here, and my neighbors don't exactly live within peeping distance. Besides, where would you go? You don't know anyone, you don't know the area, nor do I think you'd get very far in that outfit without someone questioning you. It's more likely you'd be picked up on a charge of drunkenness."

"That possibility has crossed my mind."

"You really don't have much choice."

"If I were not so tired I'd continue this argument a little longer, but as it is," he sighed wearily, "I will have to trust your judgment." He drained his glass. "Where would you like me to sleep?"

"In the small bedroom upstairs," I reminded him, and then I noticed the glint in his eye. "Well, I can always lock my door."

"That will not be necessary."

He was watching me, and I made a motion to get up.

"Please, be still. I've put you to enough trouble already." He reached over, took my hand and dropped a soft, warm kiss on my fingers, "Good night, Jessica. Until tomorrow."

"Until tomorrow." I watched him walk away, his head high, his shoulders still squarely straight, tired though he was. I listened to his footsteps as he climbed the stairs.

Only then did I gather up the dirty dishes and busy myself washing them and picking up the kitchen. It was ten o'clock. I felt as exhausted as if it were twelve, mentally and physically drained from trying to absorb too much of the unexpected in too short a time. All was quiet upstairs. He must have been sleeping. I turned off the lights, blew out the candles. I started up the stairs, wondering what tomorrow would bring.

THREE

I sat up quickly, still half asleep, yet knowing there was something different about this Saturday morning I couldn't quite recall. Then I remembered Christopher and the extraordinary events of the day before. Had it all been a dream?

I stumbled sleepily to the dresser, pulled out jeans and a light sweater, and dragged them onto my tired limbs. My ears strained for a sound of movement in the next room. All was silent, and when I slipped across the hall to the bathroom, the other bedroom door was closed. I caught a glimpse of my reflection in the bathroom mirror as I washed. My eyes shone with anticipation. How foolish! It must have been a dream. I opened the bathroom door and returned to the hall.

He was standing there, a sleepy look on his face. For a moment he didn't speak...just stared. Then he smiled.

I couldn't suppress the sigh of relief that escaped my lips. "Good morning. Did you sleep well?"

"Surprisingly enough, though I had the devil's own time when I woke up trying to remember where I was —thought I'd gotten foxed and spent the night with one of my paramours." Grinning, he moved his still hazy eyes to mine. "Fortunate for you I remembered my actual circumstances in time." He was in stocking feet and wore his blousy white shirt tucked into his pants. Dark, tightly curled hairs lay in a soft mat on his chest where he'd left the upper buttons undone. He'd begun rubbing his bristling chin thoughtfully, "I do not suppose you'd have a razor about I could use? Since my valet is not to be had, I shall have to do something about this myself. You know," he added thoughtfully "I never appreciated Parkins so much in my life as I did this morning when I looked over to my wrinkled clothing and realized I had to put it on as is."

"I'd be glad to iron your shirt and pants if you like."

"Not necessary. A razor would be sufficient if you have it."

I turned back to the bath, found my plastic razor in the medicine cabinet and handed it to him. "It looks a little different from what you're used to, and I'm afraid you'll have to use soap. I don't have any shaving cream."

Frowning, he flipped the razor over in his hand. "Interesting, but how does it work?"

I gave him a few pantomime instructions then turned toward the stairs. "Let me go make some coffee. You do like coffee in the morning?" He nodded. "Good. Come down when you're ready."

I was about to step down the first tread when his voice stopped me. "It is the style now for women to wear trousers?" He was staring in open appreciation at my well-outlined backside.

"I'd forgotten—you've probably never seen a woman in pants."

"Certainly not in decent company." He hadn't taken his eyes from me.

"You'll get used to it." I chuckled. "If you're around here for a while. And I can promise you, they're a lot more comfortable than long skirts."

"Leaving a great deal less to the imagination."

"If I'm not mistaken, dampened muslin was the rage in your day, and if that's not revealing I don't know what is."

He made no comment, but as I swung round and hurried down the stairs, his laughter burst forth and followed after me. I was beginning to think he was going to thoroughly enjoy this little sojourn into the future.

He arrived in the kitchen a few minutes later, still in his shirtsleeves but clean shaven and smelling spicily masculine. He joined me at the table, and over our coffee we began discussing what we might do with the coming day.

It still felt strange to be with him, to look across the breakfast table and see his alert and handsome face, knowing that yesterday I hadn't even dreamed of his existence. Even today, how could it seem altogether real? But he was unarguably there, and it seemed obvious that even if his stay with me was to be of short duration, there were several things we'd have to do. I pointed out the need for him to obtain a change of clothing. Then there were other personal items he'd be needing, too. We talked it over and decided on a trip that morning to a local men's clothing store. I thought it would be interesting to see his reaction to rack after rack of ready-made clothing, considering his background of exclusive, expensive, fine personal tailors.

We left the house about nine-thirty. Without his long-tailed jacket and elaborate tie, he didn't seem as conspicuous as he had the day before. Still, as we entered the downtown men's clothing store, I noticed the raised eyebrows of some of the salesmen as they spotted us. To me he looked dashing with his full-sleeved, open-necked shirt and gleaming leather boots, but I knew I was being romantic and just kept my fingers crossed that people would pass him off as an eccentric and not make any fuss. Thankfully, one of the salesmen walked very casually over to ask if he could help us, and took Christopher off with him in the direction of the clothes racks. We were out of the store in thirty minutes with most of what he needed packed in four shopping bags.

Next we stopped at the drugstore and the supermarket. During the entire morning he behaved exactly like a hungry tourist, but of course he was touring not only a strange country, but a strange century as well. He exclaimed approvingly over the convenience of the supermarket with its huge amount of merchandise, spoil-proof packaging, and long aisles of neatly sorted cans, bottles, boxes, and refrigerated meats and vegetables. He was ecstatic over the system of traffic signals, the high quality of the roadways, and the amazing cars and trucks that plied the streets. To him it was extraordinary that anyone could move so quickly or cover as much distance in as short a period of time as we were that morning. It made me realize how much I was taking my life and its conveniences for granted. But his comments took on a negative tone when he remarked on the unsightly sprawl of concrete block shopping centers and the hastily constructed buildings that sometimes appeared to be no stronger than cardboard boxes and were certainly no more attractive. He wasn't pleased with the plastic quality and impersonality he found evident in our rushing lifestyle compared to the dignity and grace of his era, left behind in our headlong flight for progress. His delight pleased me; his displeasure made me sad.

As soon as we arrived home he went upstairs to change, and came down looking very self-conscious in a pair of jeans tight around his hips and a shirt open at the collar. He looked entirely different from the nineteenth-century stranger I'd met the day before. He was waiting for my reaction.

"Well, what do you think?"

I looked him over appraisingly. "You look good. You wear clothes very well."

"You are sure?" He glanced down stiffly in inspection.

"I'm sure."

He relaxed. "Then I will take your word for it. And now,

I'm famished. I would invite you to a charming restaurant for luncheon and try to repay you in some small way for your generosity, but I find myself sadly lacking in exchangeable currency." His eyes grew serious all of a sudden, and he took my hand in an easy clasp. "Truthfully, Jessica, I do not know how to thank you for all you've done. You know I am deeply grateful."

"I know...and you don't have to thank me. Think of the adventure I'm getting in return." I slid my hand gently from his grasp and went to the refrigerator. "What would you like for lunch?"

We ate simply—sandwiches and coffee—and talked about what we'd do with the afternoon. He wanted to see as much of my world as he could during the indefinite time he was here, so as soon as the lunch mess was cleaned up, we were in the car again. This time I took him away from the flashing signs and symbols of twentieth-century civilization. We drove south a short distance to the Eastport Beach, parked the car and looked out over the blue waters of Long Island Sound, rippling in the clear sunlight.

Although it was early May, there were a few boats out on the water, mainly power boats carrying weekend fishermen.

He scowled out at the view, then asked, "Where are the ships? Where are the sails?"

"Victims of the internal combustion engine, like the one that powers my car."

He shook his head sadly. "All that grace and beauty gone."

"There still are sailing ships around, preserved and new, but they're mostly used for passenger cruises or training ships. I can understand how much you'd miss them. A fleet of tall ships from all over the world sailed up the Sound in '76 in celebration of the Bicentennial. It was magnificent to see."

"Another point on which we agree."

From the beach I headed north, out of the industrialized sprawl of the coastal Connecticut towns and into lands of rolling green meadows, untouched woodland, and red-barned farms.

We found a narrow country lane that threaded its way up into the low mountains. I stopped the car beside a stone wall that sprawled along the edge of the road.

The land sloped gently downhill, ending at a meandering brook that cut through the valley in a glimmering streak then vanished into the trees. The sky was a brilliant blue found only on occasional spring days, the air so clear it was electric. We could hear the wind whispering across the grass, the call of the birds searching out food for their young, the water as it rippled over its rocky bed. We settled ourselves near the stream, where the fragile new grass made a rich carpet.

"This reminds me of England," he said, "These rolling hills, the greenness. You enjoy it here?"

"Very much."

"You would enjoy England as well."

"I did—I was there."

"Long ago?"

"About two years back, on a vacation."

"Vacation?" he quizzed.

"In England, they call it a holiday."

"I see. Then you can tell me what it is like today."

"I've been meaning to, but there seemed to have been so many other things to tell you."

"Has your family been in this area long?"

"In Eastport? Yes, quite a few years. I was born here, as were my parents. Both their families came up here in the early nineteen hundreds and farmed. My parents built a house on some of the farm's former pastureland, and this is where I grew up. Since my father retired from his job, they've moved to a smaller home in Florida. My brother and sister have moved out of the area, so I'm the only one left."

"From the little I've seen, it's a lovely area. You must have had a happy childhood."

"We were an average family. My father was an accountant with a firm in New York City, my mother a housewife. My brother and sister and I all attended local schools until we went away to college. All in all we were happy...not remarkable in any way, but happy."

"I have been thinking of your marriage, wondering what brought you to divorce."

I glanced over at him, expecting to see a curious smile on his lips. He was quite serious. "At one time I thought I was in love. In my infatuation I built my ex-husband into a fairy-tale character that didn't exist. It wasn't long before my bubble burst. He wanted nothing I wanted. He couldn't see me as a person in my own right. The little frictions I'd ignored before we were married suddenly became raw wounds as we grated against each other day in and day out.

"It was as much my fault as his. I should have been perceptive before the wedding and not run so blithely down the garden path. I'd been brought up to think marriage was my ultimate goal. All my friends were married, and I was twenty-three, the age when I thought I should be married, too. The unhappiness got to the point where we were tearing each other apart emotionally. I couldn't please him without giving up my identity, and he couldn't please me because he was asking too much. I wouldn't change, and he couldn't. After three years we decided to get a divorce while we still had the chance to find happiness with someone else."

"Still it must have been a hard decision for you to make."

"It was the only decision we could make. I know in your time couples in our position would have been forced to stick together come hell or high water, but divorce is easier now— people have begun to realize that life is too short and too important to be wasted away in an unhappy relationship. Divorce doesn't carry the stigma it once did, though I hope I've learned from my mistakes. I wonder sometimes if I could ever be happy in marriage. Can I give enough of myself? I know all marriages have their ups and downs, but I need a true fifty-fifty relationship, and few men I know are willing to accept those terms, to share all the responsibilities of keeping a house. Or to understand that if a woman desires a career outside of housekeeping and motherhood, her career is just as important as his and demands just as much of her time and energy. I can't pamper a man's ego or take a subservient role. I've worked too hard all my life at being an individual, and I take pride in what I've accomplished on my own."

He nodded. "And where are you going now, Jessica Lund?"

With these words he flicked his eyes in my direction, and I felt that warm tingle again in my spine. I drew my own eyes away, unable to think clearly under his penetrating gaze, looking instead at the pale green treetops shimmering in the sunlight. "I don't know where I'm going. I don't think about it as much as I should. I guess I live each day to see what it will bring, and for now I have my work, my house, and my independence. I travel when I want, see my friends, come and go as I please. No one tells me what to do, where to put my pennies, what's important and what's not."

He didn't say anything for a while, yet I knew his eyes were upon me. I could feel them etching patterns on my profile.

"You are a lovely woman, Jessica. You deserve to have the right man at your side."

It was strange to hear those words from his lips. I swallowed and continued to stare at the landscape, not knowing what response to make.

"Please go on," he spoke up. "You were going to tell me about England. What is my country like today?"

"It's changed—just about everything has changed since your day—but I think you'd still like it. You wouldn't know where you were if you stood by St. Paul's Cathedral and looked at the Old City, yet some of the country estates, the tiny villages, and the acres surrounding them beyond the metropolitan area haven't changed at all. London is still elegant and full of history. Would you believe that they've uncovered part of the old Roman wall not far from the Tower and have left it standing amid the skyscrapers—that's an anachronism you'd enjoy seeing—but St. James and parts of Westminster have remained pretty much untouched since the early eighteen hundreds. The parks are all there and just as beautiful—I really had a love affair with Hyde Park. I could have spent hours there, roaming down the paths, through the gardens, around the Serpentine. I don't think you'd be disappointed if you saw it today. There are still horses in Rotten Row. The Queen's Guards exercise there. Thankfully they've banned cars on all but a few of the park roads, so there's a timelessness, especially when you're deep inside and cut off from the noise of the city traffic."

I rested my chin on my hand. "But there are other changes you wouldn't like. For one, your style of life is a thing of the past. The aristocracy still exist, in title if nothing else, but the lord of the manor is gone."

"The ruling class is now made up more by the men who tilled your fields than of men like yourself. High taxation, the lack of cheap labor, and the coming of the industrial age drew farm workers off to the factories and the hope of better wages. A lot of the large estates had to be split up and sold off. Only the very wealthy could afford to keep them up. Some of the estates are now owned by an historical trust and are open to the public."

"And the Royal family?" he asked.

"You still have a queen, Elizabeth II, but the royal family are figureheads. Parliament makes and keeps the laws, and the Royal family are sort of like goodwill ambassadors who help keep the tourist dollars coming in. There really isn't much except the physical you could identify with anymore."

I glanced quickly at his grim face. "I know how you must feel. I know how I would feel if it were my world we were talking about—but somehow I think you can handle it. You give me the impression you're the kind of person who can cope with change."

"I was expecting to find things very different. I just wasn't certain in what manner they would change. I suppose one could almost see it coming. But to go back a bit. What ever became of Napoleon? Did Wellington succeed in capturing the Fox?"

"He did, at Waterloo. I don't remember the year offhand."

"One piece of encouraging information, at any rate. And what of the prince? Did he outlive his father to become king?"

"He became king, but I don't think he had many years left before he died. It was his niece, Victoria, who went on to become one of the greatest queens in English history, right up there with Elizabeth I." I clarified. "During Victoria's reign the British Empire stretched around the world. There was a saying, 'the sun never sets on the British Empire.' Then in 1914 we had the First World War. The Germans began it, as they did the Second World War in the nineteen thirties. They lost in both cases, but not until most of Europe was a wasteland."

"A pity that I cannot use any of this knowledge when I return. My doing so might change the course of history, though, mightn't it?"

I changed the subject, feeling the conversation was too dark for the brightness of the day. "Tell me about Cavenly. What does it look like—one of those stone mansions with millions of tiny paned windows, Grecian columns at the door and a winding drive to the entrance?"

He laughed, and his pensive mood vanished. "You would be amazed how aptly you have described it, considering you have never seen it. Or have you? You said you have been to England."

"Not as far as Kent, and until you mentioned it yesterday, I've never heard the name."

"The house is three stories, stone. There are a great many windows, but I am afraid we are sadly lacking Grecian columns. The original structure was Norman, but it has been added to and disguised beyond recognition. The building I own was designed by Wren and is rectangular with three wings off the back, one the original Norman structure. There is a small lake in the front, and in the rear are my stables, training ring, and pasture lands. Beyond the park are the estate farms and my tenant farms, which keep the place running." His eyes were clouding with that misty, faraway look that disturbed me when it came. "I love Cavenly, Jessica. I wish I could show you its beauties instead of using these inadequate words."

"You spend most of your time there, you said."

"I go up to London only when necessary, but I believe you know enough of your history to realize that too many of my fellow gentry leave their estates in the hands of overseers while they carouse and gamble away their fortunes...unfortunately, I see now, giving the lower classes a very valid reason for despising them. Much as I hate to admit it, I did that myself for a while when I was younger, but the novelty quickly paled. My home and inheritance are too important to squander away, and Cavenly is as successful as it is only because I have put so many hours into its management, balancing crops, easing frictions with the tenants, being an equitable landlord, and trying some of the new agricultural methods many of my friends tend to scorn."

"Don't you ever get lonely?" I said, and silently reproached myself for asking a personal question.

"With all my lovely ladies of the evening only too anxious to ease my aching heart?" But after a moment he sobered and added, "I suppose I get lonely sometimes...but it is nothing I could put my finger upon. And I have my town house in London, where I can repair when the country life becomes too isolated. Lately, though, I have been going up only for business or when I felt my presence was needed at the House of Lords. While I am there the invitations pile up. There is no way of escaping them all, and it has become a bore. You see the same faces, hear the gay, insincere laughter, the quips and gossip, the desperate battle to squeeze some happiness from life when people are too blind to realize that happiness usually stems from the simplest things, not the hectic whirlwind they are creating. Ah, but I am becoming philosophical, am I not?"

"What you say is true. People don't change."

"That seems to be the nature of mankind."

I sighed. "You've given me such a different perspective on your life. I always thought it was so glamorous."

"My cynicism should not be taken to heart. You might very well enjoy these things I have grown to despise."

"You can't always have been such a cynic."

"No, as a child I remember I was very happy, and as a young man before I got a taste of my world. I was born at Cavenly, and when my parents were alive it was a very different place. They were happy together. They entertained, but not the London crowd. Usually they had in the local gentry, occasionally a hunting party down for the opening week of the season. The house would come alive. To me as a child, every day brought a new adventure, from riding about the estate on my father's saddle, to sneaking down to the river for some fishing when I should have been at my studies. When there was company, I would steal out of the nursery to peek over the banisters and wish for the time when I was a man and could join those gathered in the library for port and talk of politics. I had a lot to learn about life.

"I received more than my share of attention, since I was the only child, with my father already into middle age when I was born. His first wife had died in childbirth during her fourth attempt to beget him an heir. He married my mother while she was in her middle twenties, a few years after his first wife died, and despite the disparity in their ages, they were very much in love.

"She was a wonderful woman—full of life and love and laughter, deeply devoted to my father and our home. She died suddenly of pneumonia while I was up at Oxford. The shock nearly killed my father. In fact, he never recovered. He followed her a year later. I returned home then to take over the estates and claim my inheritance as the Ninth Earl, but the place had changed. The life seemed to have gone out of it. I suppose a home needs a family to keep it vital."

"Haven't you ever wanted to start a family of your own?"

"I have thought of it, yet I seem to keep putting it off. I never have had any great longing for the entrapment of a wedding ring, much as it is almost my duty to try one day to produce an heir. To this moment I have drifted along very complacently."

"You certainly don't have a very high opinion of marriage."

"And you do, I suppose?" He eyed me, and I laughed.

"Well," I insisted, "it might be different if you were in love and the two of you truly compatible."

"Oh, I was in love—some time ago. She and I turned London inside out and the *haut ton* on their ears. I still hear occasional gossip about that old affair, although she is now safely imprisoned in the country, where her husband can keep a watchful eye on her. Such a pity, too, for her. She was so full of life and must be withering away with only her ancient spouse to keep her company." He chuckled to himself. "Fortunately, I have been wise enough not to repeat that particular mistake." For a moment his eyes leveled on me, and I didn't know where to look, but soon he was off on another tangent.

"It is a shame I cannot show you a season of the social whirl in London. What a lark it would be to sponsor you, to see the stir you would cause with your modern-day thoughts and that quick tongue of yours. Of course, I cannot say I would do much to enhance your reputation. Not that that would bother you, I am sure, but we would have to find a suitable chaperone— some lady of upstanding morals and irreproachable virtue. I have several austere aunts who fit that description to the letter, but they would also dry your spirit to dust and drive me mad in the bargain. No, it would be much more delightful to do it on our own...Tell me, do you ride?"

"Oh, yes. I love horses. I have a place to ride not far from here."

"Do you? Marvelous. Then we could have gone riding in the park together, and in the evening I could escort you to all the proper balls. At least I could have tolerated them with a fetching maiden at my side. My only obstacle would be holding you there, with all the ardent competition I would have."

I laughed outright at his fantasy. "You're letting your imagination get carried away."

"You have something against imagination?"

"No, I think it's wonderful."

"Good, then let me imagine, and try to put some spark into an existence that has grown tedious and that I may never see again. Are there no flourishes you would like to add to your own life?"

"With you here, how many more flourishes can I expect?"

He grabbed my hand and, with a start, pulled me to my feet and began jogging with me toward the brook at the bottom of the meadow. "Come girl, let us be imaginers again. Do you feel like wading?"

"It's too cold!"

'No, it is not. Use your imagination. It is midsummer, and we are two children running across a field. Come dip your feet in the cool waters."

I was laughing merrily with him. I took off my shoes and joined him in splashing through the rock-strewn stream bed. We walked up and down its length, from woodland to woodland, skinning our toes on the slippery rocks and freezing our feet in the icy waters. Then, to warm our chilled bodies, we left the stream and ran like careless children to the top of the meadow and back. We paused to pick early spring flowers from the grass and count the blue jays flashing across the sky. I tripped in a woodchuck hole, and he caught me up, his arm resting a moment more than necessary on my waist. I smiled into his eyes, and he did into mine, and we reeled down the hill, forgetting for the time who we were.

As I dropped onto the crushed grass where I'd sat before, I looked up into his cheerful face. "This has been fun."

His eyes were full of afternoon fire, his voice a whisper. "Hasn't it, though."

His body was no more than a foot from my own, his face so close I saw every feature in detail. I was astonished once more by the brightness and depth of his vivid blue eyes, how easy it was to rivet my own upon them and lose sight of every other feature in his face. So easy, too, to lose track of any thoughts that had been passing through my mind at the time our glances met.

His gaze remained on me, washing over my face. I could feel myself being drawn to him...heedless...seeing nothing beyond his magnetism.

He reached over and placed his hand gently but firmly on my shoulder, pulled me toward him across the grass. I didn't protest, but let him lead me to discover at closer range the masculine perfection of him, from the tiny laugh lines at the corner of his eyes to the strong, inviting lips that were almost touching mine. I inhaled the clean scent of him, felt his breath on my face...his eyes never leaving mine until our lips met.

I wouldn't have wanted it to happen that way if I'd had all my senses in focus. We were behaving impulsively, but I couldn't deny my pleasure. The kiss was firm, warm, and devouring. Our lips might have been intended for each others', so well did they mold themselves together. I heard his breath catch. His hand slipped from my shoulder to my back. He pressed his body over mine, and without conscious thought, I was opening my mouth to his tongue, moving my lips softly under his. It would have taken only a second more for our limbs to become entangled and our emotions to carry us away, but in that second, realization came to us both like a stark flash of lightning.

He drew his mouth away, but his arm was still tight about me. "I am sorry...that should not have happened."

"Don't be sorry."

"I do not know what came over me. You are angry?"

I smiled, shook my head. "No."

"And here I promised you I would be a gentleman. Will you forgive my impetuosity?" His voice was husky.

"Of course," I whispered.

Neither of us moved. We studied each other for a long time in silence. Then before I could think much further, he dropped a soft kiss on my brow and rose.

FOUR

We were in a quiet, contemplative mood during the drive home. I wished I had the courage to tell him I was a modern woman, free to enjoy what we'd just found. But I realized, too, that with Christopher I could fall in over my head. Then, if I woke up one morning to find him gone, I'd be shattered.

As he helped me from the car, there was nothing in his manner to indicate how much things had changed between us in the last hour. Yet I suspected that the thoughts hidden by his silence were much the same as my own.

I needed some time alone...to compose myself, build up my defenses, and shield the feelings that were too close to the surface and too ready to explode with the memory of being held tight in his arms.

I shooed him off to the other room while I made dinner so that I could be alone with my thoughts. Throughout the meal his easy, steady conversation covered nearly every topic except the one we both wanted to avoid. And after dinner, surprisingly enough, the rest of the evening took care of itself when I decided to give him lessons on the old bicycle stored in my garage. He'd need some form of transportation other than his two long legs, since I wasn't located near enough either to stores or to the downtown area to make walking a practical means of getting around.

His expression was leery when he saw the spindly two-wheeler, yet once I'd made a few demonstration runs up and down the drive, he was more than eager to try it himself. It looked easy, he told me, but he was soon eating his words. He was off to an amazingly good start for about two feet. Then, as he concentrated on the peddling mechanism, the front end of the bike began to wobble crazily, the wheel skittering first in one direction, then the other, and over he went. When he tried to steer a straight course, his pant leg caught in the chain, sending both him and the bike over once again in a skidding slide on the gravel. He wasn't hurt, although I knew it must be humiliating for him to appear in such an ungraceful light. He wouldn't give up until he had it down pat, and then only after he'd run down several of my most promising flower beds.

Justly proud as he whipped by me finally on a straight and steady three laps around the drive, he laughingly called out, "A marvelous contraption, Jessica, but damned if I wouldn't feel safer on the back of a horse!"

"We'll try that, too," I shouted back, and waited until he'd brought the bike to a fairly steady halt beside me. Dusk was heavy upon us by the time we'd packed his marvelous contraption back into the garage. My mind had been free of any troublesome thoughts during the hour of his bicycle instruction, but now that I was faced once again with devising a means of entertaining him, I felt lost.

He walked on ahead of me through the kitchen and into the living room, where he headed for the bookcase. I was seriously considering leaving him on his own for the rest of the evening when I spied the television set, and I decided his introduction to this particular marvel shouldn't wait any longer. I gave him time to find a comfortable seat on the couch and open a book before I casually moved in the direction of the set and turned it on. Just as casually, I continued to a nearby chair to watch his reaction as the set flared to life.

It was a moment before the blaring sound of strange voices penetrated his concentration. When it did and he looked up, his expression was worth a thousand words. His eyes widened in utter amazement, and he sat upright in a quick movement that sent his forgotten book falling to the floor. "What is it?"

I was laughing too hard to answer him. The show was a typical police drama. He was so taken with it, he paid little heed to my silence and watched with avid interest as the cop and the villain battled it out with smoking guns until one of them caught the bullet and fell in a heap on the pavement.

"I do not believe it," he burst in. "By God, it is like having the theater brought into your home in a nutshell. How does it work?"

"I don't know the first thing about electronics or television. That it works has always been enough to satisfy me. I thought you'd enjoy it."

"I never in my life imagined anything like it!"

I lost him as a commercial came on—a winsome blonde in her underwear describing in sweet tones the bra with invisible support.

He was back in a flash. "They show this for public view?"

"They show a lot of things that would surprise you a great deal more."

"Have people no modesty?"

"Not the kind you're used to. Besides, don't forget these are anonymous models."

"Still. Well...who am I to judge?"

He smiled with the delight of a small boy as the police story returned, and I gave up any hope of recapturing his attention.

I left him then, rousing his attention long enough to ask if there was anything he needed before I went up to bed. He gave me a quick smile and said he'd manage very well for himself. I said my good nights and walked away feeling far less satisfied with his response than I would have wished.

FIVE

The next days were so full, they flew by. Already May was drawing to a close, and Christopher could hardly believe he hadn't yet made the journey back to his own world.

We were getting to know each other, the little habits and idiosyncrasies, the traits that were distinctly our own and set us apart as individuals. The days together were satisfying, but there were awkward and uncomfortable moments, too. The discomfort stemmed from his never-ending impatience to be home...the worry that always filled his thoughts of what might be occurring in his absence. The awkwardness came as he tried to make the personal adjustment to a lifestyle so very different from the one he'd been used to. He'd been a man of independent habits, used to doing what he wanted, when he wanted, and now he was forced into small living quarters with a single woman whose own standards were modern, liberal...nothing at all like those he'd known. As a person in the habit of having his every need premeditated and fulfilled by anxious servants, I sensed his frustration at times that certain mundane tasks now fell to his care alone.

If the transition was more difficult for him than for me, his entrance into my life had the effect of turning my world topsy-turvy. I'd been used to running my life on a certain schedule and had been guaranteed a certain amount of privacy, which I certainly wasn't getting now. Not that I minded his elegant body decorating my house—the last thing I wanted was for him to leave—but no more Saturday mornings spent in my grubbiest jeans and a sloppy shirt, my hair pulled up in an untidy mass on top of my head. I didn't want him to see me looking anything less than attractive. Neither could I run downstairs in the morning in my nightgown and robe, as had been my habit before his arrival. Now my morning coffee was postponed until after I was dressed—a hardship I didn't cherish.

It was difficult for both of us, yet it was a time of adventure, of discovery, of never knowing what lay in store for tomorrow. How much time did we have?

We came to the conclusion that we should create a plausible-sounding explanation for his being in my house—a story to forestall and satisfy the curiosity of friends who'd heard of my surprising house guest. Quite frankly, it didn't bother me

what people might be thinking, but they were talking and to
pacify him and, in a way protect him, we fabricated an intricate
fib, making up the existence of an old-time friendship between
our families taking place enough years in the past that even my
closest friends wouldn't question the truth of it. We told them
that Christopher, born in England, had been brought to this
country as a child when his father was transferred to New
York on business. Our fathers, having become acquainted in
England during the war, renewed their friendship, and it was
then that I'd first met seven-year-old Christopher. We'd been
playmates and friends until our middle teens when his family
had returned to England, where he'd completed his education
and later taken a post teaching history at Eton. Over the years
our families had kept in touch with each other, and when it
came time for him to take a sabbatical in the United States, it
seemed only natural to contact my family and me for assistance
while he did research and consultation work at the colleges and
universities in the area. Eastport seemed a good center axis
from which to travel to the Ivy League and city universities
he'd chosen, and I'd invited him to stay with me until he'd
found a place of his own. My parents were the only ones who
could disprove the story, and since they lived in Florida, they
weren't likely to catch wind of it except from my own lips.

As casually as I relayed my story and answered curious
questions about him, I'd see the winks and half-disguised smiles.
But what other people thought didn't faze me, just as long as
each morning I woke up to find him still in the neighboring
bedroom.

He was recovering from his absorption in the television.
His attention turned toward books, which he was borrowing
from the library with my card—books of history, of science, of
politics, of medicine...of any worthwhile subject that could be
digested by his intelligent mind and—should he retain it
permanently—be used to advantage if he returned to his own
world. While he read, I'd often sit down at the piano to play for
an hour or so. He enjoyed this. One of his favorite pieces was
a Chopin nocturne, lyric and flowing, and he encouraged me to
play it for him as often as I was in the mood.

Always an avid reader, I sometimes picked up a book to
join him in companionable silence. I found I had trouble
concentrating on the pages of fiction when my real-life drama
was so much more exciting. Too often my eyes would drift up

from the printed words to glue themselves to the picture of him, unselfconsciously reclining on the couch, a lock of hair falling across his brow. He looked so boyish, so romantic, relaxed as he was with his feet propped on the cushions, his tall frame covering the length of the couch. It was difficult to realize, when I saw him in this setting, that in his own world he was a man of great stature. Were our situations reversed and I deposited in his time, I'd probably be sitting in his library at Cavenly, my knees knocking in awe. Now he was just a man, and I liked him that way.

We tried playing cards. He taught me loo and whist, and I introduced him to gin rummy and five-card stud, which he loved. He was too good for me: he beat me at my own games, and I did horribly at his. We'd play poker for pennies, with my losses at the end of the evening totaling well over a dollar. And as much as he teased me that if I kept up this way he'd own my house at the end of a month, I enjoyed every minute of losing.

Our good nights were said below stairs. I'd go up first and be safely imprisoned in my own room behind a closed door before I'd hear his footsteps on the stairs. I'd listen to the sounds of the taps being turned in the bathroom, the water running, then the sound of his door closing firmly. As I snuggled between the sheets in my thin nightgown, my thoughts would run wild, and I would imagine his naked body sliding between the sheets of his bed, separated from me by no more than the boards and plaster of a wall. I never imagined he might be thinking about me, too. His self-containment and unapproachable friendliness grew, rather than diminished, with the passing days, and there was no fertile ground for my glorified daydreams. In self-defense I perfected my ability to disguise my feelings, so that he never guessed how much more I cared for him as each day went by. He seemed to be existing only from one day to the next—not really living. His heart and mind were in England, and as long as they were there, the thought of his return consumed him. I often felt he was only half with me—the rest of him one hundred and sixty years away.

One evening as we were having coffee after dinner, he suddenly broke away from the thoughts that had been absorbing him and said in a speculative tone of voice, "I may be entirely off course, Jessica, but have you ever seen a copy of a British peerage anywhere about, in a bookshop or library? There were several in publication in my day, though I am not sure such a thing is still in existence."

"The books giving the genealogy of different families? They probably have one at the local library. Didn't you look when you were there last?"

"The idea just occurred to me, but do you think it might be our answer? If we find a peerage and it contains what I am thinking it will, I shall have all the answers. I can discover the identity of the current earl, the facts on all his predecessors, and the details of my own tenure. The dates will be there—all the facts I should need to determine whether or not I return...possibly even when!"

Why, I asked myself, did he want so desperately to leave? Couldn't he find something in my world worth remaining for? I answered his queries in as level a tone as I could manage. "There's one way to find out, isn't there? I'll take you down in the morning."

We were at the library moments after they'd opened their doors. As much as I tried to fight the feeling, I was choked with trepidation—part of me hoping we would find the information that would put an end to his anxiety, and the rest of me praying not to see the words that would leave me no doubt as to the futility of my dreams. He gave no indication of any tension he was feeling except for a certain sternness to his expression as we proceeded toward the reference shelves. We uncovered a massive leather-bound copy of Burke's Peerage, found a free table, and spread the pages open before us, thumbing rapidly to "W." The Westerham coat of arms seemed to jump from the fine print, along with the heading beneath:

The 14th Earl of Westerham (John Charles Dunlap) of Cavenly, Kent; b. 9 September 1934; Educated Eton, Oxford; Captain Fifth...

The words went on, but we were interested in other matters. Quickly our eyes scanned down the column of ancestors and preceding earls, and there it was. I spotted it before he did, and my finger jabbed at the paragraph that bore his name:

Christopher Robert Julian George, 9th Earl of Westerham; b. 26 June 1780; Succeeded by James Dunlap, Tenth Earl; cousin.

That was all. The paragraph above it pertained to his cousin. My eyes scanned that, too, thinking there'd been a mistake:

James Algernon, 10th Earl of Westerham; b. 2 February 1784; Son of Hon. James Terrence Dunlap and Lady Althea

Webster; m. 12 December 1814 Lady Eleanor Watte...

I didn't dare say a word to him as his own eyes perused the paragraph and went back to read it again more thoroughly. His expression told me of the shock he'd just received. But how strange! The information was so incomplete—no date of succession, no explanation. Did this mean that he'd never gone back to reclaim his land and title?

When he looked up at me, his face was a chalky white, his mouth hard and unflinching.

"I'm sorry," I began, but halted at the brittle glint in his eyes. "What does it mean?"

Without answering, he flipped back toward the copyright page and introduction. His eyes moved rapidly, then halted at a paragraph standing by itself. His voice, calm, belied the anger I'd been expecting.

"I am not sure what it means, Jessica, though several possibilities come to mind. First of all, the publishers themselves admit a possibility of error through omission or faultiness in the information given them. You have noticed that nothing at all is mentioned of me beyond my name and the date of my birth. That there is no mention of issue, date of death, or reason for the succession. Don't you observe that in the other biographies, even if one of my ancestors or successors died without heir, his date of death or the reason for succession is mentioned? Look at my father's history, for instance: 'Robert Julian, eighth earl of Westerham; born 4 April 1736; married 1761 Lady Elizabeth Hodge, daughter William Hodge, sixth viscount Edgemare, died 1777, no issue; married 1779 Mary Windover, daughter Sir George Windover and Lady Madeleine Hants, died 1800, issue; died 19 August 1801; issue, Christopher R. J. G., ninth earl of Westerham...'"

He continued determinedly, "Both you and I know something occurred to me in 1812, but there is no way to even guess at a disappearance or ultimate return by looking at what is written here. There are no dates, no details. True, it appears my cousin succeeded me—but when? Shortly after I had vanished? Or years later, after I had returned from this journey in time and succumbed to illness or some other mishap? Of course, it also occurs to me that James may have used my untimely disappearance to his advantage. You would have to be acquainted with the history surrounding my cousin James, my father's brother's eldest son—and my heir if I were not to produce another. There never was any love lost between the two of us. James is—was—a despicable cad...he could never stoop too low to gather the laurels another had earned. The smaller the amount of effort he put into a task, the more it was to his liking, and so had been his character since the time he was in knee breeches and tagging along after me during visits to my father's estates. He always envied me, and despised me because I was heir and he was only the son of a younger son. He felt that because of the injustice fate had served him, the rest of the world owed him a great deal. He was in and out of trouble from the first day I can remember. When he was a youth, he played mischievous pranks—cruel ones. As he grew older, there were gaming debts, unsavory associations, tangles with prostitutes. And lately his intrigues have been far more infamous. He has always wanted the title, and I have sometimes felt, especially in the last year or two that he would consider taking almost any measures to reach that end.

"About six months ago from the lips of an astute gentleman who is often in my employ to ferret out information pertaining to my business dealings, I caught wind of a scheme in which my dear cousin was involved. This was no ordinary scheme, and its implications were shocking.

"It seems my cousin was well over his elbows into a Bonapartist conspiracy to assassinate the Prince of Wales—an act intended to cause enough upheaval and distraction in England that a sneak invasion by Napoleon would be successful. Nonetheless, the gentleman I mentioned was fortunate enough, by watching the mails coming and going from my cousin's house in London, to intercept several very damning letters written by and to James—not using his name, of course—tying him into the assassination plot so tightly there could have been no hope for his defense.

"Before I had the opportunity to do something with the letters, the plot blew apart. One of James' accomplices in England apparently panicked at some unfounded suspicion. He spilled the story in a pub to the wrong set of ears and fled the country. Agents of His Majesty caught two other accomplices red-handed with a small arsenal of arms in a flat in East London, and in the ensuing altercation the accomplices were killed. The prince was saved, but with the silencing of the only known tongues that could prove witness to his guilt, so was my cousin—except for my own damning evidence. I was waiting for a few more pieces of information and the right moment to produce it to the proper authorities to end his career for good. Unfortunately, my trip here intervened."

He took a long breath. "But do you see why I have gone into this long story? After learning of this espionage in which James was involved—for which I am sure he received a healthy payment in gold—I realized that nothing was quite beneath his touch. Reading this grievously short history of me now, it is tempting to think that when he heard of my unexpected disappearance, he took the bull by the horns.

"How simple it would be for him to twist the facts completely about, especially with his full knowledge of them, and throw the blame for the assassination plot on me since I was not around to defend myself. If my gentleman friend who had originally put me on to James' misdeeds had heard of his further intrigue and tried to speak up in my defense, I'm sure it would not have irked James' conscience to expediently dispose of the fellow to silence his tongue. Then it would have been an easy matter for him to put forth my disappearance as a timely departure when I had known the plan had failed and feared for my own skin. And even if not all of my loyal friends believed him, if the record as to my integrity seemed to contradict what he was saying, I was not present to show it for the lie it was. He would have been cunning enough to mention my supposed guilt to only enough of the right ears to promote his own easy succession."

"But you have the evidence against him," I interjected. "You could have cleared your name. Doesn't this prove you're not going back?"

"No, because I might not be able to get to the evidence if James is already installed in Cavenly. The papers are hidden in the house, and it is not likely James will allow me ready access in order to retrieve them.

"As you can see, I do not consider the information in this peerage final proof of my destiny. The vagueness alone seems to defend my position."

"Yes, but it's still supposition. Or hopefulness," I added gently.

"I know. I can see why you might think the odds are fifty to one against me. I choose to believe they are with me, though I admit the road ahead of me doesn't appear a pleasant one."

I sighed and closed the massive book in front of us. "So, in fact, we're back where we started."

"I am afraid so."

"And what do we do now? Just wait and see? If you are here another two or three years, are you going to spend those years marking time?"

"I must dig further into this—try to turn up some long-buried facts that might point me in either direction. But I need time to consider it all. I feel right now as though my head were spinning."

"Mine, too." I checked the clock. "Christopher, I want nothing more than to sit here and talk further, but I have to get to work. Do you want me to drive you home?"

"I would rather walk, if you do not mind, and hope that the exercise clears my head."

"All right, then I'll see you tonight."

He nodded. The expression on his face as I rose and left the room was that of a man plunged into very serious contemplation.

SIX

His determination to go back was the foremost thought in his mind. I gave up trying to get him to consider otherwise and began to live from day to day, enjoying his company and the friendly companionship of our conversations.

I took him riding. His delight at being on horseback again was heartwarming. He was an excellent horseman, putting me to shame, but he was a generous teacher, too, showing me how to improve my seat and hands. "Remember, Jessica," he said to me, "though the size and strength of your mount may intimidate you, the horse is a beautiful but dumb beast. Treat him as though you are indeed his master, and you will always be in control."

I tended to disagree with his view of horses being dumb beasts. I saw all other mammals as being intelligent in their own way, and we had to learn to communicate with and understand them, so that they could communicate with and understand us.

But soon I was more confident of myself, feeling proud as I rode beside him, mixing my silent beliefs about the needs for kindness and understanding with his obvious skills at horsemanship. We trotted down the woodland trails. He talked more freely during our rides. He spoke of his fear for the future of his estates in his cousin's hands. He dreaded what would happen to his breeding stables and tenant farm under James' jurisdiction.

"He has no sense of the land or the work necessary to keep it prosperous. He'll think only of women and gaming, and bleed Cavenly into bankruptcy."

"He may not, Christopher. He may turn over a new leaf."

"You have a greater belief than I in the perfectibility of an ignoble nature."

Gradually the cool evenings and clear-aired days of late spring rolled into the humid stickiness of summer. The Fourth of July was upon us. We participated in the excitement by watching a parade and, later, fireworks sent up in a glorious display from Eastport Beach over the waters of Long Island Sound. We'd been invited to several parties over the weekend, none of which he seemed inclined to attend. Not that I minded. I enjoyed the exclusiveness of his company, and at a party I'd be forced to share him with too many others.

Weeks earlier, my friends, tired of waiting for an invitation to visit, began dropping by of their own accord. They came on the pretense of seeing me, but more often I would find our chats cut short when Christopher entered the room. I watched my friends become mesmerized one after one.

Christopher was no more than his usual polite and cordial self. But he had an effect on women, an inborn charm and magnetism that drew them to him. I would catch their covetous looks, twinges of envy that I and not they had been the one to snag him. If they only knew how little they had to be jealous of.

One evening Sonya Travers had dropped by. Sonya was not a close friend. As a matter of fact, I really didn't care for her. We'd meet socially, she'd call occasionally, and we were usually included on each other's guest lists. But the friendship went no further than that. I had the feeling that given the opportunity and incentive, she wouldn't hesitate to double-deal a supposed friend or steal away someone else's lover if she found him attractive. She had the looks and glib tongue to do it, which was one reason I was so dismayed to open the door to find her standing there.

"Well, hi, Jes. I was just passing by on my way over to Meg's and thought, 'It's been ages since I've seen Jes. Let me just stop in and say hello!'"

"It's nice of you to stop," I answered, lying through my teeth. "Please come in."

I ushered her into the living room and watched as she settled herself gracefully on the couch. "Can I get you something? Coffee, a drink?"

"Thanks, yes, a drink sounds lovely. A little Scotch, if you have it."

"Sure. Make yourself comfortable." An unnecessary statement on my part, as she was already molding herself into the couch, looking as if she were planning to stay there for a while. I went into the other room and fixed a drink for each of us. Christopher was upstairs in his room taking a nap, and I hoped he'd remain there for the duration of her visit. I returned to the living room and seated myself on an easy chair facing her.

"Thanks, Jes." She took a sip from the drink I'd handed her. "So what have you been up to? Haven't seen hide nor hair of you lately."

"I've been working pretty hard, doing a little riding, nothing special." While I spoke, her eyes scanned the room. I knew she was looking for some sign of Christopher.

She turned back to me, raising her perfectly shaped brows. "Nothing special?" She laughed. "That's not what I heard. The word's out that there's a certain very handsome English gentleman in your life whom you've been hiding away from the world over here. Now, I don't call that nothing. Come on, Jes, fill me in. I'm just dying of curiosity!"

I sincerely wished I'd told her I was sick when I answered the door. But as I was thinking this, I heard Christopher's footsteps on the stairs and groaned inwardly. Damn, my luck hadn't held out at all. She heard him, too, and I watched her eyes light up with anticipation.

Christopher entered the room, still a bit fuzzy from sleep, but immaculately neat and as handsome as usual.

"Oh, we have company," he said, surprised. "I didn't realize." His eyes surveyed Sonya as he spoke, and I wondered if he was having the same effect on her that he had on me.

"Sonya," I said, forcing out a polite introduction, "I don't believe you've met my house guest. Christopher Dunlap, Sonya Travers."

He crossed the room to take her hand. "A pleasure to meet you, Sonya. Jessica has so many friends, I seem to be meeting a new one every day."

Her face was all smiles now. "I'm sure it must be a problem keeping track of all these new faces. It's so nice to meet you. I've heard so much about you and can hardly believe I'm finally meeting you at last." She looked at him through her long, blackened eyelashes. "Imagine Jes keeping a man like you hidden away for so long. Shame on you, Jes." She directed the last words to me, but smiled at him beguilingly, and I could see he was flattered. She sounded as corny as hell to me, but somehow she managed to pull it off.

"We were just having a drink, Christopher," I interrupted, hoping to draw his attention away from the artful pose she was affecting for his benefit. "Can I get you something?"

He glanced at me and flashed one of his dazzling smiles. "The usual, Jessica, if you do not mind." Then turned his eyes immediately back toward hers.

I wished I'd held my tongue and let him suffer with his thirst, because as soon as I rose, I saw her patting the vacant spot on the sofa beside her, beckoning to him. "Come sit down

here and tell me about yourself. We've all been so anxious to
meet you and help you feel more at home in a strange country.
I understand you're over here from England to do a little boning
up, but really, you know, all work and no play makes John a dull
boy, as the saying goes."

I caught her last words as I walked into the next room. Her
cuteness nauseated me. I returned quickly with his drink.

"Actually, I think you've come here just to charm all of us
American girls out of our senses," Sonya was saying as she
ran her eyes quickly over him.

He laughed. "How kind of you to say so, but I fear you are
overestimating my abilities."

"Never! A handsome man like you? You're far too modest."
Her teeth gleamed as she gave him another winning smile.
"And if you had any sympathy at all, you'd be out enjoying
yourself and giving the rest of us the benefit of your company.
I don't know how Jes could have been so inconsiderate in letting
you stay fenced up here without any outside entertainment.
You've been missing a great deal. You know, I've always
wanted to meet an Englishman. That accent of yours...it just
sends shivers down my spine."

Her soft pink lips puckered for a moment, then relaxed.
"So you're a professor?"

He nodded.

"And I've always thought professors were dry, bespectacled
creatures. How misinformed I've been. What do you teach?"

"History."

"At Eton, isn't it?" He nodded. "Quite a fine school from
what I've heard. But I want to hear all about England. Such a
pretty country—as a matter of fact, I was thinking of taking a
trip over there in the next few months."

"Were you? Well, there are many fine places to see if you
do go. You must spend some time in London, of course, and
you might find Bath and Cornwall worth seeing, too." He began
sketching brief descriptions for her, while she sat with a rapt
expression on her face.

I might not have been in the room for all the notice I was
attracting. I was fuming. He seemed taken with her, and I'd
thought more of him than that. She was a red-haired, green-eyed
cat. I felt my own claws rising, ready to tear out her eyes.

He finished his description of England.

"It sounds marvelous," she exclaimed. "It's a shame I

couldn't plan my trip at a time when you'll be back home." Her look toward him couldn't have been more blatant an invitation.

"Unfortunately for me, my words will have to do. I'll be in the States for some time yet."

"Oh?" She sighed but quickly rallied. "Then we'll have to get better acquainted in this country, won't we?"

"A delightful undertaking, I'm sure." He smiled.

Then suddenly, as if recalling herself from a trance, she glanced at her watch. "Oh, my! I've completely forgotten the time, and I have an appointment to meet someone. I really must go...much as I'd rather continue this conversation."

She gathered up her purse and drained the last drops from her drink. Then her voice purred forth once more. "Listen, I didn't get to mention it before, but I'm having a few people over for cocktails next weekend. Some close friends. But there'll be a few professionals and businessmen from the area joining me whom I'm sure you'd enjoy meeting. I'd love to have you come. Of course Jessica's welcome, too, if she'd like," she added in afterthought. "Do try to make it. I'll give you a call during the week to confirm it, shall I?"

He was silent for a moment, considering her invitation.

"Actually I think I will have to pass. I am really quite busy with my research now...though I do hope you will think of me another time."

"I most definitely will. The summer's just beginning." She grinned up at him, extending her hand. "It's been a pleasure meeting you."

"The pleasure is mine, Sonya. I hope we shall have the opportunity to see each other again soon."

I rose as Sonya moved toward the door.

Christopher gave me an absentminded smile. "Do not bother, Jessica. I can see Sonya out." He left the room at Sonya's elbow, listening as she murmured something to him.

I heard their voices in the hall, the sound of the front door closing. Christopher returned to the room with a preoccupied expression and picked up his unfinished drink. "Attractive woman."

"Do you think so? I've never noticed."

His eyes flicked toward me with a twinkle. "A close friend of yours?"

"Not particularly." I went to the couch to straighten the pillows.

"Then you are pleased I did not accept her invitation."

"You're free to do as you wish."

"But you were invited as well," he reminded me.

"That's not what she had in mind, m'lord, as well you know."

"My, but you are short-tempered all of a sudden."

"I'm just tired. I think I'll go up to bed."

"Bed already? I forbid it. It is much too early— especially since I just got up. Come, I have a better idea. We will play a game of cards. Poker, if you please."

Already he was heading toward the dining room table, looking back over his shoulder to see if I was following.

It didn't take too much effort on his part to sway my decision. I cursed myself for being such a willing fool. Yet the result was a very agreeable two hours spent playing several furious games of five-card stud.

SEVEN

As we got further into summer, I put one tomorrow behind me, and another, keeping my fingers crossed that each day wouldn't be the last that was mine to share with him. I was growing accustomed to having him around—seeing his razor lying on the bathroom sink, hearing his cheery good-mornings, knowing my spare room was now his domain. And if he did leave after all this time, it was going to shatter me. It was a possibility, one I couldn't bring myself to think about.

His attitude was the same as it had been. He thought no further ahead than his plans for the day—but he was running out of things to do on his own. Boredom was finally taking hold, a restlessness stemming from a purposeless existence that no man as vital as Christopher could long endure. Then, too, our summer heat, so unlike the more temperate English summers, was annoying him, prickling his normally easygoing disposition and making him occasionally short tempered. I wanted to ask him what was wrong, but I was afraid I'd learn he'd grown weary of my company.

One morning as I woke I heard him moving about in the bathroom, the soft whir of the air-conditioner muffling his sounds. It was Saturday, and I'd slept late. I heard him make his descent to the kitchen. I dressed and followed him down.

"Ah, just in time," he said as he poured me a cup of coffee. "Let me be the cook this morning. I guess you are happy this is your day off."

I nodded.

"Well, I am glad you are home today, too. I want to talk to you."

"Oh?"

He took a few sips from his mug. "Jessica, you realize I have been here for two months."

"I'm not likely to forget."

"I never expected to be here this long. Oh, I know, you have tried to convince me of the possibility of my visit going on for some time, but I am stubborn, and I didn't believe it. Now I am forced to consider it." He drank once more from his mug as if debating how best to phrase his next thoughts. "I looked through your checkbook the other day. I know it was none of my business, and I apologize for that, but it woke me up. My

God, how much it costs to run this house each month! I have no idea how you have done it. Here I have been lazing around, playing the lord, so wrapped up in my dreams of going back I did not even stop to consider what a financial burden I have been on you. Jessica, I am ashamed of myself. It is, I hope, unlike me to be so unfeeling. Why did you not speak up? There must be something I can do to help you."

I didn't like the trend of the conversation, but wasn't sure where it was headed. "It's been no hardship, Christopher."

"It has been difficult enough. I have only to look at the money you've been piecing out here and there to know it's a fact. And I have not done a goddamned thing to help you."

"What was I supposed to say? That I needed your money when you had none to give? What can you do to help? I realize in your own world money is no object, but here it's something different. I seriously doubt you can get credit on your estates when you haven't been around to take care of them for the last hundred and sixty years."

"I am getting a job. And I should have done it much sooner." He was in one of his fighting moods, determined and obstinate, but what kind of job could he get without having to present a Social Security card and a multitude of other types of identification?

"I realize I must seem sadly lacking in practical talents when it comes to your world, but all I really need to find work are certain legal credentials, and I have circumvented that problem.

"There is a construction site downtown—maybe you have seen it—a new office complex. I made the acquaintance of the foreman. A very likable fellow and quick to talk about his problems, which appear to be major ones and perfectly suited to my needs. There are certain jobs he has for which he can not keep anyone on for more than two weeks. The men he gets feel they will do better on your Unemployment, where they can get several hundred dollars sitting on their asses rather than breaking their backs lifting steel and concrete all week. He needs someone who will stay on the job, and when I told him I was looking for work, cash work, he offered me the job— and—listen to this, Jessica—for double the wage he was paying the last man he hired! I already told him I shall take it. I start Monday."

This was the last thing I'd expected him to say. For a

moment I was stunned, but soon my mind was catching at points that perhaps he hadn't considered carefully enough. "Do you have any idea what you're getting yourself into? Do you think you can handle the physical end of it? Have you forgotten who you are? I doubt if in your whole life you've ever had anyone tell you what to do. How are you going to like taking orders all day when you've only been used to giving them yourself?"

"We are not in England now. I shall do what has to be done. I am a man. It is my responsibility. If I had been thinking clearly, I would not have allowed the situation to get this far out of hand."

"You've made up your mind?"

"I have. It is settled." He expelled a long breath. "I have been thinking about some other things, too. Perhaps it is my time for reckoning."

He looked pointedly at me. "Would it surprise you if I said that sometimes lately I am not as anxious about going back as I was?"

"It would surprise me a great deal."

"But why?"

"You've seemed to hate to admit that there could be a life here for you. Today, for the first time, you acknowledge that you can see the possibility of staying. You've never said that before."

"I have not made it easy for you, have I?"

"No, but I'm not the slightest bit sorry for what's happened. I'm glad you're here. We'll make the best of it, and if you feel this job is what you have to do, then I'm happy you've taken it."

I got up from the table in a swift motion. I couldn't help thinking that now, with a job, his dependence on me would be ending. Would he soon be breaking the news to me that he was moving out to quarters of his own, leaving me to live my life as I had before his arrival? I was afraid.

He began his new job that next Monday, and on the surface things improved. His morale lifted, and my financial situation was eased by his contributions. He was exhausted nearly every evening, but it was worth having him fall asleep on the couch by nine o'clock just to see the improvement in his attitude. I had to rouse him and send him stumbling up to bed the first few days, but soon his body began adjusting to the physical demands of the job.

Between all the busy hours at the construction site, he spent as much time as he could researching what had happened to him, trying to answer the questions that had been disturbing him since the day we'd read the Burke's Peerage. He searched through all the relevant books he could find at the local libraries, but most of them were general texts relating to the history of his period rather than studies of individuals or families. He also searched for an explanation of the phenomenon that had carried him a century and a half into the future, but here he came up with dead ends. It wasn't a topic the scientific world took seriously, and aside from the theorizing Einstein had done, he found nothing with which to comfort himself. My own theory on the subject—that it was a freak of nature and highly unlikely to happen to the same person more than once in a lifetime—I didn't repeat. He didn't need my opinions to add to his worries.

His search for facts soon exceeded the meager capacity of the local libraries. He wrote to the Department of British History at Yale University for copies of unpublished papers he'd come across in the footnotes of the texts he'd been reading. He struck up a valued correspondence with one of the professors curious to know the reason for the depth of Christopher's interest in this particular period of English history. Christopher and Professor Enright exchanged letters, and the professor forwarded the papers, together with some data on the current ruling class.

From the latter information, Christopher gleaned some details on the current earl of Westerham and his family, the state of the family affairs, and a record of both the British and Swiss residences. But more important, he learned that Cavenly was still there, intact and prospering as he'd so hoped.

The other papers he'd obtained were mainly of a political nature. They didn't delve into the histories of the noble families of the time unless their lives were meshed with politics. He did have the thrill of seeing his name mentioned in passing as one of the supporters of a bill presented to the House of Lords in 1810, but beyond that there was nothing.

He wrote again to Professor Enright, requesting further information. A letter came back, inviting him to come to Yale to see firsthand what was available. He shied at this, probably afraid he'd reveal too much to someone very well acquainted with his own period of history. But he continued to write and received more information—yet, unfortunately, nothing about

his life that would tell him what had occurred after the spring of
1812.

On our own relationship to one another, I drew a blank. His
feelings for me were as unreadable as ever. One night I came
home from work to find Christopher on the telephone. When
he hung up a few minutes later, I asked who it was.

"Sonya," he said mildly. "She calls from time to time to say
hello." Yet before I could question him further, he averted his
eyes and walked past me to the other room.

There were times when I'd sit across the room from him,
and I'd look up from whatever I was doing to find him staring
at me. I'd see a strange expression on his face, his blue eyes
gazing contemplatively at me. I never knew what he meant,
but I was very much aware that as soon as he knew I was
watching, he'd drop his glance quickly back to whatever was
before him, not permitting me a deeper look.

Could there be any question that he was a man possessing
in full measure the drives and yearnings of the male sex? Did
he ever want a woman? I wondered. Did he ever have the
urge to take advantage of what was close at hand and come to
me?

There were opportunities almost thrown at his feet. Once I
walked out of the bathroom in my nightgown to nearly collide
with him in the hall. We stood there and stared at each other. I
looked at his bare-chested body, he at the semitransparency of
my gown, and we didn't move. I saw his strongly muscled
shoulders, the mat of dark hair, wide at his chest and running in
a triangle down to his pants, and was seized with such an intense
physical longing I found it almost beyond my power to control
myself. What reactions he was experiencing I could only
imagine, but then embarrassment overcame me. I scuttled into
my bedroom, and he into the bath. Once behind a closed door,
I mused about him rushing in to take a cold shower, then chastised
myself for overestimating my attractions.

But God, how I longed to see the fire light in his eyes, to
feel the warmth of his mouth pressed against mine once more,
the caress of the kiss I remembered, and the feel of his strong
arms and the length of his virile form touching me. I wanted
him to follow me into my room and tear the gown off my back.
It didn't happen, of course. I yearned silently.

EIGHT

Temperatures stayed high for a spell that summer. There was hardly a breath of relief from the energy-draining heat and humidity. Yet despite it, one weekend in early August Christopher went out to the yard to remove a rotten tree stump that had become an eyesore. The physical exercise brought him pleasure, even though I thought he'd had enough of it during the week.

As he worked, I watched his muscles rippling under his sweat-shiny skin. He was bare to the waist, damp forelock falling on his brow, lines of determination etched in his face as he raised the axe to destroy the dead wood. I felt excited seeing his beautiful physique at work and ached to run across the yard to wrap my arm around him. The desire left me quickly when I realized my foolhardiness.

I went to the garden, in clear view of him, and began weeding. I looked up to watch him, and when I did, I found him watching me as well. He was squinting his icy blue eyes, and for a long moment he gazed at me appreciatively. Before I had time to digest his look, his expression changed abruptly to a scowl. He dropped his axe so the blade sank into the grass, and then he crossed the distance between us in a few quick strides to stand glaring over me as I remained crouched on my knees.

"What in God's name has come over you?" his voice whipped. "Has the heat gone to your head?"

"What...?" I hadn't the slightest idea what he was talking about.

"Look at you!"

I looked. "What's wrong?" I lifted bewildered eyes to his frowning brow.

"You are half naked," he stormed.

I looked again at the faded cutoffs and comfortable halter-top I wore. I couldn't understand his anger. "I have more on than you do."

"But I am a man!"

"This is the style now. You've seen other women dressed like this before."

He didn't seem to hear me. His eyes dropped from my slightly amused face to my breasts, and there they held. I felt a slow flush creeping into my cheeks.

With a sudden start, he recalled himself, and his voice hissed with anger. "My God in heaven, you're practically hanging out of that thing! Get in and put on something that covers you." It was an order, and before I could say a word, he turned sharply on his heel and stalked off, his fury written in the rigid set of his shoulders.

"Christopher," I called after him, but he didn't seem to hear me.

I ran across the lawn after him. "Christopher!" He turned to face me. His mouth and eyes still hard.

"Well! I thought you were going to change."

"I'm not going anywhere until you hear me out." I planted my feet solidly.

"And I refuse to listen while you're dressed like an advertisement for a brothel."

I grabbed his arm as he was getting ready to turn away again. "I don't understand why you're making such a big thing out of this."

"Are you going to stand there half naked, or are you going to put some decent clothing on?"

"Dammit, Christopher, you're not seeing anything you haven't seen a hundred times before."

"And that's all you need—the knowledge that everyone else is doing it—to make it acceptable to you? I thought you were different. I thought you were a lady! I do not expect to see you dressed like that again—at least not in my presence. Am I clear?"

"Oh, you're quite clear. And what gives you the right to dictate to me, I'd like to know?" I was furious. "I'm perfectly well aware of right and wrong, and if I want to dress like this, dammit, I'll dress like this. How dare you even infer—much less say—that I'm not a lady? You're the one who needs some straightening out, not me. You and your old-fashioned ideas. Never once since you've been here have I told you how to behave—and there've been plenty of times when I probably should have. I didn't feel it was my place. But suddenly you feel it's your place to boss me around as if I were some...some...serving maid of yours."

I was so angry I was sputtering, and I could have said more, but the expression of cold fury on his face put a halt to my tirade. I'd never seen a man so angry with me. For a moment I thought he was going to hit me, but I could see him consciously checking that impulse, forcing his arm to his side.

His eyes were blazing. Tension showed white around his mouth, "Does your cocksure independence know no bounds? Leave me!"

Damn him and his lofty commands. He wasn't even going to argue the issue. Instead he'd turned away from me to stand looking frozenly into the adjacent woods. There was nothing I could do but utter an angry exclamation and stamp back to the house.

I paced between the rooms, mentally abusing him, throwing at him the full vent of my fury. I thought I was beginning to understand him. How wrong could I be? I watched him pound away at the stump. He was probably wishing it were me under the blade instead of an inanimate piece of wood.

Very slowly my anger began to cool, and I supposed in his own way Christopher had been trying to look out for my best interests. Maybe his anger was a sign that he cared more for me than I expected. But I could not tolerate being ordered around. It rubbed against my grain like fingernails on a blackboard. Inevitably, as I had just done, I would lose my judgment and fling out harsh retorts that normally I would keep to myself.

It was a little late for regrets now, but as the afternoon wore on, my cloud of anger and humiliation metamorphosed into a mild depression. I was afraid that even if Christopher had begun to feel some warmer feelings for me, my unconsidered remarks of the afternoon had pushed those feelings far from his mind. It was horrible to think that a moment's impulsiveness might have made a mockery of all the good intentions I'd cultivated for months.

By five o'clock I couldn't stand the tense inactivity any longer, and to keep my hands and thoughts occupied constructively, I started dinner.

I was fiddling with some pots on the stove when he came in. He stood in the doorway, surveying me for a moment. He was dripping with sweat, his damp hair clinging like a cap to his head. Then he came slowly across the room and stood in front of me. He looked down at me, and with those knee-weakening blue eyes staring into mine, I forgot the last three wasted hours. I saw only my reflection swimming in his eyes. I wanted only to be close to him.

"Jessica." His face bore traces of humbleness and remorse. "Jessica, I am sorry. I realize it is not my part to criticize, and you have every right to be angry."

"Well, I was angry." I pulled my gaze quickly from his, then brought it back again, "Oh, I'm not angry now...I never stay angry for long. But I don't understand why you came down on me like that."

"I was not thinking. But Jessica, your attire."

"Made you angry," I finished for him. "Christopher, there was nothing that indecent about the way I was dressed."

"No, no there was not. It was more than that...it was what..." The muscles along his jaw tightened for a brief instant, as if he were thinking of something else, then relaxed as he shook his head to push the thoughts away. "It is of no matter. What is important is that our relationship not be ruined by a foolish argument. I promise in the future not to repeat that boorish display. I shall try to keep my opinions where they belong. Will you forgive me?"

"If you'll forgive me for all the horrible and hateful things I said. I was trying to get back at you."

"I know." His eyes, brilliant against the tan of his stern face, were watching me. I wanted his firm lips to come down hard on mine in a sweet kiss of forgiveness, but he squeezed me quickly and smiled. "Then we are friends again?"

I nodded, not sure of my voice.

"Good. We shall try to forget this unpleasant incident, and I am sorry, Jessica." He hugged me quickly once more and dropped his arms. "When you are finished in here, will you come in and play the piano for me?" He knew his words would mollify me, and if that wasn't enough, he took my hands to give them a gentle squeeze. "All right?" he coaxed.

"All right." I tried to ignore the weakness his touch brought to my body. It signified nothing, this action of his, except to pacify my anger. I steeled myself against the warmth of his fingers, the very near proximity of his body, and in a moment he took his hands away and left the room.

NINE

Through the rest of August I was edgy and in a very unstable state of mind. Finally one night I decided to visit a close friend, whom I spoke to or called weekly, but to whom I'd never confided the truth about Christopher. In a way, I couldn't believe that I hadn't confided in her, because we were so close and had never kept secrets from each other. But somehow the truth about Christopher's illogical appearance in my life was something I'd been afraid to share, even with my closest friend.

But that night I was ready to have a good woman-to-woman talk. Dana Wood and I had been friends since high school and had managed to keep our strong ties through the years when we both returned from college to our hometown and began our separate careers. Just as I had, she'd suffered the unhappiness of an unsuccessful marriage. I'd been tempted many times to tell her the real truth of Christopher's arrival. In the end, I hadn't. I told her only the story we'd told everyone else.

Dana was a chic, pert brunette with a nonstop smile that could warm the coldest heart. For the past two years she'd been renting a cottage that was part of a large estate. The four rooms were exquisitely decorated in a style that reflected the warmth of her personality. I'd helped Dana collect odd bits of furnishings for her cottage, just as she'd helped me decorate my own house.

She greeted me happily when I knocked on the door.

As we settled on the couch, she poured two glasses of wine. "So what's new, Jes?"

"When was the last time I saw you, three weeks ago?" She nodded. "Did I tell you I got the promotion? I'm working with Jack now. Actually doing some writing. It's great."

She laughed, "Now, isn't that a coincidence. You know, Stanwick finally broke down and gave me my raise. I pinched out a few more of his cherished pennies. Guess he got tired of listening to me dropping hints all over the place. You'd think he was sacrificing his last loaf of bread, but heck, a promotion. That's twice as good. I'm really happy for you."

"I'm pretty happy myself," I agreed.

"Got my first check yesterday," she exclaimed, "and boy, did I go on a spending spree! Also dropped by the thrift shop, and you won't believe what I found—such a deal. A Dior original, and only thirty dollars. Wait, I'll show you." She scampered from the room and returned in seconds with a chic black-and-white creation on a hanger. "Like it?"

"I'll bet it looks fantastic on you."

"Sexy! I'm going to wear it for Jim on Saturday night."

"Speaking of Jim," I interrupted, "how are things going with you and him?"

She gave me a wicked little smile. "Good...really good. Actually, I didn't expect it to work out this well. I'm kind of surprised."

"Well, I'm glad to hear at least one of us is having success," I commented dryly.

"Do I hear a note of bitterness?" she quizzed. "With that mystery man of yours around, I thought you'd be ecstatic. What's up?"

"That's the problem—nothing, with a capital N. I swear to God sometimes he doesn't even know I'm living in the same house with him."

"No, you're kidding."

"I wish I were. He walks around in his world, and go around in mine—cursing it. Dammit, Dana, he turns me into butter, but I might as well be a piece of bread for all the attention he pays me." I paused. "You know, I caught Sonya over at the house the other day when I came home from work. It's not the first time she's been over when I'm not around. That sweet little miss, I'd like to throw acid in her face sometimes. The way she's been after him. I just hope he's not stupid enough to fall for her."

"She was over at your house? What were they doing?"

"Oh, nothing. Just talking, at least this last time when I caught them."

"Then what are you worried about?"

"The fact that she was there to begin with. She and I aren't exactly bosom buddies, you know, and she obviously wasn't there to sweeten my day."

"I'm getting the message. But, Lord, you're head and shoulders above her. Do you really think you have to worry?"

"I don't know. In any case, he certainly doesn't seem to be crazy about me."

"Now, there I think you might be wrong. He has a way of looking at you....If a man ever looked at me like that, my knees would buckle right out from under me."

I was instantly alert. "When did you see this?"

"Several times, and I haven't seen him look at anyone else like that."

"You're kidding."

"Would I kid my best friend?"

"To make her feel good?"

"Never! Jes, you've got it all over Sonya, and any other woman I can think of offhand. Where's your confidence? Is it that you're so much in love with him that you've forgotten who you are?"

"Probably. I'm just so afraid. I analyze every stupid little thing I do. Instead of saying what I want to say, I say what I think he wants to hear. I am being stupid, aren't I? If he's going to care for me, it's pointless to have him care for something that's not real. But it's only lately I've been this way—when he started getting so sullen and moody. Maybe if I went back to the way it was in the beginning..."

"Just be yourself. He likes you."

"I wish I could be as sure as you seem to be. Dammit, I hate being in love! I wish I'd never met him."

"And where would you be then?"

"Oh, I don't know. But at least I wouldn't be tearing myself into little pieces."

"Give it time. He must realize by now he's probably here to stay...or maybe he's just taking what he has for granted. Why don't you try a little waking-up medicine?"

"What do you mean?"

"I mean, take the dust out of his eyes—and I've got the perfect thing. Jerry Walters called me the other night. They're having a dinner-dance at Longleaf, a closed party. They've invited all the old crowd plus some pretty swish people, and she told me to ask you. It's perfect, can't you see? You bring him, let him see you sparkling, socializing with your old crowd, you happen to run into one or two old male friends and get up and dance a couple of dances—and you know you're good—and if that doesn't wake him up, nothing will."

"He won't go."

"What makes you say that? How do you know until you ask, huh?"

"I'm afraid to."

"That doesn't sound like you."

"All right. Suppose I ask him, and he says yes. Then we get to the dance, and you know how he looks when he gets dressed up. All the other women will fall all over him, and I'll lose him for the night."

"That won't happen. For one thing, he's too much of a gentleman to leave you when he's come with you. For another, none of the other women there will be able to hold a candle to you. Put on some low-cut, sexy dress, and they'll all be eating their hearts out."

I laughed. "Nothing like a little exaggeration, but what would my ego do without you?"

"Your problem is that you're too much of a pessimist. Come on, it won't hurt to try. Why don't you ask him? The worst he can do is say no."

"And shatter what little is left of my pride."

"Well, if that happens, you know where you stand," she responded logically. "Right? Besides, I don't think he's going to say no." She clapped her hands together in glee. "Oh, this is going to be fun. I've never played the matchmaker before."

"You think maybe I should go to someone with more experience?" I put in wryly. She just laughed.

"Go home and ask him tonight. He'll go. Then all you have to do is go out and buy a sexy dress. I'll go with you."

I was giggling with her when I left, but by the time I was home I felt nervous and my stomach was tense.

He was sitting on the couch reading. He smiled when I came in. "Did you have a pleasant evening?"

"Very nice," I said mildly. "And you?"

He nodded. "I gather from the length of your visit, you two had quite a bit to talk about."

"We did a little gossiping, as usual." I took a deep breath, deciding no time was as good as the present, and plunged in. "Dana told me about a dinner-dance some of my old friends are planning. Sounds quite nice, formal...at one of the country clubs. I was invited, and, well, I was wondering if you'd like to go. With me, that is," I clarified as if in afterthought.

The blue eyes were twinkling. "First, you tell me. Would you like me to go with you?"

"Well, yes. I mean, it should be fun, and we don't get out very often."

"Then it is settled. I would love to. When is this ball?"

"September twenty-third."

"Do you think I will still be here?" His brows lifted in a teasing arch.

"That's my hope."

"And mine. I look forward to it."

I was surprised at how easy it had been to convince him. And after sitting down and sharing a relaxed conversation with him, I went up to bed with the proverbial stars in my eyes.

TEN

The skies were leaden the Sunday after Labor Day. I was trying to be engrossed in a novel while curled up in a living room chair, when I heard his footsteps crossing the room.

"I want to talk to you, Jessica." His voice held a serious note. "Put down the book. This is important."

I felt a touch of foreboding. "Is something wrong?" I waited, my gaze on his pensive face.

"I have been doing a great deal of thinking the past weeks. I have been thinking about you, myself...our situation." He fidgeted, studied a small spot on the floor as if it had particular interest for him, then looked up. "I have been thinking about our lives together. I hardly know how to express it to you, but it was not my intention to change your life. Of course, when I arrived in this world we did not know whether I would be here for more than a few days or weeks. Now it appears my stay may be indefinite." He paused, his knuckles pressing into the fabric of the couch as he sat hunched on its edge. "You and I get along well together. You do not complain of my being here. But the more I think of it, the more I realize that you are entitled to a life of your own, just as I, if I continue to remain in this world, must begin considering the life still ahead of me. I know you are too considerate to bring up the subject on your own or even hint that your life is less than it should be, but I know your social life has become nearly nonexistent, just as I know from various comments I have heard that you had a busy social life before, my arrival..."

"Your being here doesn't stop me from going out."

"The fact remains that if I wasn't underfoot, your opportunities would be much greater."

"Perhaps. But what does it matter? I'm not complaining."

"It is not exactly the sort of thing you would complain to me about, now is it?"

"If I thought I had reason to, I would. If I had a desire to change my situation."

He shook his head. "There is no point in beating around the bush, Jessica. I will say what I came to say. It is time I left you to make a life of your own and took a few steps in that direction myself."

"What do you mean?"

"I mean I am moving out—getting a place of my own."

"You're not serious!" I could feel my face draining of all
its color.

"I am very serious."

"But why?"

"Is it not obvious?" He lifted his eyes from his hands to
look searchingly at me. "We cannot go on any longer the way
we are."

"After all this time, you've decided to move?"

"That is just it—all this time."

I shook my head. "I don't understand. I thought you were
satisfied."

"It is not a matter of being satisfied. I am doing what I feel
I have to do. This is not healthy for you, and if I stay much
longer, well..." He let his voice drag, then hurried on. "I thought
you would see my reasoning."

I just stared at him. It was all I could do. "Yes," I said
almost silently. "I think I am beginning to see." It all began to
click. How had I been so stupid as not to have seen it from the
beginning? I was not a great deal more to him than a dear
friend. There was no deep emotion involved. It was from another
woman that he—would seek love.

He went on levelly, as if he was trying to make a point. "I
know your friendship with me can not be enough for you. You
need more than that, and it is not as though we shall not see
each other anymore, but we shall not be living out of each
other's pockets."

"Is that the way you think of it? Living out of each other's
pockets?" I could feel a lump growing in my throat.

He scowled. "Well, yes. Do you not feel that way?"

Just like that, as though with the snap of his fingers, he was
ending it, telling me in a few short sentences that the ember of
hope I'd kept glowing all those months had been a futile spark.
I lowered my eyes to hide the pain that was filling them. "And
when did you decide this?"

"Not all at once. I have been thinking about it for some
time, but I started making arrangements this week."

"I see." My voice sounded dead. "I had no idea."

"I thought you had guessed."

"No." I dragged out the syllable.

"I am sorry. I have done this poorly. I wish I were better at
explaining myself, but you see I care about you. I want to do

what is best without destroying our friendship—"

I cut him short. "When are you going?"

"I have been looking for a place. As soon as I find one."

"You don't have any furniture," I said nonsensically.

"I shall get a furnished apartment. I have seen several that I liked."

"Have you."

"I need something near town."

"Yes, I know." I was staring at my hands without seeing them.

"You will be happier, Jessica, without me cluttering up your life, and we can get together and go riding on Sundays." Was he making these rationalizations for me or for himself?

"We can do that," I said numbly, raising my eyes to his guiltless face.

"You do not mind if I stay on for a little while longer?" His eyes were so blue, so beautiful.

I stared at him, "Mind?"

"Yes. I know you will have your own plans to make now."

I sprang up from my chair and strode across to the fireplace to still the trembling that had begun in my knees. I gripped the mantel with my fingers. "No. I don't mind." My mouth was dry.

"It will be only for a little while, until I am settled."

"Yes, a little while." Tears were stinging my eyelids. I closed them. "No...stay. Stay as long as you like. What difference does it make? A day, a week, a month." There was really no point in asking any more questions. If he cared for me at all the way I cared for him, he wouldn't be leaving. I turned back toward him, but the soft, imploring look on his face was more than I could bear. Did he pity me? Pity for a foolish woman? "Well." I heaved a sigh. "That's that, isn't it? I guess you'll be happy." I managed a weak smile.

"Jessica..."

"Excuse me, Christopher, but I just remembered I have to go out."

"Wait, please..."

I walked out of the room, out of the house, to the car. I didn't know where I was going, but I knew I had to go somewhere. I was running, not thinking that the pain I was trying to escape was within me and would follow wherever I went. I started down the road. The rain was pouring down the windshield. I could barely see the road ahead.

I headed toward the country, somehow feeling I might find solace there. I drove for miles, speeding over the wet highways without thought for my safety. I turned off the paved road and onto a narrow dirt lane that led to the banks of a reservoir. Unable to sit still with my thoughts, I plunged out into the rain. I walked blindly, numbly toward the water, staring at its spattered surface. I followed the edge of the reservoir, walking knee deep in waving wet grass. He wanted to leave me. Was it because of another woman? Was Sonya the other woman?

We'd be friends, he'd said....I caught my leg on a log and cut my ankle. I kept walking. Oh, the wonders of friendship—could I survive them? And how was I to survive the time until he left? How was I to occupy the same space, trying to be cordial, sweet, friendly, acting as if it was all the same to me, when inside I'd be hurting so much the very sight of him was going to make me want to run to my room and lock myself away from the world.

Oh, but I would go on. I always did. I'd get over it, and it wouldn't hurt so much in time. There'd be others. I would survive. That was me. I always survived. If only I could get through today.

After the tears were shed, I'd start over. I'd been happy never knowing him. I could be happy again. Who was he to shatter my world into little pieces? I wasn't going to let it happen, not to Jessica Lund! I'd show him that my heart could be just as cold and heedless as his.

An hour later I drove home, soaked to the skin, dripping, shivering, bedraggled but determined.

I went straight upstairs and drowned myself under a hot shower, letting the water scorch my skin until the numbness was gone.

His expression was worried and questioning when he saw me downstairs, but the look of brittle aloofness I affected forestalled any consoling words he'd been contemplating. Our dinner conversation was in monosyllables, and I couldn't wait for the meal to be over so that I could escape. Later, after I'd vigorously scrubbed the kitchen in an effort to keep my thoughts at a distance, I went to the piano and played the most powerful, soulful pieces I knew. Chopin's *Prelude in D Minor*, the melancholy of Debussy, and Beethoven's *Moonlight Sonata*, interpreted brazenly and full of passion instead of softly and tranquilly. I played and played until the anguish had drained out of my body.

"I have never heard you play so well," he spoke quietly as I finally let my hands come to rest. "Do you want to talk to me, Jessica? Is there anything I can say?"

"There's nothing to say."

He came over and laid his hands gently on my shoulders, his eyes pleading. "Jessica, I did not mean to hurt you. I am doing what I think will be best." His expression was intense. He stared deeply into my eyes. Then slowly, as though without volition, he leaned toward me. My heart constricted as I watched his lips move closer. Those softly chiseled lips. But no. I couldn't endure any more pain. Couldn't become vulnerable again. I turned my head to the side.

My voice was cold. "You haven't hurt me, Christopher. Why should you say that? We're friends. That's what you wanted, isn't it? We'll be friends—you made yourself very clear. I'm beginning to think you're right —it's much better this way."

His mouth tightened, his eyes narrowing a hair's width. "Very well, Jessica." He removed his hands.

"If you'll excuse me," I said, "I'm going to bed. I'm very tired." I wanted to cry.

He stood aside, watching me strangely, and I walked past him.

"Good night, Christopher."

"Good night."

After that night our conversation became brief. I did my best to ignore him when it was within my power to do so, but the pretense of being indifferent toward him was hard to maintain. I didn't want him to know how badly I was hurt or to guess that I'd committed the unforgivable sin of falling deeply in love with him. I'd allowed myself to forget who he was and who I was. I had pushed to the back of my mind the fact that we were from different worlds and at any moment might be separated by the barrier of time. I had forgotten that if he did stay in my world, there were other women he could fall in love with.

My coolness widened the gap between us. He did what he could to make amends, but I was unable to accept his tokens of friendship at face value.

I was behaving childishly. I knew that, once he was out of my house, I'd wake up and see what an idiot I'd been. But just friendship wasn't enough for me. The emotion I felt for him was intensely strong—it was love or hate, or nothing. There was no room for subtle shadings. And to see the warm smiles he still bestowed upon me, and then a few minutes later hear him on the telephone calling about an apartment, reminding me that he'd chosen to step out of my life, had the effect of a knife blade thrust through my heart.

I talked to Dana and told her what had happened. She couldn't believe it. Christopher's decision to move was out of line with her conjectures. She tried her best to console me, but, really, what could she say?

As the days passed, I existed and healed, on the surface, anyway. I got used to thinking he'd be gone soon and knew that I would survive.

I buried myself in my job, pushing myself and working like an automaton. I'd stay at my desk until seven or eight at night and make a quick dinner when I got home. Jack, my boss, was concerned. It was on the tip of his tongue to ask me what was bothering me, but my warning look stopped him. The work helped to keep my mind busy, and he never questioned the small volume of good copy produced during those evening vigils. All I could think about was Christopher—his movements, his voice, his eyes, his broad-shouldered physique. Why did I have to love him so?

On one of those evenings when I'd come home late and was eating dinner by myself, Christopher came over to me with two glasses of wine and plopped down in the chair opposite me. "We are going to talk, Jessica."

"Are we?" I tried to be blasé.

"Have some wine with me."

I took the glass he offered and took a sip, more to cover the awkwardness I felt at the serious look in his eyes than out of thirst. He rested his forearms on the table with his hands clasped before him. He was wearing a light blue shirt. I noticed how tan his arms and hands looked against the pale color. His hair had grown a little long, but I liked the way it waved softly below his ears and down the nape of his neck to his collar. He smelled good, and it made me ache for him, as much as I tried to shut away my feelings of desire.

"What is the matter with you lately?" he asked without preamble.

"Matter?"

"Do not pretend you do not know what I am talking about. The last week and a half you have behaved like a stranger."

What did he expect? But I only replied, "Have I? I hadn't realized."

"Ever since I told you I was moving."

I looked sharply at him before I realized what I was doing, and my expression gave me away utterly.

"I thought as much," he continued. "Does my moving necessarily change things between us?"

"You can answer that better than I."

"I thought you would look forward to a chance to have your privacy again," he persisted.

"I told you before that I decided you were right, and this was the best thing for both of us."

"Then why is it you act as though you cannot stand the sight of me anymore?"

"Do I act like that? I don't mean to," I lied.

"You know perfectly well you do. You have changed. I sometimes get the feeling I cannot leave soon enough to satisfy you."

I finally put some life into my voice. "It wasn't my idea for you to move out. The thought wouldn't have crossed my mind if you hadn't decided it on your own. And now that you've made up your mind, I'm trying to make the best of it. What more do you want me to do?"

"And ending the warm and pleasant relationship we had is the best you can do?" He tightened his hands, making the muscles in his arms bulge for a second.

"I'm not the one who's ending it. I've never denied your friendship—I can't help it if I—" I stopped short, shook my head. "Never mind." I'd almost said too much.

He jumped on my words. "What were you going to say?"

"Nothing...nothing important." I abruptly changed the subject. "Are we still going to the dinner-dance on Saturday?"

"The ball?" He frowned. "I had planned on it." Was he surprised I'd asked? I saw his eyes narrow. "Unless you have become averse to my company."

I wanted to scream. It was no good. Why didn't I just come out and tell him I loved him? Why couldn't I swallow my pride? But I couldn't, knowing that he wanted to leave me. Instead, I riveted my gaze on my half-empty wineglass and said as calmly as I could, "I'm not averse to your company.

Whatever gave you that idea?"

"Everything you have said and done this evening and in the last week or so tends to give me that idea."

"Don't be silly. I like being with you."

"Look at me and tell me that, Jessica." His words held a touch of anger.

I looked up and swallowed hard to conceal my feelings. "I like being with you," I repeated, staring into his blue gaze.

His eyes never wavered as he seemed to mull over my words, then he reached out his hand and caught mine. I had to fight the urge to pull away. His touch was warm, electric. But his next words were like a shower of cold rain. "You know my reasons for leaving and that I am powerless to change them. Can you not put down your red flag and call a truce? Can we not be friends?"

"Do you really think we can?"

"Of course I do. It is not as if anything had materially changed, except that I shall not be living in this house anymore." He spoke very quietly. "To be perfectly honest, Jessica, I think too much of you to tolerate the waspish looks you have been throwing my way. I want to see you smile and laugh again—with me—not just when there are other people around."

I dropped my eyes and answered in a voice as quiet as his own, "All right, we'll try."

His tone softened. The tension had gone out of it. "Then how about beginning with a smile?" His hand released mine and touched me lightly under my lowered chin. The gesture alone was enough to make the ice begin to melt inside me, and without willing it, I felt warm excitement creep upon me. I raised my head and looked at him. My reward was one of his brilliant smiles that revealed the white flash of his teeth and made the skin crinkle at the corners of his eyes. "My sweet friend."

I just smiled. I was afraid to do more without releasing the dam on my emotions.

He went on quickly, as if he didn't want the newfound truce between us to end too soon. "Do you know how good it is to be able to talk to you again," he said, "really talk, without expecting a cold shoulder for my efforts. I have not told you, I got another increase in pay last week."

"No, you didn't tell me. You're making quite a bit now."

"Yes, a bit, but not enough to do all I want. Jessica, the

dreams I am beginning to have!" The life and spark where back in his voice.

"Will you ever be satisfied with the little you have here? It'll never compare to the wealth you had at home."

"Perhaps not, but I see no reason why I should be satisfied with drifting along. If I am going to stay, I intend trying to build my fortunes here. Even if I do not succeed, I can not sit idle and watch the world pass me by."

It was so obvious that what he needed and wanted was someone to talk to...someone in whom he could confide his plans. Was that the only reason he wanted our friendship to continue on an even keel? I was, after all, the only close friend he had in this world...until he could find another.

"I have this idea," he was saying. "Tell me what you think of it. It is just a seed right now, but if I can put aside enough of the money I'm making with this construction work—which I don't have to tell you, Jessica, is considerable, and all cash—I want to start buying up real estate. Nothing big at first, of course. Possibly something out in the country. I would hold it for a while and make some minor improvements, then turn around and sell it for a fair profit. It should work well. With the pattern of the real estate market just now, it is a sure investment. I do not see how I can lose if I invest in the right type of property."

"I see one problem right from the start. You have no identification. You can't get a mortgage."

"I have thought of that. Actually, it is my only stumbling block at the moment, but my plan was to start with something small, as I said, a few pieces of land where perhaps I would have enough to pay cash. I would clear off the land for building, cut in a drive, leave enough trees and whatnot so that it was appealing, and then sell the land for a few thousand more than I paid. I don't see any problem in that. Eventually, as I got involved in more complicated schemes, I would have to do something about identification. I have other reasons for wanting that as well," he added in an undertone. "But I think that will work itself out in time."

"Where there's a will, there's a way." I watched his eyes, full of the fire of determination.

"That is just what I have always felt, and although I am not discounting the ever present chance I shall be thrown back to my own time without warning, I want to start doing something constructive in this world. You were right all along, Jessica. I must consider a future here and stop hiding from reality. But, anyway, that is the gist of it, and once I do get some credentials..."

His enthusiasm caught me up like a fly in a spider's web. Against my better judgment, I let him draw me off into his plans for his future. I couldn't help thinking that a few weeks earlier, a conversation like the one we were now having and the knowledge that he was thinking beyond the possibility of returning to England and 1812 would have filled me with delight. Now it was different. There was no mention of my playing a part in his plans, and without that, there was no reason for rejoicing.

When I went to my room shortly after eleven, leaving him to watch the late news content in having voiced his plans to me and having won my approval, a feeling of sadness and loneliness slipped over me. I was empty again. I wasn't content being his confidante and friend. His friendship would never fill the longing within me. It wouldn't quench my thirst for his love. But unless I threw my cards on the table and made it plain to him just how deeply I cared, he'd never understand why we couldn't be just friends.

ELEVEN

Early Saturday evening, the night of the dinner party, I went to my room to dress. I pulled the beautiful green gown from the back of my closet, where it had hung ignored since the day he'd told me he was leaving. I held it up before me, taking pleasure again in its graceful, flowing lines, then laid it on the bed and went to bathe. It was no use remembering the daydream I'd dreamed the day I first saw it in the store.

When I returned to my bedroom, my body warm and scented with bath oil, I stood before the open window. Outside the birds were chattering. A low-flying plane droned overhead. Summer was singing its last song, and although the grass was still green and lush and the trees had just a few scatterings of red and gold leaves, I knew the barren grip of winter was just around the corner. Were the changing seasons a portent of what the future would bring for Christopher and me? Was tonight to be my last splash of autumn color before the cold emptiness of living without him?

The gown was silky against my skin as I slipped the soft folds over my head. When the draped lines were smoothly in place, I stepped into high-heeled sandals, fastened a long jade pendant around my neck so that it hung seductively between my breasts, then stood before the mirror of my Victorian dressing table. The green of the gown looked beautiful against my skin. My dark hair fell long and full to my shoulders and rested there in gentle curls. A warm flush was high on my cheekbones, and my eyes, though filled with uncertainty about the evening ahead, were still bright and sparkling.

It was a beautiful woman staring back at me from the mirror, but would Christopher notice, or would his thoughts be elsewhere? I picked up a white Mexican shawl and went down the stairs to meet him.

He was waiting in the living room. I paused in the doorway, unnoticed, and watched him as he stood there unselfconsciously in the lamplight with the last rays of sunlight washing over him. I let my eyes feast on the superb manliness of him that yet had the power to make my heart beat faster. He stood in profile, sipping dark liquid from a glass. Another glass rested on the table, waiting for me. He was wearing a long, fitted beige jacket from which his broad shoulders seemed to threaten to explode.

His dark locks shone. His straight nose and strong cleft chin were in silhouette. I stood silently, absorbing everything about him, even the faint aroma of his spicy cologne that drifted across the room.

As if sensing my presence, he turned, then slowly, gently let his gaze sweep over me. "You look beautiful." He smiled. His blue eyes fastened on mine intimately. Our glasses tinkled as we touched them together, and over the rim of his glass, his eyes held a promise. "We'll have a wonderful evening tonight, Jessica," he said.

My foolish heart almost stopped beating. In that moment I forgot he was leaving, forgot our differences, forgot everything except that he was here and I was with him. I was going to spend the evening at his side, and I loved him so very much.

As Christopher and I pulled to a stop on the graveled drive of the Longleaf Country Club, an attendant hurried over to take the car. We stepped out into the warm September night and, Christopher's hand on my elbow, followed the brick walk toward the front doors of the white clapboard clubhouse. Pools of brightness from scattered lampposts touched the manicured grounds nearby, and in the distance, beyond the golf course, the waters of Long Island Sound were just visible.

We were directed to the ballroom and, as soon as we were through the doors, were instantly surrounded by people, some just arriving, others with drinks in their hands. I left his side for a moment to find Dana, and it was with difficulty that I managed to squeeze through the mob to get back to him.

I emerged from the crowd, reached out and tapped his arm. As he saw me, his smile broadened. "Ah, you have returned to rescue me." He took my hand, but before leading him off, I was obliged to make some formal introductions to those I knew in the group surrounding us. I was aware of the barely concealed delight in some of the women's eyes. Even the men had a look of curious interest as they took his firm grasp in a handshake and noted the intelligence in his blue eyes.

A muted rush of conversation began behind us as we left the crowd to meet Dana and Jim. Christopher was causing a sensation, and it disturbed me.

We found our table one row back from the dance floor. The others at the table, the Osgoods and Jamesons, were old friends and witty company, making a pleasant group. Jim soon had Christopher's ear, and the two were off in a deep discussion of politics, leaving Dana and me to chat happily. I noticed her glancing curiously back and forth between Christopher and me, her dark eyes dancing with questions that, what with all the listening ears present, went unasked. We turned our conversation to other topics, Mary Osgood and Rona Jameson joining in. The four of us enjoyed a little invigorating gossip until the waiters began bringing out the first course of the dinner.

As the food arrived, conversation became general, and everyone joined in. The band was playing soft music in the background. We joked, laughed and argued, getting into quite a discussion of politics over the current city administration.

I'd glance at Christopher from time to time as the meal progressed, wondering what he was thinking, whether he was enjoying himself, and why he hadn't mentioned to any of the others that he would soon be moving into his own quarters. They all knew we lived together, but none but Dana knew the truth of our arrangement. Once, as I glanced in his direction, he looked up from his plate to meet my gaze. The smile and the light of happiness on his face sent goose bumps running down my arms.

"Are you enjoying yourself, Jessica?" A bewitching smile played about his lips.

"Very much. And you?"

"Most definitely. I had no idea there would be so many people here tonight."

"Neither did I. I see some people I haven't seen in years. I'll introduce you later."

He nodded, found my hand under the table, and held it warmly until Don Osgood called his name and brought him back into the conversation.

I took time to look carefully around the room. It was easy enough to pick out the faces I knew, but there were many, too, whom I didn't recognize. Fortunately, I couldn't spot Sonya, although I seriously doubted she would miss attending such an occasion.

The band was playing a quiet Viennese waltz as people were finishing up their coffee. A few eager couples went out to the dance floor. The waiters cleared away the last of the dishes. Christopher brought us each another drink, and together we sipped them and watched the dancers.

After a moment he found my hand again and pulled it toward him. "Would you care to show them up?"

I looked at him disbelievingly. "Us?"

"Not afraid of my skill, are you Jessica?" I blushed, but he smiled in good nature, and before I could refuse, he led me to the floor.

He pulled me easily into his arms, holding me just close enough so that I could feel the heat of his body and the material of his jacket rubbing against my arm, smell the intoxicating scent of his cologne blending with my perfume. It was delicious just to feel his arm around me.

"Ready?" he whispered.

"Ready."

He took one step, then another, and then we were swirling effortlessly across the floor, his hand firm on my back, his eyes laughing down into mine. He was a superb dancer. He led expertly, our feet moving as if we'd practiced the dance for hours together. I floated on a cushion of air, drawn into the romance of an earlier age as the music ebbed and flowed around us, my gown swirling out behind, my elegant partner with his head bent over my face. I could picture myself in a ballroom at Cavenly, candles shimmering in crystal chandeliers, elegantly dressed ladies and gentlemen moving about us, the room filled with their low chatter and laughter and scented with expensive perfume. I imagined tall windows open to the night air beyond, and its freshness caressing my cheeks. The music of violins echoed in the background as I was swirled in the arms of the master of the house, felt his embrace tighten, and saw him smile down at me with the tenderness of love. I watched the gleaming wood floor slip by beneath us, the sea of faces and tables blur as we glided past. I forgot everything but him.

His eyes, blue diamonds, were watching me. "You see what I mean, Jessica?" His voice brought me back to the present. "I promised you we would show them up."

"I see. But where did you learn to dance like this?"

"One of my varied accomplishments. What matters is whether you are enjoying yourself."

"I love dancing."

"We should have tried this a long time ago," he breathed into my ear. "We are perfectly matched, you know."

"I know...I know."

He dropped a light kiss on my brow, and I felt happily faint, aglow in the pure, unexpected headiness of it all.

I hummed softly to the music that seemed intended for us

alone.

His deep voice caressed the air. "Are you singing for me?"

"If you like. I usually sing to beautiful music when I'm happy."

"Then you are happy." His fingers tightened about mine. "No, go on. I like to hear the sound of your voice. It makes the music a thousand times sweeter."

I wanted to look up at him, but he pressed his cheek softly against my hair, and I had to be content with imagining the expressions crossing his perfect face.

We danced on tirelessly, moving together as fluidly as one. I felt his lips against my hair, his warm breath soft on my neck. He lifted his head and smiled again into my eyes. To me it was as if there was no one in the room but the two of us. It was only as the music began to fade that we became aware of our surroundings and noticed the soft echoes of applause. We turned to see the other dancers clustered around the dance floor.

For a moment we were both stunned, realizing we had been the center of attention. Christopher turned his startled eyes toward me. I shared his expression of amazement. He laughed, took my hand, and together we walked off the floor to calls of congratulations.

I touched his sleeve with my fingers, and he pulled me close to his side. "It was a pleasure dancing with you, sweet friend." His voice, his eyes, his whole expression had a quality of soft vulnerability I'd never seen in him before.

At our table the others were full of praise, Dana exclaiming, "I knew you could dance up a storm, but didn't know you could dance like that! Why didn't you tell us?"

"I didn't know myself," I laughed. "Give Christopher the honors. I just followed his lead."

"Well, you were both great!" She turned to her bemused date. "Now, James, that's how I want you to learn to dance."

"You'd have ten broken toes if I tried." He hugged her affectionately about the shoulders. "But if you can persuade Christopher to get up with you later, I'll have no objections:"

Immediately Dana swung toward Christopher.

"I'd be delighted," he answered, laughing, before she could get the words off her tongue.

He was still holding my hand, his fingers gently rubbing mine in an absentminded gesture as he spoke to others at the table. He didn't relinquish my hand until it came time for Dana's dance. She returned to the table after their dance, grinning from ear to ear and began again to coax Jim to join her on the dance floor.

Christopher and I danced again as the band played Cole Porter's "Night and Day." His eyes stared into mine, and his arms held me ever more closely, my breasts pressed against the hard strength of his chest, our hips touching in a way that sent fire through my veins. His smile seemed to be meant only for me, and his words were threaded with hidden meanings. He was weakening. I was sure of it, but I didn't dare hope too fervently. There were too many things that could happen to pull us apart. I tried not to feel doubtful as I looked up into his eyes and answered the unspoken questions he posed while we moved together in slow, sweeping steps. And when suddenly the beat quickened, he twirled me round and round, laughing at my flushed cheeks. My head was spinning, my feet barely keeping pace.

"Christopher, I feel dizzy."

"That is precisely my intention, sweet friend," he laughed. We continued to twirl, our gazes meeting, until the tempo mellowed and we danced slowly again. I could see a gleam in his eye, a spark of desire.

I thought I heard him murmur "Jessica, my sweet" as he pulled me against him. Perhaps I hadn't heard him at all, but the dance was over, and we returned to the table.

People drifted by, stopping to say hello and introduce themselves to Christopher.

I left the group to their discussions and excused myself to go to the ladies' room.

I took my time, straightening my gown, brushing my hair, and applying fresh lipstick. When I looked at myself in the long mirror to the side of the room, the glow in my eyes was evident, the happy flush in my cheeks making me seem vivacious, daringly alive. Walking back slowly across the crowded room, I anticipated a smile across Christopher's lips when he saw me.

The table was empty. I saw Dana and Jim talking to some people on the other side of the room. There was no sign of Christopher.

My eyes searched through the crowd of faces around me, trying to pick out his tall frame and broad shoulders. I left the table, winding my way through the crowd. There was nothing to worry about, I told myself. The Osgoods or the Jamesons were probably introducing him to some of their friends. I pushed

my way around the people blocking my path, saying quick hellos
and smiling at those I knew, all the while straining for a sight of
him.

I saw a group of men gathered off in the corner of the
ballroom. I spotted Christopher's unmistakable shoulders. His
back was toward me. Quickening my footsteps, I hurried in his
direction. He appeared to be engrossed in conversation, listening
now to what one of the men was saying. His head turned in
profile as he nodded and made some comment. They all laughed,
and a man in a brown suit clapped Christopher on the shoulder
like an old friend.

He turned his head again to speak to the man beside him.
Hoping to catch his attention, I raised my arm and motioned.

It was then that I saw the woman standing at his side,
hidden before by the clutch of men surrounding Christopher.
Her face was lit by a wide smile as her gaze hovered over him.
She reached out her hand to place it possessively on the sleeve
of his jacket, and her lips moved in a soft-spoken entreaty.
Christopher turned to her and smiled. It was Sonya.

My throat tightened as though a hand had closed about it. I
felt my eyes narrowing, homing in on the sight of the two of
them together. I felt sick. I stood there for what seemed an
eternity, frozen into a block of ice—feeling the anger, the hatred
for this bitch welling up inside me, the blood throbbing in my
temples.

Then I turned, still unnoticed, and rushed blindly across the
room, halting at our vacant table. But what was I doing? I had
to pull myself together. I wasn't going to let anyone see me
with tears on my cheeks. I'd been crazy to think one evening
could change things.

I stood in front of the table, my fingers gripping the edge of
a chair. My drink lay untouched on the white cloth. I finished it
off in a few quick swallows to still the shaking within me. I
waited by the table for several minutes, hoping he would come
back. When he didn't I looked around, remembering there were
other smiling faces in the room—men who would appreciate
me, old friends. I'd seen the gleam of admiration filling certain
eyes when I'd pass by. I'd show Christopher I wasn't his to
play with.

Pulling my chin up proudly, I pasted a smile on my lips as I
stopped to chat with friends.

I made a special effort to be bright, witty, and glib-tongued to whoever was standing at my side, flicking my eyelashes and pouring glittering smiles of encouragement at the attentive males who'd been too unsure of my relationship with Christopher to approach me before now.

The men were charmed. I was a gay and flittering butterfly. Tomorrow I would have regrets. At the moment, my conscience was not to be bothered. It became a game—a fast-moving game—a challenge to see how quickly I could lure a man, play with him, and watch him succumb. Drinks were placed in my hands—compliments, invitations thrown at me, sincere perhaps, but meaning nothing. I skipped back and forth between several dance partners, trying to ignore that not one of them could measure up to Christopher.

The time passed. I'd spot him occasionally through the mass of bodies. I could see the shine of his thick dark locks above the rest of the heads and the red sheen of Sonya's tresses beside him.

Only once, when I was dancing, did I look across the floor to catch his eyes upon me. He stood with a drink in his hand, making no attempt to hide that his gaze was upon me and me alone. His brow was creased by a deep scowl, his mouth hard. He stared unmoving until I felt my skin begin to burn from his penetrating eyes. Then he turned abruptly and disappeared into the throng.

His look unnerved me more than I wanted to admit. I made a special effort to block him from my mind.

My lips began to feel stiff from artificial smiles. My mouth was dry from too much empty talk. I was tired of the game and didn't know how much longer I could keep up the pretense. Just a little longer, I kept telling myself, just a little longer. I slipped quietly away through the long French doors at the side of the room, let myself out onto the terrace surrounding the clubhouse. The night air was cool. I pulled my shawl tight around my shoulders. It was a beautiful night. Stars spattered the deep violet heavens, and a half-moon sent down gray-white light.

I walked to the edge of the terrace to lean against the iron balustrade, staring out into the semivisible landscape of golf course, the rustling trees, and the silver of Long Island Sound glimmering like a length of shiny cloth in the moonlight. Behind me I could hear the muffled strains of a waltz, while in the grass at my feet, the last of the summer crickets chirped their dying song.

It was a night for lovers, and I felt lonely and rejected. I wiped a traitorous tear from my cheek and dreamed about how the evening should have ended.

I heard footsteps approaching from the far end of the patio. Probably a strolling couple. I didn't look up until the footsteps halted beside me and a hand tapped me lightly on the shoulder. "Jessica?"

I looked up into a face I'd known so very well a year before. The face of a man I might have married but whom I'd known at the last minute wasn't the right man for me for the rest of my life. He was smiling at me now, delighted that he'd found me.

"Hello, John." I spoke quietly, in the spirit of my hollow mood.

"Jes. It's good to see you." He looked intuitively at me, a certain perception written on his features. "I saw what happened in there. Is there anything I can do to help?"

John had always been able to see right through me.

"No, there's nothing you can do. I'm all right."

He placed his hand over mine on the railing in a protective, consoling gesture. "Are you sure?"

"Very sure. It was over anyway, John. Just a matter of clearing the air, I guess." I returned my gaze to the silvery light on the golf course, unable to disguise the dampness that had filled my eyes at the first sign of understanding sympathy.

John was silent for a moment. When he did speak, his tone held a brightness that was meant to distract me from my morbid thoughts. "You know, Jes, I got the *Seagull* in the water this summer. You remember her, don't you? You always told me it was a hopeless cause trying to make her seaworthy again. You wouldn't recognize her now. What a peach. I took her on her maiden voyage up to Newport and Block Island—a real warrior, a queen of the sea." He paused. I knew his eyes were on my face, but I didn't dare turn to look at him. I could almost see his gentle look and the warm smile I'd memorized a year before. "I'd like to take you out sometime, Jes. One Sunday. She's snug as a bug in the worst weather. We could pack a lunch..."

"Maybe, John. Maybe sometime." I couldn't help the flatness of my voice.

"Jessica, this isn't you! You never let things get you down— you used to fight back. He's not worth it. He's just not worth it. You've got too much going for you."

"I know, I know..." My voice broke.

"I'm sorry. I didn't mean to bother you. I know you're not ready yet, but how about if I give you a call in a week or so. Okay? We can go out for a drink, or a show." His fingers tightened around mine. "What do you say?"

I nodded, gulping. His kindness was more than I could bear.

"It's a date. Jes, I know you haven't forgotten last year. Neither of us has. But I just want you to know I'm asking you as a friend...you understand? I'm not—"

The French doors slammed shut behind us. We paid no attention.

"I understand, John, and thank you."

"Oh, Jes," he whispered as I pulled my hand from under his and made ready to return to the ballroom.

Christopher's sharp tones cracked through the air behind us like the snap of a bullwhip. "So, Jessica. I finally catch up with you. My, but you've been running a merry chase this evening. And as much as it grieves me to break apart this tete-a-tete, I am afraid it is time to go."

John and I turned in one motion to stare at the tall, dark presence. Even in the semidarkness I could see the glint in Christopher's eyes, almost as if they were gathering the weak moonbeams and focusing them into a power of their own. He looked us both up and down, his eyes narrowing as he scrutinized John.

"I hope you have had a pleasant evening, Jessica." His words couldn't have been less sincere.

"Very pleasant. And you?" I replied with ice to equal his.

"Passable, but it is after one o'clock. Time we left."

I wanted to snip back at him that after the way he'd behaved this evening, he could find his own way home and another bed in which to spend the night, but somehow I couldn't get the words off the end of my tongue. All that came out was a cool, "Oh, do you."

I glanced at John. He looked like a bull ready to charge. The shock of Christopher's entrance was wearing off. John's expression had grown hard in anger and resentment at Christopher's presumptuous attitude toward me. Christopher didn't miss John's look and turned his cool gaze fully on him, examining him as he might a specimen on a laboratory table. "I do not believe we have met," he said condescendingly.

I interrupted. I knew if I didn't, the two of them might be

fighting it out right there on the terrace, so dangerous was the look on John's face, so supercilious the one on Christopher's.

"John Wilenski, Christopher Dunlap. Christopher, John," I said. The two men shook hands. My words were enough to bring them back to a sense of their surroundings, but their handshake was aggressive and crushing, that of two men who dislike each other intensely on sight.

"A pleasure to meet you, Mr. Wilenski," Christopher drawled sarcastically.

"I'm sure," John growled.

I had to get away. My evening had been bad enough without this scene to top it off. I grabbed Christopher's coat sleeve. "Let's go," I said, "I'm ready." Christopher turned on his heel and headed for the French doors. I took a quick look back over my shoulder and mouthed a silent "I'm sorry" to John. He seemed to understand. John's quick, still angry smile and the nod of his head were all I had time to see before the door banged shut behind me.

We said nothing to each other on the way home. I'd been a fool to imagine for a minute the evening could have been anything but a disaster.

He stared out the windshield at the black landscape. I watched the road weaving before the headlights. When we arrived at the house, he opened the back door for me without a word, then promptly walked past me. From the abruptness of his manner, I took it for granted he'd go immediately upstairs to close himself in his room. I remained in the kitchen to make myself a cup of tea, grateful for the respite. There was nothing we could possibly say to each other.

I heard his footsteps recede, and when my tea was ready, I took my cup into the living room, thinking I'd be alone. He hadn't gone upstairs after all, but was standing before the fireplace, his back toward me, his elbow resting on the mantel. He heard me enter, although he showed no sign of moving, and I took an uncomfortable seat in the chair that faced his rigid back.

The room was as silent and cold as a tomb. I tried to ignore him, but my eyes kept returning to him against my will, watching the fabric of his jacket tighten and ease across his shoulders with each breath he took, his long legs planted firmly on the floor.

He turned suddenly to face me. I had never seen his eyes

so cold, so condemning. His voice was cruel. "Do you think you can use me, Jessica? Do you think just because you have a beautiful face, you can play with me as if I were a toy? You are wrong! No one does to me what you did tonight! Am I such a great bore that you cannot bear my company for more than a few minutes before throwing yourself at every man in sight? Never have I seen a supposedly decent woman so patently suggesting the uses that could be made of her body." He was demonic, beyond control. "All this time I have been handling you with kid gloves, holding myself back...for what? Tell me, for what? So you could play around with those weak-livered fools tonight who would not know how to handle a woman if she were thrown at them? To think I even went so far as to plan to move out just for the sake of your reputation...because I had so much respect for you! And after I told you I was leaving and I saw your reaction, I actually deceived myself into thinking you had some feeling for me in that frigid heart of yours. Feeling—ha!" He slammed his hand down on the mantle. "Damn, but I've been a fool!"

I gaped. "What's the matter with you?"

He crossed the room in a few swift strides, reached down and pulled me to my feet with fingers that bit into my flesh. My head was flung back with the suddenness of his action. His teeth were gritted. The eyes that burned into me with icy fire were only inches away. He thrust the words from himself as if trying to cleanse his system: "Matter with me? The matter with me is that I love you, woman! I love you so much that I want to tear the clothes from your body and take you like a whore for what you have done to me tonight!"

I was utterly amazed. I felt so confused, so torn by the conflicting emotions of the last few hours and weeks, I had trouble believing the words were coming from his lips. "You love me?"

"I am saying it. Like the madman who can no longer control his passion. Yes, I love you. And where has it gotten me? To the point where I am confessing my soul to a callous, uncaring woman. I curse the day I met you!"

"And what about tonight?" I exploded. "What about Sonya?"

His eyes narrowed. "You do not imagine I have any feelings for that calculating woman!"

"Then why did you leave me? Why did you spend half the

night with her, if you dislike her so much? Do you know what it did to me? Have you any idea how much it hurt me to see her standing there with her hand on your arm?"

"I could not get rid of her—I thought you knew better than to think there was anything between us. She has been chasing me for weeks, and I have been trying to avoid her. Could you not see her little game?"

"I only see what's in front of my eyes. You couldn't even wait for me at the table. If you wanted to be with me, why didn't you come find me? A man of your experience shouldn't have any trouble extricating himself from the clutches of one small woman."

"I tried calling to you. You would not look. You were too wrapped up in making an ass of yourself over those other cads."

"Ass of myself? How dare you! And I suppose there was something preventing you from walking over and finding me?"

"I became so angry watching your exhibition, I would not have lowered myself."

"And why do you think I was putting on that exhibition? Because of you—because of you and your rottenness! What other way did I have of trying to forget you and what you were doing to me? Did you expect me to sit on the sidelines and watch you lolling around with that bitch? What a lovely wallflower I would have made!"

"You didn't seem to have too great a difficulty in forgetting me, with those lapdogs at your feet. And what about the gentleman on the patio and that lovely little hand-holding scene I witnessed?"

"Don't include John with the others. I almost married him."

"How interesting. Are you planning to resume the relationship?"

"No, of course not! He's just a friend—a very sensitive and understanding friend. At least he was concerned enough to come out and give me some sympathy."

"Sympathy—ha!" he scoffed. "I know enough of men's intentions to know it was not sympathy he had on his mind."

"Why are we even discussing John? I'm not in love with him. Everything I did was a result of what you did to me. The last few weeks have been living hell for me."

"And what do you think they have been for me?" he barked.

"Don't give me that—not now. You must have known what

you were doing before you made that lovely declaration that you were moving out. If you had any feelings for me, you wouldn't be able to walk all over mine as if they didn't matter in the slightest. Oh, but I forgot...you told me we'd still be friends, didn't you?"

"I planned to leave because I thought you did not care! How was I to know what was going on in that self-contained skull of yours? Have you once shown me any sign of encouragement in the past months? Oh, you have been kind, and most helpful and generous, I grant you that," he said reluctantly. "But beyond that you are as unapproachable as a mist maiden. Did you expect me to continue to impose myself on you when I thought I wasn't wanted? I have my pride, too. You once told me you could never pamper a man's ego or take a subservient role. By God, I should have listened!"

"It seems to me your ego is all that's really bothering you tonight. And no, I'm not willing to give up my identity—but that doesn't mean I can't love and share and want to make a man happy. I've loved you for months. Don't tell me you couldn't see it. It must have been as obvious as the nose on your face. You knew it, and you've been using me!"

"Damnit, I have not been using you. How can you even consider that, with the circumspect way I have behaved? I loved you. What do you think I have been trying to tell you the last few minutes?" He pulled me closer. He closed his eyes briefly, as if in pain. "If I had not been so afraid of giving in to the feeling I was beginning to know for you, I could have saved us this hurt. It is done, it is said—and I cannot in a million years live through more tortures like the ones I have lived through tonight and the past month. The battles I have fought with myself, knowing I was growing to love you, wanting to tell you, yet realizing how unfair it would be to entangle you in a relationship that had no future. What if I'm gone tomorrow, Jessica? I can take memories of you with me, but what can I leave you in return?" His fingers dug deep into my shoulders. "It takes more than you can imagine for me to make this admission. I never thought I would say these words to any woman. But they are said, and if that is not enough for you, there is nothing more I can add. I will go."

I watched his burning eyes and saw joy and sorrow etched in his gaze. I flung myself against him. My anger evaporated like raindrops on a dry summer day. I knew only how much I needed him, how much I wanted his love. I pressed my cheek against his chest. "And all this time I thought you didn't care."

"I cared, sweet friend. I have cared for a long time."

"How could you let me think that all you wanted was my friendship?"

"It was all I could offer you honestly. I wanted more than that. I wanted you—your love. I knew I was losing hold on my willpower. Another week in your presence and it would be over—I would take you whether you liked it or not." He looked at me with deadly serious intent. "Tonight I am going to have you. I do not care about the rest anymore. I cannot deny the need I feel for you any longer."

His muscles tightened, and my head was thrust back as he lifted my chin to look deep into my eyes. Then slowly, very slowly, we drew together. My arms wrapped around him, and I watched as his lips drew closer...until I could taste their sweetness and feel their burning softness on mine. With a long sigh, he drew me tight against him.

There was no feeling to compare with that of being held in his arms, as though I was suddenly in a warm, secure nest—cherished, protected, and desired. This was right. He was my perfect complement. I couldn't get enough of him. I ran my fingers through the thickness of his hair. My cheek brushed against his. My lips nibbled his neck, his ear, the sharp planes of his face, and his mouth that was so eager to greet and devour me.

His breath grew ragged as desire seized him. His hands grew more demanding. His tongue pushed between my teeth to touch mine and taste the inner sweetness of my mouth. I could feel his need building and swelling against me. When he finally tore his lips away to bury them in my hair, we were both trembling, a single fire consuming us.

"I want you, Jessica," he murmured into my ear. "I want you now." In a swift motion he lifted me into his arms and carried me effortlessly up the narrow staircase to the bedroom.

He put me down gently then pulled me into his arms, close to the heat of his body. His fingers touched my cheeks, his eyes stared into mine. His hands loosened the ties of my dress. "I want to make love to you as you have never been loved before...so you will want no other man to touch you again."

He pushed the dress off my shoulders, sliding his hands over my bare back, then around to close tenderly over my breasts. A shiver of delight coursed through my body. I slid my hands under his jacket, pulling his shirt free to let my fingers roam freely over his naked skin. He trembled, then pushed me away to remove his jacket and vest. He began unbuttoning his shirt, and I stepped close again to finish the task. I pushed away his shirt to expose his broad chest and then buried my lips in the curly mat of dark hair that covered it. He flung his shirt to the chair, and I saw his hands go to his pants, loosening them. His thighs brushed against mine as his pants fell. I stood away briefly to see his nakedness and felt a girlish blush tinge my cheeks at the exquisite sight of him. I turned my head. He reached out, took my chin, made me look at him.

He brought me close again. I felt his skin meet mine. He didn't hesitate this time. He surged against me. I felt the hard muscles of his thighs, the tautness of his belly, and the warm strength of him drawing me toward oblivion. My breath came quickly as he slowly urged me to the bed. His body slid against mine as his lips dropped down along the curve of my throat to close and linger over my breasts. His hands grew insistent, making me forget everything—except that I was his. At last I was going to feel his body within me. I let my hands rove from his back to his chest and stomach. He urged me lower, moaning with desire as my fingers reached their destination.

We grew impatient. Our fevered endearments were husky in our throats. I felt nothing except the heady sensations flooding through my body, and the need that grew stronger with each second our hands lingered. Then he was above me, pushing into me gently but urgently, lying like a heavy, sweet blanket upon me, calling my name, telling me to love him and be his forever. I cried out in joy that at last I'd found the man with whom I could spend the rest of my days and never be sorry...the one man in the world I could love without reservation. And tonight he was mine. He was mine! I could sense his extreme pleasure. I felt the quickening of his movements, and waves of pleasure began to wash over me. Our bodies moved as one, struggling to be as close to each other as two separate entities could be. I heard moans deep in his throat, and I knew that nothing could ever go wrong in this world again as long as this man was beside me.

TWELVE

I wakened to the unaccustomed warmth of his nakedness pressing against me. His eyes were already open, watching me in the soft yellow sunlight that streamed through the window to form a halo about us.

"It wasn't a dream this time," I whispered.

"No, my love, it was not a dream." He slid his hand gently over my body. "You are mine now, every beautiful inch of you."

With one lazy finger he traced the hollow of my cheek and the outline of my lips. "When I think of these months of waiting, never knowing. I do not understand this spell you weave over me, sweet witch. I have always been able to hold the reins of my heart in check. I have played; I have toyed; I have flirted and dawdled. I have been propositioned, cajoled, and approached in every devious manner imaginable, but no one has been able to do to me what you have done—and not even known you were doing it! Never have I met a woman so oblivious to my charms as you seemed to be."

"I wasn't oblivious."

"Then you were an expert at deception."

I curled my fingers in his hairy chest and traced the cleft in his chin.

He lifted one brow. "Have you any idea what you are getting yourself into?"

"Nothing I'm not going to enjoy with every ounce of my body."

"But I am a greedy man. I expect all of you. You will never know how many nights I spent dreaming of being in this bed. I swear I knew every valley and curve of your body without ever having seen them." His eyes drifted closer, his chin squared. "I have no intention of losing you."

"I'm not going anywhere."

"No. You are not." He wrapped his leg over mine and left it there meaningfully. "I have found happiness —something, with all my cynicism, I was not expecting to find, much as I know there may be no future in which to enjoy it." His voice had a bitter note to it. "How I despise this uncertainty. I want to give you so much, yet I cannot be sure of giving you anything beyond these brief hours of loving. I cannot even promise you tomorrow."

"It doesn't matter." I tried to smooth away the harsh line in his cheek. "I have today."

"But that is not enough."

"Suppose we had been born in the same century. I in your time, for instance. Do you think we ever would have met?" I asked reasonably. "Think, Christopher, of all that would have separated us then—even more than separates us now. With our different backgrounds, is it likely we'd have been thrown together as we are now? The differences in our class would have divided us. And even if by some slim chance we had met and fallen in love, wouldn't my common ancestry have kept that love behind closed doors? You might have offered me protection, put me up in a lovely apartment in a fashionable section of town, provided me with a carriage and team, servants, credit at all the best shops—but never would I have been permitted into any stylish drawing room to sip tea with the wives of your friends. I would have been excluded, ignored, gossiped about behind ladies' fans. Your family would have pretended I didn't exist. And eventually, with pressure from all sides, you'd have married a lady of your own class and raised a family. I would have been left hidden in the darkest of corners to persevere with a love that would never be totally mine. I couldn't have tolerated that. I'm far happier having you the way I do now, even if we can't count on our tomorrows. If you ever go, at least I know the time we've had together has been ours alone...honest and loving."

With a tender touch he pushed a few stray hairs from my forehead. "Then we shall think only of today."

The first few weeks we spent in our awakened state were like a prolonged honeymoon. Each day our love grew more tender, more consuming. We forgot for a while how suddenly Christopher might be swept out of my life forever, and I out of his. We thought only of the need between us and were determined that for whatever time we had left, we would be together.

I loved to hear his laughter and see the fire in his eyes, to have him teasingly join me in the shower and douse me under the spray. To know his sensuous eyes were upon me as I was undressing, to feel the warmth of his body pressed against mine at night.

For a while, except for the necessity of going out to our respective jobs, we shut ourselves off from the rest of the world.

It was enough to spend our evenings and weekends together in the coziness of the house, perhaps going out for a quiet dinner together or to a movie, or spending a Sunday afternoon horseback riding through the crisp fall foliage. The trees were putting on a glorious display as the October chill turned the leaves brilliant orange, gold, and crimson.

Gradually we began to develop a social circle, first including Jim and Dana. The four of us went out dancing, and I had a chance to introduce Christopher to the vibrations of modern rock and disco. He took to the new dances with delight.

One evening, Dana and Jim invited Christopher and me and Don and Mary Osgood to have dinner with them at Jim's apartment. Dana had been helping him decorate his wide-windowed living room with low white couches, plush carpeting, chrome and glass tables, and bright Impressionist paintings. A fire burned in the freestanding fireplace, and there were bouquets of mums in tall vases in each corner of the room. The effect was lovely.

After dinner, as we sat over our coffee, Don Osgood brought out a roll of house plans. His and Mary's eyes were alight as they told us of the two acres of land they'd purchased in a town ten miles to the north. They spread out the blueprints and hashed over the details with us, asking our opinions, speaking of their own numerous trepidations, but of their excitement, too. I wished as I listened that Christopher and I could be making similar plans. Perhaps he was thinking the same thoughts, because I noticed the wistful look on his face. And later when we'd left for home, he questioned me.

"What do you think of their house, Jessica?"

"Oh, it's nice, for them, but not quite to my taste."

"And what is your taste?"

"Something very old like we have now, or very new...though I think I tend more toward the old. A house with some history, odd-shaped rooms, crooked floors, tiny paned windows, big fireplaces. But if we were ever to build something new, I'd want lots of windows and natural wood siding that looked as though it fit right in with the land."

"But lots of land," he added thoughtfully.

"Yes. I like the land as well as you do. Do you remember the beautiful old colonial homes along the road where we go riding?" He nodded. "If we were to buy something old, I'd like one of those homes. Do you remember the house on Southfield

Avenue? It sits up from the road a little. It's a white brick house with a big barn behind. The fields around it are mowed, and there are two big maples in the front on either side of the drive and lots of old stone walls. It looks like it might have been built about 1750."

"I do not recall it."

"Next time we're riding, I'll point it out to you. I'm afraid, though, even if it were for sale, it would be well out of our price range. There must be at least ten rooms in the house, probably about a hundred acres of land..."

"Show it to me anyway." He seemed thoughtful. "I sounds very much like what I would want myself."

He surprised me when we reached home by laying a gentle hand on my arm, forestalling my departure to the bedroom.

"Wait, Jessica." He smiled, but his eyes were serious. "I have something I want to give you."

I wondered fleetingly why he would choose this moment to give me a gift. I watched the expressions flickering across his face in the dim light. He stood silently for a while, studying me as if he were drinking in my face and body. Then he took my hand and slid a ring on my finger. I looked down. It was the ruby signet ring he always wore.

I lifted my eyes to his, not understanding quite what it meant. He was watching me quietly with the light of love in his blue eyes. "I want you to marry me."

That was all he said. It was a statement, not a question, as if he knew as well as I what my answer would be.

"I know it cannot be legal, Jessica, but between the two of us we can make our private vows, hoping that someday we can make them a reality."

I could hardly speak. "Is this what you want?"

"More than anything else in the world, except perhaps the knowledge that we shall never be separated. I cannot go on thinking of you and knowing you are not tied to me, listening to your dreams and only wanting to make them a reality. It struck me how foolish we are to go on living as if the end were tomorrow. There is no reason why we cannot hope to live out our desires, be like other people. Tomorrow will come anyway. I want you to be my wife for what time we have left."

"You want me that much?" Tears of joy stung my eyes.

"I do, Jessica. It is not enough, living the way we are." His arms came around me, cradled me in the warm security I needed so much from him. "The love we feel was meant to be shared by a husband and wife."

"I know, but it never seemed possible...I didn't think..."

"We will make it possible." He caressed my hair and let his lips kiss away the tears on my cheeks. "We will be one in all ways. Take my ring. Think of it as your wedding ring, as it would be in truth if there was a way to get around the legal tangles. Someday we will make it a real one, with a ceremony, so there will never be any question again that we belong to each other."

"My sweet earl. Do you know how much I love you?"

"I am your husband now."

"My husband..." I let the words slide over my tongue. We kissed deeply for a long time, sealing the bond between us, making us married. There were no formal vows spoken, nor clergy to bless the union. Nor did there need to be. Our decision to join as husband and wife was just as meaningful to us as the ceremony we might have shared before an altar.

Later, as we lay side by side beneath the covers of the bed, he dropped a gentle arm over my waist and pulled me close. "You are Mrs. Dunlap now, my countess. You are my wife."

"I know." I snuggled closer against his warmth and let his kisses spark the fires within me until my yearnings for his flesh were more than I could bear.

He hovered over me, his hands on my skin, his breath warm, rapid, sweet. His voice a husky invitation. "Come, wife, we have new worlds to explore."

THIRTEEN

Knowing he loved me to such an extent that above and beyond all obstacles he had made me his wife, made my world an incomparably richer place than it had ever been. I felt as though a door had opened to a whole new future where there was always room for hope and for dreams. And Christopher was intensely serious about our marriage. It was to be no halfway agreement between the two of us. It was to be as full as if we had a legal document in our hands. He wanted me to change my name to his, and I did. At another time, with another man, I might have hesitated, but with him I had no doubts.

I changed my name on all my identification, including my payroll records at work, hoping there would never come a time when the government investigated into my records to discover my husband was a nonentity, an alien with no current background. I wanted to find him false identification. It was becoming a necessity now, but I didn't know where to begin. Just a few simple scraps of paper could make such a difference to us by erasing the subterfuge that was too much a part of our relationships with others.

Despite this concern, we skipped happily through the balance of these crisp fall days, content with our love and with each other.

One day in the middle of November, Christopher went to New Haven to meet with Professor Enright. I had a good feeling about this journey, an intuitive feeling that the professor would be making Christopher a job offer that could take him off the construction site and into a suitable profession. Before their meeting, Christopher kept whatever hopes he had to himself and stifled any anticipation he felt. But when he returned from New Haven in the early evening, it was a different matter. He seemed barely able to hold his elation in check.

"Good news, Jessica. He has asked me to work as his collaborator on a history text of eighteenth and nineteenth century England. Also to take a post in his department as a research advisor. I have accepted. Of course, I had to make the stipulation that he pay me in cash. I think he wondered at it, but fortunately he asked no questions. He is allotted enough money to pay for a research advisor out of his own salary. The work can be done in the evenings, which means I can keep the construction job and pay the bills. Professor Enright and I will meet every few weeks to compare notes, and if everything goes well, I should be receiving the first money at the end of the month."

"I'm delighted. But how are you going to manage both jobs? Half the nights when you come home now, you're exhausted. It's one thing to research the material on your background on your own time, but this work for Yale is serious."

"It is not that demanding, and do you not realize I must do both? I could hardly keep us alive on what I shall make at Yale."

"Have you forgotten my salary? It's not much for two people, but it's enough to keep us out of debt. You could afford to lose that construction job income, and we could still get along. Then you'd have more time to spend on the Yale work."

"I have no intention of putting a burden on you again. There is always the possibility this job with the professor will work into something more substantial, but until that time, I am not leaving my other job. Besides, I want to feel that someday you will be able to leave your job."

"I have no desire to leave my job," I retorted. "I like working."

"So you do, but someday you may have no choice."

"Why not?"

He stared at me as though I'd suddenly lost my reasoning abilities. "Because, Jessica, you could get pregnant."

"It's out of the question. In our position? There's no way we could have a child. What could we offer it?"

"I know your sentiments—I share them myself. As much as I would like to see a young brat of ours running around the place someday, I know it is not only impractical, but unwise. Yet mistakes do happen. You should think of that."

I ignored the knowing look in his eye and dismissed the subject with a cool, "As long as we're careful, nothing can go wrong."

Christopher turned his former bedroom into a study, and soon the bookshelves were overflowing with research material and note pads.

He also investigated the real estate he'd been speculating about at the end of the summer, and found a five acre piece of onetime farmland for sale a few miles north of the area where we went riding. The price was right, and we were able to come up with the purchase funds without going to a bank for a mortgage. Still, Christopher put the deed in my name alone, which I wondered about until he explained that this was an insurance measure in case anything should happen to him. I knew what he was thinking. I knew that, should that unhappy event occur, with the property in his name, I'd be left with nothing. I didn't question him further.

As busy as he was, we managed to steal a few hours for ourselves alone—a night out for dinner, a trip to New York City to see a play, Sunday afternoon rides in the country before the cold weather forced us indoors.

I showed him my dream house on Southfield Avenue and hadn't been surprised when he found it as lovely as I did. Perhaps in time—if there was time—we could save enough money to afford it, or one like it.

When the November winds turned bitter, rattling the bare branches over a barren landscape, we spent many evenings before a roaring fire, sharing a bottle of wine, making plans, building dreams, trying to escape the omnipresent threat of separation. It became more important than ever for us to discover whether or not there was evidence that he had returned to his own nineteenth century world. Christopher felt the answer lay in the family records he hoped were still kept at the ancestral home, Cavenly. If his suppositions about his cousin were close to the truth, however, the records at Cavenly or elsewhere might have been distorted or disposed of by his cousin to protect his own interests. We could only surmise.

Christopher wanted to go back—by modern means this time—and find the records and put an end to our uncertainties. I was afraid. Perhaps the answer wouldn't be there, and we'd suffer countless more years with our uncertainty. But perhaps the records would show an answer that I didn't want to see. Would I be able to face the future knowing we had only a few days left...a month...a year? Could I go on at all normally, knowing that each passing day would bring me closer to a living death? For myself it seemed more merciful to exist with the uncertainty of not knowing. He didn't share my opinion.

He was determined. What if he found that the Ninth Earl of Westerham, Christopher Dunlap, had disappeared for all time on May 5, 1812? Think of what that would mean to us, he kept telling me. We could make our dreams a reality at long last. We could have children without fear, knowing Christopher could never return to his own time.

He was right, and I agreed hesitantly. But then there was the problem of getting him out of the country. I checked into the requirements for getting a U.S. passport. What I learned was not encouraging. Even if Christopher became my legal husband and adopted my citizenship, a husband and wife could not be included on the same passport. In order for Christopher to obtain his own U.S. passport, he would have to produce a birth certificate, naturalization papers, or an official identification card. In trying to obtain either of the latter two, it seemed only logical that the authorities would want to see a British passport and to know how Christopher had gotten into the United States in the first place. The feat of his travel in time was something we obviously couldn't try to explain to anyone.

We had mulled over the problem for several days when I came across a magazine article on black-market passports. Here was our answer.

The logic was very simple, really. When you were born, a birth certificate was made up and duly filed away in the courthouse of the place of your birth. It remained there, forgotten and dusty, for posterity or until you called for a copy. When you died, a death certificate was issued and duly filed in the township where you had passed away. There was never a correlation between the two, except in the memories of those who survived you.

It could work for Christopher. It was only a matter of locating a deceased male of approximately his age, determining the city of that male's birth, and writing the local town hall for a certified copy of his birth certificate. In receiving the birth certificate for his passport, what official would know that the facts contained therein didn't apply to Christopher? He'd be acquiring a name very different from his own, but Christopher, smiling mysteriously, assured me that was a minor inconvenience in comparison to all we had to gain, and he would handle it. The problem was finding a deceased male to fit our requirements. The obituary column seemed the place to look, but there was too much chance someone would remember a man recently deceased. We had to go back further and find a very young man or child who, had he lived, would now be in his early thirties. It was morbid, but it was our answer.

It would be many days before we came up with the name of the man Christopher was to become. In the interim we celebrated our first Christmas together. The Farmer's Almanac predicted winter was to be very cold, with heavier snows than we'd had in the past two years, but except for several icy days when the thermometer dropped close to zero, the snowstorms skirted us, and the ground remained naked and frozen through Christmas Eve.

I spent many frustrated hours searching for the perfect gift for Christopher. It was in desperation I entered an antique shop one lunch hour, not knowing what I hoped to find. I was rewarded. On a small table in a dark corner, all but hidden from the eye, stood a statuette. The white marble glowed softly, even though only the weakest rays of daylight reached it. Upon a low marble knoll, its stone grass forever bent in the rushing wind, posed the perfectly executed figures of a thoroughbred mare and her nuzzling foal. I quickly called the dealer over, wondering why he would push a prize like this into a dusty corner unless it was a piece whose beauty was only in my eyes. In a flurry of protestations, he assured me that it was quite valuable, and the reason for its present location was that it had arrived only the day before as part of a large consignment. In the bustle of getting the pieces marked, numbered, and assigned, he said, he just hadn't had the time to put it in a deserving place.

He carefully lifted the statuette to show me the fine markings on its base. The sculptor was well known, he said. The statuette had been made in the early eighteen hundreds. I wasn't sure if these were the facts or a sales pitch, but I knew I wanted it. It was perfect—both a memento of Christopher's own time and a representation of one of his greatest loves, horses. The price was high, and I spent the next half hour bargaining the dealer down, finally agreeing on a price. I quickly wrote a check for a deposit and promised to be in the next day with the balance to pick up my treasure.

In the days before Christmas I decorated the house in pine branches and garland and red candles. I arranged a miniature snow scene on the mantle and hung Christmas cards on ribbons down the walls. Together we chose a bushy, five-foot Scotch pine, which we placed before the front window and covered with colored lights, shiny balls, and handmade ornaments I'd collected over the years. The house was a heaven of red and green and sweet-smelling pine. The scent mingled with wood smoke from the fire we lit every evening.

By the twenty-fourth of December the Christmas spirit had firmly captured us. We invited Dana and Jim to share our Christmas Eve dinner and waited impatiently for them to arrive. We put on Christmas music and arranged our presents under the tree. Christopher laughed and teased me when I poked and prodded the packages that were for me, telling me I was just like an impatient child. Nonetheless, I caught his own curious eyes hunting out the tags that bore his name, registering surprise and puzzlement when he spotted the large box that contained his statuette.

Our guests arrived at seven o'clock, arms laden with cookies, wine, and gifts, full of good cheer. Their cheeks cold, their hearts warm. We helped them settle their packages, took their coats, and started the evening with a toast to health and happiness. The room had a mellow glow from the blazing fire and candlelight, and the food cooking in the kitchen filled the house with mouthwatering scents.

We stood in a cluster by the fireplace as we drank the spicy holiday punch Christopher had concocted.

"You two look awfully sparkling tonight," I said to Dana and Jim as I intercepted a conspiratorial glance between the two of them.

"I noticed," Christopher agreed. "What do you think, Jessica, could they be keeping secrets from us? Or is it just an infectious case of Christmas spirit?" He winked at me, and we turned to study Dana and Jim.

Dana broke into a wide grin that covered her pretty face. "I can't wait any longer. Look." She thrust her left hand in front of her and waved it before our eyes. The flash and glitter of the diamond adorned her finger.

I put my drink on the table and took her hand. "Oh, it's beautiful. How wonderful! Why didn't you tell us? When did this happen? Tonight?" I threw my arms around Dana and kissed her cheek, "Congratulations! What a wonderful Christmas present."

Christopher shook Jim's hand and slapped him on the back. "Best of luck. You are a sly fox—we did not even guess." Christopher kissed Dana warmly on the cheek. "This calls for a celebration. I have a special bottle of champagne stashed away just waiting for the occasion."

Jim followed Christopher, and I pulled Dana to the side, full of questions. "When did you get it? Why didn't you tell me?"

She laughed, "I didn't know myself. Oh, we talked about getting married from time to time, but I had no idea he'd gotten the ring. When Jim picked me up tonight, he handed me a little box, all wrapped up with a bow, and told me to open it. It was an early present, he said. I was surprised when I saw it was a ring box, but when I looked inside—Jes, I was floored! I'm so happy."

"That much is obvious. I hope you find all the good things that Christopher and I have."

"I know we will."

"I know it, too." I hugged her once more quickly.

Christopher uncorked the champagne and distributed the glasses of bubbling liquid. "To Jim and Dana and their happiness."

"Cheers!" we chorused.

The rest of the evening, too, was wonderful. Dinner was delicious, and feeling replete, we gathered around the piano to sing carols. Christopher laid more logs on the fire, and we sat within the circle of its warmth to open our gifts. From Dana and Jim we received a beautiful pair of candlesticks. Dana held up an antique music box, and Jim exclaimed over the desk set we'd given him.

Shortly alter midnight Jim and Dana left, and Christopher and I settled on the couch, cuddling close. "Shall we open our gifts, my love?" he asked as his lips muzzled my hair.

"Wouldn't you rather wait until morning?"

"No, I wouldn't." He grinned. "Curiosity has gotten the better of me."

"I thought you weren't interested in your Christmas presents." I smiled smugly.

"I lied. Just get the presents, my love."

Yes, my lord and master," I said, and curtseyed. I made two neat piles of gifts on the floor at our feet.

He took one small package from my pile and placed it away from the others. "Save that for last," he told me. He picked up a larger box and handed it to me. "You start."

I ripped off the colored paper, throwing it untidily to the floor, and lifted the lid. Inside was a beautiful silk print blouse. I held it up before me. "It's gorgeous. I love it." I leaned over and kissed him. "Now it's your turn."

We made our way through the piles of gifts. He gave me perfume, two scarves, a crystal bell for my collection, and a tiny but beautifully executed oil painting of a New England landscape that depicted a house very much like our country dream home.

He worked his way through my gifts to him, discovering a tie tack, a wallet, a shirt, and a classical tape. Finally he tore the paper from the large box containing the statue. I waited anxiously, hoping he'd like it but afraid he'd be disappointed.

I needn't have worried. As he tore off the last bits of packing encasing the statue, a look of astonishment came to his face and blossomed into delight. With both hands, he raised the lovely object from the tissue to place it on his lap.

"My God, Jessica! Wherever did you find it?" His voice was filled with excitement.

"In an antique shop. Do you like it?"

"Like it? I love it! But how did you know?"

"I thought you might like it because of the horses, and because the dealer told me it was an early nineteenth century piece."

"You are telling me that you bought this piece not knowing it came from Cavenly?"

I was incredulous. "From Cavenly? Christopher, you can't be serious...I didn't know."

"Yes, yes. This piece came from my house. It is Carlotta and one of her foals. I had it done especially for me and had it on my desk in the library. What stroke of fate could have brought it back to me?"

He was dumbfounded, and so was I. It was an uncanny coincidence that I should have found a piece that once belonged to Christopher and decided it was the perfect gift for him.

He looked at me earnestly. "I cannot tell you how much this means to me—accident or not. Thank you, my love." He carried the statue to the table at the side of the room and stood there lost in thought as he stared at the marble images of his beloved horses, consumed, no doubt, by all the memories they brought home to him again. It was poignant and touching to see him fighting the desires and longings he'd thought he'd learned to keep in check. But after a few moments he shrugged his shoulders and turned to me, his eyes clear and only the present reflected in his gaze.

He took up the small box that was to be my last treat. "Now, my special gift to you." He smiled and placed it in my hands.

I could only guess it must be jewelry of some sort, but beyond that, I had no idea. I carefully removed the red wrappings to reveal a velvet-covered box. It looked like a ring box, but he had already given me his signet ring. I snapped it open and was startled to see a white gold band with a row of sapphires set along its crown. It was beautiful.

I removed it from its slot and began to slide it onto my right hand.

"No, Jessica." He reached out to stop me. "It belongs on this finger." He deftly took his signet ring from my left hand and gently slid the new ring on in its place. It fit perfectly and gleamed against my skin. "I want you to have a real wedding ring, Jessica, and this one is modeled after my mother's ring, which I had at home and was saving for my bride. Now that you are my bride, you should have one like it. I only wish it were in my power to give you the original." He looked on me softly, his fingers caressing my hand.

I wrapped my arms about him and laid my head against his broad chest. "I love you," I whispered against his shirt.

"And I love you." He held me tight and dropped his head to plant a gentle kiss on my cheek. "Has it been a good Christmas for you?"

"The nicest I've ever had."

"That is because we have each other. Shall we go up to bed?"

I nodded.

After checking the fire and gazing once more at the image of Carlotta and her foal, he turned off the lights, and we walked arm in arm up the stairs.

FOURTEEN

The snows of winter were at last upon us, the rivers and streams frozen solid as the cold bit in with a vengeance, but the hostile weather bothered us less than it might have had we not been so wrapped up in our togetherness.

By mid-January a candidate for Christopher's alias had been uncovered. How Christopher came across the information he never told me, but one evening he came home with a few short, cold facts written on a piece of paper, and we were ready to proceed. The name he would be taking, if all went smoothly, was Robert C. Branford. Robert C. Branford had been born in Bridgeport, Connecticut. He had died a mere child of two. But had he lived, he would have been Christopher's age.

Within a few days Christopher had penned a brief letter to the Bridgeport City Hall, requesting a photostatic copy of "his" birth certificate. We waited with our fingers crossed for seven days before it arrived. Christopher forged ahead with the passport application and photos. In fact, it all went so smoothly, it troubled me. Yet why should suspicions be aroused over what appeared to be a routine request of an American citizen for permission to travel abroad?

Now there was no holding him back. We set a date for our legal wedding ceremony, and we made plans to go to England— back to his home. We visited a travel agent, making arrangements for a four-week trip beginning April second. We would stay in London the first two weeks, then go to Cavenly. I almost choked when he told the agent to book us reservations for the Dorchester, which was one of the most expensive hotels in London. Had he forgotten he wasn't a rich earl anymore? I grabbed his sleeve on the way out the travel agency door. "Christopher, what are you be thinking? We can't afford a hotel like that. It's going to cost a fortune for that room!"

"I'm well aware of it,," he said nonchalantly.

"Don't you think that's a little ridiculous? We'll hardly be spending any time in the room. Just as long as a room is clean and the beds are comfortable, we could use the money we'd be saving on other things. There're several hotels along the park that would cost half as much."

"We will have enough money to have a good time, too. Let

me be the judge. I intend for this trip to be the most glorious in your life."

"Oh, it'll be that, all right, if we don't end up in debtor's prison in the process."

"You're overdoing it a bit, don't you think?" He gave me one of those heart-melting smiles of his.

When we got back to the house, Christopher detailed the rest of our itinerary, leaving me with the feeling that my practical protests were no more important than deciding in the supermarket whether to buy chuck or sirloin steak.

His plan was to find a room at a country inn in the vicinity of Cavenly for the second two weeks of our trip. We would rent a car to get there from London and to use in traveling around Kent. What I couldn't understand was what he felt he would gain by spending a full two weeks at the back door of his old home, except self-inflicted misery. I doubted the present earl would greet him with open arms, let alone give him free access to the grounds. Who did he plan to tell them he was? Not the ninth earl returned from the grave, I hoped! Or was he planning to steal into the house in the middle of the night to get his hands on the records he needed?

We knew parts of Cavenly were open to the public for a fee, but would that be tolerable to the man who had once been its lord and master? He was made of sterner stuff than I if he expected to get through the ordeal without some serious bouts of depression. But he was well ahead of me.

"Professor Enright and I have discussed our trip to England," he explained blandly. "I do not think there will be the slightest problem getting into the house as often and for as many hours as we wish, since I am going there on a research project for Yale. Enright has written the present earl, describing the project and requesting permission for access to the family historical papers. The professor has come up with such a persuasive piece of arm bending, with his flattery and implications as to the worthiness of the project that the Earl would feel very brutish indeed to refuse us." He laughed. "At any rate, the earl should give us carte blanche shortly, and then it will only be a matter of a letter of introduction to identify myself, and we are home free."

"Why is Enright doing this?" I asked. "You didn't tell him why you really wanted to go to Cavenly, did you?"

"Obviously, I did not tell him the truth. Although I did mention a very distant connection to the family, just close enough to give him the idea that I knew of certain information contained in the family histories that had never before been made public knowledge and could be invaluable to us in our work."

"Is there?"

"Well, you know that, Jessica. The information about my cousin, of course, and his connection with Bonapartist spies."

"You can still find the proof?"

"If there has not been too much redecorating in the past century and a half, I believe I can find what I am looking for—once I am inside the house and do not have someone watching my every move."

"You realize what the publication of those papers will do to blacken the family name," I said mildly.

"I am well aware, but since the present family send their roots back to my notorious cousin, I shan't let it bother me."

"I can't see what you'd be gaining by smearing his name and embarrassing his descendants at this late date."

"Nothing except a vindictive joy in seeing a traitor finally exposed for what he was."

I shook my head. "Sometimes I don't understand you. Isn't it enough for you to find the proof that you're going to remain in this century? Why do you need to pull skeletons from the closet, too? And aren't you a little bit afraid of what the records at Cavenly are going to show? I'm frightened. I have this horrible feeling that we'll learn the worst—and if that's the case, I'd rather not know."

We stood beside the dining room table with brochures spread out in front of us. "It will not be the worst, my love. Chin up," he said optimistically. "I can kiss you better that way, you know, with your chin high in the air and your lips facing mine." He kissed me with a passion I wasn't expecting.

"Christopher," I whispered, "we're getting off the track."

"Delightful, isn't it?"

"But we haven't finished talking."

"Haven't we?" he mocked me. His voice was lazy as his lips gently caressed mine.

I pushed him away playfully. "Later."

"Oh, be fair, Jessica," he teased.

I laughed. "Be serious, you idiot. Let's get back to business."

He sighed regretfully.

"Now, about the trip. One small question. Aren't you going

to be nervous traveling with conflicting identification? Your passport will read Robert Branford and the letter of introduction from Professor Enright says Dunlap." I raised my brows.

My passport will not read Robert Branford by then, so there is really no problem at all."

I scowled. "What are you talking about?"

"We are getting married in two weeks, Jessica— legally, I mean."

"Yes, I know, but what's that got to do with it?"

"A great deal. When we get married, I shall take your name."

"You'll what?" I exclaimed.

"Well, actually I shall be taking back my own name. I shall have my passport changed accordingly, and the question of Branford will never arise."

"Do you think we can get the passport changed in time?" I asked.

"Plenty of time. We have over two months."

"Don't you think the passport office is going to think it strange that you're changing your name when you only applied for it less than a month ago?"

"Stranger things have been done than a man taking his wife's name in marriage. You worry too much." He laid a reassuring hand on my arm.

"I can't help it. I'm not used to all this intrigue and subterfuge. I still get nervous jitters every time I think of you confronting that passport clerk and pretending to be an American."

"It is really very simple. When you have grown up and lived in this area all your life, who is going to take you for a stranger," he replied with so good an imitation of my all-American New England accent that I stared at him wide-eyed.

"God, that was great!"

"Only for short distances," he laughed. "After that I am afraid the ingrained Englishman in me slips to the fore."

"Well, if you can do that well in the passport office, I'm not worried. But I still have visions of traveling to England all by myself because my husband is locked behind bars trying to explain who he is, how he got here, and what he's doing with an illegal passport."

"That is not going to happen. Now, I believe we have some

unfinished business," he said with a positive leer, tightening his arm about my waist and pointing me in the direction of the stairs.

"So we do," I said, letting his capable hands push me where I was only too delighted to go.

FIFTEEN

On a February afternoon, with the sun shining in long shadows on old snow, we entered the home of a justice of the peace to say the vows making us legally husband and wife. The ceremony was nearly as simple as our first, with only the justice's wife and son as our witnesses. But now no one could question that we were a wedded pair.

In celebration we had a quiet dinner alone in a tiny restaurant overlooking the Sound. At a small table close to the windows, with a flickering candle to light the tabletop between us, we held hands and sipped vintage champagne to seal our happiness. Outside, only the light cast from scattered houses along the shoreline broke the darkness stealing over the cold gray waters, while stars twinkled in a velvet winter sky.

The warm yellow candlelight reflected the dreamy glow in our eyes and the rosy, high color peculiar to lovers who are aware of no sounds, sights, or happenings around them, but only of their own exchanged glances and sweet-spoken words.

"We have done it, my love," he said in soft, deep tones.

"We have done it, Mr. Dunlap."

"Mrs. Dunlap." He lifted his glass. "To your many years of happiness with me. I love you."

"I love you," I answered with all the feeling in my heart— so much feeling that I felt it must be overflowing. "We've come a long way, Christopher."

"Let us hope it is just our first step together. There's a further way we still can go, God willing." The hand clutching mine clutched it a bit more tightly. "Never did I think I would find myself sitting across the table from a bewitchingly beautiful woman, knowing her to be my wife, and telling her that I loved her with all my soul, every bone in my body. That without her I could never find happiness again."

"There would have been other women, Christopher, if we hadn't met, and one woman in particular who would have carried off your heart. I'm just so glad that I met you first."

"When we return from England, I am going to buy you that house in the country. We are going to have our horses and our children. Two—one for each of us—to fill the rooms with laughter and noise. We are going to do the things we want to do most, strive for the things that make us happiest, grow content and lazy and old together and never regret a moment of it."

I grinned at him. "You make it sound like a fairy tale."

"It will be," he said with conviction.

"I just hope it's one of those fairy tales with a happy ending."

"We can only hope. I have so many dreams I want to build with you. We will have time for that when we return from England."

I looked at him over the rim of my wine glass. "Aren't you even a little bit afraid of what we'll find?"

"I am very much afraid, but I have chosen to look at the good side. If I dwelt on the other, I doubt I could even function."

When we arrived home, he lit a fire, and there on the rug before the warm, flickering flames, we made love with a greater tenderness than ever before. As our hands moved slowly yet hungrily over each other's nakedness, we spoke without words of our joy, and our need to be one in all ways. My skin tingled as his lips teased over every inch of me from my neck to my toes. I listened to his deep breaths of barely controlled desire as I reciprocated and tasted his warm maleness. Then he possessed me, filling me so that I thought I would explode with the love I felt for him. His hips surged down against me, and mine rose to meet him, and we became lost in our own world of pleasure and oneness, where nothing could intrude.

We lay tight in each other's arms, satiated, whispering quiet words of love, until the fire was in embers and the chill of the room brought goose bumps to our flesh.

He rose and brought a pillow from the couch, and a blanket. We cuddled together again and slept.

During the next two weeks we finalized our travel plans, changed the names on our records, and sat back to wait for the event that was daily becoming a more momentous one.

One Saturday morning—as I was dusting the spare bedroom that had become Christopher's study—I came across a large envelope. He was in New Haven for the day with Professor Enright and had left the house in a rush that morning, barely making his train. He must have absentmindedly left the envelope on the desk in his hurry.

Normally I wouldn't have pried, but my eyes couldn't miss the large square brown envelope as I tried to dust around the objects on the desktop. Several large papers had partially slid out, and I couldn't miss them, the green scroll borders or the print upon them. Stock certificates? But where would he have gotten them? I pulled the top paper the rest of the way out of the envelope and examined it.

"Ten Shares," it read, "Common Stock." The corporation named was one of the rapidly growing outdoor sporting goods chains quickly spreading across the country. I picked up the next. Fifteen shares of another stock. I leafed through them. I couldn't believe my eyes. There were about a dozen certificates, two or three blue-chip. Where had he gotten these?

I wasn't sure of their value, but I knew it wasn't insignificant—and the most surprising thing was that they were all in my name. Christopher had obviously bought them for me, but where had he gotten the money? I knew that he'd been putting aside some of his construction earnings. I didn't know how much, but even so, in the six months he'd been working, he couldn't possibly have set aside enough to buy all this stock.

I was eaten up with curiosity and couldn't wait until he got home. The hours dragged by, as they always do when you're anxious for them to fly. I did the best I could at distracting myself with vacuuming, laundry, washing the kitchen floor, and finally I sat down at the piano, hoping music would make the hours go more quickly.

At three-thirty he called from the station, and I was I there within ten minutes. As soon as he jumped into the car and landed a light kiss on my cheek, I burst out, "Where did you get all that stock, Christopher?"

My words had taken him completely off guard. He looked disconcerted, slightly guilty, just the way I knew I always looked when he caught me sneaking a cigarette.

"You left the envelope on the desk. Some of the papers slid out. I couldn't help seeing."

I could sense his mind racing, trying to backtrack over his movements of the morning. "I guess I did leave them out," he mused thoughtfully. "I was in such a hurry this morning." He turned to me with a smile and continued composedly, "Well, no harm done. You would have known about them shortly, anyway."

"What about them?" I couldn't help my impatience. "How did you get them? Have we suddenly come into a small fortune?"

"No, nothing like that. Shall we say I have accumulated them over the months?"

"That's no answer."

"They are very legal, if that's what you're worried about," he said blandly, smiling. "Bought, paid for, and all yours."

"It's the money I'm talking about, Christopher Dunlap, as you know perfectly well. I'm not such an idiot that I don't know those stocks are worth a lot of money. How much? Where did you get it?"

"Oh, several thousand—probably between twenty and thirty—if the market goes up," he replied, as if he were discussing the weather. "It will be enough to take care of our needs for the immediate future. Later, I have a few different schemes I would like to try with a little better profit margin."

"Twenty to thirty thousand dollars! I don't believe it. You couldn't have saved that much in six months."

"No, that I could not. Although a portion was out of my earnings."

"And where did you get the rest?" I felt it was like pulling teeth without anesthetic, trying to get the information out of him.

"What if I told you I am not going to tell you?" he asked, with such a devilish twinkle in his eyes, I wanted to shake him.

"I won't go to bed with you again for the rest of my life."

"In that case, you remember those gold coins I had with me when we first met that I showed you to prove who I was? Quite a purseful I had, if you will remember—about three, three hundred fifty pounds sterling in my own currency and about ten times that on today's market. They are worth a considerable bit *more* than that on a collector's market. Well, I pawned them."

"You pawned them?"

"On a more genteel scale than that, of course. I did not pay a visit to the corner pawnshop. I followed up a few advertisements in a coin collector's journal. Very rewarding. I expected the coins to be worth something, but I was not expecting some of the newly minted and uncirculated coins to be worth as much as they were. Apparently, several of the coins are quite rare today in perfect condition."

"You sold all of those beautiful coins?" I said, appalled.

"No, I have quite a few left—the most valuable ones. I sold only what I needed to buy the stock that I thought would give you security in this modern day if anything should happen to me. Originally, when I discovered their value, I was simply going to leave the coins with you, but I was afraid someone might question you as to how you came to be in possession of them, and I was not sure you would know the proper routes to follow in getting the most value for them. Then again, knowing you, you probably would have held on to them for keepsakes."

"I certainly would have."

"Which would not have served my purpose at all, which was to provide the woman I love with some financial security should I suddenly disappear from her life. Now, of course, I intend the proceeds for us. We'll sell a few shares for our trip, and eventually we should have enough to put a down payment on a house. I would rather not sell any more of the old coins unless absolutely necessary. They will be our insurance policy against the future."

"So that's why you've been so sure all this time." He didn't answer. "But how did you get involved with stocks?"

"I have always fiddled with investments, long before I arrived in this age. That was one way in which I kept myself and Cavenly solvent. So when I began looking into the market here, I found it fascinating and followed it for a while for my own amusement. Then I tried a few small investments—nothing hazardous. What I did not realize was that, even in this country, the government has its finger in every pie, and in order to purchase stock, I needed a Social Security number. I did a little snooping in your wallet and used yours. I gradually added to the stock as I learned more about it."

He was speaking matter-of-factly about his ventures, as if his feat of financial prowess on the part of a stranger, from not only a different country, but also a different time, could have been carried off by any schoolboy.

"Will you please drive, madam," he continued complacently. "I was looking forward to a nice drink by the fireside with my beloved before dinner."

I reached across the seat and hugged him impetuously. "What a man I've married. You never cease to amaze me."

"I was not trying to amaze you, but if you would like to put me up on a marble pedestal," he teased, "I have not the least objection."

As we drove out of the station parking lot, he laid a hand on my arm. "You are not angry I've kept this from you so long?"

"No." I smiled happily. "How can I be angry knowing I'm on the road to riches? I'm proud of you."

He smiled. "I am glad you are pleased."

SIXTEEN

There was just the slightest breath of spring in the March air, enough warmth to melt the top layer of frost from the frozen earth. The first sign of spring usually brought a feeling of elation, but that day shock had its hold on me.

I'd suspected nothing that afternoon when I walked into the doctor's office. I'd gone for an annual checkup and a change in my prescription. The birth control pill I'd been using had begun to give me unpleasant side effects, and I'd stopped using it the month before. I was surprised to see the doctor's raised brows when, during the examination and routine questioning, I'd told him I was two weeks late. I wasn't worried, because I figured my system was upset. The doctor finished the examination, asked me a few probing questions, and then told me to come into his office after I was dressed. I had a chilling feeling that I wasn't going to like what I was about to hear.

"Sit down, Jessica," he said calmly, motioning me toward the chair. He finished scribbling something on his pad, then looked up and folded his arms across the desk in front of him. "I take it from what you haven't told me that you and your husband are not trying to have a baby."

"No...no, we're not." I clenched my hands together to stop them from shaking. "Since I went off the pill last month we've been very careful."

He smiled gently. "Apparently not careful enough. I think you're pregnant."

"Oh, God!"

"Is it such a catastrophe?" he asked kindly. "Babies sometimes have a way of bringing themselves into the world when they're least expected, but I've seen from experience that it often works out very happily. I can't be positive you are pregnant. It's too early for an examination to tell me anything definite, but Mrs. Wallace will take a specimen before you leave today, and I can tell you conclusively."

He must have noticed my face paling before his eyes. "Before you get upset, why don't you go home and talk it over with your husband? I think you'll feel differently about it. I'll talk to you tomorrow."

I stood up, knowing there was nothing more he could tell me. But he didn't understand. Christopher and I weren't like other people. This wasn't just a case of having an unexpected baby.

I left his office, shaking badly. Christopher wouldn't be home until five thirty. It was only four. I made several cups of strong coffee and sat at the kitchen table. I knew he would want this child. It was the fulfillment of his dreams. But was I ready? I wanted it—I knew deep inside I wanted his child to fill my body, to know that his seed was within me. But what of the rest—the years of raising this child, a child whose father might not even be here to see its birth? I would have living proof of our love, but was I capable of raising his child alone?

At last I heard his footsteps coming down the path, and I ran to the window to be sure. I was at the door waiting, opening it before his fingers touched the knob, and flung myself into his arms.

I hadn't shed a tear until that moment, but now, feeling his warm, strong arms about me and seeing his understanding face alight with surprise and happiness at finding me so eagerly awaiting him, a flood of tears burst forth. I buried my face in his jacket.

"I thought you'd never get home tonight," I cried.

His hands were immediately on my shoulders, one of them sliding under my quivering chin to lift my watery eyes to his, "Jessica. My Lord, what's the matter?" He glanced at the clock. "You are usually not home so early. You didn't lose your job, did you?" I wagged my head no. "Then what is it that has upset you like this? Was the house broken into?"

"No, no," I sobbed. "Nothing like that at all."

"Well, tell me! What could possibly have happened to get you in a state like this?"

"I had a doctor's appointment," I muttered.

"A doctor's appointment?" He scowled. "You're not ill?"

"No...Christopher, I'm pregnant."

His blue eyes seemed to darken a fraction as he tried to make sense of my stumbling words. "You're pregnant?" His voice was harsh. He looked as if I'd dropped a bomb on him.

"Yes...I...I think so," I stammered. He wasn't happy, after all.

"We are going to have a baby?" Now he sounded astonished.

"Yes."

Suddenly a smile flashed across his face, as radiant as a

sunrise after forty days of rain. He picked me up in his arms so that my feet dangled several inches off the ground. "You mean it?" A hint of suspicion that he'd misunderstood what I'd said flicked across his face, then cleared as I nodded in affirmation. "Jessica, that is wonderful," he exclaimed.

He hugged me even more closely. "But why in heaven's name are you crying? I've wanted this. I know it was not the sensible thing to do, but now that it has happened, it is wonderful!"

"You're happy?"

"Of course, I am happy. How could I be anything but happy at this moment, knowing my wife is to bestow me with our child." He paused. "But your tears— you don't want it, do you?"

I didn't know how to tell him the multitude of feelings in my heart—the joy of carrying his child, the trepidations for our child's future and our own. Could I tell him that deep inside I didn't know if I was ready for the responsibility? Would he accept that in me, when he was so strong? Or that my vanity cried out in protest at the thought of a body that would be swollen and misshapen, one that he might no longer love because of its awkwardness? Could I tell him that up to this moment I'd never craved a child? That they'd always seemed nice if they were someone else's, but I'd never pictured myself with a child of my own? Could I tell him these things? I knew I couldn't—a man couldn't understand these strange turnings of a woman's mind.

Suddenly I felt it wasn't such a horrible thing anymore—the world wasn't ending for me or us with this unexpected seed in my belly. In fact, it might just be beginning. I lifted my eyes to his and felt some of his strength and joy flowing into my veins and knew that if there was ever anything in this life he could give me as a remembrance of him, he'd just given me his most precious gift, his child.

I was finally able to smile, and when I saw his smile, the strength I'd felt before flowed even stronger from him to me. It was like a current, and it steadied my wobbling knees.

His eyes were knowing, seeing the torment in my mind. "You are afraid I will not be here to see our child born."

"Yes, and more than that. But it doesn't seem so important anymore. You're happy...your happiness makes me happy. I can do it, Christopher. We'll do it together, if we can."

"Oh, Jessica?" He took my chin again to study my face. "Why did you not tell me what you suspected? We could have talked it over. You would have known sooner how happy I am and not have worried yourself into a dither."

"But I didn't suspect..."

"You must have had some idea. Weren't you late?"

"I was. But I thought it was because of the pill...because I'd gone off last month. We were careful..."

"I know, I know. Perhaps it was simply meant to be. With all our care and caution, we still have begotten a child. Do you not think that it might be a sign to us? That nature is telling us we are not meant to be separated? We will find out soon, Jessica, and until then, if it is in my power, I will be beside you. Let us not think beyond the fact that I am here, and will be indefinitely. That is all I want to contemplate. I do not want to go back anymore—not when my life is so full in this world." He pulled me close.

"I love you," I whispered. I thought how wonderful this love of his was that it had the power to turn my confusion into a happy moment and take my body, cold with fear, and make me feel warm with protection.

"And I love you," he said. "But why are we standing here in the kitchen? We have plans to make, and there are so many questions I want to ask you."

He fastened his arm about my waist and led me into the living room. "I will light the fire, and we'll talk." The beautiful smile that had lit his face a few moments before was bright again as he plopped me gently against the cushions.

We talked for hours that night. He was curious about everything—he'd never been a father before, he told me unnecessarily. He wanted to know how I felt. Fine, I told him, no different than before.

"When is the baby due?" he asked eagerly. "Let's see, this must be your first month." He did a quick calculation. "Sometime in the late fall, then?"

"Middle of November."

"But you're sure you are all right? None of that morning illness?"

I laughed at his over-protectiveness, "No, not yet. Give me time. By next month I'll probably be sick as a dog."

He pulled his arm a little more tightly about me. I leaned my head against his warmth as we nestled on the couch before the crackling fire. By the time we rose for the bedroom, a light snow had begun outside the window.

But the winter didn't penetrate as far as our bed that night, as we settled between the sheets and released our bodies to the desires that were always with us. His embraces were especially tender, as if I'd gained a certain fragility in my pregnant state. But we were one body again long before either of us could relax into sleep, still holding each other close, afraid to let go.

The relaxation that followed didn't stay with me long. As I heard his deepening breaths beside me and knew he was asleep, restlessness entered me and I rose, pulling my robe about me. I tiptoed quietly from the room, trying not to waken him, and went to the darkened hall. The drapes were open, revealing the full fury of what had now become a storm. The back yard was eerie in the snow-brightened night...cold and uninhabitable...and I was glad I didn't have to face its wrath.

I thought of Christopher, sleeping peacefully in the bedroom, and pressed my hand to my flat stomach, amazed that life could already be starting there. How tiny was this seed that could bring such drama into my life, and how uncertain its future.

Outside, the cold wind whistled through the branches. The heavy snow swirled past the windows, whipped by the wind into funnels and pushed into drifts over the ground. I prayed my love-conceived child would never know the angry tumult nature was displaying for me tonight and that its father would be here to see its entrance into the world and know the beauty of the life he had created. Then I turned and joined my husband in our bed.

SEVENTEEN

The big 757 was lining up for the runway, the jet engines roaring. Any moment now we would feel the sudden thrust of energy that would take us off the ground and high into the air above New York City. I could feel a ball of excitement and nervousness in my stomach. It had been a hectic month building up to this point, between the last-minute travel plans, the letters and briefs from Yale and Professor Enright, setting our affairs in order at home for our four-week absence, buying clothes, and packing. And, for me, the biggest adjustment of all had come during these last weeks—that of mentally and physically accepting this new bundle I carried. I was happier now. My pregnancy lay easier with me, and I was more content. I still had my fears, but now my uncertainties were overshadowed by the greater fear of what we'd discover in England during the next few weeks. My husband's destiny was still more important to me than anything else, and my hands turned cold at the thought that I might soon discover he'd be leaving my life forever.

My ears were ringing as we gained altitude, and I turned my attention to Christopher's excited face. He'd been looking forward to his first experience of air travel, and the delight in his eyes told me it was measuring up to his expectations.

Below us, like a toy landscape, lay the southern coast of Long Island beside the blue waters of the Atlantic. The loudspeaker clicked on. The captain's voice sounded in a smooth British accent, "Welcome, ladies and gentlemen, to British Airways Flight Nine-oh-two. We hope you'll have a pleasant trip with us this morning, and thank you for joining us. We have clear weather ahead, good tail winds, and should be arriving at Heathrow in about six hours to partially cloudy skies and a temperature of sixty-eight degrees. I'll be checking back with you again before we reach our destination. May I wish you a comfortable journey."

I squeezed my husband's hand. "Well, my love, we're off."

"London in six hours," he sighed. "This is absolutely fantastic."

"I had a feeling you'd enjoy it." We settled back and unfastened our seat belts as the flight attendant came by to take our drink order.

Although six hours is a long time to sit crushed into a small seat, especially when you have legs as long as Christopher's, the time passed quickly. We talked to the gentleman in the seat beside us. He was a gregarious London banker, returning from a business trip to the States, and was only too eager to fill the hours of his trip with lively conversation. He introduced himself as Eugene Morris, and he was full of suggestions and hints for our stay in London. He gave us a list of good restaurants where the atmosphere would be to our liking and the prices not exorbitant, told us which of the London shows currently playing would be worth seeing, and where the best buys were to be found on Bond and Oxford streets that year.

Lunch was served about midday, but I was so wrapped up in our conversation, I'd lost track of the time. While we ate, Christopher and Eugene discussed the economic situation in England and a little of the current politics. Eugene, of course, was curious about Christopher's accent. Christopher answered that he'd been born in England but had been out of the country for many years, which I suppose was close enough to the truth.

I asked Eugene for a refresher course in British coinage, which both Christopher and I needed if we were not to insult the cabbie who would take us to the hotel in London, or the porter at the Dorchester. The coins themselves had taken on a different appearance in the hundred and sixty years and were now based on the decimal system, but Christopher didn't seem to have any trouble grasping the system and quickly calculating and extracting a fair tip from the coins in his hand.

Before long, the pilot announced our approach to Heathrow. I felt the jar as the wheels of the plane hit the runway, then the smooth, slow ride as we taxied to the terminal. Disembarkation began. The waiting, the long walk down what seemed to be miles of glassed-in corridors; the bustle of travelers at once eager and tired.

At the luggage racks we bid Eugene good-bye, Christopher accepting his card and promising to give him a call for an evening together with him and his wife while we were in London. After more delays and long lines clearing through Customs, we hailed a cab and within minutes were leaving behind the madness of the airport, heading east on M4 toward London.

It was difficult to see details of the scenery in the fading light, yet our eyes were glued to the windows. Christopher's expression was one of alert observation, but as we neared

London, it became one of shock.

"But this is entirely changed," he exclaimed. "There were only fields here for miles on end, a village or two, all the way to Hammersmith."

"I warned you things had changed."

"Yes, but to this extent? My God, native Englishman though I am, had I not studied a map before we left New York, I would not know where I was!"

We were now on the outskirts of the city. Five-story Victorian apartments, with their high, ornamented facades and windows, lined either side of the roadway. Many had an unkempt, tired look to them—windows boarded, trim faded. It was almost impossible to believe that at the time of Christopher's last visit to London, these buildings had not been constructed.

When we pulled off the highway onto London streets, traffic immediately became more congested. The slow movement of the taxi gave us ample opportunity to examine the street signs and watch the pedestrians on the sidewalks. I was too busy alternating my attention between Christopher's amazement and the glimpses of scenery to pay much attention to the cab driver.

I remember the car picking up speed as a space cleared in the traffic, then hearing a raucous squeal of brakes, the sickening sound of metal hitting metal, glass smashing. I remember a sudden flash of pain...then all was darkness.

EIGHTEEN

I opened my eyes to a white glare, blurred outlines, a strange, throbbing pain in my head. I tried to clear my vision by blinking my eyes, but the motion brought greater pain. There was someone standing beside the bed. I couldn't distinguish clearly, but it was a male figure. I willed my eyes to focus. He was tall, trim, and wore a crumpled yet well-made suit. There was a shadow of unshaven beard on his cheeks, dark smudges under his eyes.

His head turned, looked down at me. He took a step closer, reaching out his hands.

"You are awake...thank God."

It was difficult to concentrate. I scowled.

"Do not move. Lie still. I will get the doctor." The man's voice was filled with a strange jubilation.

He was back in a second with a white-coated figure, the two of them speaking in low, rapid dialogue that ceased as they approached me. The white-coated figure came forward to stand by my side. I turned my head a fraction. The fog was gradually clearing from my eyes, the fuzzy outlines sharpening. I could distinguish the man's features.

The doctor took my wrist, listened to my pulse, then held a small light before my eyes as he peered into my pupils. "Can you see me?" I was able to make out two warm brown eyes.

"Fairly well," I said uncertainly.

"You're having a problem with your vision?"

"Yes." Just to speak demanded too much effort.

He examined my eyes again. "I don't think there's any damage. Any other aches or discomfort?"

"My head."

"Not surprising. You've had a concussion, but the worst is over. Fortunately, aside from some bruising, there are no broken bones—no other injuries. I think you'll begin to feel yourself in a few hours. Try to get some rest now. I'll be back later on."

A dreamy drowsiness was slipping over me. All I wanted to do was sleep. I closed my eyes.

When I awoke later, a set of piercing blue eyes was gazing down at me. They belonged to the man who'd been standing beside me when I'd first wakened. I could see him clearly now. He had a strong-boned face with a straight nose and cleft chin, and slightly curling dark hair.

He was sitting on a chair pulled close to the side of the bed. "Feeling better?"

I nodded, noticing the pain in my temples seemed less severe.

"Good." He reached around to a rolling table near the foot of the bed. "They have brought you something to eat. I think it's still warm. Are you hungry?"

I looked at the plate of food but felt no appetite.

"You should eat. It is the only way you'll regain your strength." He pushed the tray in front of me and propped pillows behind my back so that I could sit more comfortably. "Do you want some help?"

"No." It seemed an indignity to allow him to feed me. There was a bowl of soup in front of me, still steaming. I lifted the spoon with a shaking hand. It tasted good, and I finished it, then went on to a small meat pie with an appetite I hadn't imagined I had.

He grinned as the food disappeared from the dishes and gave me a satisfied nod when I motioned for him to take the tray and leave me just the cup of tea. With a full stomach, I felt a new surge of energy.

When the cup was drained, he removed it as well, having said nothing in the interim. Now he took a seat on the edge of the bed, grasped both my hands in his own and held them gently. I was too shocked to do more than gape.

"You do not know how wonderful it is to see you coming back to life again," he spoke softly. "Of course, you are not yourself yet. The doctor said it would take a day or two—but when I think of how I felt when I saw you lying on this bed, looking like death itself! I was so afraid I was going to lose you and our child...after all that you and I have been through together." His fingers tightened around mine, then loosened as he raised his hands to let them rest tenderly on either side of my face. His eyes became more serious. They seemed touched with a yearning. "Do you have any idea how much I've longed to kiss your beautiful lips these last days, to hold you in my arms and give you strength...make you well again?"

His face drifted toward me. His arms slipped behind my shoulders. I felt his mouth as it covered my own—a soft touch that soon burned with a fire as it pressed down in hunger. For a suspended moment I was caught by the animal strength that vibrated from him like a current. But it was a stranger's kiss, a stranger's embrace. Gasping, shocked, I pulled away from the hungry mouth.

"Jessica, what is wrong?"

"Why are you kissing me? I barely know you!"

"Barely know me? My God, I am your husband!"

"No!"

He tried to pull me back into his arms. I shrugged him off. "Get away from me! Get me the doctor!"

"Listen...please listen."

"Get out of this room," I screamed.

I watched him lift his weight off the bed. He was a man in a daze, shaking his head, unable to take his eyes from me. He moved slowly backward toward the door, staring at me all the while. Finally, as he reached the door, he spun around. I heard his footsteps as he rushed off down the hall.

My insides churned and clenched against themselves. I didn't know what to think. He'd called me by name— Jessica. But that wasn't me. What was my name? I couldn't seem to remember. And he'd mentioned a child. No, this was only shock. It would come back to me in a moment. Yet everywhere I searched, I came up with a void, an empty page. Everything that had come before the moment of my waking in the hospital bed was a shadow. There was nothing to tie myself to. There were no memories!

The doctor rushed into the room, and I reached out my hands to him in my eagerness for reassurance.

"What's happening to me? Who was that man?"

"Please try to relax, Mrs. Dunlap. Distress cannot help your condition. That man was your husband. Before you say anything, let's talk for a while. You were involved in an automobile accident three days ago when you and he were traveling into London. Obviously you don't recall, but that accident was the cause of your head injury and is the reason why you are in this hospital. Unfortunately, one of the effects of your concussion appears to be amnesia. Now, don't become frightened. I've seen many cases like yours over the years, and your memory will return."

"Who am I?"

"Your name is Jessica Dunlap. You're an American, traveling to England with your husband, Christopher Dunlap. From conversations we've had, I've learned he was born here in England, but is now an American citizen. You are twenty-nine years old, three months pregnant, and, aside from concussion, in excellent health."

"It can't be."

"I wouldn't be telling you this if it wasn't fact. You've given your husband quite a turn. I've told him to wait until I'd spoken to you and you had an opportunity to reconcile yourself to the situation."

"But how can I have forgotten so completely? There's nothing...nothing."

"A shock to the brain—a blow that has temporarily blocked your memory."

"When will it come back? When will I remember?"

"That I can't tell you. It could be a few days, a month, a year. It would depend upon the circumstances, how much healing is necessary. I realize you can't tell me now, but perhaps there was something in your past you subconsciously wished to forget. I'll know more when I get a full history from your husband."

"I don't know what to do."

"For the time being, I want you to remain in hospital a few more days to rest. With your strength recovered, you'll be much better able to cope. It won't be an easy adjustment for either you or your husband. You will both need to be patient and keep in mind that your memory will find its own time to reinstate itself. It's not something that can be forced."

He rose, laying a hand on my shoulder. "Would you like to see your husband?"

"No, not yet."

"I'll speak to him, and I'll be in to see you later."

I awoke the next morning from a restless night's sleep, plagued with dreams that meant nothing to me. I'd started awake several times during the night and had stared blankly at the nightstand, then looked out the window near my bed at the streetlights, searching for familiar signs, anything to ease the feelings of emptiness.

The nurses brought me breakfast and a fresh nightgown, and helped me to the bathroom. I saw a stranger's face in the mirror as I tried to straighten the tangled mass of long, dark hair. Even when they gave me a purse containing my identification and certain articles of makeup no bells rang.

The doctor came to check me. We sat and talked for a while, but I wasn't ready to see my husband. I was secretly afraid of our next meeting. Though I went over and over in my mind the details of his face as I remembered them from the day before—each feature, each expression, the shape of his hands and the line of his body beneath the well-fitted clothing—he was still an unknown entity. I had no idea what to say to him, how to behave. Certainly I desired no intimacy. Yet apparently I was carrying his baby. The thought pressed home the point that at one time I must have been very intimate indeed with him.

I procrastinated, avoiding the inevitable meeting until, that evening, he walked into my room unannounced.

The long stride was firm as he approached me, yet there was a wariness in his eyes, a gray pallor to his skin and a tautness about his mouth, attesting to the trial he was undergoing. He took a seat in the chair and studied me. As two strangers meeting, neither of us knew what to say.

Finally he spoke, his voice tired but steady. "I know you do not remember me or anything of your past. I've tried to reconcile myself to that fact as best I can, but we cannot put off confrontation indefinitely. We have a lot to talk about."

"Yes."

"We are legally husband and wife. Is there any question in your mind about that?"

"No. The doctor told me everything, and I found some identification."

"You still have no recollection of me...nothing at all?"

"Nothing."

He sighed. "You will be leaving the hospital the day after tomorrow. We should consider our plans. Originally we were going to spend two weeks vacationing in London, then go on to Kent, where I have some research work to do. These plans can be changed now, of course, if you would rather go home."

"Home?"

"Connecticut. We have a small house, which was yours before we married. Very lovely."

Strangely enough, as he spoke I could picture the outlines of the state on a map, but I had no recollection of the landscape or ever having lived there.

"I'm willing to continue with our trip here. I can't think what else to do."

He nodded. "I have already checked into the hotel. I think you will like the room. Since we will lose six days because of your stay in the hospital, I will extend our reservations another week here and make the necessary arrangements at our other stop."

"The doctor told me you're an Englishman."

"I was born and raised here, yes."

"Then how did we meet?"

"I made a trip to the States, and we met at that time."

"We've been married long?"

"Two months."

I stared at him. "I'm three months pregnant."

"We lived together before we were legally married."

"Is that why you married me—because I was pregnant?"

"No, I loved you. I still do."

I glanced away to the opposite wall and the small print hanging upon it. "I feel very uncomfortable."

"And you think I do not?" He paused. "I'll be as understanding as I can, Jessica...do anything in my power to make it easier for you. I trust you will meet me halfway."

"I'll try, but I don't know anything about you."

"We will have to become reacquainted, then."

I was remembering his lips upon mine the day before — the passion that had been beneath the surface—and wondered what he would expect when we were alone together in our hotel room. "I can't be a wife to you. At least not as I was before."

For the first time his mouth turned up slightly in a smile. "If you are trying to tell me you would rather not have me in your bed, I did not expect you would, for a while. We'll take each day as it comes. We'll see London, go to the theater, try to relax and enjoy ourselves as much as possible under the circumstances."

There was something about this man that attracted and frightened me at the same time. He was certainly very attractive, and so strong. It came through in the decisiveness of his speech, and in his desire to face the situation head-on and his expectation that I do the same. I fished around in my head for something to say to relieve the awkwardness I felt every time I looked in his direction. "Why did you come to America?"

"My reasons are something we can go into another time. Suffice it to say it proved a beneficial trip."

"Are your family still here in England?"

"Some distant relations. We are not on the best of terms.

Actually, when we go into Kent, I will be doing my research work in my former home. The family will be away at the time, and I have no desire for them to become acquainted with my real identity."

"Why?"

"I cannot answer that now. You will understand when your memory returns. You look tired. Perhaps I should go and let you sleep. I'll see you tomorrow." Rising, he took my hand for the briefest moment, squeezed it, and then left me to my thoughts.

He came and went, spending a few hours with me over the next morning, afternoon, and evening, sometimes sitting quietly beside me as my thoughts followed their own course, other times striding restlessly about the room, an underlying urgency to his conversation. Having seen him as much as I had, I no longer found his face a stranger's face, but our discourse still lacked the informality of husband and wife. He told me a great deal about us and about myself, but I sensed a vagueness in his descriptions of his own background—there were no precise dates or details of his life before he came to America.

He spoke, too, of less personal things—of what we would do in London—of the entertainments, the restaurants, the beauties of the countryside, all of which he intended to show me. I was more relaxed when he spoke of impersonal things. It required no emotional commitment on my part.

The next evening was my last in the hospital. Physically I was ready to face the world beyond the hospital doors, but mentally I was not. I was uncertain, even afraid. It would be just the two of us in a frighteningly large city. But then, he'd said he'd give me all the support I needed.

He arrived for his visit that evening shortly after the nurse had cleared away my dinner tray. Coming straight to the bed and sitting down, he handed me a colorfully bound paperback.

"A London guidebook," he advised me. "I thought you might like to look through it before we embark on our adventures about town."

"Yes, thank you. I'd like that very much." My fingers quickly flipped through the pages as I scanned it.

When I glanced up, he was watching me with a deliberate intensity. Unexpectedly, his hand reached out to take my shoulder. The other hand cupped my chin.

"No..." I whispered.

But in an instant he'd slid across the bed and was pressing me back against the pillows as his lips sought mine, found them, claimed them. I fought to escape the ever tightening circle of his arms, but he wouldn't allow it. Even when I wrenched my head to the side, out of reach of his lips, he forced it back.

"Jessica...look at me. Tell me there is nothing there."

"There isn't."

"I do not believe you've forgotten so completely that you cannot respond to me anymore!"

"I can't!"

In his distress he loosened his arms, and I shoved him away from me and slid from the bed.

"Or is it that you won't allow yourself to respond?"

"No."

"Jessica...please."

"You're going too fast."

"But I love you."

"Don't say that."

"I must. For the past three days I've held it inside, all my need, until I am burning up with it. I want you to feel for me what I feel for you."

"I feel nothing."

"It will come back—it will all come back."

"When? When will it stop being a blank wall?"

"Do not make it harder for us than it already is."

"What am I supposed to do? Pretend I know you? Pretend it is all as it was? Is that what you want? But you see, I don't remember what it was."

"I want to help you. I want you to love me again."

I shook my head.

"Jessica, what we had was so good. Please come back to me. It can be good again."

"I can't...I don't know you. I..." My eyes were filling with tears I couldn't stop from rising to the surface. I couldn't face the love I saw in his eyes, or my failure to remember him. Everything that had been dammed up in me during the last days came flooding up. I didn't know what to feel, what to think.

I rushed to the window to bury my face in my hands and sob. The strong arms reached out to turn me, to cradle me as I cried.

"I am sorry," he said softly. "I did not intend to push you like that. Only promise me that you'll give us at least a chance...give yourself a chance to remember all that we had—and will have again. Do not close your mind."

He held me until the last of my sobs had subsided and I lifted my head to wipe the remnants of tears from my cheeks.

"Come, you shouldn't be up like this. You should be getting all the rest you can. Tomorrow will be time enough to test your stamina." He led me back to the bed and helped me under the covers, suddenly all meekness and solicitude. "Comfortable?"

"Yes."

"Again, Jessica, I'm sorry. The last thing I wanted was to upset you."

"Perhaps I'm acting like a child. There are responsibilities to be faced. I know I must learn to face them."

"In time. The adjustment you've had to make is frightening you, and I have hardly helped. You will be leaving the hospital late tomorrow morning. Is there anything I can say now, or do, that would make it easier for you?"

"No. I think I'd like to be alone. I have a lot to think about."

"I understand."

He moved toward the door, flicking off the overhead light to leave only the reading lamp burning beside me. In the doorway, he hesitated. The light from the hall cast him in shadow. His face was indistinguishable, yet his tall frame seemed larger, more powerful, more unsettling than ever. With a barely audible sigh, he left me.

NINETEEN

The London buildings we passed on our way to the Dorchester Hotel were lovely: mellow, proud in their dignity and age. The sidewalks were lively with shoppers, and tourists, too, it appeared from the number of cameras I spied clasped in hands or slung over shoulders. We reached a busy intersection marked by an equestrian statue in a grassy rotary. To one side I saw a large stone arch and, beyond that, glimpses of green trees and lawns and beautiful flowers. As we rounded the rotary and turned off to the left, a park stretched out the length of the road, set off by iron gates and well-matured trees.

"Hyde Park, Jessica. We are almost at the hotel." There was a certain tone in his voice I couldn't identify...nostalgia?

I was busy watching the scene around me. There were automobiles of every description, from round black taxis to sleek sports cars to bright red double-decker buses, all vying with each other for the right-of-way. We headed down the roadway parallel of the park, then circled back on the other side of the grass-covered island that divided the roadway.

Our cabby pulled up before an impressive building attended by a neatly liveried doorman. He hurried over to the cab as we came to a halt and held the door for me as I stepped out onto the pavement. "Good afternoon, madam. Welcome to the Dorchester."

My husband paid the driver, and we stepped through the doors into the elegant lobby. After collecting the room key from the desk, he led me toward the elevators. We exited at one of the upper floors, into a long corridor. He paused before a door at the end, opened it, and waited for me to precede him inside.

It wasn't one room, but two. I could see the bedroom door open to my left and a bed within. The room in which we were standing appeared to be a sitting room. It was furnished with a small couch and chairs, a tea table, a desk and a bookcase. At the front, looking out toward the sky, were three tall windows draped in heavy green curtains. I went to stand before them, resting my hands on the broad sill. We were at the front of the hotel, facing the park, and the view was spectacular.

My husband came to stand beside me at the window. I turned toward him, and he smiled. "Do you like it?"

"It's beautiful. I don't know why, but being in the midst of a city, I somehow felt we'd be cooped up between soot-covered buildings. The park is lovely—especially looking at it from this height. Can we walk through it later?"

"It would be my pleasure. London abounds with parks. If you like, we will see them all."

"I'd like that very much." I glanced up at him and caught such a warm, wistful look in his eyes, I turned away. "When we were in the cab, you spoke as though the park meant something special to you. Does it?"

"A long time ago. I used to ride on the paths across the way here every morning...meet friends...talk." His eyes were focused out the window as though he was seeing something more than just trees and grass. "I cannot explain to you now, but it means a great deal to me to see it again."

I was wondering why none of the objects or people around me seemed odd. On the ride over, I'd not been amazed at the sight of cars or traffic lights or tall concrete buildings or the hordes of people and the way they were dressed. I knew that there was a light switch inside each doorway and that in the bathroom I could turn the taps and get water. It seemed I remembered all the basics that enabled me to get around in this world. Only the most personal memories were an absolute blank.

My husband turned to me. "I thought perhaps we would get some tea, then take a walk in the park. Would you like to freshen up first? You'll find the bathroom off the hall between these two rooms."

"Yes. I'll be right back."

It was a huge room, with tiled walls and a tub in which you could drown yourself. I checked my hair and makeup in the mirror. As I unwrapped a bar of the scented, labeled hotel soap to wash my hands, I was aware of a building excitement within me. Perhaps it was being amid city life, in this elegant hotel, feeling the clash of life around me, so different from the isolating protection of the hospital. For a brief moment I stopped thinking of problems and began anticipating the days ahead.

When I left the bathroom, Christopher was still standing by the window, gazing away from me, lost in thoughts of his own. He heard my footsteps, turned, and smiled.

We had tea downstairs and left the hotel for the park, stopping at the curb to wait for a break in the traffic. I don't remember which one of us it was who finally looked down the street to see the sign for a pedestrian subway, but soon we were walking toward it, descending beneath the street, coming up at the opposite side near one of the small gates to the park. We entered, then headed down a narrow, tree-shaded pathway.

"Does it remind you of anything?" he asked as we walked through the speckled sunlight that drifted through the branches.

"Not particularly. It's pretty. I feel a sense of comfort here, but it reminds me of nothing."

"I thought perhaps it might remind you of home. New England has many of the same qualities in spring, except that it is much more hilly and the grass is not this vivid shade of green. I often thought of the greenness of English grass when I was with you—it's a memory that always stood out in my mind." He took my arm to lead me around a puddle of water. "Of course, when we go to Kent, you'll find more similarities than here, but I thought since you'd been to London two years ago, this park might seem familiar."

"I was here two years ago?"

"From what you've told me, yes."

"Strange...it seems an entirely new place to me— although I do feel comfortable here."

"Perhaps by the time we leave London, you will remember."

We walked a while longer in silence, then his mood seemed to grow more frivolous. We passed a bed of late daffodils growing in the grass. He reached down and broke one off and, with a wide smile and a dramatic bow, presented it to me.

"For you, madam. A small token of the great bouquets I would lay at your feet."

I laughed at his comic pose and, in spirit with his eloquence, accepted the flower with a curtsy. "You're too gracious, my lord, but I shall treasure this bloom from your noble hand."

I didn't expect the odd, startled look that swept across his face.

"Is something wrong?"

"No...it's nothing. A memory." He changed the subject. "Would you like to see some of the countryside while we're in London?"

"I thought we were going to Kent."

"We are, but some of the northern country. Kent is to the south, you know. From what I've read in the hotel, they're offering excellent tours of Oxford, Shakespeare country, Cambridge and Norfolk."

"You'd rent a car?" I held his daffodil as we walked and

tickled it across my nose.

"We could, or we could take a bus tour. Do you think you can still drive?"

"Yes, I think I can. I thought of it as one of the insignificant things I could remember when I've forgotten all the important ones."

"We'll take turns, then. You never did enjoy being chauffeured about."

"Didn't I?"

"Not particularly. I had an awful time persuading you to teach me to drive."

"I taught you to drive?"

"You did. "

We found a spot under the trees that we decided would make a nice place to rest. I folded my legs under me, and he sat with his knees drawn up. I laid my flower on the soft grass and looked across the park to a spot where a young man was lying prone on his stomach, reading or studying, his book propped up before him.

I let my mind drift off to less tangible things. "What kind of woman am I?"

"You are much like you are now. You don't change people by wiping out their memory."

"I have a feeling there is a lot more to me than that...a lot more than I can understand of myself right now."

"You are talking about the deeper things—the part of you that you will not find until you stop drifting, until you are able to trust in yourself and in others again." Absentmindedly he pulled blades of grass from the carpet at his side to scatter them carelessly over my skirt. "You are thinking of the woman who knew what she wanted, who had goals, convictions, who knew love and hate, her friends and her enemies, from experience. You cannot be that woman now because you have had all your experiences taken away from you, but basically you have not changed, and you'll be the same woman again when your memory returns."

"And if I don't remember?"

"You will find new convictions and goals, new incentives, but I think you'll discover that they will be the same as the ones you had before."

We began walking again as I thought over what he'd said. Our steps led us to a long, narrow body of water. There was a boathouse halfway up its length and a few rowboats cutting its surface. This was the Serpentine, he told me. Young children at the edge of the water trailed small boats attached to strings gripped tightly in their little hands. Nannies and young mothers pushed carriages or clutched the hands of toddlers, some of whom were filled with excessive high spirits and difficult to control. Many other people, young and old alike, were seated on the wooden benches or sprawled out on the grass, reading and relaxing. Several held leashed dogs by their sides, yet others ambled with their pets across the parkland.

We found a bench in sight of the water where the weak spring sunshine would fall on our backs. Christopher was smiling as he watched the children. "Just think, Jessica, one of those will be ours in a few months."

I channeled my gaze in the direction of his.

"I never thought I'd see the day," he mused, "when my own flesh and blood would be scampering before me on fat, stubby legs. I had a much more detached outlook on the whole phenomenon of offspring."

"When did you change your mind?"

"When I knew it was happening to me...when we discovered you were pregnant." He studied my face—a face that reflected none of the happiness or excitement written plainly on his own. "When will you accept it, Jessica?"

"I accept it. I've never questioned that I'm pregnant, but it's a little difficult being joyous about the occasion when I can't remember the child's father, or any of the feelings that led up to its conception."

"It seems that you are making little effort...fighting me every step of the way."

"I can't pretend to feelings I don't have."

"Recall that underneath that cloud in your mind are strong feelings for me and the child."

"Perhaps."

"These are facts, not conceits of my own devising. You cannot pretend they don't exist," he pressed on sternly.

"'I'm not pretending. I just don't know."

"You must have some feelings, some inkling. You've had your memory blocked out, not your emotions."

"I don't know! Why are you battering me with questions?" I rose and strode off in the direction of the side gate. He followed me and was at my side once again as we approached a wide dirt track where several horseback riders were exercising their mounts up and down its length. I admired the skill of the riders and the graceful lines of the animals. I felt a certain rapport with them and their obvious pleasure in horses. I sensed I could ride and, sometime in my forgotten past, must have shared their pleasure.

My husband spoke up at my side. "Rotten Row, Jessica. It's a shame you do not remember how we used to ride."

"We did ride, then. I knew there was something about horses..."

"We rode often at a place up in the country not far from your home. As a matter of fact, we were thinking of buying a house in that area and raising a few horses of our own."

"A big colonial with lots of land," I said without thinking.

He caught my shoulders and swung me around. "Why did you say that?"

I was startled now, too. "I don't know," I said dumbfounded. "It just came out. What does it mean?"

"It's the place we wanted to buy—the place I was just going to describe."

"I didn't know."

"Are you sure you're not remembering things?"

"No of course not. The thought just came to me."

He stared at me. "I wonder if it's a sign the rest will come back soon."

"I'd like to think that. You don't know how much I'd like to think that."

TWENTY

We had dinner at the hotel that night, neither of us having the energy to travel too far afield. Lingering over coffee, we were careful to speak mainly about our itinerary for the next day and the remaining two weeks in London, steering clear of sensitive topics. I had scanned the guidebooks he'd purchased and left in the hotel room, and checked off the places that interested me. I wanted to see the Tower, St. Paul's, Buckingham Palace, Westminster Abbey, Parliament, Chelsea, and several elegant old homes in and around London. At first I mentioned only a few of my goals to him with the Tower first on my list for our next day's excursion, but I saw his expression becoming increasingly mutinous as my ambitious list unfolded. I had to suppress a grin. He was probably picturing our vacation in London spent on the back of a tour bus or on sore feet, hoofing miles over the pavements and along museum corridors.

"I have a better idea, Jessica," he interrupted. "We'll see the Tower tomorrow, if you like, and St. Paul's, since they are each in the same direction, and on each succeeding day we will see one more of your sights, but the balance of each day and the evenings are to be my jurisdiction. Are we agreed?"

I smiled across the table at him in the dim light of the room and nodded. As we'd been talking, I couldn't help noticing how often his brandy glass was drained and refilled. Granted, our conversation was on a lighter note than it had been that afternoon, but his drinking made me uneasy. I couldn't say he was getting drunk—but then, of course, I had no recollection of stages and warnings of drunkenness in him. Foremost in my mind was my dread of the evening hours that still faced us— the events that might occur once we were behind the door of the hotel room.

It was after eleven before we left the table. The dining room had been crowded, but the waiter, instead of making hurrying hints and asking if we were ready for the bill, had ignored us as we tied up our corner table for three hours. In the end, we had to get his attention.

I felt tired, worn out by the events of the long day, but now my husband was in high spirits, reenergized. He unlocked the door of our room and flicked on a light. The curtains hadn't been drawn, and the lights of London were fully revealed beyond the bare windows.

He walked to one of the chairs, stripped off his jacket, and sat down with a sigh. "Very pleasant evening, Jessica."

I wandered over to the window. "Yes. Very nice. I liked the atmosphere."

"Did you?"

"Yes, the old-fashionedness."

"I thought perhaps you were referring to the company."

"That was nice, too."

I wasn't quite sure what to do with myself, so I laid my purse down on the windowsill and riveted my eyes on the scene beyond. What was in the back of his mind as he sat there in the chair watching me? Even as tired as I was, I didn't want to go to the bedroom, afraid that he might take the departure as a sign to follow. His mood was so uncertain. I would wait.

He loosened his tie, pulled it off, and threw it in the direction of his jacket. He undid the first few buttons of his shirt and let it hang open. "You don't sound very convinced, my wife," he said tauntingly.

"Oh, it was nice." I had to look at him. The small section of his chest and the curling dark hairs exposed by the loosened neck of his shirt were very attractive, suggestive. I wondered if he'd done it deliberately.

He leaned farther back in his chair, watching me with a wicked gleam in his half-closed eyes. "Why are you standing by the window, Jessica? Does the London scenery attract you that much?"

"I just thought I'd get a view of the city at night," I said quietly.

"You'll have plenty of time for that in the next two weeks."

"Is there something wrong with looking out the window?"

A knowing look was in his eyes. "Why don't you close the drapes, Jessica."

"Why?"

"It is time for bed, and I do not want all of London looking at your silhouette in the window."

I fingered the marble sill. "You can go to bed if you want."

"And what about you?"

"I am not tired."

He laughed.

"Well, I'm not," I lied. Maybe if he went to bed, I could make myself a spot on the couch out here.

"Which bed did you want? The right or the left?" he persisted.

I stared at his grinning face.

"Oh, you'd rather share mine?" He smiled devilishly. "How nice!"

"No!"

His brows came up in a smooth sweep. "You had something else in mind?"

"Of course."

"You say that with such aversion, my little love. But you are talking to the wrong man, you know. Remember I've been in your bed before."

"Well, you're not going to he there tonight," I flared.

He laughed again. This time the deep-throated sound filled the room.

"You'll wake someone," I said.

"These old walls are thick. It would take more than that to wake our neighbors."

"Christopher, stop it!"

Just as quickly as the laughter had lit his eyes, his seriousness darkened them. "So, it is Christopher, is it? Why is it, my dear, you can force my name past your lips only in your most heated moments?" He studied me darkly.

"That's not true."

"And shall I remind you of the many other times when you called me by far more intimate names than that?"

"That was in the past."

"It was not in the past, Jessica—it was before you lost your memory, and there is a great difference between the two."

"I can't help it."

"You could if you tried. But you do not want to try." His voice was biting.

I wanted to run, but wherever I went in these small rooms, he would follow me. I could almost picture the scene upon the mattress in the next room.

"Please," I pleaded. "You promised me you'd give me time."

"Promises are made to be broken." He laughed again, but it was a harsh sound. His blue eyes bored into me as he let me fidget with my uncertainties. Then abruptly he turned his head away from me to stare at the wall. "All right, my wife, go to your bed. I am sure I shall be very comfortable out here on the couch."

I didn't know whether to believe what I'd heard or not, but I didn't wait for him to change his mind. I was out of the room in a rush, with a hurried "Good night" over my shoulder and, when I'd reached the bedroom door, a softer, "Thank you." He gave no indication whether he'd heard me.

In the morning, as I opened my eyes, I wondered for a startled moment where I was. It came back quickly enough, and I rolled over to look at the travel clock on the nightstand. It was just after seven. Still early, but I was wide awake. I went to the window and pulled back the drapes. The sky was watery blue in the morning sunlight slanting over the city and washing the park with misty light. Traffic was already moving determinedly in the street below, and a few pedestrians were on the sidewalk.

I opened the closet and pulled out pants, a blouse, and good walking shoes. After I'd dressed, I used the phone in the room to call down to room service for coffee to be sent up. I opened the bedroom door cautiously and peeked out.

The sitting room was shadowed by the drawn drapes, but I could distinguish his form sprawled on the couch. He was sound asleep, lying on his back with one arm thrown out and dangling on the floor. His legs were twisted in the blankets, which had slipped down to leave his solidly muscled torso bare to the waist. The clothes he'd been wearing the night before were flung haphazardly over the chair. It was obvious from the articles collected there that he was naked under the slipping blanket.

I went into the bath, making as much noise as possible with the intention of waking him before I left the bath. I was rewarded soon by shuffling sounds, a muffled yawn, the sound of drapes being pulled, and a hearty, "Good morning, Jessica!"

"Good morning," I called back over the rushing noise of water turned on full force.

I gave him more than enough time to get dressed, wondering as I did what his mood would be like this morning. Then I stepped out into the sitting room. He'd put on his pants and was gathering up other clothing off the chair. We hadn't had time for more than a quick smile of greeting before a knock sounded at the door. Christopher left for the bathroom as I admitted the waiter with our coffee and busied myself the next few minutes pouring out two cups, automatically dropping one sugar and a dab of cream in his, and only cream in mine. As I placed the cups on the table, it suddenly struck me that I'd remembered how to make his coffee exactly as he liked it. It shook me up, but I managed to keep a calm expression on my face when he returned to the room and sat down on the couch beside me.

He took his cup. "Why, thank you, my dear." He took a sip, then another, and looked slyly at me from the corner of his eyes. "So you've also remembered how I drink my coffee?"

"It was just an accident," I said hurriedly. "Probably reflex."

"Mmmm." He continued watching me. "I wonder."

"And how are you feeling this morning? I thought you might have a slight headache after last night. Did you enjoy yourself?"

For a moment he was puzzled, then my meaning clicked, and his smile was sheepish. "Well it was diverting to see my wife acting the virginal maiden facing her abductor. Did you think I was going to devour you?"

"You know perfectly well what I thought."

He laughed. "Was I behaving like a cad, my dear?"

"You were."

"Seems to me there was a time you didn't mind my behaving that way at all." He let the statement lie, and I couldn't think of what to reply.

I finished my coffee and got up restlessly. "What time do you want to go to the Tower?"

He was eating a pastry, unperturbed. "About ten. We can take a cab from the hotel."

I glanced at my watch. "It's not even nine yet."

"I for one need a more substantial breakfast than this before we begin our day. We have time to get something downstairs. Are you ready?"

"In a minute." I left for the bedroom while he made a few finishing touches to his own appearance.

We left for the Tower promptly at ten, taking a taxi from our hotel to the Old City, now the business district and filled mainly with modern high-rise office buildings. We stopped at St. Paul's on the way and went into the great church for a brief tour. He said it had been many years since he'd been inside these portals, yet it seemed the church was the only landmark he recognized in this section of town. I didn't question him on the point. I supposed a lot of building had been done in the last several years.

We picked up a cab again and were dropped at the admission gates of the Tower. Here, standing in the midst of a modern city, was a picture out of the past. Beyond the battlements and

Tower were the Thames, rolling in the morning sunlight, and the Tower Bridge, impressive in itself.

Christopher was smiling at me, amused by my enthusiasm, but I didn't care what he thought. The history gathered within these walls was awesome. We saw the armories, the central and original tower begun in the time of William the Conqueror, Traitors' Gate, the Queen's House—a lovely building of black-and-white Tudor construction where Anne Boleyn had lived during her days of imprisonment—the site of the block in the Tower Green where many famous personages had breathed their last as they lost their heads to the ax. Last we visited the Jewel Room, where the Crown Jewels were on display. The security was intense in this part of the Tower because of the many robberies that had been attempted. I was impressed with the magnificent collection of precious metals and stones, but not nearly as much as I was by the buildings themselves.

It was close to lunchtime when we left the fortress and hailed a cab to bring us back to Westminster. The cabby dropped us on Piccadilly toward the park, where we found a little pub on one of the side lanes that was open for lunch. After my first remembered taste of traditional English fare—steak and kidney pie—we were out on the street again, once more looking for a cab to bring us to the Victoria Embankment and the Charing Cross Pier, where we would pick up the boat to take us down the Thames.

It became slightly more overcast that afternoon than it had been the day before, but there was still enough sunshine to make the river sparkle and enhance the scenes along its banks. We went down as far as Greenwich, past the Tower, and then turned and made our way back. We stood by the railing for most of the trip, letting the breeze ruffle our hair until, on the return journey, the chill began to seep in and we retreated out of the path of the wind.

When we reached the dock, instead of taking a taxi back to the hotel, Christopher took my hand and we began walking along the Embankment toward Westminster. Visible in the distance were the towers of Parliament and Big Ben. "I thought we would walk for a while," he explained. "Do you mind?"

"I'd rather walk than ride around in cabs all day."

"We'll go as far as Westminster Abbey, and by then I think we'll both be ready for tea."

He was still holding my hand, but it was a careless gesture, and comfortable. We hadn't argued or exchanged double-edged words once since we'd left the hotel that morning, and the unspoken truce between us contributed to the easy feeling I had about him that afternoon.

That easy mood remained with us the balance of that day and evening, through our dinner at an elegant, soft-toned restaurant on Regent Street, and an uncomplicated good-night when he allowed me, without any insinuating remarks, to depart for the bedroom and close the door behind me.

I was more confused than ever. It was a game of hide-and-seek we were playing, and I did not know what next to expect from him—or from myself.

TWENTY-ONE

The next morning we boarded a red double-decker bus at Piccadilly Circus for an abbreviated tour of the major spots of interest in the city. There were no stops, but the driver maintained an interesting dialogue throughout the trip. We sat on the top level near the front, and had a wonderful view.

My husband didn't say much during the trip. I noticed he was in a very thoughtful mood, almost withdrawn, with a pucker on his lips and a tiny frown creasing his brow.

The tour ended back at Piccadilly Circus, and it was only a short walk from there to Bond Street and the shops Christopher wanted to show me. The beautiful things I saw were in such abundance that I grew bleary-eyed trying to draw comparisons. I made mental notes of the best buys—the fine English china, the plaids and woolens from Scotland.

We ate at a little restaurant on Bond Street, resting our weary feet, and when the meal was finished, Christopher suggested we walk towards St. James's Park.

Our course led us down Old Bond Street, and within a few minutes we were crossing Piccadilly onto St. James. I liked this section of older, well-kept buildings immediately, all with their neat fronts and unostentatious dignity. It looked to be a residential section, although he told me he doubted it was any longer. Probably offices, perhaps apartments, he thought.

Suddenly he stopped and paused in front of one of the buildings, a strange expression on his face.

I wondered at it. "Is something wrong?"

He was staring through the windows. "Wrong?" Shaking his shoulders slightly, he answered, "No, nothing's wrong. It's just that this used to be one of my old haunts. Funny seeing it again."

"One of your old haunts?" I studied the bowed windows. "What is it? A restaurant?"

"Not quite. A men's club. One of those wonderful places where a man can retreat from family problems, business worries, and all the other troubles to have a quiet drink with his friends, a game of chance or a pleasant dinner without harassment. This, my dear, is White's. As a matter of fact, you're the one who told me it was still in existence, back in the days when you had a sharp memory."

"And you used to go here?"

"Very frequently."

It didn't quite fit in with my picture of him. The stories he was telling me seemed to be contradicting themselves. I'd thought he'd told me that he hadn't been to London for many years, but wouldn't that have made him a very young man...too young a man to frequent a place like this? And why did I get the feeling when he spoke of things he'd known before in London that he was speaking of the distant past? He was only thirty-three. How distant could the past be at that age?

We walked down the street and came to a road branching off to our left. He hesitated. "If you don't mind, Jessica, I'd like to make a short detour. What I wanted to see is down this way."

I shrugged my shoulders. "Fine. Lead me where you will."

At the end of the road, we entered a square of buildings looking much like the ones we'd just passed. In the center of the square was a small green park bordered by a wrought-iron fence. I looked over to where a sign was fastened to the fence. St. James Square, it read. This wasn't the famous park he'd been telling me about, I hoped. But no, he'd said we were making a detour.

We started down the sidewalk, past rows of windows and stone facades. When we were about halfway 'round the square he began to slow his steps, his eyes glued to the front of one building in particular. It looked much the same as the others to me. It was four stories high. The windows on the top floor were much smaller than the tall, slender ones in the lower three. Marble steps led up to a door in the center of the building. Brass lamps, now tarnished, were on either side of the door, and a narrow, cobbled drive ran down one side of the house to the back. There were no curtains at the windows, and the house looked empty and forlorn, deserted.

He stopped in front of the steps and let his eyes roam over every stone, every detail of the building. His face was serious...as serious as I'd seen it. I noticed a muscle twitch in his tightened jaw, and his eyes had that faraway look that I'd noticed when he'd looked out at the park from our hotel room window.

"Is this place important to you?" I asked quietly.

He nodded, although I think he barely heard me, so deeply was he buried in his thoughts.

"Do you mind my asking why?"

His eyelids flicked down.

"No...I do not mind your asking. I used to live here."

"But I thought—"

"This was my London house. I lived here when I was in the city."

"Oh. I didn't realize you had two homes."

He smiled whimsically. "I guess I didn't tell you, did I? There are probably quite a few details I have omitted in your refresher course."

"Then I knew before?"

"Oh, yes." His eyes watched me, but they were sad. I knew the sadness had nothing to do with me.

"I wondered why you got that blank look in your eyes," I said.

"I was thinking about the last hours I spent inside these rooms...what happened to my life shortly after I closed that door and walked down these steps for the last time." His eyes were focused on the front of the house.

"What was it that happened?"

"I left England...I found a new life."

I couldn't understand his expression. I studied it. "Why did you leave?"

"For reasons I cannot explain now. Someday, Jessica."

"Your parents?"

"They were dead."

"You must have been very wealthy."

"I suppose you could say that," he answered. His voice seemed to be coming through a long tunnel of which we were at opposite ends.

"We're wealthy now?" I persisted.

"We have our wealth in other ways."

"I see." But I didn't. I didn't understand anything of this new aspect he was showing me. Two homes, seeming wealth, a mysterious departure, a space of time unexplained. "Just when did you leave, Christopher?"

He turned his attention to me then, a melancholy smile on his lips. "Sometimes it seems like yesterday...sometimes a hundred years."

"Did you have to sell this house?"

"Sell it? Not quite, though it still may belong to the family. As I told you, after I left England I lost touch with all of them."

"I can't understand why you left."

"You knew once—you'll know again when your memory returns." The look on his face told me not to press the issue further, but I wasn't to be held off that easily.

"Were you in trouble with the law?"

"No."

"Running away from a bitchy wife who wouldn't divorce you? You're not a bigamist, are you?" Even as I said it, the thought seemed preposterous.

He laughed outright and grabbed my hand. "Come on. I have seen what I came to see. Besides, I have a feeling the longer we stay here, the more questions you are going to ask."

"Leaving here isn't going to stop me from asking," I said as I made an effort to keep up with his long strides.

"No, but if we are walking, perhaps you won't have the breath to get the words out. We still have to go to St. James's Park, don't forget."

"Is it much farther?"

"It shouldn't take us more than ten minutes." He kept up the brisk pace.

We crossed Pall Mall and continued onward until we descended into a tree-lined roadway liberally spattered with pedestrian traffic. I could see the greenness of the park on the other side.

"The Mall," he explained. "And across there is St. James's Park. Down to the right, Buckingham Palace. Which would you like to see first?"

"As long as we're here, let's go through the park."

He nodded, and we crossed over and entered the park. The path we took eventually led us down to the water. St. James's wasn't as big as Hyde Park, but the gardens were more abundant and more formally designed. The flowers were gorgeous. We sat down on the grass for a while near the water and watched the ducks floating by. The park was crowded, but I noticed that there was no litter strewn about. We didn't stay long. It was a little too busy that afternoon for our taste. We headed out of the park in the direction of Buckingham Palace, passing on the way a fountain spouting forth a cool, misty, sparkling spray. We climbed a short series of steps that brought us into a large paved square with a statue at its center. In the distance beyond that was an imposing building enclosed by high iron gates.

People were milling about, most of them carrying cameras and dressed in vacationers' clothing. I could hear conversations and chatter in several different languages, all blending into such an uproar I could barely hear my voice when I spoke. "Buckingham Palace."

"Yes, but look at these people!" He frowned with displeasure. "It must be time for the changing of the guard." His voice was raised over the noise. "Do you want to stay?"

"I did want to see it," I said. His answering scowl changed my mind. "No, let's go back to the hotel."

I thought I heard his breath expel in relief, but with all the noise, I wasn't sure. He took my arm and determinedly pulled me through the throng of bodies. We were well out of the crowd and into the shady coolness of a cluster of trees before he slowed to a more leisurely walk.

"This is Green Park," he explained. "If we follow it through, we'll come out near Park Lane and the hotel."

"Is it far?" My feet were beginning to hurt.

"No, not far, and we'll take our time."

I noticed the long file of tour buses lined up along the side of the park near the palace. I pointed them out to him. "That must be the reason for the crowd."

He grunted. "Not my idea of the way to see London."

"Nor mine, either."

"Well, I'm glad we agree on that point, my wife. My blood cannot take too much of this madness."

As we neared the park exit, I spotted an arch in the distance and recognized it from our drive into London two days before. We found the appropriate pedestrian subway—conveniences he found very amusing, but practical. They must be fairly new, I thought, if they'd been introduced since his last visit to London.

We ascended to street level on Park Lane. Ahead I could see our hotel. Instead of going straight up to our room, we went to the teashop and sat by a window looking out toward the street and Hyde Park. It was bright and cheerful inside, and we relaxed in comfortable silence as a rosy-cheeked waitress poured our tea and placed a tray of small sandwiches and cakes on the table. I took one and began nibbling. The exercise had made me hungry.

Christopher enjoyed several of the tidbits and then lazed back in his chair with a contented sigh. "It's been a busy day."

"I've enjoyed it."

"I'm glad to hear you say that, because the day is yet young. What do you say to a night on the town? Dinner and dancing?"

"You're joking, of course."

"A little nap before dinner, and you will be full of energy. What do you say?"

"Fine, I guess."

"I know just the place," he continued. "I'll make reservations while you take your nap."

I was tired, and when we reached our room, I'd no sooner laid my head on the pillow then I was asleep. When I woke, it was to find him seated on the edge of the bed looking down at me. There was a light coverlet over me that he must have provided sometime while I was asleep.

He seemed full of pep and very cheery. "Have a good nap?"

"I don't know. I'm still half asleep."

He placed a light kiss on my brow. "Well, I think it's time you got up. It's seven, and we'll have to start getting dressed."

"Seven! Have I slept that long?" I could see now that the last rays of sunlight were just barely slanting through the window.

"Here. Maybe this will help bring you around." He placed a cup of coffee in my lap. "I had room service send it up. I thought you might need it. You always were slow on the uptake after a nap."

"Was I?" It annoyed me that he knew more about me than I did myself.

"Short tempered, too," he added, grinning. "Drink up. I'll be back when you're not so likely to bite my head off." He left the room, whistling softly to himself. I didn't recognize the tune.

I remembered that I hadn't thought about what I was going to wear that night. I threw back the coverlet and jumped out of bed. When he entered the room a few minutes later after a discreet knock, I was rummaging through the closet and the collection of evening dresses hanging there.

"Let me," he said, reaching past me and grabbing hold of one of the garments. He pulled out a slinky black gown, extremely simple, with a low V neckline and softly draped long sleeves. The flowing material was sewn in formfitting lines that flared slightly at the ankle-length hemline. "Wear this," he said decisively. "You look good in it." There was a slightly suggestive gleam in his eye, but I ignored it.

I laid the dress on the bed. "Do you want to use the bathroom first, or shall I?"

"You go ahead. I'll read the paper while I'm waiting."

Lying back in the scented water of the tub, I could actually feel my vigor being restored. I would have stayed there much longer, enjoying the luxury of the relaxation, but Christopher was waiting. I dried myself with fluffy white towels and attacked my hair and makeup. When I was satisfied, I belted my robe about me and slipped into the bedroom. He was reading his newspaper in the sitting room.

I saw the dress lying on top of the bed where I'd left it. Beside it was a white fur shoulder stole. I hadn't remembered seeing it in my luggage or in the wardrobe,

Well, perhaps I'd overlooked it. The fact that I didn't remember owning a fur stole didn't signify anything. I slipped into the dress and a pair of high-heeled, open-toed sandals, put on the stole, and went to inspect the result in the full-length mirror. The dress did fit very well, and with the long fur piece draped seductively about my shoulders, I looked, I thought, very much the rich and pampered lady about to embark on an evening on the town.

His knock on the bedroom door roused me from my daydreams. "Come in," I called.

He entered wearing a tailored suit of deep blue. He was extraordinarily handsome. My breath caught for a second in my throat as he walked into the room.

"Did I not tell you that you look beautiful in that dress?" he said.

"You look very nice yourself."

He smiled. "I see you found the wrap. Do you like it?"

"I didn't realize I owned a fur." I stroked my fingers over the silky white pelt as I spoke.

"I saw it when we were out shopping this morning and thought it would be perfect for you. I picked it up when you were sleeping. And don't worry. It isn't an endangered species."

"Christopher! Why did you do that? It's beautiful...but you didn't have to."

"I wanted to."

Without thinking, I crossed the room to embrace him in thanks. Immediately his arms began to tighten about me, warmly, familiarly. The tips of his fingers pressed through the fabric of my dress to my back. I leaned back to look up into his face, but couldn't read his expression. His eyes were bright, sparkling, but I wasn't sure I wanted to know what was going on in their unreadable depths.

"Well, my beautiful lady," he said finally, "shall we go and set London on its ear?"

Downstairs the doorman called us a cab. We settled back for the short ride to the restaurant. Christopher took my hand as I exited from the cab and walked me up the crimson-carpeted pathway to the double doors of the restaurant.

The hours that followed were filled with laughter, luxury and a sense of adventure. Christopher had chosen the perfect restaurant, with its intimate tables in the corner, French cuisine, soft dinner music, and dancing.

We sipped champagne and nibbled at morsels that were all the more delectable for their French names that appeared in graceful calligraphy on the menu. We waltzed about the floor immersed in one another, the clientele and atmosphere all blending into a background of elegance and old-world romance.

As the evening drifted by in one happy moment after the next, I could feel my resistance melting. I began to forget all my reasons for holding my unremembered husband at arm's length. Christopher was so interesting to talk to. Our conversation flitted from one topic to another. He danced well, very well. He could speak to the waiters in just the proper tone and have them fawning over our table. He could read the menu and order in fluent French just the right vintage champagne. He made me feel so alive, so desired, and so very much respected.

Heads turned as we passed by, yet he seemed unaware of it. He devoted himself and his evening entirely to me.

All too soon it came time to leave. As we stepped past the other diners, the waiters, and the maitre d' and exited through the massive doors, I felt as if I were the Queen of England. He held his arm tightly around my shoulders on the ride home, and I laid my head against him. Dimly, I wondered if he would carry me off to his bed...

When we reached our room, my mind still floating away on silk-lined clouds, he led me into the bedroom, and as I leaned dreamily toward him to lay my head against his chest, he gently slipped the stole from my shoulders.

"Tired, aren't you, my love."

"Mmm, very."

My eyes closed. His hand went up along my back, a slow,

soothing movement drawing me closer to the heat and strength of his body. I felt so comfortable, so protected, so warm with his arms around me. I snuggled closer, and when his fingers reached for the fastening of my dress, I didn't push away. I heard the soft whir of the zipper, felt the cool air of the room touching my skin. Then his palm caressed my long hair. I felt my gown slipped off my shoulders and over the contours of my body until it fell in a silken puddle on the carpet.

Only my black lace slip was still in place as he sat me on the bed and knelt beside me on the floor. He lifted my feet one at a time, loosening the buckles of my sandals and drawing off the elegant bits of leather. Then his fingers returned to my feet, massaging away their weariness. I felt warm tingles of pleasure at his touch. But as I yielded to the melting sensations, he rose, lifting me with him. With one hand he reached down to pull back the covers of the bed, and then he gently eased me onto the soft linen.

His lips touched my cheek, lingering there as I felt the warm covers being drawn up over me. He withdrew a few inches and looked deep into my eyes. "Sweet dreams, Jessica, my love." Then he was gone, closing the door quietly behind him.

I lay there, wondering what had happened...why was he gone? But a pink cloud swirled dizzily in my brain and I couldn't think.

When sleep finally enveloped me, it was to dreams of the two of us sharing happy hours like these for all time.

I woke up decidedly queasy the next morning—too much rich food, reminding me that I was indeed pregnant. I remembered the events of the night before—how could I forget them—but I recalled too well how my loss of memory left so many empty pages. I knew that although I'd discovered once more that I was susceptible to so many of my husband's charms, I still couldn't overlook the unknowns of my past because of one evening.

He didn't expect anything extra of me that morning, for which I was thankful, but if he hadn't been aware of my bedazzlement the night before, he'd been blind. At least he didn't remind me of it.

As I cautiously sipped my tea, my stomach still queasy, he looked over at me with a frown. "Are you feeling all right?" he asked, concerned.

"My stomach's a little upset." Then I clapped my hand to

my mouth and rushed to the bathroom, where I promptly lost to the toilet the little bit of tea that I'd drunk. My stomach heaved dryly as I took deep breaths. When I finally felt steady enough, I rose and went to the sink to splash water over my flushed face.

He was waiting anxiously when I came out. "Morning sickness," he said in sympathy.

I nodded, though I had no memories left of previous episodes before the accident.

"Try a glass of this. It seemed to work in the past." He handed me a fizzling glass of water. "Alka Seltzer," he explained with the touch of a smile.

As shaky as I felt, I returned his smile, took the glass and settled into one of the chairs to drink. He hovered around like an anxious hen, until I finally said, "Relax, Christopher. I'll be fine in a minute." And in fact I was already feeling better.

"Perhaps you'd like to skip today's plans," he said. I shook my head. "Well, if you're sure, I'll go take a shower." He cast another worried look my way, and I smiled to myself. This pampering wasn't half bad, I thought.

That day we toured the museums and, after lunch, more shops, this time on Oxford Street. Christopher talked me into trying on a dress and a lightweight suit he saw hanging in one of the department store windows. He liked how they looked on me, so we left the store carrying packages. A little later on he saw a beautiful leather handbag he thought I should have, and we added that to our collection.

I began to feel overindulged and insisted it was time he spent a little money on himself. At the next men's store I saw a handsome sports jacket displayed in the window and urged him in. The jacket looked better on him than it had in the window, and we added yet another parcel to the ones already weighting down our arms.

We acted like frivolous kids, spending money freely, forgetting responsibility. As much as I wanted to continue in a carefree mood, on the next corner I grew suddenly very sick to my stomach again. Christopher hurried me to a convenient ladies room, where I unceremoniously lost my lunch into the bowl. I felt much better after that, but he was worried. He was sure my sickness had been brought on by our trying to do too much during the last few days. He was adamant about returning to the hotel and turned a deaf ear to my assurances that a few bouts of sickness were to be expected in my condition.

Once back in the room, to pacify him I agreed to lie back on the couch for a few minutes. He remained in the room with me, and out of half-closed eyes I watched him as he leafed through the *Times*.

The paper obscured his face, but from the part he'd folded back, I observed that he was reading the financial section. I was reminded how little I actually knew about him. It seemed he had an avid interest in the business world, although I didn't understand how he was involved with business at home. And there were many other things I didn't understand. Why the mysterious air and evasions when I asked him about his life in England, his reasons for leaving, our past, our real purpose in making this trip? There was more to this trip than he was telling me. I could sense it. What was he hiding from me? By what steps had our lives met, joined, and progressed to the precipice where we now stood? I felt it was a precipice, and that something in the ensuing days would be happening to carry us one way or the other.

My most disturbing thought at that moment, however, was about the child of his I was carrying. Deep inside me I rejected it, and would until I could remember the history of its conception. It was an alien being in me, one that had entered an unremembered past when the doctor in the hospital had told me of my pregnancy. It was the seed of this man before me now—this man I didn't understand—and that frightened me terribly.

TWENTY-TWO

During our first few days in London, Christopher had gotten in touch with Eugene Morris, a gentleman my husband told me we'd met on the plane coming to London. They had lunch together one day while I rested in our room, and the following evening we had dinner with Eugene and his wife who introduced us to several of their friends.

These acquaintances provided us with a carte blanche to some of the best of the city's private clubs and parties, though it seemed my husband's main objective in going out was to chat, mingle, and discuss business with the men he'd met. When he left my side I tried to converse with the well-soled Londoners who made an effort to be friendly, but I found it difficult to overcome the hindrance of my amnesia. I needed Christopher's steadying presence in these social situations more than at any other time, yet he seemed unaware of my need, and his seeming neglect rubbed a raw nerve. I hid my annoyance and persevered, but the enjoyment I'd felt in his company during our first two evenings in London was gone.

I met several women my own age and a few older, well-established socialites. Some were nice. Some I disliked with a passion for their shallowness and condescension. But all of them were only too eager to question, probe, and pry into the where, why, and who of Christopher and me. I didn't reveal that my husband was practically a stranger to me, but I was honest about my amnesia and there wasn't a great deal they could ask me about our past. Yet still the questions came.

"Such a pity," a silver-coiffured woman remarked one evening, "that you don't remember London, dear. I understood from your husband that you'd been here before."

"Yes. But my injury, you know."

"Ah. But how extraordinary for you. Surely your husband's an Englishman."

"He was born here."

"And what part of the country did you say he was from?"

"Kent."

"I see. From Kent. Oh, then perhaps you know the Conrad Dunlaps. Quite an old branch of the family."

"Afraid not."

Someone else chirped up, "Your husband was educated

here?"

I nodded.

"Oh? Not Cambridge, I don't suppose."

"No, Oxford, I believe."

Eyebrows rose. "Would he know Thomas Medford, then? About your husband's age. Probably up at Oxford at the same time."

"You'd have to ask him."

Another question was thrown out. "You were born in America?"

"I was."

"Whereabouts in the States, may I ask?"

"Connecticut."

"Oh, yes. New England. One of the older families?"

"I guess you could say my family's been there for a while."

"And your husband's been in the States for many years?"

"A few."

"Yes, of course. If he was educated at Oxford, it couldn't be too many years. He's still a young man. Strange we've never met him before. Did he spend much time in London before he left for the States?"

"I'm afraid I don't know."

The silver-haired lady spoke again. "I was just trying to recall if I knew any Dunlaps from Kent, and it occurred to me the earl of Westerham has family estates in that area. He's a Dunlap, you know." Then aside to a friend, "You know Westerham and his wife, don't you, Monica? Yes, I thought so." Back to me: "Your husband wouldn't be related to that branch of the family?" Speculative eyebrows. "I don't recall my husband mentioning any nobility in the family tree. Of course, there's always the possibility I've forgotten."

"Quite so. Although I understand the earl and his family are in Switzerland just now. Tax situation, you know."

"Yes, I understand it's quite rough for the aristocracy right now."

"Will you be in London long?"

"Another eight days."

"Ah. Then back to the States?"

"No, actually, we're going to Kent. My husband has some research work to do."

"Research? How interesting. What business did you say he was in, or is this undertaking purely for personal pleasure?"

"He has a number of business interests at home. I'm afraid that my amnesia...but I believe he's doing some work for Yale University."

"I see. Well, perhaps we'll be seeing you again before you leave?"

"Perhaps."

The conversation dwindled. The women drifted off, and new faces strayed by briefly, to ask more questions.

Then I met Charles Raintree. A hundred people can enter a room in one evening without making a difference at all, then one person in particular enters and you can't draw your eyes away. So it was the first time I saw him. He wasn't as handsome as my husband. He was a few years older—closer to forty—and elegant, a man of the world. He had the look of a Norseman, tall and like chiseled stone, with gray eyes and thick, flaxen hair. His nose was perhaps a shade too long, his smile a shade too broad, and there were lines of determination that etched his cheeks. As he stood in the doorway of the club, hesitating before he stepped down the short stairway into the room, the light in the hallway behind him glanced off his thick hair and accentuated the contrast with the dark evening clothes he wore. He looked about in a cursory way, his eyes not holding to one object for more than a few seconds. His glance swept the room and stopped as it reached the table where I was sitting. We stared at each other for a long moment. Then he looked up and away and started down the stairs in the direction of the blackjack table.

It was an hour before I saw him again. He arrived unexpectedly at the table with a couple I'd met earlier, and they introduced him to me. My husband was in the barroom, deep in discussion, and I was alone as I felt Charles's steady gray eyes penetrate me. I felt his hand in mine, heard his soft voice. "It's a pleasure to meet you, Jessica." He smiled. I don't remember whether I said anything at all.

We spent several minutes chatting with the couple who'd introduced us. Then he asked me to join him at the roulette wheel. I lost miserably at first, but quickly he took over, standing behind me, coaching at my ear, directing me where to lay my chips. In the next three turns of the wheel, I'd tripled my meager investments. I played several more turns, making moderate winnings, and then decided it was time to quit. He helped me cash in my chips. With the money safe in my purse, I was led in the direction of the dance floor. I didn't hesitate, strangely enough. I gave no thought to my husband. I didn't stop to consider that I was letting a strange man take control of me.

We danced three dances to the soft music from the orchestra. His hand was strong and secure on my back. He asked polite questions in an unprying way that made me feel at ease with him. I felt no restraints—I spoke honestly about my accident, my amnesia, my estrangement from my husband— and he listened with a patient ear, making no comment condemning or approving. In turn he told me in brief sketches of his own life: of oil rigs in the North Sea; of a wife and two children, a home in the north of England, business interests in London; of a loneliness and unhappiness that slipped through his words unintended. I listened, absorbed, completely caught up in the sensation of being with him, of hearing his soft, liquid voice. We seemed to be two people searching for the same kind of answers.

I watched the way his lips moved when he formed his words, the way his broad smile could light up his otherwise serious face. I felt the solid strength of his chest beneath his finely tailored evening jacket, saw the tiny crow's-feet at the corners of his eyes and the laughing twinkle within them that turned to soberness when he mentioned his life away from London. I lost all track of time and forgot the forlorn feeling I'd experienced earlier at being left alone with so many strangers. With him I was suddenly comfortable, sure of myself. I felt free to speak whatever was on my mind.

I was daunted when I looked up from some comment he was making to see Christopher standing on the other side of the dance floor, glowering at me. I'd almost forgotten about him. I must have stiffened, because Charles sensed it, and in a moment he turned to look in the direction of my glance.

"Your husband?"

I nodded.

"I think it's time you returned to him."

"Yes."

Gently he released me and led me to the spot where Christopher stood. Charles was dignified, the essence of a gentleman as he complimented my husband on my loveliness, yet he made no excuses or apologies for leading me off as he had. My husband's response, though within the bounds of polite behavior, was curt and short, and he wasted no time in taking

my arm and decisively directing me off the floor. Charles
vanished into the crowd.

My husband asked no questions, but his eyes watched me
steadily, and for the balance of the evening he didn't stray from
my side. There was no opportunity for me even to survey the
throng of people in the room for Charles's tall figure, his tousled
blond head. He had left such an impression on me, I couldn't
get him out of my mind. I felt warmed and deeply excited,
confused that such a brief meeting should have such an effect
on me—that the man should exert such magnetism. If I'd paused
to think clearly, maybe I would have understood the source of
my infatuation—the need to find an outlet for my frustration—
the need for a man to confide in who understood me and was
unconnected with conflicts or unremembered mysteries from
my past.

I saw Charles again two days later. I was in the park for an
afternoon stroll alone, and had wandered in the direction of
Rotten Row. As I stood under the trees watching the dozen or
so riders, my attention was caught by a magnificent, long-legged
chestnut and the neatly groomed man on his back. The rider's
seat and form were perfect, the chestnut's strides smooth and
unfaltering. Viewing them with no more than a fellow horse
lover's admiration, I was startled when on their next pass the
rider pulled to a sudden halt before me.

He was off his mount in an instant, striding purposefully
toward me, his voice calling across the short distance, "So it's
you! I never expected to see you again."

"Charles Raintree...my goodness..."

He reached for my hand and held it warmly. "What a
pleasant surprise! Do I seem foolish if I tell you I haven't been
able to forget our meeting the other night? I came to the club
feeling so disgusted, so embittered about things...but then, after
talking to you..." A bright smile adorned his lips. It was
contagious. "What an idiot I must sound," he laughed. "Here
we are practically strangers, and yet somehow I feel we're
not."

I smiled in answer, and he laughed again, a reckless spurt
of joy that creased his weathered cheeks. He was the Viking
on the deck of his ship, his face to the wind, taunting it.

"So how have you been, Jessica? Your husband wasn't
angry the other evening? I'm afraid I put you in an awkward
position."

"No, no, not at all. Well, actually, I suppose he was a little miffed, but he didn't say anything to me. And if he had, it wouldn't have bothered me."

"I've been thinking about you."

I nodded.

"I take it to mean you've been thinking about me as well?" His eyes twinkled with the question.

"I have. Not that I understand why...on such short acquaintance..."

"Don't you?" The way he looked at me! I swallowed hard. "I think you're beginning to," he continued. "It's really not hard to put the two and two together." Suddenly he was very serious. "Do you have a free hour or two, Jessica, to spend with me?"

"I do." The response was ready on my tongue.

"Let's take a walk, shall we? There's a quiet pub over toward Knightsbridge. You don't mind tagging along while I stable my horse?"

We headed toward the stables, then on to the pub as he'd promised. We were both silent at first. A barely contained excitement vibrated in the air around us. He took my elbow, and my skin tingled at his touch. He turned his head to look down at me, smiling softly, and my knees felt like water beneath me. I didn't fully understand what was happening, but I hadn't the least desire to fight it or return to a more levelheaded state.

We entered an old barroom with black-beamed ceilings and smoke-darkened walls that must have been witness to many generations of man's comings and goings, conflicts and achievements, sorrows and joys. We would soon be part of that history, Charles Raintree and I.

Over mugs of ale for him, orange juice for me in a small back booth, we began talking, talking as though we'd never been allowed the joy and release of conversation until that moment. He told me more about the discontent that filled his life, the bitterness of a miserable marriage with a clutching wife who refused him his freedom. About two lovely children whose security was uppermost in his thoughts. He'd reached a plateau in life where the contentment and joy he'd always hoped for seemed child's dreams, nothing to do with reality. He told me that even his tremendous success in business left a sour taste in his mouth, when the rest of his life was so lacking. London was his escape, his place to come and be alone, to concentrate on his work and, after hours, find forgetfulness in a maze of unfamiliar faces. He was a lonely man, and in my own isolated, memoryless state, I understood.

Our hands gripped each other's across the table as we spoke. Our touch was like a lifeline encircling and forcing the bond that was growing more substantial with each word that passed from our lips. We weren't strangers. We were a man and a woman who had known each other for an eternity, yet had only now had the privilege to meet in the flesh. The attraction I felt for him was so great that just to think of it was enough to knot my stomach. I knew from the way his eyes caught mine and trapped them, from the softness in his expression and the firm clasp of his fingers, that he felt the same.

Too soon our hour was over. He walked with me back to the center of the park, and there, his body seeming taut with repressed desire, he kissed me gently on the cheek. "Tomorrow?"

"Yes, tomorrow."

"I'll be here." He turned. I hurried off in the direction of the hotel, already afraid of the explanations my late arrival would necessitate. Now that I was alone, all the obligations I'd pushed from my mind came tumbling back at me in a wave of guilt. The rest of the world had seemed so far away and unimportant while I was with Charles. But there was Christopher to consider, and some fiber of moral right and wrong ingrained deeply in me balked at the deceit I was about to adopt.

Fortunately, excuses weren't necessary. Christopher himself had been out, and at the time of my return was engrossed in the evening *Times*, hardly conscious of the hour.

When I left the hotel to meet Charles on the following afternoon, I whispered a promise to myself to make our visit short. My conscience had been nagging me during the hours I'd been apart from him, and I was almost convinced to turn around and head back to the hotel. Yet, moments later, when I saw him and was once again standing beside his tall, lean figure, all my resolutions were forgotten. His hands were waiting to close over mine.

We took his car and drove toward the outskirts of the city, no destination in mind, wanting to be alone without fear of watchful eyes. There wasn't time to stop, not even for a quiet drink, but at least we were together, our thoughts and feelings rushing from our lips. Something terribly important was happening between us. We both knew it, and neither of us had the will to impede its progress.

I arrived back at the hotel at dusk in a daze of happiness, thinking of nothing but Charles and our lovely afternoon.

Christopher was waiting at the door. I hadn't expected him to be standing there, and the look on his face wasn't one that warmed my heart.

"You are out rather late this afternoon," he informed me. "It is after six. Where have you been?"

"Is it that late?" I stumbled. I didn't have time to gather my thoughts, and my response seemed weak even to my own ears. "I must have lost track of time. I was in the park.

"What did you find so interesting to keep you?"

"Oh, nothing. I was walking...and when I went over to Kensington Gardens, I sat there for a while."

"Did you?"

"Yes, you know that fish pond and fountain I'm so fond of."

Silence from him...only a penetrating stare. "Strange we didn't meet each other, then. I was over there myself not an hour ago looking for you."

All color must have left my face. Of course he hadn't seen me—I hadn't even been near the park at that hour. My God, did he know? Had he seen Charles and me say good-bye to each other near the park gates?

I was saved any more awkward remarks when he straightened his frame and moved to let me pass. "Well, I am afraid you will have to forgo your nap this afternoon. We are due to meet some people for dinner at seven. I trust you can be ready by a quarter to?"

I nodded and made my escape, but my heart was beating like bird's wings against my ribs. There'd been no softness in his tone, no understanding.

His mood was taciturn and preoccupied at dinner. His conversation, gracious and flowing with the other members of the party, was constrained to the bare minimum with me. He said only what was necessary, and even that seemed forced from his lips. I was horribly uncomfortable during the meal, and was thankful to hear him decline an invitation to one of the clubs after dinner.

We returned to the hotel, but long after I'd closed the bedroom door behind me, I heard his restless movements in the other room, the sounds of pacing and repeated clink of bottle and glass. I closed my mind to the noise, the reasons for his insomnia, the possibility that he knew more of my activities of the past two days than I wanted to imagine. I turned my thoughts to Charles, his clear, gray eyes and warm understanding, and fell sleep.

Time dragged slowly the next morning. Christopher left for a long lunch meeting with Eugene Morris, leaving me alone with my anxieties and anticipation. He still hadn't returned at three o'clock, when I left the room and made my solitary way across Park Lane.

The excitement between Charles and me was electric. Our hands had barely touched before he gruffly pulled me off into a hedgerow and into his arms. His mouth came down upon mine without preamble, hard and insistent, then became more tender, more searching. I poured out my feelings with a lack of inhibition that startled me. I wanted him. I wanted him near me. I wanted the warmth his arms could provide.

"Ah, Jessica," he sighed into my ear, "the hours seem so long when I'm not with you. I can't seem to do anything but think about you."

"How do you think I've spent my day?"

"We need some time together—alone. Will you come to my hotel?"

I didn't need to consider my response.

He led me to the opposite side of the park, far from the rooms I shared with my husband. I wasn't conscious of where we were going. I felt only the driving need to be at Charles's side.

When we reached his rooms, he shut the door behind him, turned toward me and took my hands. "Alone at last," he said quietly, "away from all the watching eyes. What a wonderful three days these have been for me, Jessica."

"For me, too."

"I can hardly believe what's happened between us is real. I'm afraid at any moment I'm going to wake up to discover it's all been a dream." He drew me closer. His arms went around me.

Pressing my cheek against his shoulder, I returned his embrace.

"I could love you," he murmured. "Do you know that?"

I nodded.

His words hung suspended in the stillness of the air as he

looked down at me and saw my eyes devouring him. Then his lips were on mine, burning with barely contained longing. His body was strong and supple as he drew me down onto the mattress and pressed his warm length against me. We clung together, letting our flesh speak as our words had done on the days preceding. The verse eloquent. I felt his lips on my cheeks, my eyelids. His hand slid down over my hips then rose to my breasts. I felt his fingers at the buttons of my blouse, then against my bare skin. "You're like velvet," he whispered, "soft as velvet."

I responded to his caresses with a hunger of my own, wanting him, needing the completeness our lovemaking would bring. Yet even as I yearned for him, my husband's face flashed before my eyes, intruding between Charles and me, reminding me of vows I'd made and forgotten.

Suddenly I reached up to grasp Charles's hand.

"Charles, stop...please..."

His breath was ragged with the passion that gripped him as his gray eyes stared at me in confusion. It took him a moment to steady himself.

"I'm sorry." I whispered. I wanted to cry because I didn't understand my own hesitancy. " Charles, I care for you so much. It's just that I need time...I'm not ready... I'm..."

"Hush." He pressed his fingers gently across my lips. "Don't try to explain, Jessica."

"But I must."

"Don't. I understand."

"You do?"

"Yes."

"But I don't understand the reason myself."

He was silent as he looked into my eyes. His lips turned up in a slight smile, yet there was pain written across his face, cut into the furrows of his brow. With a deep sigh he pulled me close in his arms, cradling me.

When we left his room, he walked with me through the deepening dusk toward my hotel. He was quiet, thoughtful. I held tightly to his hand, as if it were an anchor, as aware as he of the step we'd almost taken. I didn't understand why I'd held back. There was no flimsiness here. Our attachment was no watercolor that could be swished away by a careless brush. We'd entered a new realm, and the road could lead us either way. There could be sadness and uncertainty ahead, yet I felt a joy—an invigorating, marvelous joy I wanted never to let slip from my grasp.

We walked in silence for some minutes before he pulled me to a halt beside an old maple. He ran a gentle finger across my face, let it rest in the hollow of my cheek. His expression told me of a conflict going on within him. When he spoke, his voice was filled with pain.

"Ah, Jessica, how does one say good-bye? You're a small ray of sunshine that's flickered into my world to dispel the darkness. I'd give anything in the world if I thought there was some way we could remain together.

"But I've been thinking about us...thinking a great deal. I've weighed the pros and the cons...considered what I want as opposed to what is right and what is honest. My feelings for you are honest, and everything I've told you has been the truth, but my asking you to join in a relationship with me now isn't honest. You've come to me these last days—all warmth, the embodiment of love—but I don't think it's in me you'll find your answer, or find the fulfillment I know you crave. I'm afraid I'm just a man who came along at the right time to fill the void that your loss of memory has created inside you."

"No, that's not so, Charles." How could he be saying this? He was breaking my heart.

"This afternoon when you told me you weren't ready to make love to me, I didn't want to see the truth, but sometimes the truth is unavoidable. I knew then that under all the mist and confusion in your mind, you still love your husband. That's why you couldn't commit yourself to me. Your love for him is there, waiting for the right moment to come back to you. If I took you away now, as I'm so, so tempted to do, someday your memories would come crashing down on you...and at that same moment, you'd despise me."

"I could never despise you."

"You think that now." He laid his palm against my cheek. "Jessica, I don't want it to end...I don't want to give you up, to lose you. I love you. I do, you know. There are times when strong feelings like love are there from the first. I think you love me, too, now....but later..." He shook his head. "We're only torturing ourselves...or do I mean prolonging the ecstasy?" He smiled.

"Please, Charles, consider—"

"If I'm wrong—and I pray I am—come and find me. Just

tell me you want me, and I'll give you everything I have. If after your memory returns you find your feelings for your husband are still empty, I'll be waiting." He reached into his pocket to pull forth a folded sheet of paper and pressed it into my hand. "My addresses...everything you'll ever need to get in touch with me. Until then, it has to be good-bye."

He took me in his arms. His kisses were soft petals falling gently on my cheeks and brow, crushing their sweetness onto my lips. Tears poured unheeded down my cheeks as I clung close to his body one last time. "I can't say good-bye, Charles. I have no strength. I need you..."

Gently he disentangled my clinging arms, shook his head sadly as he spoke in a voice almost as choked as my own. "I think it best we part here, where we've spent our happiest hours. I don't mean to cause you pain. For every pang you feel, remember that mine are doubled, and everything I'm doing, I hope I'm doing for your eventual happiness." A mistiness slowly clouded his eyes as he stared down at me, then he held close once more, briefly, fiercely.

"I'll never forget you—never. Good-bye." And he was gone, moving briskly away toward the edge of the park, his stride telling me that if he were to hesitate now, he'd turn back.

The pain was unbearable. To think that hours before I'd been filled with a heady joy, and now there was only a horrible emptiness inside me. I wanted to run after him, but I knew it would be futile. He'd made his decision—the one he thought was best—and I had no choice but to live with it. I felt sapped of all strength, all ability to carry on. I couldn't think what lay ahead for me, yet I knew there was a future. There always was a future...and he hadn't closed the door forever. There was hope. Someday soon I would remember. I'd have my answers. I'd be able to understand the things that were important to me, and those that were not.

I watched Charles until he was just a dim figure in the distance, fading into the long sun and shadows of the afternoon, becoming one with the leafy trees and green grass. When his image had disappeared, I turned to make my uncertain way back to the hotel. I knew my pain wouldn't end quickly, but I would try—I promised myself I would try—to make the best of it with Christopher and me, to have the patience to persevere until my memory returned and I could be honest with myself.

TWENTY-THREE

Our stay in London was almost at an end. We would depart for Kent in two days. It no longer mattered to me where we went, or when. I couldn't forget Charles, and I was aching and empty. I hardly paid attention to my husband.

We went out to the clubs those last two evenings. Our conversation was strained when it existed at all. More often than not, he left me at the table alone as he pursued his discussions with other men. In a way it was a relief to be alone—at least I didn't have to speak platitudes. My thoughts were in a jumble. I thought constantly of Charles. I wondered over and over again why I had allowed myself to plunge so recklessly into a near-affair with him.

Nothing seemed real, and as I sat pondering, trying to make idle conversation, my eyes searched the room for the sight of him, knowing it was a wasted effort, knowing he was gone...gone back to the north of England to his family. Christopher was cool to me. I had the impression he was trying to slight me. I didn't know if he suspected what had been going on, and didn't care one way or the other.

Our last night in London, my husband curtly excused himself from the table, and I went to the powder room. I was returning to the table when a distinguished-looking man stepped in front of me and blocked my way. At first I thought I'd bumped into him, and I looked up to apologize.

"Sorry...wasn't looking where I was going."

His smile was easy. "No need to be sorry. You didn't bump me. I've been waiting all evening for an opportunity to speak to you."

"Oh?" I was in no mood for it, and I started to walk on, but he reached out his hand.

"Jonathan Trevelon," he introduced himself. "But I already know who you are. Jessica Dunlap, is it not? Delighted to meet you."

"How do you know me? I don't recall meeting you before."

His boyish grin seemed somehow out of place on his aristocratic-looking face. His hair was dark. His long face was sharply featured, but the fullness of his mouth helped to offset his angled looks. He was tall, thin and wore an expensive, three-piece suit. "No," he continued, "I'm afraid we haven't had the pleasure. Saw you at Annabel's the other night...wondered who you were. I made a few inquiries, and here we are."

"I see." I didn't know what to make of him.

"I understand you're only in London for a short time," he said.

"Yes, we'll be leaving for the country tomorrow."

"But you're enjoying your stay."

"Certainly. England's a lovely country."

"I see your husband has quite a few acquaintances in London. Are you here on business?"

"Business and pleasure." I began to move on. "If you'll excuse me, I—"

He laid a hand on my arm. "Don't run off. Surely there's no harm in our chatting for a few minutes. Let's move over to the side a bit. I think we're blocking traffic." He led me over a few steps to the side of the room, where we were still in plain view.

"I really think, Mr. Trevelon, that I should be getting back to my table. My husband will be looking for me."

"Jonathan, please. And your husband is well occupied elsewhere at the moment. I just saw him in the other room discussing business with Aston Longwood."

"Oh." My voice fell. Quickly I cast about in my mind for another excuse. There was something very disturbing about this man's forwardness.

"Tell me about yourself," he inquired. "You're an American, obviously."

"I am."

"But your husband is English?"

"He is."

"Your first trip to London?" His eyes watched me as I looked uneasily about the room for a sign of Christopher.

"No."

He laughed softly. "My! So free with the information. I don't bite, you know."

"I'm sure you don't, but there really isn't much to say, is there?"

"Oh? I thought we might have a great deal to discuss." He hesitated, his eyes searching my face for a reaction. "I've heard about your untimely accident on the way over from the States. So sad to have no memory—especially of one's own spouse."

He smiled slyly.

I'd told no one but Charles my amnesia was that complete. I turned on Trevelon. "How did you know that?"

His triumphant smile was my answer. He hadn't known. He'd been baiting me, and I'd fallen neatly into his trap. "That is a pity, but you've made a brave showing. I'm sure no one else has guessed."

My face felt as it must have looked—cold and immobile as stone—but he went on, digging further. "How trying it must be to live with a man you don't remember."

"Really, Mr. Trevelon, I don't see that it's any of your business."

"You're quite right, and I apologize." He changed the subject abruptly. "You know, if it weren't for your accent, I'd take you for an Englishwoman, or at least a European."

"Oh?" I was short, ready to break away from him again, forcefully if necessary.

"You have a cool shell of class about you. Very different from the other American women I've had the pleasure of meeting."

"Have you thought that it might be your company that brings out the coolness in me?"

He laughed heartily. "What an interesting woman you are. I curse my luck for not having made your acquaintance sooner. But perhaps it's not too late after all."

"What are you talking about?"

"I mean that under the circumstances a little *affaire de coeur* might not be so objectionable to you."

I stared at him.

"Perhaps you could arrange to get away from your husband for a few hours tomorrow, no one the wiser?" His lips curled.

I was too shocked by what he was saying to notice anyone approaching, until a heavy hand was placed on my shoulder and an angry voice barked from behind me, "I am afraid, Mr. Trevelon, that my wife's time has been well assigned for her already. I'll thank you to remember that. If you will excuse us."

With a forceful grip on my upper arm, Christopher pulled me away. If the pain his fingers were inflicting was any indication of his anger, he was ready to explode. At the table he held the chair for me stiffly. I sat down. He took the chair opposite me.

"I didn't realize you were acquainted with the honorable Mr. Trevelon." His eyes were dark with ire.

"I've never met him before. He stopped me as I was coming from the ladies' room."

"I'm sure."

"Oh, come on. Did you hear what he was saying?"

"I had trouble believing my ears. Does he interest you?"

"Interest me? Of course not!"

"I thought he might."

"You're being ridiculous. He's not at all my type. How do you happen to know him?"

"I've heard talk. He was pointed out to me on several occasions. Being the heir to a cosmetics fortune in this country, most of which is invested in Swiss bank accounts, he's very well known. Then, too, he has the reputation of being one of the most eligible playboy bachelors in Europe."

"I didn't realize who he was."

"And if you had, perhaps you might have been more attentive to his comments?"

"I was trying to find a way to excuse myself."

"A slap across the face would have been appropriate," he snarled. "I didn't hear your earlier conversation, but you must have been leading him a merry dance if he'd progressed to the point of trying to arrange an assignation."

"Christopher, for goodness' sake, you have things all out of proportion. It wasn't like that at all, and I certainly wasn't attracted to him."

"Then why, may I ask, didn't you just turn on your heel and walk away?"

"I don't know. It happened so fast."

"Yes." He was barely able to contain his emotions.

"Believe me," I said, trying to sound reasonable, "you're making too much of this."

"We'll discuss it later."

"But—"

"In fact, I think it is time we left." Abruptly he rose to his feet and turned toward the door, not waiting as I grabbed my wrap and purse and hurried after him through the swinging doors to the street. I felt a cold knot in my stomach.

On the sidewalk he paused for a moment, then turned and strode down the street. He didn't seem to care if I followed or not.

I felt my breath coming quickly as I rushed after him. "Where are we going?"

"We are walking."

"Where?"

"To the hotel. Come if you like. Otherwise call a cab."

"I'll come." My voice was a whisper. My high-heeled evening slippers barely stayed on my feet as I tried to keep up with the murderous pace he was setting. I followed along, not daring to say a word. A wall of silence stood between us. In the distance I heard the evening sounds of a busy city, but only our own staccato footsteps echoed along the street. We reached the end of the block. He swung around the corner. We had walked halfway down the dark expanse when suddenly he stopped and turned to face me. The black fury in his eyes was like a physical blow.

"Now we'll finish our discussion."

I swallowed. Was he going to hit me?

He spit the words out in a growling fury. "Do you think me blind? Blind, that I do not know what has been going on? These so-called solitary trips of yours to the park, your flirtations? You were meeting Raintree, were you not? And now Jonathan Trevelon! A pity we are leaving London tomorrow—or are you arranging a rendezvous in Kent?"

I gasped. "It's not what you think."

"I'm sure," he sneered.

"Please...listen..."

"Jessica, I saw you and Raintree together! Are you trying to deny what was right there in front of my eyes? And now Trevelon! What is it about him that attracts you? His charm? His fortune stowed away in Swiss accounts? Goddamnit, isn't it enough you have carried on an affair behind my back these last days? Must you make a complete ass of me with a piece of slime like Trevelon? A half-man who prefers a male in his bed to a woman!"

"No...no!"

He glared at me. "What are you denying? Your guilt? Or didn't you realize Trevelon is bisexual? I'm sure you would have discovered the fact soon enough." His voice showed his disgust as he gripped my wrist in his strong fingers so tightly tears sprang to my eyes.

"Christopher, please! I'm telling you the truth. I never saw Jonathan Trevelon before in my life. He means literally nothing to me. Believe me..."

"Believe you? After the way you have been sneaking around behind my back, I should believe you?"

"It's the truth."

"And the rest...your affair with a veritable stranger."

At my silence, his teeth clenched. "Well, it is over! Do you understand? Finished! You have not given my feelings a thought since that first day in the hospital, but you will not make a fool of me again. If it was not for your amnesia, that child of mine you are carrying..."

Without another word he turned on his heel and strode off down the street, leaving me to follow at my will.

TWENTY-FOUR

We left London by car about eleven the next morning. Christopher was moody and withdrawn. My own frame of mind didn't lend much to lively conversation. I hadn't slept well the night before. I had gone up to my room and listened to the night sounds outside the window on the street below. Once in bed, I tossed restlessly against the cool and crumpled sheets. It was much later before I heard the outside door click open and shut, and heard his movements in the next room.

When I'd wakened, unrested, in the morning, he was still asleep. I used the time to pack the suitcases and empty the rooms of the effects that had made them ours during our stay in London. About ten, I heard his first movements, and the sound of running water in the bath. A few minutes later I looked up to see him standing in the open doorway. He was dressed and immaculate, but he carried a tired air about him. He watched me as I folded the last of my blouses and his shirts into one of the tightly packed cases.

"You are ready?"

"In a few minutes."

"Then I'll fetch the car." Aside from his first, probing, look, he didn't seem to want to allow his eyes to dwell on me any longer than necessary. He turned in the doorway and added as an afterthought, "Call the porter when you are finished, to bring down the bags. Have you eaten?"

"No."

"We'll eat downstairs, then. I'll be back in a few minutes." He left, closing the outside door soundly behind him. I finished the packing and met him downstairs. His spirits didn't seem to lift as we ate in silence. He hadn't forgotten the last evening, the last few days, or my actions and his opinion of them. It was as though I was sitting at a court of judgment, hoping for a sentence of mercy from the magistrate. His looks to me were solemn, not softening under his dark brows. His mouth kept its rigidness. We climbed in the rental car after breakfast and left for Kent.

Christopher did the driving. The job of checking the road map fell to me. Our conversation was limited to only those occasions when he needed directions. About noon we stopped on the road for lunch. I should have sought to finish our conversation of the night before—clear the air, get all the grievances to the front while they were still fresh and before they left too many traces of bitterness. Several times the words to broach the subject were on the tip of my tongue, and each time I swallowed the courage to speak up. I tried to believe his anger had been a momentary thing. But then, too, Charles was still a pain in my heart, and I was selfishly thinking of him and not my husband.

Our silent drive continued down the four-lane highway to Kent. We left the highway near Tonbridge for narrower roadways that led us north again through the countryside toward our destination, a small town near the place of his birth. I watched for road signs and turns and didn't have much time for thought. He said the country had changed greatly since his last visit there, and I didn't question him.

The scenery was lovely, though. There were low hills, and rolling fields interspersed with woodland. Bright-green meadows and quaint houses snuggled cozily in tiny valleys. Livestock dotted some fields, orchards and freshly dug furrows marked others. It was peaceful, so very pretty and so very old. I felt the years emanating from the old stone or cross-timbered houses we passed, from the old arched bridge we crossed, from the width of the timeless trees that seemed to hover protectively over picturesque dwellings.

I had the sensation that I was part of an endless cavalcade of people and events, wrapped up in all that had gone before and would come after. The conflicts in my life seemed inconsequential against this sudden sensing of time passed, time to come.

We drove down a two-lane roadway, hedged in on either side by tall trees that blocked out the afternoon sunlight. The sun was growing fainter and fainter. Heavy cloud cover shouldered in over the lovely spring skies and held the threat of a downpour. Before the clouds had completely obliterated the sunlight, we rounded a corner on an otherwise deserted roadway to enter a small town. In the center of the village, gathered about one main roadway, were several two-storied timbered buildings, some barns, a gas station, and, predominant among them all, a three-story Elizabethan structure that bore the sign "The Green Bottle" jutting out on a metal arm from its timbered and stuccoed front. We pulled into the dirt parking lot at the side of the inn.

A low picket fence enclosed the grounds, a profusion of small patches of soft green lawn and flower beds, bright with color even in the cloudy afternoon light. Behind the inn was a copse, beyond that open fields. Christopher parked the car, and we let ourselves in through the gate, up the flagstone path to the heavy, oak-studded front door.

There didn't seem to be anyone around. I checked my watch. It was three—an in-between time, too late for lunch, too early for tea. We went through the front door into a low-ceilinged hall. I could see a dining parlor on the right, tap room to the left, and at the back of the hall in front of us, a stairwell. Christopher rang the bell on the small front desk, and within seconds footsteps could be heard scuffling up the corridor from the back of the building. A portly but neatly dressed man arrived, looking as though we'd disturbed him from a nap.

"Sorry. We're closed. Open again at four for tea. Bar opens at five," he said brusquely.

"We're Mr. and Mrs. Dunlap," my husband spoke up. "I made reservations for one of your rooms."

"Mr. Dunlap? Ah, forgive me, sir. Not used to having people arrive here in the middle of the afternoon. Your room's ready. If you'll just sign in, I'll get my wife to show you up."

My husband took up the pen while the gentleman departed for the back of the inn. He returned in a few moments, trailing a smiling middle-aged woman.

"Good afternoon." The hospitality was warm in her voice. "I'm Mrs. Barr. I've given you a lovely set of rooms to the back so you can enjoy the view. Have you luggage?"

"Still in the car," answered Christopher.

"Mr. Barr will bring it in. Won't you follow me?"

We climbed the paneled staircase to the first landing, where Mrs. Barr led us to a door at the back of the hall. There was a beautiful diamond-paned window in the hall, and through it I could see the view she had mentioned. The land behind the inn gradually dropped off to a valley that seemed to stretch for miles before meeting the hills in the distance. The whole of it was a study of green, fenced fields alternating with forest, with a tiny cottage here and there. The view was breathtaking yet serene.

She unlocked the door to our room and held it open for us to precede her in. We entered a large room with the same low-beamed ceilings we'd seen downstairs. A series of casement windows faced the back and offered the same view as the diamond-paned window in the hall. There was a fireplace along one wall, with two easy chairs beside it, and a round table with straight-backed chairs. A desk stood in the corner. Next to this room was a bath. It was charming. As we quickly inspected it, I found the plumbing old but serviceable and the room spotlessly clean. The other room, separated from the main room by a short hall, was the bedroom. Heavy red drapes hung by the windows, and a patterned red rug covered the floor, leaving sections of polished wide-board floors exposed about the edges. Another fireplace occupied one wall, but what immediately caught the eye was the magnificent four-poster canopy bed hung in red brocade. It was the kind where great romances begin and dreams are dreamed for the very first time.

Only one thing marred the perfection of the rooms. There was only just the one bed...no couch, no day bed or other similar furnishing. The state of rapport between Christopher and me was not such that I dared question the accommodations. I would have to wait and see, and hope that with evening some solution would present itself. After our confrontation the night before, I was less willing than ever to share his bed.

A sidelong glance at Christopher's satisfied smile told me he was pleased with the rooms.

"This will do very nicely, Mrs. Barr. We should be quite comfortable."

"I thought you'd like it, sir," she beamed, "from what you wrote in your letter."

He nodded. "It is exactly as I expected it."

"Good, good, and if there's anything you might need, you'll find a pull rope over by the window. One by the bed, too. We kept the old system, so much more pleasant than these new buzzers and telephones. Would you and the lady like a bit of tea?"

"Marvelous idea," he answered easily.

"I'll send up a tray, then, and my husband should be right up with the bags."

"Thank you."

"You're quite welcome, sir. Enjoy your stay with us." She backed out the door.

We had our tea when it arrived and unpacked some of the luggage. His mood, now that he was again alone with me, was still somber. He said barely more than three or four words, and those only to tell me we would take a drive around the area before it got dark. He intended to show me his former home, which we'd be visiting daily during the next two weeks, and to renew his acquaintance with the countryside of his birth.

We left a few minutes later, the threatening overcast brooding over our heads in a solid gray blanket. As we drove, a light rain began falling. The scenery around us was blurred slightly by a mistiness that clung to the trees and slipped across the valley.

We were about five miles from the inn when he pointed to the first portion of a stone wall, commenting that this was the western limit of the Cavenly land—or at least had been when last he'd been there. The road we were following skirted along the wall. Over the top of the wall I caught a glimpse of fields and thick clusters of wooded land.

The mental picture I'd conceived of a moderate-sized estate did not prepare me for this immensity, these unending acres that rolled by the car window. Could this truly be the home of my husband's birth? If so, I was more confused than ever about him.

"The main drive is just ahead now." His tone was as lackluster as a tour guide's. "Over this next crest."

The walls became higher—well over seven feet—entirely blocking the view of the lands behind. As we topped the crest, he slowed the car and stopped completely before an imposing set of iron gates. The heavy stone walls had given way to a graceful iron fence some yards before, which was connected to the ornamental gates in front of us. They were closed tight, locked with a heavy chain and padlock as if warning away unwanted visitors. My eyes were riveted on them in awe and confusion...a feeling, too, of not belonging. A place like this had no part in my past.

It was several moments before my gaze drifted to the unobtrusive sign posted to the left of the entrance. "Cavenly House," it said, "Residence of the Earls of Westerham. Open to the Public Mondays, Wednesdays, Fridays and Saturdays. 10:00 A.M. to 7:00 P.M. Admission £5.00.

I blinked and read it again, my eyes glued to the words Residence of the Earls of Westerham. I swung toward my husband, my mouth gaping.

His own mouth was drawn in a hard line that could only mean displeasure. His eyes were dark as they skimmed the gilt letters of the sign, his voice bitter when he spoke. "My God, it's a common amusement park."

I looked from him back to the sign, then to the gates and the green lawns and shrubs beyond. "But what does this mean? You never told me..."

He wasn't listening. He stared at the grounds that rolled in a low rise into the distance. Not daring to interrupt his thoughts, I watched his face and the emotions that flitted across its surface. His fingers clutched the steering wheel. I could sense the churning anger within him. He was immobile as rock, yet I gazed back to the grounds and the beauty of the place—the lush carpet of lawn, the shrubs neatly manicured, the brilliant flowers. The gray gravel drive curved left and disappeared into an avenue of elms. There was no view of the house itself.

His bitter voice called me back. "So now that you have seen the gates of my former home, Jessica, what do you think?"

"Didn't you know...about the tours?"

"I was not prepared for this." He flung his hand toward the sign. "Five pounds for a peek!"

My mind was following a course of its own. "You never told me you were a nobleman..."

"I'm not."

"But you were."

"Not necessarily."

"Yet you were born in an earl's home. You bear the same name. The women in London told me that much."

"A poor relation many times removed, living on the family's generosity, can also carry those credentials."

"You admitted the house in St. James was yours."

"It was."

"So how can poverty be the case with you?"

"The story is a long one."

"I don't understand. Why must you be so mysterious? What is there about your past that you don't want me to know? And if it's so terrible, why did you come back here at all?"

"There is nothing terrible, and there are sound reasons for my return...my work, for one."

"I don't believe you. There's more to it than that."

"Perhaps there is. All of which, as I told you in London, you will remember in due course. You are beating a dead horse, Jessica, if you think I am going to enlighten you now." He swung away from me and gazed once again through the gates. "The

house is beyond that rise over there." The lightness
in his voice was forced. "It sits at the end of a small valley with
the parkland surrounding it. But you'll see it all tomorrow when
we come to introduce ourselves."

"And I'm not to mention your relationship to the family, or
that you've ever been inside these gates before?"

"You are not. We come here solely on behalf of Yale for
the purpose of research. If you have any doubts about what to
say, let me do the talking." I nodded, watching his hands knot in
his lap as he stared blindly at a small section of the dashboard.
"We are to see the earl's secretary. I have papers with me to
identify us, a letter from the professor with whom I work and
another written by the earl that gives us permission to look at
the family records. Beyond that, we know nothing of Cavenly,
and if by some chance anyone should mention the coincidence
of our bearing the same name, you are to play dumb."

I nodded again. "But isn't there a chance some member of
the staff will recognize you? And what about the earl and his
family?"

"They are away. I believe I told you. And as for the staff,
enough years have passed so there is little likelihood I'll be
recognized."

"Just how many years has it been?"

If I thought to catch him off guard, I was mistaken. He
looked up sharply, then away. "That's enough." The tone of his
voice closed the subject.

With every word from his mouth, the mystery around him
deepened. I frowned and muttered spitefully, "You know, I
can't figure you out at all—you're a mass of contradictions!"

"Then we have reached a common ground of
understanding." He turned the key in the ignition. "We had
better go back to the inn. There is no more we can see here
this afternoon."

I was nettled, my temper short. I wanted to know more. It
had been difficult enough the past few weeks, struggling against
amnesia, without him putting me off at every corner. What he
could tell me might give me some insight into myself and my
past. Why was he constantly throwing roadblocks in my way
when my questions became too prying? But how convenient
for him if I should remember only what he wanted me to
remember! I stole a glance at him as he drove. His blue eyes
were cold and his face blank except for the tension in his square

jaw. Would I ever reconcile myself to this situation? And Charles...how I longed at that moment for his quiet, understanding ways.

Once at the inn, we went directly to our rooms. At seven we changed for dinner in our usual manner, taking turns in the bathroom, but the tension was thick between us, and I wondered how we were going to survive the days ahead.

The dining room was crowded, which surprised me. I hadn't expected there to be many people in this quiet neck of the woods, but apparently the inn had a reputation for good food, prompting people to go out of their way to eat there. Mr. Barr found us a quiet table not far from the fireplace.

The warmth of the fire, welcome against the chill of the late April evening, didn't touch my husband's mood. He was abrupt, and I didn't know if it was anger or his own deep thoughts that were troubling him. Somehow I had to make an attempt to clear the air. If he shunned my overtures, such was life, but at least I'd have tried. I lightened my voice. "Cavenly is lovely. At least what I've seen so far."

"You'll get no argument from me on that."

I stumbled on. "Are you nervous...about tomorrow, I mean?"

"Why should I be?"

"Seeing your home for the first time after so many years?"

"I have mixed feelings, but nervousness certainly is not one of them."

"Aren't you afraid it's changed?"

"I'm sure it has. It has been some time. I do not expect to be overjoyed at what I'll find, but that cannot be helped." He took his glass and swallowed the contents in one long gulp, gripped the stem and twirled it between his fingers. "And you seem to forget, Jessica, that our purpose for being here is not a family reunion."

"I haven't forgotten." I watched as he continued to twirl the glass, staring at the glittering reflections it made in the firelight. He poured another glass, took a few sips, pondered as he stared into the fire, then lifted the glass to his lips and drained it again. His eyes seemed to sparkle unnaturally, but perhaps it was just the quality of the light creating that effect. I hoped the waitress would bring our dinners quickly.

"We must have more pleasant topics to discuss, my dear," he was saying. "How do you like Kent—the little you have seen so far?"

"It's pretty country. You told me that this was something like our home?"

"It is." He glanced up. How transparent his eyes seemed, and how they reflected the light of the candle on the table between us. "It is a pity you cannot remember, my wife."

"Yes."

"Yes, a pity. And there are so many other things you should be remembering, my love."

"I know. You've told me." I could only watch his eyes.

"So I have." A slight smile crossed his lips, and he filled his glass once again. "I thought by now some of it might have come back."

"You know it hasn't."

"Hasn't it?"

"I would have told you. What reason would I have for keeping it a secret?"

"I wonder." His eyes gleamed. I knew he wasn't drunk, but there was something unsettling about his manner.

The plates of food finally arrived, and for a short time we concentrated on eating and let our conversation lapse. Instead of attacking his dinner with the healthy appetite he normally possessed, he stopped eating when his steak was only half finished, dropping his knife and fork upon the plate and balling his napkin upon them. The wine was gone by now. He leaned back in his chair, calm and in control of himself but for that underlying current of leashed anger that smoldered below the surface, giving off just enough spark that I could sense it.

I tried conversation again. "Do you think I could help you tomorrow with the research? I realize I don't know much about it, but maybe I could take notes for you or do something to make myself useful."

"I had not thought of it, but I'm sure you could. You used to help me a great deal with my work at home. I do not suppose you have lost the touch. I would hate to find you getting bored and roaming about in search of other pleasures." The words were double-edged swords that couldn't help nicking me. "Though even I must admit this countryside can provide you with only so many novelties."

"I'd rather help you."

"Would you? Sweet music to my ears, to think my evasive wife would rather be with me." He laughed, and the undercurrent of anger was stronger than ever.

The waitress came to clear away the dishes. Instead of coffee, Christopher ordered a brandy.

He was silent again, staring into the flames that licked brightly at the huge logs in the fireplace. He seemed to have forgotten me. I glanced around the room at the other diners. No one was paying attention to us. They were all absorbed in their own conversations in the dimly lit room. It was a well-dressed group, and I wondered whether they were businessmen and their families, or gentleman farmers.

Startled from my reflections by the sound of his chair scraping back across he board floor, I looked up to see him rise abruptly and throw a note on the table. "Let us go, Jessica." Hurriedly I followed him as we weaved our way through the tables and out of the room.

Climbing the stairs, I felt a chill draft sweep by my ankles. I shivered, yet our rooms when we entered them were warm. The heavy drapes had been pulled across the windows, closing in the heat from the fires, and lamps had been turned on in each room, giving off a mellow light that cast long shadows across the ceilings and into the corners. I walked across to the bedroom to hang my jacket in the wardrobe. The kingly four-poster bed stood beckoning in the rosy light of the fire, the covers thrown back invitingly across the soft mattress. I hurried back to the main room, with its chaste and unsuggestive furnishings. Christopher was fiddling with the fire, resetting a fallen log and adding another for the night. When he'd finished, he brushed off his hands, rose, and, taking off his own jacket, went on into the bedroom.

I glued myself into the armchair by the fire, taking advantage of the small security it offered. From my position I could look at an angle into the bedroom, and I saw him settle on the edge of the bed to remove his shoes. This done, he began unbuttoning his shirt, leisurely, seemingly unaware of my gaze. I turned my head and riveted my eyes straight ahead on the uniform brickwork of the hearth. I heard the wardrobe doors open and close, his bare footsteps, the sound of running water in the bath.

Fifteen minutes must have passed, each one increasing my discomfort. He'd left the bath, and for a while all was quiet. I didn't trust the silence, though. It didn't necessarily mean he'd crawled innocently beneath the covers of the bed for a night alone. Unable to bear the suspense any longer, I glanced toward the doorway.

He was standing there, leaning lazily against the doorjamb, his bare-chested, broad-shouldered body filling the small space. The sardonic smile that twisted across his lips made me tremble. The firelight filtered from behind him, giving a larger-than-life look to his tall frame. The planes of his face were accentuated. His strong chin seemed stronger, the cleft in it deeper. The thick curls of hair on his chest were masculine and enticing.

"Are you planning on spending the night in that chair, Jessica? I do not think you'll be very comfortable." His voice was threaded with amusement.

"It will do, and under the circumstances I haven't much choice." I looked down at my hands, away from his penetrating eyes.

"Oh?" He smiled. "Have you somehow overlooked the large and very comfortable bed directly behind me?"

"You know as well as I only one of us can use it."

"I thought tonight you might change your mind."

He drawled the words lackadaisically, yet there was a sharp tone to his voice. I tensed. "I don't know why I should."

"I seriously suggest you consider it. I am tired of playing cat-and-mouse, my wife."

"It's not cat-and-mouse. You know my reasons for—"

"I am well acquainted with your reasons. There is no need to reiterate them, since they no longer disturb me in the slightest."

"What do you mean?"

He laughed. "Have you grown obtuse in your old age, Jessica?"

"I'm not obtuse, but if you think for one minute I'm going to spend the night in that bed with you..."

"I do not think anything of the kind, my dear. I know it."

"That's where you're wrong. You can't force me. I have no intention of coming to bed with you tonight or any other night until I remember and do it of my own free will."

"I am tired of waiting, Jessica."

"You'll just have to find the power within you."

"Come here!" As he straightened his tall frame, his expression was deadly serious.

"No!" I gripped the arms of the chair with my fingers to anchor myself.

"I said come here."

"I will not! I'm not some twig you can bend to your will."

Suddenly his voice became very quiet. "And I am finished playing games." With tightened jaw and hard mouth he left his easy pose in the doorway.

I cringed back into the chair. His intent was obvious. He grabbed my hands where they were trying desperately to hold fast to the chair and, with an ease that frightened me, pulled them free and jerked me to my feet. He seemed unconcerned by my ineffectual efforts at resistance. I wrenched one hand free and lashed my fingers across his cheek. Small drops of blood oozed out where my nails had done their damage, but it didn't affect him. Instead he hauled me up as he would a child and carried my protesting body toward the bedroom.

"Goddamn you," I cried, "What are you doing?"

"Taking back my wife, woman. Something I should have done two weeks past." Then he smiled, and all the lust and passion within him was evident in the baring of his even white teeth.

"I won't let you."

"Oh, you will, woman, you will. You don't have much choice in the matter now."

My strength was no match for his. The more I fought him, the tighter his grip came around me, trapping my flailing arms against my sides. He dropped me to my feet beside the huge draped bed and gripped my shoulders with fingers that bit through to the bone. "You will be mine tonight—you will be the wife you should have been before. Instead of teasing me out of my mind, you will be between those sheets beside me. Nothing is going to stop me from taking what is meant to be mine."

"It's not yours! It's not yours to take until it's given, and I haven't given."

He didn't hear me. His hands grasped my face so that my eyes were forced to stare into his. "Do you know what it has been like for me these weeks? Do you have any idea what your taunting has done to me? You are a beautiful woman—a beautiful, tantalizing seductress who happens to be my wife! You turn me away again and again—you're indifferent, cold— yet I must stand by and watch you. Watch you warm to other men, flirt with them, give them the freedoms I am denied. Once you wanted me, too, but you have forgotten that. Pity that I haven't! Pity that I can't forget the moments we had together...the desire...the need to be one. Pity I can't forget you. But I cannot. And now I have had enough. Not one moment longer will I walk around like a crazed, sex-starved idiot. You are sharing that bed with me tonight, and there is nothing in this world you can do to stop it."

I swung free of his hands in a quick gesture and made for the door. He caught my arm and threw me against the bed.

"You are not getting away that easily," he said quietly as he approached again.

"You're drunk," I cried in last defense.

He laughed demonically and moved closer, his eyes filled with fire.

I backed toward the bed until my knees were braced against its edge. "Don't touch me."

He stopped a foot away and stared down. "Get undressed."

I shook my head.

"Get undressed. We are going to bed."

"No!"

"Shall I help you?"

I glared at him. "I'm certainly not doing it of my own free will."

"Then I will help you." His hands reached out. He took hold of the neck of my blouse and ripped it open as if the buttons didn't exist.

"You bastard."

"Are you going to get undressed, or shall I continue to tear your clothing to pieces?"

"I have no intention of aiding your demented cause. Go ahead and strip me. At least then there can be no doubt it's rape."

"You would have a great deal of trouble proving that in a court of law, my love. We are husband and wife."

"And you're a son of a bitch! If you do this, I'll hate you," I cried. "Hate you!"

He drew me against him and pushed his hands up under my loosened blouse to caress my skin. His mouth came down hard on mine as I tried to turn away. He bruised my lips with the impatience of his passion. I couldn't escape him. He was a man possessed, blinded by desire. I kicked out with fury at his legs and caught him a punishing blow in the shins. He winced and reached reflexively for his leg, but it was only a moment, and before I had time to escape his grasp, his arms were about me, forcing my head against his chest, into the dark hair, against the sweet, clean aroma of his body. His hands roved madly over my body, speaking to me in a language all their own. His lips were in my hair, against my ear, finding my mouth again, suddenly making me forget who I was and why I was fighting the fire he was arousing in me. Before I knew what had happened, he had stripped me with expert movements and was pushing me back on top of the bed and into the soft mattress. His own hard body followed me down, covered me, moved against me.

Then he rose quickly to stand by the side of the bed. The light of the fire was behind him. All I could see was the outline of his clean-limbed, perfectly proportioned body as he towered there. Then his pants fell, and in one sinuous move he slid across the sheets toward me.

This time his hands reached for me gently. He smiled ever so slightly as the ice-fire of his eyes beat upon me. His fingertips began to swirl over my naked skin in slow, sweeping motions that started at the back of my thighs and worked up to my shoulders. I couldn't stop the shiver that went through me at his touch. He was only too well aware of it.

His lips were soft when they once again dropped over mine, his tongue pushing between them, tempting them to part. I wanted to close off my mind to the sensations he was prompting in me. I didn't want to enjoy his touch. I wanted to lie there a mute, feelingless body.

He was whispering in my ear, "Love me, Jessica. Lie against me. Let me show you how wonderful it can be." He spoke seductive words that sighed from his throat to fog my thoughts, feeding the fire within me. I fought myself, forced back my desire, but his hands caressed me, bringing tingles of pleasure. He brought his body closer. I felt the warmth of him, the heat of him, the desire he was controlling with an effort. He took my hands and moved them to where he wanted them. He made my lips move against my will to return his kisses. And the soft, husky voice continued. "Come, my love...closer...ah, yes...let yourself go...touch me...let me make you mine."

My breath was coming in rapid gulps. I couldn't control myself. He'd turned my body traitor, into an aching, throbbing hunger. I didn't know what was happening to me. I only wanted to lose myself in the pleasure, ease the yearning in every fiber of my body.

"You want me now, don't you," he whispered. "You want

me."

His caresses became more urgent, his breathing heavy as he recognized the desire he'd roused within me. As his body began moving rhythmically against me, I felt his hands exploring me delicately, tenderly. I moaned and tried to pull him closer.

"Easy, my love," he murmured, and pushed me back against the pillows. His hand took mine and closed it around him. He was over me, bearing down, pressing into me gently, inch by inch, heightening my ecstasy until my body was a warm, throbbing fountain, until my flesh ached to feel him full and deep inside me.

Again I heard his soft voice. His fingers brushed my cheek. "Open your eyes, Jessica...look at me. Let me set the tempo, my love. It has been so long since we shared this joy, let it linger..."

And as I stared deep into his eyes, his hips began a gentle movement, up and down, side to side, a butterfly touch that gradually, so gradually, became more intense. My body responded exquisitely to the tender pressure of his loins as he catered to me, seeking my hidden spots of pleasure, finding them, sensitizing them so that each thrust of his hips sent tingles of white light through my veins, until I was crying out to him, telling him never to let it stop.

He held me lingering on that plateau for a long moment. Only when he heard my cries and saw the desire clouding and lidding my eyes did he let me move with him.

"Now, Jessica. Press against me...come with me...now...together!"

There was a moment of suspended animation, our bodies united and alive with a joint spark growing brighter and brighter, then bursting with the light of a thousand candles to send us shuddering against each other and to raise from each of our throats a low cry of ecstasy, of release.

His body melted in warm relaxation over me, yet we clung to each other. His face was buried in the pillow against my neck as his ragged breathing slowed. As I moved my hands over his sweat-dampened back, my mind reeled. What had I done? I'd made him my husband again. I'd let him take me and show me what it had been like between us in the days before my memory became a blank page. And I'd enjoyed it. I'd enjoyed every moment of his conquest, every second of his body touching mine. I still didn't love him, but I felt something very deep drawing me toward him. Was this feeling the beginning of something new, or was it a trace of forgotten love resurfacing from the darkness? Was this what Charles had meant?

Christopher lifted himself on his elbows to look down into my face. With one finger he pushed the tangled hair from my brow. "God, how I love you, woman."

I watched him, but didn't speak.

"Is it too much to ask that some of that feeling be returned?" he asked quietly.

"Yes." I barely breathed the word.

"Why?"

"I don't love you."

"Are you sure of that? It was not hate that spoke to me through your body a moment ago." His face was only inches away, and his breath brushed my cheek.

"I should hate you for what you've done tonight."

He smiled. "But you do not...and you will not, because you knew it was going to happen soon enough. You needed me, my little wife. You just would not admit to yourself how much you did."

"You're taking a lot for granted, aren't you?"

He shook his head. "No. I know you well enough...I have watched you enough to know that behind your protestations, it was fear that held you back. Not fear of me so much as fear of the feelings you might find hidden within you. You are afraid to remember you once loved me." His eyes gleamed. "You are afraid to discover you still might."

"No," I denied.

"Yes. But I can be patient. I'll have my reward soon."

I wagged my head. He was wrong, I told myself emphatically, so wrong. There was Charles. He'd given me what I wanted, made me feel whole. But had he? The nagging doubt my husband had planted couldn't be stilled.

"I shall not press you now, my love," he said. "I've had enough for a beginning." He touched his lips to my brow, rolled away from me and climbed from the bed. He went to the fire, his body taut and straight in the flickering light. I let my eyes move over him slowly. He seemed unselfconscious as he knelt to place another log on the fire, as if he realized what visions his lithe, muscular form was creating in my tormented mind.

The log in place, he rose to cross the room and turn off the lamp. Then I felt his body, chilled by the cool air of the room, slide against me once more as he pulled the blankets up to our chins. His arm slipped beneath my neck, and he drew my head into the cradling nook of his shoulder. He leaned over to place one last, soft, lingering kiss on my lips. Then he settled his head against the pillow, drew me imperceptibly closer to his side, and sighed. "You are back where you belong, my wife." He closed his eyes.

There were many days ahead of us, and too many things I had yet to learn about myself. And although my husband had gained possession of his wife by force, the one thing that meant the most to him and without which the rest seemed meaningless, could not be gained by physical struggle.

TWENTY-FIVE

I opened my eyes slowly to a hint of daylight sifting into the room. His broad back was facing me under the blankets. His dark, tousled head lay against the whiteness of the pillowcase. I reached out my hand to touch him lightly. He didn't stir.

Without waking him, I slipped from under the blankets into the cool air and went to the wardrobe to find my robe, then into the bath. When I was washed, dressed, and wide awake, I slipped back to the side of the bed to look down at his sleeping form. His rugged face seemed more like a child's with his dark lashes against his cheeks and all worry and care erased from his features by sleep. Again I reached out my hand, sliding my fingers across his brow, down his cheek where the bristle of new beard showed, along his jaw, finally to the cleft in his chin.

He wakened then, his eyes opening lazily, blinking closed, then open again. The blue eyes looked down toward my hand, then followed a course up my arm to wash across my face. They held there for a moment. Then he smiled, and I could only smile in return.

"Good morning, my wife," he said hoarsely. He surveyed my kneeling form. "Up and dressed and ready to go, I see."

I nodded.

"I'm surprised you have not taken the opportunity to desert me." He lifted one lazy brow, but he was teasing.

"No."

He hoisted himself on one elbow and ran his hand through his disheveled hair. "And you've let me sleep...What time is it?"

"Early."

"Good. I was afraid we might be late getting to Cavenly."

"We have plenty of time."

Drawing his legs out from under the covers, he sat on the edge of the bed, stretching once to get his blood moving. He didn't seem concerned that his nakedness was now exposed to me. I stood up quickly, but he caught my hands, grinning evilly. "A good morning kiss, temptress?"

I obeyed, and our lips met. Laughing, he pulled me down onto his lap and squeezed me against him. "A lovely evening, wasn't it?"

"I'd say that depended on how you looked at it."

"If you looked on it other than I did, you would not still be here." It was a statement of fact, and I didn't bother replying. He pushed me gently to my feet and rose to stand beside me. "I had better get going if we are to get anything accomplished this morning." He glanced toward the still-drawn draperies. "Have you looked outside? How is the weather?"

"Clearing."

"Good. Yesterday's weather was not much of an introduction." And then his voice came to me over the sound of running water in the bathroom. "Have you called down for coffee?"

"I will." I pulled the old-fashioned bell rope, and picked up the clothing scattered during our battle the night before. My blouse, it seemed, would need extensive repairs if ever I was to wear it again. The other garments I neatly folded and put in their proper places. At Mrs. Barr's knock I ordered coffee and rolls and returned to the bedroom to pull wide the heavy drapes. A bright morning light flooded the room. Christopher came out of the bath and began to dress as I stood looking out the window.

"The weather is definitely clearing," he called from over my shoulder.

"Yes. It should be lovely."

"Only the best for my sweet wife. A perfect English spring day." He came to stand behind me, resting his hands on my shoulders, his mouth nuzzling my neck just below my ear. I shivered involuntarily at the scent of his after-shave lotion and the feel of his now smooth cheek rubbing against mine. I didn't trust the sensations he was rousing in me.

"Do I feel a tremble?" he taunted. "A tremble for me, perhaps? Or does my wife have some trepidations at the thought of visiting my former home?"

"Neither," I lied.

"No?" He reached around my waist from behind to fold his arms over my stomach. His hands slid up toward my breasts.

"Christopher, not now..."

"Why? Cannot a man feel a passion for his wife in the early morning hours as well as in the dark of night?"

A firm knock on the door saved me from having to respond. I pushed free of him and walked with a steadiness I didn't feel toward the front room.

Our hostess was there with a laden tray, which she placed on the table, smilingly commenting on the beauty of the day. I answered her with what composure I could muster. We passed banalities back and forth until my husband entered the room, at which point she suddenly remembered she had other pressing duties waiting for her and left us.

Christopher didn't seem inclined to continue in the amorous vein of our earlier conversation. We chatted quite easily about the work that lay ahead of us at Cavenly as we drank our coffee.

When we arrived at the high iron gates, the sun was trickling its golden rays over the landscape. My husband turned the car through the open gates, down the long, graveled drive that wound through the exquisite parkland. The azaleas banking the drive were in glorious full bloom. To the left a natural pond lay glistening in the morning sunlight, Two arched-necked swans cut gracefully across its surface.

We rounded the last corner, and there before us in all its elegance, grace, and beauty stood Cavenly. The dark gray stone facade rose three stories in majestic splendor. Two stories of evenly placed, many-paned windows, and a third story of smaller ones above, reflected the sunlight streaming across their surfaces. A fountain played in the center of the half-moon drive that curved before the imposing porticoed entry. The house was huge, but every line was perfect. I sighed at the fairy-tale quality of it all. Never had I expected anything quite so lovely.

To the left of the house were acres and acres of parkland with age-old trees and seemingly carelessly designed flower beds scattered across the undulating green surface. To the front was a pond, better described as a small lake, and farther on, a heavier growth of woodland that screened the house from the road.

"Has it changed?" The awe in my tone made my voice a whisper. "It's so beautiful...is this the way you remembered it?"

He nodded slowly, as if in a daze. "Yes, Jessica, it is. Except for small changes here and there, it is exactly as it was. I feel as though I'd never left."

He said nothing more as he turned into the newly installed parking lot to the right of the house. We parked, and as I climbed out I looked back to the land behind the house. A formal garden sat directly behind and, beyond that, pastureland. Trees had been left standing to separate each field from the next and to provide some shade in the midst of the pastures. I couldn't see any sign of a barn or outbuildings. No doubt they had been built far enough away from the house to be out of view of its occupants. But I did see a few stray thoroughbreds grazing in the lushness of the nearest meadow, and marveled at the beautiful lines the animals presented as they roamed peacefully with their heads to the grass. I saw a dam and her spindly-legged foal trotting valiantly behind her, the disdainful looks of the other, older horses as the foal's scamperings interrupted their grazing. I nudged my husband, wanting him to enjoy the scene as well.

His eyes were already fixed in that direction, but the expression on his face was one of pain, not joy. I wanted to ask him what was wrong, but he turned his head sharply away from the scene before him and, grabbing my hand abruptly, led me toward the side entrance of the building, intended for visiting tourists.

Our business was with the earl's secretary, and it had seemed the easiest way to find him would be to ask one of the tour guides. We entered a small hall, plainly furnished, its walls lined with benches and folding chairs and tables covered with brochures. It was clearly intended as a waiting room for the visitors prior to their guided tour. Near the door was a desk manned by a tall, spare-framed woman with hair wrapped in a bun at the back of her neck. A few stray, loose strands of hair escaped the tight bun to fall about her face. Her warm and hospitable smile as she greeted us revealed a set of white, slightly protuberant teeth. Her gray, fitted tweed suit and sturdy shoes fit exactly my image of the typical English country-bred woman. She nodded her head briefly, speaking in well modulated tones. "May I help you?"

I smiled at her. Christopher reached inside his jacket pocket to remove the papers that would verify his reason for being at Cavenly. He unfolded these and handed them to her.

"I am Christopher Dunlap. My wife, Jessica." He motioned to me. "I am here to do some research for Yale University. I think the letter I have given you will explain it. The earl has been kind enough to give the university permission to go through some of the family and historical documents at Cavenly. I was advised to speak to the earl's secretary, if you would be kind enough to direct us to him."

Her sharp, intelligent eyes quickly perused the papers he'd handed her, pausing at the letter written by the earl himself. She scanned the signature at the bottom of the page as if checking its authenticity and, apparently satisfied, smiled and handed the documents back to my husband. "A pleasure to meet you, Mr. and Mrs. Dunlap. If you will have a seat for a moment, I'll ring up Mr. Wadsworth and tell him you're here. His offices are in another part of the building."

We sat on the rather uncomfortable bench. I picked up one of the color brochures about the interior of the house and leafed through it. Magnificent. The beautifully laid out rooms were preserved, it said, unchanged since the time they were designed by Sir Christopher Wren. The brochure credited Wren as the genius who'd designed Cavenly in the late sixteen hundreds around the ruins of a Norman tower. Christopher looked over my shoulder as I turned the pages.

I was alarmed to see the torn look on his face. Did it bother him that much to be in his old home once again? I could see how it would bother anyone to leave a place like this. Yet apparently he'd left of his own free will. What was beneath the surface that I didn't understand? His eyes stared at the color photographs of the finished rooms, the paintings, the objects of art, but his face was drawn, his mouth hard. I didn't dare ask him, in his present mood, to answer the questions I had, so I sat silently perusing the brochure until he spoke of his own accord. I stopped at a page showing a floor plan of the house.

His hand reached across my arm, his finger pointing to an area on the plan. "These are the formal rooms—the state rooms, if you like. Drawing room, dining room, anterooms. Here is the muniment room, where we will be working, and here the library. I don't imagine any of these rooms have changed greatly since I was last here. At least from the photographs, it doesn't appear that they have. The family would want to keep the treasures intact if they could afford it, and from the look of the house and grounds, they can." He slid his finger to the next drawing. "On the first floor are the private rooms. Here in the front are the family drawing room, sitting room, music room, tower room. In these two wings are the bedrooms, and this entire wing is the ballroom. On the top floor, of course, are the servants' rooms and the nursery. These rooms on the first floor were the ones used most often. The state rooms, with the exception of the library, were generally used only for entertaining..." His voice trailed off.

"You entertained often?"

"On various occasions."

"It's just so hard for me to believe you actually lived here."
He smiled gently.

"This is more like a palace."

"It is far from a palace, although I suppose you could say it is quite large."

"Where was your bedroom?"

Without hesitation his finger moved to the first room in the east wing, where the plans showed a large room facing out over parkland. "This was my room while I was here."

My eyes widened as I cast him a puzzled look. "But it's huge. I thought you said you were a poor relation."

"So I did," he said mildly, but I couldn't question him further, since his finger had already moved back to the plans for the ground floor, and he was describing to me in businesslike tones the rooms that filled the space of the lower wings. "Here was the estate office, and here the servants' pantries and whatnot. The kitchens were below stairs, although there was talk of moving them to a more practical location so the food would still be warm when it reached the table."

We were interrupted by the sound of a door being closed and brisk footsteps approaching. A pale-faced man in a sporty tweed jacket came toward us. Christopher rose and extended his hand. "Mr. Wadsworth?"

The man's eyes swept over my husband in critical assessment before he extended his hand in turn, but perhaps it was my imagination giving me this impression. "Yes, and you must be Mr. Dunlap." He raised a questioning brow. His eyes were a pale, watery blue. "It is Dunlap?"

My husband nodded mutely. The men released hands, and Mr. Wadsworth stood with his own behind his back. He wasn't tall, the top of his head reaching only slightly above my husband's shoulder.

There was a moment's silence. Wadsworth's smile was weak, but his eyes were probing. When he spoke, his voice held little warmth. "I understand you had some difficulties during your journey which delayed your arrival here."

"Yes. We were involved in a car accident." My husband did the talking.

"So you mentioned in the note you sent here. Well, it would have been more convenient all around had you arrived according to schedule. However, these things can't be helped. Let me welcome you to Cavenly."

"Allow me to introduce my wife, Jessica, who will be working with me."

Wadsworth turned to me and smiled in condescending fashion. He ignored the hand I'd extended. "Delighted to meet you, Mrs. Dunlap." He returned his gaze to my husband. "You've found suitable accommodations, I presume? There was no mention in the earl's notes of your staying here."

My husband's answer was terse. "We have a room in the village. I am quite familiar with this part of the country and knew the Green Bottle."

"Are you. How interesting. You're an Englishman, aren't you? I was expecting an American."

"Yes, I was born in England and lived here for some years—in Kent, as a matter of fact—although I am now an American citizen." My husband's eyes wore a dark gleam that would have made me cringe were I the recipient of their stare. Mr. Wadsworth seemed unconcerned, his smile growing a shade more insincere.

"I see. That was long ago...that you lived in England?"

"Close to ten years ago."

The man studied my husband minutely, his fingers pulling at his lips. "Interesting that you haven't picked up the American accent or manners."

"I find people tend to hold on to the habits acquired in their youth—don't you find that true, Mr. Wadsworth?"

The man ignored the question and straightened his shoulders slightly. "Well, now that we've become acquainted a bit, you have some papers for me?"

My husband handed the folded packet to Wadsworth. The little man carefully scrutinized them, pausing as he came to my husband's passport. "I see your passport is made out in the name of Robert C. Dunlap. Christopher is your second name?"

"Yes. I prefer it."

"You're aware, I imagine, that the earl of Westerham's family name is also Dunlap? A strange coincidence, wouldn't you say?"

"I was aware of it, although I assure you there is no connection."

"And your living so long right here in Kent?"

"What are you saying, Mr. Wadsworth?"

"Oh, nothing. It's just that your face seems to strike a familiar note with me."

"Does it? Well, I am sure in your business you've met a great number of people, and no doubt one bore some resemblance to myself. Now, if you have no objections, I would like to settle whatever arrangements are necessary to begin my work." My husband had changed the subject briskly. "We have only two weeks in the area and a great deal to do."

"How thoughtless of me. You are here to work, aren't you? I thought perhaps before you embarked on your task you might enjoy a tour of the house—those rooms open to the public, of course. It might give you a bit more insight." He glanced toward the door where a group of people had been milling about for the last few minutes. "Mrs. Cribbs!" He motioned imperatively to the lanky woman who had met us on our arrival.

She hurried over.

He continued as if he were talking to a serving maid. "As you know, Mrs. Cribbs, Mr. and Mrs. Dunlap will be working here during the next few weeks on some research. First, they'd like to see a bit of the house, and I think it would be convenient if you would include them in your next group. Afterward you might show them to my office."

"Of course, sir."

"And I noticed some papers on the steps outside the main entry. See that they're cleaned up." He dismissed her with a wave of his hand as though demonstrating to us his sway of authority, and turned back to us. "I'll see you shortly, then. Enjoy the tour." He strode off without waiting for our acknowledgment.

"I don't like that man," I muttered as soon as the door closed behind him.

"Pompous ass, isn't he," my husband replied tightly. "I think he might be singing an altogether different tune if he only knew who..."

"Who what?"

Quickly he took my elbow. "Come, wife, I believe Mrs. Cribbs is motioning to us." He pulled me along.

It was too late to question him any further when we reached the tour group. Mrs. Cribbs was already beginning her dialogue, instructing us to follow her into the next room.

We entered a room of moderate size with a high, graceful ceiling, a huge crystal chandelier hung in the center. Along one wall was a fine white marble fireplace, and grouped about it were various small couches and upholstered chairs. To the side of the room were odd tables holding flowers upon their gleaming surfaces. Beneath our feet, protected by a plastic runner, was a lush oriental carpet showing barely any signs of wear.

Our guide's dialogue was interesting, still I much preferred the more personal comments and information my husband was directing quietly in my ear. This was the small sitting room, he told me, to which I raised my brows, wondering what I'd find when we entered the large sitting room. We passed quickly through a small anteroom and then through a set of graceful double doors into a long, elegant room furnished with several arrangements of Chippendale pieces. The main salon, Christopher explained, where most of the formal entertaining was done. Fireplaces graced opposing ends of the room, and another oriental carpet covered the shining wood floor. The ceiling was a peaceful mural of dancing nymphs and angelic babes.

We passed through another set of double doors, matching those on the other side of the room, and were in the formal front entry hall. Here the floors were marble, the walls hung with a multitude of paintings, scenes, portraits. To our left were the wide, heavy doors that opened onto the front drive. To our right, at the far side of the hall, a graceful staircase rose in smooth lines to the floor above, where the railings branched off in either direction and widened into a semicircular balcony on two sides of which were more double doors, leading, Mrs. Cribbs said, to the private quarters of the house. On the ground floor on either side of the staircase, wide halls tunneled on into darkness. We proceeded directly across the front of the hall into yet another small salon, masculinely appointed in leather and deep colors. Then on into the dining room, which occupied the far corner of the house. The dining room had windows and French doors on both outside walls, revealing a beautiful view of the side park. We headed toward the back of the house to see the card room and the dark-paneled library, then circled back toward our embarkation point, passing the music room, another sitting room, the morning room, and various smaller rooms to which I didn't pay much heed. As we passed the central core of the house on our return trip, my husband pointed out a round, stone-walled room closed off by heavy oaken doors. The muniment room, he explained, where the family histories and records were stored, and where we would be spending most of our time during the next two weeks. The rounded wall was the only part of the original Norman structure that remained.

For Christopher's sake, as we'd gone through each well-preserved room, I was happy to see that here at Cavenly there were no worn chair covers, faded or damp-stained paint, carefully mended but threadbare draperies.

I said little during the tour, listening to my husband's quiet comments and, in the distance, Mrs. Cribbs's well-enunciated speech. I was aware that although Christopher's voice was calm and his conversation limited to purely informative remarks, his eyes were dark, brooding and distant, seeing visions and pictures from his past that were invisible to all eyes but his own. He grew increasingly more constrained as we proceeded through the rooms, to the point that I was actually pleased when the tour ended just to see some of the sadness leaving him.

We waited near the benches until our guide detached herself from the group and came to direct us to the earl's secretary. I smiled. "You're quite an authority on Cavenly, Mrs. Cribbs."

She flushed slightly. "Oh, dear, when you do it as often as I, it becomes quite automatic. But it is a marvelous house, isn't it?"

"It certainly is. I find it hard to believe that anyone could actually live in a house like this and call it home."

My husband's brows lifted a fraction in amusement. Mrs. Cribbs, however, nodded understandingly. "You know, my dear, I often get that same feeling myself. And you, sir," she turned to Christopher, "did you enjoy it?"

"Very much, although, being an Englishman, I can't say the size of the place astounds me as much as it does my wife."

She smiled and studied his face for a moment as though there was some troubling thought in the back of her mind. Then, remembering her mission, she hurried on. "Well, I'd better escort you both to Mr. Wadsworth's office. He doesn't like to be kept waiting. This way."

She opened the door at the side of the room through which Mr. W, as I was beginning to think of him, had entered and departed, and led us down a long, somber corridor to the back of the house. This must be, or had been, the servant and office wing Christopher had mentioned. Down the hall on either side, doors broke the line of the wall, probably all leading to small cubicles or workrooms. At the very end of the corridor, where a single long window faced out to the rear parkland, she indicated a door to our left and knocked on its surface. The knock was so quiet that I doubted, unless the party on the other side of the door was anticipating it, that it could be heard. But the door was almost immediately opened by Mr. W himself. Mrs. Cribbs bowed to us a hasty farewell and scurried down the hall in the direction from which we'd come.

"Ah, so you've finished the tour." The small man motioned us into the room. "Come in. Have a seat. Quite a place, isn't it? Or am I mistaken in thinking this is the first time you've seen it?" Again a quality of innuendo was in his voice.

"Oh, yes, this is our first visit," I answered quickly since my husband didn't seem inclined toward courteous comment. "And we loved it. Quite breathtaking. We don't have anything to compare to this at home...the grandeur of the house and grounds, the fine paintings and furnishings." Why was I talking so much? Perhaps because I could sense the barely concealed antipathy between Christopher and Mr. Wadsworth. Their eyes critically assessed each other. "Of course, if it was up to me, I'd spend all our time touring through old homes, but then, my husband, who's lived in England, can't appreciate the novelty like I do."

"I'm sure, Mrs. Dunlap." He had a small smile on his lips, although I doubted he'd been listening. If he had been, he must have concluded I was a complete ass for prattling on the way I was. It hadn't done much good anyway, since Wadsworth's eyes remained glued to my husband, to be met by a silent frown.

"Then it's down to business, isn't it?"

"Yes," my husband said dryly. "I think the first item we should determine are the hours that will be convenient for me to have access to the records. Obviously, the more time I have to work and the fewer interruptions, the sooner my task will be completed."

"I realize that. The earl, you know, has given his full accord to this project and has commissioned me to give you full use of the muniment room for whatever hours you require, within reason of course. My own thinking," he added smugly, "in order to coincide with the shortened hours of the staff in the earl's absence, would be the hours between nine in the morning and five in the afternoon."

"And on the weekend?"

"Since it is only Monday, we have time yet to consider that." Mr. W frowned. "I suppose if it's essential that you have the extra time, we can arrange something."

"I was under the impression I was to have unlimited access...at least from my interpretation of the earl's letter to the university. Or are these restricted hours your own decision?" He was testing the little man, but he'd underestimated him if he thought Mr. W would back down that easily.

"I am acting on direct orders, Mr. Dunlap, none of which should concern you. I should think instead you might be grateful for this generosity on the earl's part."

"We are fully appreciative of that generosity, Mr. Wadsworth. I was only clarifying a point in my own mind."

"Quite." But the little man's eyes were cold as he leaned forward in his chair to brace his arms against the top of the desk. "Before I bring you to the muniment room, there are a few other details of which you should be aware. Since the earl has requested luncheon be provided for you, I have arranged with the staff of the cafeteria in the visitors' section for you to have your midday meal free of charge. It's quite adequate, and Mrs. Cribbs or one of the other ladies will be happy to show you where it is. You may have free access to any of the documents contained in the muniment room and are welcome to use the library upon request. Should you have need to visit the state rooms, advise myself or one of the staff, and they will be at your disposal—so long, of course, as you don't interfere with the tour groups. This sort of thing does keep the estate solvent these days." Toying with the pencil he held in his fingers, he studied Christopher. "Might I stress—although I'm sure you're well aware of it—that the private family rooms above the ground floor are positively restricted."

"Just how long have you been at Cavenly, Mr. Wadsworth?" There was only a faint note of curiosity in my husband's voice.

"Nine years, Mr. Dunlap. Nine years this month, as a matter of fact. Why do you ask?"

"Only curiosity. You speak with the authority and familiarity of an old and valued retainer." The slur my husband gave the words belied any compliment that might have been taken. For the first time the little man's complexion took on the tiniest hint of color, but Christopher gave him no opportunity for comment. "If that takes care of the instructions, Mr. Wadsworth, I believe my wife and I are ready to begin our work."

The man had no choice but to rise, as my husband had already done, and make his way around his desk to the door. His nod was curt as Christopher held the door for him to precede us. "If you'll follow me. The muniment room is down this corridor in the central wing."

In a moment we were standing before the wide oaken doors Christopher and I had passed earlier in the morning. Mr. Wadsworth swung them open to reveal the room within. The thick stone walls of the original tower were themselves the motif of the room. Two narrow slit windows, now glass paned, were set in the walls at one side, and a tremendous fireplace, whose hearth could easily have held a six-foot log, covered another. Tall, crammed bookcases lined the remaining two walls, leaving only enough room for the wide doorway. From the oak-beamed ceiling several electrified chandeliers hung from heavy wrought-iron chains. The furnishings were simple: two long tables with straight-backed, rigid looking chairs around them, a desk pushed between the two windows, and—the only bow to comfort—a leather easy chair in the corner by the fireplace, with its own floor lamp. It wasn't the coziest and most welcoming of rooms, but it did give the impression of great age. I felt a damp chill as I walked to the center of the floor. It was probably due to the stonework and immense proportions of the room.

Mr. Wadsworth observed my shiver. "I'm afraid this is one of the few rooms in the house to have escaped the niceties of central heating. If you find the chill intolerable, I'll see what I can do to get you an electric heater."

It would take more than one small electric heater to make this room even moderately comfortable, I thought, but I kept my opinion to myself, sure that our comfort was not Mr. Wadsworth's main concern.

My husband had turned his back and wandered to the tall bookcases. Surveying their contents, he didn't seem interested in Wadsworth's continued discourse. "You'll find any paper supplies you might require in the cupboards to the side of the fireplace. Of course, any additional materials we would expect you to furnish yourself. Should you require me for any reason during the course of the day, the intercom system will save you steps. A line runs direct to my office, and you'll find the mechanism over here beside the door."

"I'm sure everything will be quite satisfactory," I answered.

Still he didn't leave, and his gaze swerved from me to Christopher's unconcerned back. He cleared his throat.

At last Christopher turned to give the man a cold stare. "Is there something else, Mr. Wadsworth?"

The watery eyes narrowed slyly. "Are you quite sure we haven't met before? The more I see of you, the more I'm certain we have."

"Having once met you, Mr. Wadsworth, I think it is not likely I would have forgotten."

The man ignored the sarcasm. "Still, your face is very familiar...perhaps someone who bears a close resemblance to you." He smirked as he fingered his chin.

"Perhaps, because I know for a fact our paths have never had occasion to cross." Short to the point of rudeness, Christopher turned his back, signaling his dismissal of the subject. Over his shoulder he threw his parting, words, "Now, if you will excuse us, we have work to do."

I saw Wadsworth redden in anger. If it was my husband's wish to make an enemy, he'd certainly succeeded. The little man reached for the door handle and banged out of the room.

Christopher turned back toward me at the sound of the closing door. I smiled uncertainly. "I think his ears are burning," I said.

"Precisely my intention, although I fear his skin is far too thick. I am sorry, Jessica. It was never my desire to introduce you to this house in such a way."

"It couldn't be helped."

"No, not now, but once. If the blasted clock could just go back for a few moments—just long enough for me to show you the grace of Cavenly as it was meant to be. I knew before we came it was not possible, but I never expected quite this state of affairs."

"It doesn't take a great deal of insight to realize things were different here once. Perhaps because the earl is away so much of the time, Mr. Wadsworth has taken his authority a little too seriously. It seems he more or less does have free rein."

"A pity, that. I wonder at the earl's judgment of character, placing such trust in the man."

"It's not worth it to let it upset you so," I tried to console him. "We won't be here for very long. I know you're thinking about how it was ten years ago when you left, and I can't blame you for being bitter, but this isn't a part of your life anymore. After two weeks, you can go away and forget it."

"It is not that simple, my love."

"Then why did you ever come back? Knowing how you'd

feel, why torture yourself?"

"I had to come. My mistake was not realizing how vulnerable I would be to the situation. Well, no matter. When we are finished here, I think my trials will have been justified."

I studied him quietly. "I hope so."

He squeezed my hands once, released them, and went on in a businesslike tone. "We should get started, shouldn't we? Suppose we begin with this bookcase over here." He motioned. "The dates on the record files appear to be the right ones, leaving off just after the turn of the nineteenth century. Unfortunately, even at a quick glance it seems completely disorganized. I am afraid we have our work cut out for us."

My husband had already told me that his purpose in coming to the house was to research the family history of the early nineteenth century, in particular the years 1808 through 1825, looking for facts that might have escaped other historians and might be included in a text on which he was collaborating with a professor at Yale. We would be working with family diaries, newspaper clippings, and other memorabilia, all sorted and stowed away at the discretion of some earlier occupant.

All other thoughts were put aside as we began our search into the past. What was left of that morning and most of the afternoon we spent sectioning the voluminous pages of verbiage and putting them in separate piles by year. It was staggering to see the amount of information his ancestors had seen fit to store away or set down on paper for posterity's sake.

Both eyesore and dusty after an afternoon of close work, we stopped around five o'clock. We'd gone down at noon to 'partake' of the lunch so generously offered by Mr. Wadsworth. I think my husband's pride was pricked at having to eat in the visitors' cafeteria, but he didn't comment. The food was fairly good, and we found a little table as far removed as possible from the noisy vacation crowd that filled the cafeteria. He eyed the coarser, pushier tourists with distaste, although he said nothing, as was par for his reserved emotions when it came to insinuating too much to me about his past at Cavenly.

After we'd eaten, we wandered in the gardens for a time, enjoying the glory of spring flowers and the fresh smell of new-cut grass. But the tourists were all over there as well, and we didn't stay long.

Christopher was visibly tired by the time we packed to leave later that afternoon, and when we reached the car he handed me the keys. "Why don't you drive. I somehow don't feel in the mood."

The park was lovely in the afternoon light. The shadows slanted in a different direction. The sunlight was golden and the leafiness about us deep green.

As we neared the road, he looked toward the right at a small stone gatekeeper's cottage set a few yards back from the drive and nearly covered by the ivy that clung to its walls right up to the tiled roof.

"Looks deserted," he mused. "Last I was here the place was immaculate. Jons, the gatekeeper, left not a blade of grass out of place. Pleasant old man...long dead now, I guess."

"He may have been pensioned off. There's not much use for a gatekeeper nowadays."

He made no answer as I swung out onto the road, but leaned back, stretching his arms out before him to lessen the tension in his muscles. "So what do you think, Jessica, now that you have spent your first day at Cavenly?"

"Should I think any differently than I did this morning? I thought it was exquisite...a little overwhelming."

"Have you no homier feelings about it? That it might be a place where you could spend happy days?"

"I have enough trouble picturing you living there. How I could ever fit in is beyond my imagination. Tomorrow, though, I'd like to see more of the grounds. I don't think anyone would mind, do you?"

"It would not bother me one way or the other if they did. We are not anyone's bonded servants, and if I find I can spare the time, I think I shall join you. Actually, it is the grounds that mean the most to me."

"Oh? How do you mean? A love of the out-of-doors?"

He laughed. "No, I used to breed horses. Or did I not tell you that?

"Weren't you kind of young?"

"Young?" He shot a glance at me. "No..."

"If you'd been in the States for ten years, you could only have been about twenty."

"The love of horses is a passion that develops in youth."

"So you started your training as a boy."

Without confirming my statement, he kept to the topic. "I see the earl has carried on the tradition. I would like to get a closer look at that stock we glimpsed this morning."

"They seemed to be well-bred."

"If they are anything like the animals I bred, no doubt they are."

"Were you breeding for racing?"

"Primarily, although the stock that did not have the speed for the racecourse generally turned out to be good hunters. They were more lanky than your typical hunter, but had wind and muscle power. I had no trouble getting top price at the auction block."

"You arranged the sales yourself?"

"Usually. I think if I ever try it again, as I was considering if we buy the place we want in Connecticut, I shall breed hunters, and perhaps a few good saddle horses. Though you never know. If I can get my hands on a good stallion without going over our heads in debt, the racing market might not be a bad one to consider."

I left him alone to his calculations and musings, directing my attention instead to the narrow, high-banked, winding road that was carrying us back toward the inn. Something instinctively told me that I wasn't used to driving on roads as narrow and unshouldered as these, where the only way to get past an oncoming car was for one or the other to pull over in a narrow dirt layby. They couldn't pass side by side.

"You know, Jessica," he said, "I can remember as if it were yesterday taking my stallion down this very lane. It was dirt then, of course."

"Oh? It was paved recently?"

"We used to cut off across the farmer's fields about a half mile down, picking up the highway again near Brasted and paring a neat five miles off the distance to London."

"You used to ride to London on horseback?"

"Ah..." He faltered, momentarily seeming to have lost his voice. "Ah, yes...that is, purely for fun, of course. Just for fun." He continued, on a steadier note, "Actually, it was quite the thing among my friends to outdo each other with various physical feats."

"Oh, I see," I said, although I didn't. To me, it seemed pretty strange to think of a bunch of young guys racing to London, or other places, on horses, when they usually did that kind of stuff in a fine-tuned sports car to bring on their early deaths. And how did I know that? I asked myself, with another flash of past memory shooting back at me. My head suddenly throbbed, and I became breathless.

Christopher didn't seem to notice. He grinned, a wide, flashing smile of white teeth, seemingly deep in a memory. "We'd take bets at White's about who could beat the last record without driving his horse into the ground. Any rider who brought in an injured or overstressed horse was disqualified."

"I guess you miss those younger escapades," I said, still trying to imagine horseback races to congested London even so recently as twenty years before.

He answered, "I do miss those escapades very much, from time to time."

"Which makes it so strange that you left when you did."

His expression changed quickly as he glanced over at me. "I sincerely hope we are not getting into that again, Jessica," he warned.

"Sometime I would like us to talk about your past."

"If it puts your mind at rest, we will very shortly."

"Shortly when? Christopher, don't you know all this mystery is driving me mad?"

The agitation in my voice must have showed. He turned to study my profile. "You know perfectly well that I do, and that it is to my benefit as well as your own that you do know and remember quickly. I am not being a cruel brute by holding back information. I have reasons for doing so."

"Do you? And I suppose it was just my imagination today that sensed the insinuations behind Mr. Wadsworth's words?"

"No, it was not your imagination. As for Mr. Wadsworth, perhaps because of the similarity of names, he thinks he sees some family resemblance. And perhaps he does. There is that possibility, although he has never seen me. Then again, it is the nature of a man like him to look for faults where none exist. My own suggestion would be that he look to himself for a change." And with a careless shrug of his shoulders, he turned from me.

It would have been difficult to guess from his manner that the undercurrents connected with Cavenly bothered him as much as I could feel they did, that he was eaten up with bitterness at the status he now had to endure in his own former home. But it was obvious from his feigned relaxed pose, with his eyes closed and his head back against the headrest, that he considered the subject closed.

My own mind was jumping to some uncertain conclusions.

Was Christopher the illegitimate son, not necessarily of the current Earl, but of the previous one, or the illegitimate offspring of one of the other family members—brothers of sisters of this Earl or the previous one? Why did he know Cavenly so well, claimed to have lived there, yet left it so suddenly?

I was angry—not angry enough to spout any more spiteful words, but provoked enough to find out the truth, whether it was he who enlightened me or not. After all, it was my future hanging in the balance, too, and the sooner I discovered the truth, the surer the chances for my own sanity.

When we arrived at the inn, we had tea downstairs and, after a quick shower and change, left for a brief stroll before dinner.

In the fairy-tale mistiness of dusk, we walked down a quaint village street, past old but well-tended buildings, to a country lane. The air had chilled slightly, and we pulled our sweaters tight about us. The breeze that wafted occasionally across our faces was clean and pleasantly moist. The world was still but for the random sounds of a bleating lamb, a barking dog, the rustle of a leafy tree limb as we passed tiny cottages, each with its own patch of garden. I loved the blossoming gardens, not knowing at the time that many visitors before me had wondered at and admired these fertile plots of color in a climate that was supposed to be so chilly and damp. I took mental pictures of them—the green, green fields, and the hedges bordering the roadways—used as fences because they grew so thickly and with such abandon. But most of all I loved the houses —old English structures with beckoning, wide hearths and low-beamed ceilings, emanating warmth, and all the more amazing because they'd been so well preserved down through the centuries.

We walked until we could see a crimson-and-purple sky ushering out the sun. Then, in the light that remained, we found our way back to the inn.

Mrs. Barr was hovering between the entranceway and the dining room as we entered. She smiled at us. "Have a pleasant day? I've often wanted to drive over to see the house at Cavenly—lived with it most of my life, yet I never seem to get the thought and the motivation at the same moment. Pretty, is it?"

"Oh, absolutely lovely," I answered honestly.

"Not relations, are you?"

Christopher laughed. "You noticed the similarity of names?

No, I am afraid we cannot claim the honor."

She grinned in turn. "My husband tells me it's always been Dunlaps over at Cavenly. Thought perhaps you might be family who'd migrated to America years past. I was a Hatfield myself, before I married Mr. Barr."

"Hatfield of Hatfield House?" I questioned, the interest I'd recently taken in English history sparking my question.

"Of Hatfield House? Ah, yes, visited the place myself some time back, but I couldn't tell you for sure, Mrs. Dunlap. Could be I'm the descendant of some high servant taking the name for prestige."

"But I thought all Englishmen had their ancestry traced back to the time of William the Conqueror. At least to Elizabeth I."

Her good-humored face registered mild surprise. "Is that what Americans think? I know my great-grandparents' names and that they were from Suffolk, but we don't have much written down."

I smiled. "No, I shouldn't make the generalization. It's just seemed to me, since history's gone on so long here, you knew all your ancestors."

"You're interested in history, are you?"

"I seem to be since I came to England. It's fascinating."

"Fascinating. Yes, I've always thought that. Seems to me if we paid more attention to our history and our ancestors' mistakes, we might make fewer of them on our own. Ah, but don't pay any attention. I'm just a plain woman speaking my mind."

"You make a great deal of sense, Mrs. Barr," Christopher imparted. "I must say I agree with you."

We were hospitably escorted to a seat not far from the fire. I watched Christopher that night, catching him at moments when his thoughts and eyes were concentrating elsewhere. I took note of the way the light of the candle on our table played across the worry lines on his face. There was much under the surface of his sculpted countenance. His fingers idled with his glass of wine; the long, square, well-shaped fingers of a creator's hands, a doer's hands. His eyes spoke so much about him— intelligent, perceptive, at times emotion-filled eyes—they could speak a hundred words in one glance, yet in other moments were veiled mysteriously. And beneath that intriguing mask were the wheels of his undecipherable mind.

TWENTY-SIX

Slowly, steadily, each day brought us closer together. Christopher's constant, uninterrupted presence was having an effect upon me. I took each day as it came, working with him, living with him, sleeping with him, but never looking too deeply within myself. All the while, I told myself I was keeping Charles apart and above the rest. But in my heart I knew I was lying.

We'd been busy at Cavenly and had, by now, sorted through a good portion of the vast store of information. Christopher had set aside whatever papers he thought he might require for his notes. The rest we returned to the shelves somewhat more neatly than we'd found them. It reminded me of cleaning closets—a job I hated. But I put up with it because of him—because I was beginning to realize I respected him. As I collated the information, he periodically came over to check my progress. It was near the middle of our first week when I looked up to see him beside me, a deep frown on his brow.

"Is something wrong?" I asked.

"I am just noticing that there is no information here at all covering the years 1812 to 1816. Are you sure you have not overlooked anything?"

"I've tried to be careful."

Quickly he went to the bordering stacks to examine them with his own eyes, flipping through the papers, looking up finally with half-lidded eyes harboring thoughts I couldn't read. "It is just as I feared..."

"A lazy ancestor?" I spoke in a voice barely audible.

"No, Jessica. I am afraid it is more than that...quite a bit more." His hands fell flat on the stacks of paper as if his burdened mind couldn't bear more, yet when he spoke it was with determination. "Well, no matter. Perhaps I can find the information I seek from other sources."

We resumed our labors, the missing years of history forgotten for that day. I found myself becoming more and more intrigued with the work, understanding more of the subject matter and growing increasingly curious about the events that had occurred to affect the lives of the people of Cavenly.

The details we were pulling from the various journals and memorandums pertained primarily to the political role the family had played in late eighteenth and early nineteenth century government. Christopher added tidbits, too, about the personal side of life during those times of growth, war, and change that culminated in the all-powerful and far-reaching British Empire under Queen Victoria.

Our hours at Cavenly were well occupied. In the late afternoons, we'd strike out across the parkland to explore the far corners of the estate. We trespassed into the budding woodland, mossy and musky smelling, out into the open fields of green grass and bluebells, and back to the paddocks and stables to survey the horses. Christopher was a practiced judge who confidently pointed out the strengths and weaknesses in each animal: the breadth of the chest, the length of the leg, the slope of the back and hindquarters. We were left at peace outside, under the blue-and-white sky, but whenever the idea occurred to my husband to show me the private sections of the house, a prying Mr. Wadsworth would poke his nose around the next corner, keeping us in subtle surveillance. The man aggravated me beyond reason, not so much by his overt actions, but by the snide smile always perched on his lips and the condescending manner in which he'd greet us when we passed in the hall.

Fortunately, the rest of the staff were friendly and courteous. Christopher did have an inborn way with people, charming them with his natural cordiality. As a result, members of the staff went out of their way to stop for a chat or to inquire how our work was progressing. Mrs. Cribbs was especially nice, taking me around the State rooms on the days when business was lagging, bringing me beyond the roped-off barriers to show me some of the glorious treasures and to relate a little of the history of each. I found her to be entertaining company and a storehouse of information when it came to any detail pertaining to the house, its furnishings, and its occupants. Obviously she was reluctant to say too much about the present earl and his family, but she would babble on happily for hours about previous earls, and she was well versed on the biographical facts of them all, right down to the first ancestor, who'd taken title to the hamlet and the lands surrounding it during the reign of William the Conqueror. The hamlet was gone, but that first ancestor had constructed the great stone keep, the tower that still stood in the center of the house. The thought was humbling that Christopher and I were now working within walls that had echoed the jests, arguments, petty squabbles, and victory cries of its inhabitants for over a thousand years, and that we were treading upon stone floors that had felt their footsteps.

I was tempted several times to ask Mrs. Cribbs how long she'd been employed at Cavenly, wondering if it were possible that her path and my husband's had crossed before. I wondered, too, since she was so knowledgeable about the other inhabitants, if she knew the story behind his sudden move to the United States. I was stopped from asking by the memory of Christopher's clear warning on the day of our arrival not to give any indication of his association with the family. And then again, if Mrs. Cribbs had been acquainted with my husband or his role at Cavenly, wouldn't she have recognized him and spoken up on her own?

Leaving the gates of Cavenly behind us each day at five, it was still possible to have a quick cup of tea at the inn, then return to the car to drive about the countryside and view it in the repose of late afternoon, when the farmers were leaving their fields to join their families for the evening meal, and small herds of cattle were winding their way back to the barn. I saw more than a glimpse of the country Christopher loved and, just as he hoped, was learning to love it myself.

And later, after darkness, I was finding I was no longer afraid of his advances. In those brief spells when I forced undiluted honesty upon myself, I had to admit I enjoyed seeing the fire dance in his eyes, hearing his teasing remarks and his husky voice, feeling his hands reaching out to touch me. And in the morning, wakening to see his dark head decorating the next pillow, his eyes watching me lazily.

My pregnancy was increasingly sapping my energy. Some days I couldn't seem to pull myself from the bed, but he was there, pleasant and as understanding as a nursemaid, tugging me from beneath warm covers to place two pillows behind my back, then handing me a hot cup of coffee.

"Not feeling too brisk this morning, my mother-to-be?" He laughed.

"No, obviously, and I don't see any reason for you to chuckle about it. I certainly don't think it's very funny."

"Perhaps you had better spend the day in bed and rest. Judging from your temper this morning, you could use it."

"Consider my mood one of those fringe benefits," I said tartly, "of expectant fatherhood. Just bring me some more coffee. I'll be all right in a minute."

"I come well prepared with a full pot."

"Good." I drained the cup I had.

He continued casually, ignoring my glowering eyes. "We have quite a bit of work to do today, but I thought if I could find a few minutes I'd sneak you up to the first floor through the private rooms. I've decided to make use of my trump card in bypassing Mr. Wadsworth and getting us up there unnoticed."

"I thought I heard Mrs. Cribbs say yesterday that our friend would be going up to London for the day."

"Oh? And you neglected to tell me? I thought you wanted to see my former room?"

"I do, of course. I just remembered now, and I'm not even sure I heard her correctly."

"Well, whether you did or did not," he uttered mildly, "his presence won't stand in the way of my plans."

I handed him my cup, feeling a small ration of energy dribbling through my veins, and swung my legs over the side of the bed.

"You are enjoying a remarkable recovery, my dear." He grinned. "I thought we'd find you in the grave by dusk."

I made a face at him. "Just get me my robe. It's chilly in here."

He hesitated, his eyes on the flush of my naked body.

"Perhaps it wouldn't matter if we got started an hour late."

"And perhaps if you push me back into that bed you won't get me out of it."

The robe landed like a ghost's shroud over my head, and through its folds I heard his laughter. "Well, get up and dressed. Time flies on hurried wings. The rest we'll take care of tonight."

I untangled myself from the warm material and headed for the bathroom.

He was waiting for me in the other room, making a good show of concealing his impatience. As I entered, slipping a pair of gold earrings to my earlobes, he smiled appreciatively. "What wonders a splash of cold water and a comb will do. One would never guess that a few moments ago you were the crotchety, pregnant lady of the neighboring boudoir."

I glanced down unconsciously at my stomach, lately just beginning to show the barest suggestion of roundness. "I don't imagine it will be long before one would guess."

"I wonder how my beautiful wife is going to look when it is no longer possible to disguise the fact she has a loaf in the oven."

"Like an overstuffcd sugarplum, dearest husband. And I don't care for your lowly form of description."

"A sugarplum, yes...a very round one. I shall enjoy the spectacle." He laughed.

"I'll bet you will! Just remember that the bigger and rounder I get, the more distance it will put between us."

He moved closer, slipped his arm around my shoulder, and nibbled my ear. "But such a different type of distance. I shall love you no matter what girth you may reach. The only hardship I can foresee is perhaps our son will decide he is not in the mood for love play and kick me away."

"I've already decided it's going to be a girl."

"Oh?" The blue eyes gleamed. "A girl? Shall we wager on that? What would you consider fair stakes?"

"None," I said coolly. "A child isn't something to wager on."

"Not the child, my love—its sex. I don't consider it an unfair wager. I can recall in my gravy days putting up stakes on far less sensible things, such as the progress of two fleas across a dog's back."

"You?"

"Oh, my, yes. And I won. Mine was the flea with the longest legs."

"Well," I reproved, "I'm not interested in any bets. With nothing to wager, it would be rather foolish of me." I slid from beneath his arm.

"What about your freedom?" he threw forth suddenly.

The words spun me 'round in my tracks. I was too startled to try to disguise my reaction.

"So, I've touched a raw nerve?" His mouth twisted. "Would you care to reconsider my bet now that you have something to gain?"

"What makes you think I want my freedom?"

"Nearly everything you do."

"Well, I don't."

"Or is it that you are afraid of the consequences if I win? Perhaps once our son is born, you have already made plans to bolt and run from my side?"

"I've planned nothing of the sort."

Suddenly he turned on me with blazing eyes. "Do not lie to me, Jessica! I know you care no more for me now than you did the moment of our reunion. The only difference is that now you put up with me and the situation...put up with it because you have no alternatives at the moment or the clearness of mind to make a decision of your own. You are biding your time, are you not? Biding your time until you find that opportune chance to make your escape with as little discomfort or unpleasantness for yourself as possible."

I was stunned—too surprised by his unexpected accusations to refute them.

"But let me set you straight. I may love you—more than most men would admit to loving a woman—but I will never love any woman to the point where I cannot exist without her. I have been lenient and understanding of your problems beyond the bounds of what is expected. I have steeled myself against your cool lack of love, smiled and gritted my teeth when I wanted to tear into you for your selfishness—forgiven you and come back for more. But do not expect it to last forever. I, too, can reach the end of my rope, and that day is fast approaching. Think of that as you trip along in your daydreams. Someday you are going to wake up, Jessica, and when you do, you may find it is too late."

He stormed from the room, leaving in his wake the reverberations of a slammed door and a white-faced woman with hands clenched trembling against her sides.

We worked in utter silence that morning. His temper, I'd begun to realize, usually didn't continue seething and tormenting him for very long. Once released, it subsided and was soon forgotten. But this morning's argument was different—a tempest of bitter origins. The healing would take longer, and until the sore was once again smooth skin, I sat justly chastised, with a quivering stomach that gave me no peace. Perhaps he understood my self-reproach and for that reason let the argument lie, but whatever his motive, he didn't reopen the subject, and by noon his mood was visibly brightening.

During lunch we managed to pass a few inane remarks between us, meaningless except that they served as a white flag. After we'd eaten, he led me out into the back gardens for a stroll—our habit before going back to work. We hadn't gone far when he took my arm to lead me back to the house and in through the side door of the east wing.

I didn't question him, still unsure of the mood between us, but he spoke up quite cheerfully in explanation. "Do you feel in a daring mood? We could use the conventional means of getting upstairs and take our chances of being spotted—or you might prefer the priest's stairs instead?"

I looked at him dumbly. "Priest's stairs? In this house?"

"Several. Not recorded, of course, although the family is aware of them. Young boys into mischief and anxious for adventure discover them by knocking about on the wall panels until one springs open. That was how I found them myself. I had a good many hours of fun eluding my old nanny, until one day she caught on to me and, perhaps thinking to teach me a lesson, locked me in. If a lesson was what she had in mind, it was well learned. I do not think I have ever known a more frightening experience than suddenly finding myself entombed in a dark, smelly, and airless maze of passages, with the walls about me so thick I feared no one would ever hear my cries for help." He chuckled. "Come on. There is a stairway in the library that will bring us out into my old bedchamber."

"What if someone's blocked them over?"

"We shall find out soon enough." He opened the door at the end of the hall. "The main entrance to the library is at the front, but using this door, we won't been seen." We went inside. "Over here." He indicated one section of the bookcases that covered the walls on all sides except for the breaks where the long windows let in the daylight. "I hope I can remember the spot."

Removing several books, he reached behind them, then smiled in satisfaction. "Found it! Step back a few feet, and I'll swing it open." He reached into his pocket to hand me a flashlight. "Hold on to this—we are going to need it."

I watched amazed as the shelves slid slowly and silently forward, leaving a space just wide enough for a person to squeeze through. I flicked on the flashlight as he motioned me to precede him. It smelled dank inside, damp and unused, but by swinging the light around, I was able to see we were in a narrow passageway running parallel to the back of the library and leading to a set of dangerously steep stairs.

"We can get out again?" I asked nervously as I heard the panel click shut behind us.

"I would not lock us in here, my love. As romantic as it sounds, I am afraid we would get very cold and very hungry. No, we can get out with no trouble. All of these panels have catches on either side. Well, lead on."

Cautiously we started up the stairs. "Whatever you do," he added, "do not drop that light. It is damnably black in here without it."

At the top of the stairs we reached a miniature landing and proceeded straight ahead, down another narrow corridor, before the passage turned abruptly to the right, leading us back toward the front of the house. We had followed this for a good hundred feet when, face to face with what looked like a blank wall, I came to an abrupt halt.

"Here," Christopher said, running his hand over the wall. I directed the flashlight so he could see what he was doing. Jutting out from between the brickwork, and unnoticeable unless you knew what you were looking for, was a tiny handle, which he pulled toward him. My eyes widened as the solid wall in front of me began sliding slowly to the right, revealing a glimpse of the room beyond.

"You know," he whispered, "I am really surprised at the condition of these mechanisms. I seriously doubt they have received much use in recent years."

"Unless there've been other curious young boys tapping on walls," I suggested.

He chuckled. "Yes, there is that. Take a peek in the room first to see if anyone is there. I do not want us to be caught."

I squinted out. Seeing no one, I stepped into the room, my husband following.

His expression was one of delight.

"Of all things amazing...they have not really changed it! A few odds and ends, but basically it is as it was when I left. What do you think?"

I was silent, trying to take it all in. We were standing on a plush oriental rug covering most of the floor. Across the room was a huge, dark wood bed with a canopy, which I was beginning to think was an essential fixture of a traditional English bedroom. On either side of the bed were long, draped windows, and to my right on the front wall of the room were two more of the same. A closet behind us bordered on a large marble-trimmed fireplace with marble hearth and a leather upholstered lounge chair placed enticingly before it. Over the fireplace was a large gilt-framed yet masculine mirror that must have reflected every movement of anyone occupying the bed.

Around the room were various dressers, tables, and side chairs, all arranged most comfortably. On the walls were paintings of horses, hunt scenes, and the like. Another mirror hung over a trim piece of furniture that looked like a man's dressing table or shaving stand. The colors in the room were all deep, vibrant blends of reds, blues, and golds.

My overall impression was of unostentatious richness and beauty, yet one thing puzzled me. How had Christopher ever come to occupy a room this lavish? Wasn't it far too grand for a poor relation? I hadn't seen the other bedrooms, so possibly this room would seem shabby in comparison to them. Somehow I doubted it.

"Well, do you like it?" he asked again impatiently. He was like a small boy, anxious for my approval.

"Of course I like it...how could I help it?" I began walking about, examining things more closely. "And this was your room?"

He frowned for a moment. "Yes."

"It seems awfully elegant."

"But there is more." He turned, and I noticed the double doors on the wall to the left of the fireplace.

"Through here." He reached for the gold knobs. "This was my study."

Holding my breath, I followed him through the doors into a second room of about equal size to the bedchamber. I would have known it to be a man's study without his having told me so. Everything in the room was sturdy and functional and gracefully beautiful at the same time, from the large desk to the leather couches to the dark paneling covering the walls.

He strode almost possessively across the wide-board oak floor, where a few small rugs were scattered, to the large desk. "This was my favorite room in the house. As a matter of fact, last Christmas you gave me as a gift a small statue of a dam and foal that once graced this very desktop. You did not know at the time that the piece had come from Cavenly and had once been mine. I still wonder at the coincidence of it all."

"I wonder, too," I said quietly, momentarily bereft as I yearned to remember the details of an incident I'd totally forgotten. As I watched, he sat down in the chair behind the desk and opened each of the drawers to leaf through the papers within. Apparently finding nothing of interest, he reopened one of the small top drawers and let his fingers explore the empty interior. I heard a click and watched as a secret compartment popped out in the ornamentation above the drawer. He removed a roll of papers, yellowed with age, and, after unrolling them and scanning them quickly, stuffed the roll into his inside jacket pocket.

"What are those?" I asked, marveling at yet another of his secrets.

"Letters written many years ago by a certain cousin of mine. There was quite a story involved with these papers, the facts of which you knew at one time. Let us just say now that they were damning evidence against him in a case of treason, and because of their importance, I hid them away safely in this desk."

"But how did you know they'd still be there?"

"Since I had this desk built to my own design, it is doubtful anyone else would have knowledge of that secret compartment."

And here was another puzzle for me. How could a poor relation afford to have a desk built to his own design? What was I missing? What was the connection I should have been seeing but was overlooking entirely?

I didn't bother asking. I knew he wouldn't give me a straight answer, so I held my tongue as we returned to the bedroom. Instead I occupied my thoughts with trying to imagine him living in these rooms—finding, surprisingly, it wasn't difficult at all. He seemed to fit. The undefinable air I'd noticed in him right from the start blended very well into the atmosphere of luxury surrounding us. I could picture him seated behind the desk in the study, poring over a stack of papers pertaining to estate matters, or plopping down in the lounge chair before a crackling fire as a winter wind blew damp and chill against the windows. I imagined him rising and going to the finely appointed bath adjoining the bedroom to shave and change for an elegant dinner party below stairs. I saw him in a black tailored suit, his ruffled white shirt and formal black tie immaculate as he mingled with his guests, all as faultlessly mannered and well-dressed as he. And I saw him charming them with the same ease that he charmed nearly everyone else of his acquaintance. Why did he fit so well into the pattern? Why did these rooms, without his having to tell me they'd once been his, seem to radiate his personality?

My mind unsettled, I resumed wandering around the room until I stood not far from the oversized four-poster. "Such a large bed for one person," I teased. "It couldn't have been very cozy for you."

Though I didn't turn to see his expression, I could hear his footsteps approaching me. "It would have been my marriage bed had things turned out differently." He halted directly in back of me and dropped his hands lightly on my shoulders. His deep voice held a husky hint. "Would you care to try it out now, since we won't have another opportunity?"

"Hardly."

"It will be our only chance, wife."

"I'll live with the loss," I retorted with a smile.

"I am not of your prudish leanings." Before I realized what he was doing, he picked me up and heaved me onto the satin coverlet. A gasp of surprise escaped me as he pushed me down into the pillow and lowered his own tall frame over me.

One look at the horror on my face was enough to make him shake with laughter. "What is the matter, wife? Afraid to be caught making love in your husband's former bed? Or do you not think I will do it?"

I pressed my hands against his shoulders. "No. I mean, yes, I think you might, but don't! Think of where we are!"

"My dear, although it may surely seem so at times, I have not entirely lost my sense of balance...not yet. The possible consequences of such an act outweigh even the formidable benefits." He lifted himself to a sitting position. "But at least I have had the pleasure of seeing your body so charmingly decorating my bed. The first woman who has had the honor, I might add."

"I'm overwhelmed." I made a wry face.

"You should be. There were many who would have been only too pleased, under almost any circumstances, had I ever felt so inclined..."

"Your conceit is unmatched!"

He chuckled, rising. "One more thing before we go on to the other rooms—please try to keep your voice to a whisper. I do not want our progress overheard."

I brought myself quickly to my feet. "Yes, your lordship."

He ignored my mockery and strode to the door to the hall, but I thought I had seen a startled spark in his eyes.

He motioned to me. "Come quickly."

I stepped into the wide hall that seemed to stretch for a mile, then curved behind the half-moon balcony at the head of the main staircase. The hallway was carpeted and ornamented

here and there with paintings, chairs, and side tables. Almost
directly opposite us was another corridor leading off at a right
angle down into the first wing. We walked quietly as he
whispered descriptive comments to me. Off the first wing, he
explained, were all the family bedrooms and sitting rooms, but
we wouldn't have time to see them now. Farther along the hall,
past his own suite of rooms, he opened a door on the left and
indicated that the large, well-furnished room which was the
private family drawing room where less formal entertaining
took place.

He frowned. "Now this room has changed considerably."
He motioned to the overstuffed sofas and chairs. "But it does
look more comfortable than in my day."

Directly across from this room, on the right of the hall, was
the old-ladies' sitting room, as he tersely described it, hardly
ever used in the past except during formal parties when the
matrons retired there to their sewing and gossip.

"Sewing?" Had I heard him correctly? He was already at
the next door, and the next, showing me large, airy, well-appointed
rooms, some of whose furnishings, he advised, had been changed
drastically since his departure from the house.

We slipped past the bend in the hall, across from which
was the central wing which housed the guestrooms. I saw the
tower room, which, although not connected to the stonework
of the original Norman tower, contained many historic artifacts
and occupied almost the whole front corner of that side of the
house. Here were suits of armor and tattered banners, carefully
preserved tapestries and heavy hand-carved chairs so old I
hesitated to sit on them. It was a miniature museum that spoke
more loudly than words of the long, distinguished lineage of the
earls of Westerham.

We left the tower room to cross the hall, where I expected
to find the entrance to the third wing. Instead we faced a set of
wide white-and-gilt doors, which he opened to show me the
ballroom.

My head spun at the sight of it. Parquet floors seemed to
stretch for miles. Mirrors graced the walls to reflect upon
themselves and throw back an image of a room that seemed
even larger. Drapes of a golden fabric framed the windows.
Crystal chandeliers hung suspended from the tall, plastered
ceilings, their dusty pendants sparkling dimly in the light. Long
windows too numerous to count gave a breathtaking view of

the parkland. There were no furnishings, just ghostlike shadows of long-dead lords and ladies flickering in the no-longer-shiny mirrors, their laughter echoing in the stillness of the room. It was a lost, forgotten room, a figment of the past that raised the skin along my arms.

I was awed by the splendor, and would have stood hypnotized if Christopher hadn't at that moment taken my arm and hurried me away, back down the long corridor to the secret passage.

As the panel slid shut behind us, I reached for his arm to steady myself on the journey back. "I can't believe it," I whispered, though the need for hushed voices was gone.

"What is it?" he inquired quietly.

"That you lived here and spent your time in these magnificent rooms as casually as you would a tiny cottage."

"Surely not as casually as that."

"But you hadn't hinted at how beautiful they were. It's one shock piling up on top of another...I feel dizzy"

"Perhaps I did take it for granted at times."

"My God, when I think of living here for any length of time, even as a ladies' maid...just to be able to roam through all this luxury and beauty day after day, trying to absorb it..."

"Were it so, you would not be a ladies' maid, my love. And I have thought of it, too...thought that if things were different..." His wistful voice drifted off, to come back on a harder note. "I think about it, yet it is beyond thinking. It cannot be and will not be...at least not in this time."

I pulled him closer in the darkness. "I'm only dreaming...wondering what it would be like..."

"And I can see you here as my wife, within these walls as Cavenly's mistress."

"You dream too far."

His arms tightened around me. "Not so far as you might think, my countess. Were it possible, I would gladly wring the necks of the current earl and all his heirs to put you here." His bright eyes swam above my face for an instant before his mouth came down hard on mine.

His breathing was heavier when he released me to take my arm again and lead me the rest of the way down the passage to the narrow stairs.

"Christopher," I whispered, my mind in a turmoil. "I won't ask you what it is you're not telling me. None of it makes sense to me. I understand it no more than I understand myself and the way I feel about you. There's something instinctive, perhaps, that keeps me at a distance. But it's not deliberate...I don't mean to throw your love for me back in your face..."

"I understand the present turnings of your mind better than you realize. My weakness is that I have something equally troubling on my mind, and when the two worries come at me at once, it is sometimes more than I can handle. If you will bear with me, I will bear with you, my love. I am not ready to give up."

The rest of the day passed by in a blur, but when we were beneath the sheets of our bed, his warm hands upon my skin, the events of the hours preceding came back to haunt me in my sleep. In the haziness of my dreams, I saw my husband wandering through the rooms and corridors of Cavenly, first as a lord and then as an outcast. I saw him dining with the guests, gliding across the polished floor of the ballroom, dancing gracefully. The lady on his arm wore long skirts, her blond hair piled high with jewels, not like mine at all. She was smiling. I heard her laughter. I knew his arms held her tightly, but I couldn't see his face. And then he was riding across the parkland on a sleek, dark stallion. The sky was overcast, the wind whipping at the tailed jacket he wore. His white neck cloth was in disarray and his dark curls tousled. He halted in the midst of a wide field and swung around. He lifted his arm, motioning me to come. Instead, I ran in the opposite direction. I couldn't hear him following. I ran to the front doors of Cavenly. I flew up the great staircase and down the hall. I reached a door at the end...the door that opened into his room. Mr. Wadsworth was there, in the center of the carpet, standing over a heap on the floor. I stepped closer and saw it was a body...a body with my husband's face. He was so still. Then I heard him moan. Mr. Wadsworth lifted a club in his hands and swung it down, screaming, crying in frenzy, "Imposter, you must pay for your lies...you lie...you're not he...you can never be he...he's dead...dead...dead...do you hear me...dead..." The words echoed on and on.

I jerked awake in a cold sweat of trembling fear. I found Christopher in the bed beside me, and I wrapped my arms around his strong back, pressing my trembling body as closely to his living form as I could. I didn't want him to die.

TWENTY-SEVEN

My chilling nightmare didn't return, and I was too busy in our race with time and the work still ahead of us to analyze the dream's strange content. I absorbed myself in the lives of the people who had dwelt within this house so long ago. As I dug deeper and deeper into their written words, I thrilled to the extravagances they'd enjoyed, lived with them through their eternal parties, hunts, balls, and social teas. I shared their tragedies, their moments of joy, their political triumphs and travails. Individual personalities emerged, making these long-dead people very much alive and, underneath all their glitter, very real.

One day as I was glancing through a pile of clippings, I came across a tidbit in a society column that caught my interest. The writer of the article described an evening party given by one Lady Sefton during the London season of 1810. The article recorded in overabundant detail the noble and consequential attendees, their dress, their conversation, the entertainments of the evening provided for their amusement, the variety of food and drink set out on the great tables, and the latest morsel of gossip circulating the crowd.

Recorded meticulously was the entrance of each new lord and lady to the already blooded gathering, with comments summarizing their behavior while in the rooms.

I read in mild interest until the writer went on to describe the stir caused by the entrance rather late in the evening of "the Great Christopher," the young and excessively handsome earl whose wealth, fortune, and fame for a scathing tongue and unpredictable behavior followed him into every drawing room he entered. Being the most eligible bachelor in England also contributed to this outsized reputation, the writer noted.

I read on. "His Lordship made his entrance, nodded to acquaintances in the crowd, took a glass of champagne from the footman scurrying about with a loaded tray; and then, with no more than a passing smile to his hostess and other notable ladies present, including the lovely heiress and reigning belle of London, Lady Jane Liston, he made a determined path through the crowd to the side of one Miss Monfort, an attractive enough young woman, but one with social connections so slim she'd barely procured a voucher for Almacks. His Lordship proceeded to stand at her side in conversation for several minutes, scorning the more affluent personages nearby, and, when the musicians tuned up, did the unheard-of thing of dancing two successive dances with her. Outrageous! Especially for someone who usually preferred the company of other gentleman at cards and rarely set a toe upon the floor at a fete such as this.

"After spending several more moments speaking to Miss Monfort, much to the chagrin of the other ladies in the room, 'the Great Christopher' took himself off to spend the balance of the evening lost in conversation with George Brummel. Yet before departing from the party, rather earlier than the rest of the gathered ton, he once again sought out the dark-haired Miss Monfort, pulling her from conversation with Lady Dean, a stout and pretentious dowager, and bestowing upon the fortunate young woman one of his most dazzling smiles, a deep bow, and a gracious kiss on the back of her white glove. This done, he beckoned imperiously to the head footman to call his carriage."

The writer went on to recount the whispers that passed about the room as soon as the door closed behind him, and the appraising stares directed toward the still-rosy cheeks of Miss Monfort. Though "the Great Christopher" might never set eyes on the blushing lady again, and if he did, might not recognize her, he had succeeded that night in launching her into society. "Typical of the man," the writer commented dryly, "to amuse himself with an escapade such as this.

"It appears the fortunate Miss Monfort suddenly finds herself the center of attention, when an hour before she'd gone unnoticed by even the most insipid swain. All it has taken is for the earl of Westerham to set his seal of approval."

Just the sort of situation to appeal to my sense of humor, provided I was the female in the shoes of Miss Monfort, and at that moment I almost wished I had been. I wondered about the handsome earl. He even carried the same Christian name as my husband—who fit the description and characterization cited in the paragraphs amazingly well. I handed the article to him to read.

By the time he'd finished, his face was split by a wide, honestly amused grin. "I'd like to hold on to that. Put it in a safe place."

"Quite a character, your ancestor."

"You think so?" He raised an eyebrow, chuckling.

"If we'd ever met, I think I would have liked him very

much."

"I think you would have, too, my dear." He winked and returned to his work, a small smile still lingering on his lips.

Much to my delight, Mr. Wadsworth relieved us of his presence several times during the next few days. I didn't know whether it was the vision of him I'd seen in my dream, or the man himself, but the sight of him bothered me. I was glad when he was gone, and took each opportunity to stroll freely about the rooms on the ground floor. When there wasn't a tour group nearby, I let myself into the rooms beyond the velvet barricades and explored at random, testing the comfort of an ivory satin chaise or the feel of a fine china vase, checking the view from each of the windows and imagining someone long ago gazing across the parkland much as I was doing.

A few days before we planned to leave for home, I wandered into the music room—a lovely, bright, yet cozy room tucked into the back corner of the main rectangular structure of the house. Golden sunlight swept into the room and gave a glow to the pastel decor.

I liked the feeling of the room, its cheerfulness. I felt myself drawn toward the baby grand piano in front of the windows. I walked over, touched the soft, satiny wood, let my eyes roam over the keyboard and the sheet music resting above it. Tentatively, I slid onto the polished wooden bench.

I had a funny feeling about the piano, a sort of bound-up excitement that made my fingers yearn to move across the keys. I knew I couldn't resist it and turn away. The music open before me was a Chopin nocturne. Chopin...what did Chopin mean to me? I reached out my right hand and placed it upon the keys. I looked at the music, then slowly, hesitantly, began picking out the notes of the melody, listening to the beautiful tones as they echoed in the empty room. Unbidden, my fingers began to move more quickly, more assuredly, bringing the notes to life. Then I brought my left hand up to join. My fingers moved unwaveringly, gaining tempo and strength and confidence.

I knew how to play...I knew how to play well. I couldn't believe it! And I knew this song. I'd played it before, I was sure of it. My head was reeling. I let the flowing melody be my guide and let my feelings flow out of my body into the beautiful, lilting tones. I played on, bringing forth every silvery note, to the last chord.

When I finished and let my hands rest easily on the keys, I

was shaking, trembling with the knowledge of the unrealized talent I'd just discovered in myself. I didn't want to stop. I wanted to experiment more, taste more completely of this unexpected insight.

I was going to search through the other music on the piano, but I suddenly had the sensation that I was no longer alone, that someone's eyes were watching me, staring into my back. I swiveled around on the bench. The intruder was standing in the doorway, his eyes strangely alight, his cheeks creased by the smile on his lips. It was Christopher.

"Oh...it's you." I sighed in relief. "But what are you doing here? I thought you were working. Do you need me?"

"I heard the beautiful music and came in search of its source." He paused, still leaning against the door. Something was hidden in the expression on his face. A secret knowledge? A deep pleasure? He stepped over the velvet cord and came toward me. "You used to play that at home for me, Jessica. I knew there could be no other fingers playing it now but yours."

He came closer. I sat wondering at his words, wondering at my ability, wondering about the past he spoke of, yearning to bring back the memories.

Still smiling when he came to stand behind me, he gently ran one finger down the side of my cheek. "Play some more...for me, my love."

I heard his husky voice and the double meaning that seemed to whisper through his words, and reached for the next sheet of music. It was the "Moonlight Sonata," and I felt I knew it, too. When I began to play, I was sure of it. Had he once listened to me playing this melody as well?

He said nothing, resting his hand warmly upon my shoulder as I trickled my fingers across the keys in mood with the serenity of the music. When I finished, he reached over my shoulder to place the Chopin piece in front of me.

"Play it again," he said quietly. "This time for us."

I looked up into the face so close to mine. There was a difference in his expression...something I'd never seen before. It was gentle, soft, unhurried, and at the same time bespoke passion leashed by the strongest of wills. As I fingered the notes once more, without actually intending to, I played the song more poignantly—for us, for lovers.

The room was very still when the last chord drifted off into silence. I sat with my eyes still fastened to the keyboard, and he stood behind me, one hand resting on my shoulder.

When I rose, his hand reached to take my elbow. We walked from the room into the hall. Only then did he lean closer to say, with a certainty, "We will come back before we leave, my love, and you will play for me again...only then, I think you will know the truth."

I gripped his arm more tightly. "The truth?"

"About us."

"You're going to tell me?"

"I am. But not today. If you have not remembered on your own by tomorrow, I have chosen a special place." He looked down at me through his translucent eyes. "Tomorrow." It was a promise.

TWENTY-EIGHT

In the morning he was up first, striding over to the windows to pull open the drapes to a sunlit morning. I studied his naked back through half-closed eyes. I liked looking at the ripple of the muscles in his back and the broadness of his shoulders tapering gradually down to his trim waist and hips, his long legs.

He returned quickly to the bed to pull me unceremoniously into the cool air. "Up, my love. No time for dawdling this morning."

"Give me a chance to wake up."

"You can wake up in the shower." He pushed me toward the bath. "Too lovely a morning to be wasting in bed. We have much to do."

"All right. I'm going, I'm going."

I heard his casual voice from behind. "Would you mind if I joined you in the shower?"

I pivoted on my heel to face him.

"It would save time, aside from the other added advantages."

"Yes..."

"I can?"

"No. I mind."

"Surely, my wife, you can't still be holding on to some lagging modesty?" He made a gesture with his hand, indicating my obvious nakedness as I stood there confronting him, and laughed as I blushed red.

"You're teasing me again."

"I? Never. Well, get in the bathroom. We have not got all day."

I fled, tempted to lock the door behind me, but in the end I didn't, knowing that if it was in his mind to follow after me, he'd be just as likely to break down the door as pay heed to the lock.

Waiting for the water to reach the right temperature, I listened with one ear for the sound of his footsteps or the creak of the door handle. I heard nothing. Pinning my hair on top of my head and grabbing a bar of soap, I climbed in under the warm spray. I was lathering my arms and rinsing them when the curtain was suddenly zipped open. The surprise nearly sent me sprawling on the slippery porcelain, but he grabbed my arm to hold me steady. All the while, his eyes danced in amusement.

"Startled you, did I?"

"I thought—"

"That I would not be joining you? Ah, but you see I am. My back needs a scrubbing that I feel can only be obtained from your delicate hands."

He climbed in beside me and held me about my waist. He laughed into my disgruntled eyes, and in a moment wrested the bar of soap from my hand and began to lather my back in easy strokes.

"You see the advantages, my love?" he intoned.

"I could have done just as well."

"Unless your elbows are double jointed, I seriously doubt you could touch that spot..." His hands caressed an area between my shoulder blades. "...as well as I."

I gave up. What difference did it make, anyway. I soon found out, as his hands lathered in broader sweeps across my body, straying farther and farther afield. I took the soap from his fingers. "Well, turn around. I'll wash your back if you're so determined." I pushed him around so that his back was toward me.

"Is that all?"

"Of course." My reply was short.

He made no comment, but when I told him to stand under the spray, he grabbed my wrist and swung me around to face him. "My chest, wife, is also in need of gentle ministrations."

Without hope of deterring him, I began soaping the hairy expanse. His eyes watched me the whole while, and I kept mine averted. His hands were about my waist, then he brought up one hand to halt my busy strokes and move my hand lower, across his flat belly. His fingers didn't leave my wrist.

He again shifted my hand lower. "You don't mean..."

"I do."

"Christopher..."

"Remember, you are my wife."

"But—"

"No excuses." His fingers tightened.

I swallowed hard, and as I touched him, his fingers slid from my waist down to my thigh, and there began to move slowly, sinuously. His eyes, when I dared to look, were hazy, full of desire—the desire I'd already discovered with my fingers.

He edged us slowly back into the jet of water to wash the

soap from our bodies. Then, suddenly turning off the faucets, he nearly dragged me from the tub toward the huge bed. Our bodies were still wet as he threw me upon the covers and pressed his own tense body over me, smothering me with the urgency of his kisses. He bore down against me. His hips heaved. His lips were on mine, his body within me, and as much as I wanted to hold myself apart, I was lost to him again.

"Oh, God," he whispered. "Goddamnit, Jessica, love me soon." Then he seemed to abandon himself to the wild sensations that were coursing through his body and concentrated only on reaching the peak of pleasure.

He rolled on his side with me still in his arms, held me tightly and closed his eyes. As I studied his relaxed, now peaceful face, I felt a longing to reach out and touch the chiseled lips, the closed eyelids with their black fringe of lashes, the unshaven cheeks—to cradle the whole tenderly in my hands. I'd fought the feeling for so long, yet I knew I needed him. I needed the sound of his voice, the touch of his fingers, the spontaneity and honesty of the love he showered on me. Did I love him? Were these the ingredients? Coming so unexpectedly, the realization was frightening. Still, I couldn't deny that I'd made a place for him in my life and that without him there wouldn't be any warmth.

We were late getting to Cavenly, much though Christopher had wanted an early start. He had a lot to do in finishing up and sorting his notes and being sure we'd missed no details, but the work that was left to him now, he was better able to do alone.

Shortly after ten he looked up at my impatiently idle figure with a smile and suggested I take a walk in the garden. He'd meet me there when he was ready.

I didn't stray far into the gardens, wanting him to be able to find me when he came out. The sun was warm that day in an almost cloudless sky, and I found a convenient stone bench to take advantage of it. I was burning with anticipation, wondering nervously what he would tell me about the past that eluded me.

It was there that Mrs. Cribbs found me about half an hour later. I looked up as she called out to me and watched her stride briskly in my direction. I smiled a welcome.

"Lovely day, isn't it?" she remarked. "Really too fine to be inside."

"It certainly is. It's a shame you can't be out enjoying it."

"I don't think I'll have much time for that today, dear. The parking lot's already near filled, and that's usually a sign of a hectic day."

I patted the bench beside me. "Can't you sit for a minute?"

She smiled. "No, I'm afraid not. I only have a few minutes before my first tour, but I thought while I had the chance I'd come and ask you if you'd like to see something in the house. I came across it yesterday afternoon. Actually, I've known about it for some time, but it slipped my mind. I tried to find you or your husband yesterday, but you weren't around."

"We may have been in the music room."

"I know you'll be leaving in a few days, so this morning may be my last opportunity to show you. We'll have to hurry. I only have about twenty minutes." She checked her watch.

I was reluctant to leave the garden. I didn't know what time Christopher would be joining me, and what he planned to tell me seemed far more important than anything I might find in the house. "What is it you want to show me?"

"I think it would be more fun if I let you see for yourself." She twinkled. "You'll be surprised, I can promise you that."

I shrugged my shoulders. "All right. But my husband's going to be joining me out here in a little while, so I don't want to be too long."

"We won't be." She motioned for me to follow her, and I rose and fell into stride beside her.

We went into the house through one of the back entrances. She led me down the corridor until we were in the hall behind the grand staircase. Here she turned and directed me to the front entrance hall. "We'll have to go up to the gallery at the head of the stairs. You haven't been up here before, I imagine."

"No. Mr. Wadsworth said it was off limits."

"To the general public, but I wouldn't think that included you."

The hall was empty, although we could hear the muffled noises of a tour group a few rooms beyond us. We climbed the wide carpeted stairs and halted for a moment at the top. The balcony was larger than it appeared from below, its circular walls painted in a light color and adorned with rows of portraits.

She turned and followed the curve of the landing, toward the wing Christopher and I hadn't explored. In fact, we hadn't gone anywhere near the gallery for fear of being seen from below. Halfway down the gallery hall, she stopped before a large, gold-framed painting. The hallway was dim, and she flicked on the small light attached to the top of the frame.

"Here's what I wanted to show you," she said eagerly.

My eyes widened. I couldn't believe what I was seeing. I stepped closer. I looked up to the blue eyes that seemed to be staring at me from the canvas—the slight smile that curved on the lips, the dark, loosely waving hair that surrounded the handsome face. It couldn't be. The features were the same. The eyes, the suggestive smile. I might have been looking at my husband. Yet the plate on the frame read Christopher R.J.G. Dunlap, Ninth Earl of Westerham. What did it mean?

I turned my eyes to Mrs. Cribbs, who was smiling at the disbelief written on my face. "Quite amazing, isn't it? I thought you'd be surprised, dear. I was a bit taken aback myself yesterday when I saw it again. You know," she rambled on, though I hardly heard her, my eyes back on the painting, "I had the strangest feeling when I saw your husband that first day you came to Cavenly that I'd met him before. And now I know why. It's extraordinary, don't you think, that two unrelated men could look so much alike? And it's especially extraordinary when you consider that they both bear the same name. It would make you wonder, if you didn't stop and think that this gentleman lived and died over a hundred and fifty years ago."

I was feeling very strange. There was a buzzing in my ears.

Mrs. Cribbs's voice continued, "There's an interesting story connected to the ninth earl, and quite a mystery. He inherited the title at the age of twenty-two during one of the most flamboyant periods of English society. From what was written about him, he was quite some gentleman, and by the time he'd reached his late twenties, his exploits and reputation had earned him the title of 'the Great Christopher.' "

"Yes," I interrupted her in dazed tones. "I read an article about him just the other day. I showed it to my husband."

She chuckled. "Quite a fellow. He was handsome, as you can see, and was one of the most sought-after bachelors in England. Very wealthy, too. All reports indicate that he had a sharp mind for managing the estate and his other holdings, but be that as it may, apparently no lady was fair enough to capture his heart, because at the time of his strange disappearance he was a bachelor and without heir. That was in 1812. As the story goes, he'd been in London to attend some sessions in the House of Lords. He'd returned to his London house and left there early in the evening with all intentions of going on to

Cavenly. When he didn't arrive there that evening or the following morning, a search was instigated. At the age of thirty-two, he was already an up-and-coming member of the House of Lords and certainly was well known enough that his disappearance caused extensive stirring in both government and social circles. The search for him was continued for several months, if I'm not mistaken, but except for his riderless horse found grazing in a nearby pasture, no trace or clues to the earl's whereabouts were ever found."

"How do you know all this?" I asked. "I mean, we never came across any of this in the family documents."

"Isn't that strange. But, of course, I didn't get the information from any of the archives here, and since this part of the house is never open to tours, I hadn't given much thought to the Ninth Earl or his story, nor had any of the other guides. You see, years ago I inherited some old letters from my grandmother," she smiled fondly. "I was a history buff even back then. They were letters and papers that had been handed down to her. I went through every one of them—and there were quite a few. Some dated back the first half of the nineteenth century. That's where I read about the story of the Ninth Earl. My grandmother's family goes back a long time in this part of Kent. They weren't gentry, but they were prosperous and liked to keep up on the news and gossip. As I guess you can imagine, the disappearance of the young earl was very big news indeed."

"But there are no records in the archives," I said almost under my breath.

She frowned. "Very strange, as I said. Perhaps they were lost."

I was standing before the portrait, unable to tear my eyes from the familiar face. The dizzy feeling was intensifying. My hands were trembling uncontrollably. The portrait started to reel before my eyes, the room to spin. The floor seemed to tilt and rush up toward my face. I reached out a blind hand to steady myself. I was seeing images in flashes thrown upon the wall like movies. I saw the face in the portrait, then the face of my husband, then the face in the portrait again, coming to life, stepping from the frame, walking toward me in the deep-blue jacket and flowing neck cloth of another era. He was smiling, reaching out a hand, calling to me. I saw a dimly lit room and candlelight, the dark-jacketed man sitting across the table from me. I saw him on horseback, running through a spring meadow,

laughing on a blanket on a sunny beach. I saw a wedding. Soft
embraces, and suddenly felt an overpowering love. Then there
was a crash...

I stumbled to the wall and leaned against it, shaking. Mrs.
Cribbs came rushing over, reaching out an arm to steady me.

"My goodness, dear, are you all right? Come, sit down.
There's a chair over here. You look faint. Can I help you? Shall
I call your husband?"

I collapsed into the chair, still shaking, but trying to smile
weakly. I didn't want her to know. "I'll be all right," I whispered
breathlessly. "I have these spells. You see, I'm expecting a
baby..." I grasped at the first excuse that came to mind. "It will
pass in a moment. I must have been standing too long."

"Oh, dear, I didn't realize. Are you sure I shouldn't call
your husband?" Her voice was filled with concern.

"No. I'm sure. He's so busy finishing up, there's no need
to bother him." I shook my head quickly. I took several deep
breaths, then forced a false brightness into my voice. "You see,
I feel better already. If I could just sit here for a minute..." I
couldn't believe what was happening to me. I couldn't believe
what my memories were telling me.

"Of course. Sit as long as you like," she said consolingly.

I forced out another tremulous smile. "Why don't you finish
your story? It was very interesting."

She frowned in worry. "Well, there isn't a great deal more
to tell." She hesitated, then went on, seeing the interest in my
eyes. "As I said, the earl disappeared without trace, and at
least from what letters said, he never returned."

Knowing now, in full and frightening clarity, the real truth
behind the ninth earl's—my husband's—disappearance, I had
no need to question her further. I could only sit there, barely
breathing under the weight of all the memories that were rushing
through my mind.

"It would be nice," she continued thoughtfully, "to think our
earl met with a happy end. But then, too, there are others of us
who would rather have a friendly and restless ghost lurking
through these corridors."

"Yes, a ghost," I whispered. If she only knew. That ghost
of whom she spoke so lightly was at that moment seated below
in the muniments room, very real and very much alive. What
would she think? Would she think we were all mad, as I was
beginning to think myself? I had to get away. I had to think, to

be by myself to sort through the confused and illogical jumble of the things I was remembering.

I started to rise. She was instantly concerned again. "Are you sure you're all right? I didn't upset you by bringing you here? I didn't realize your condition," she said apologetically.

"Oh, no. I'm fine, Mrs. Cribbs. As a matter of fact, I'm very happy you brought me here." I can't tell you how happy, I said silently to myself.

"Well, at least let me get you a cup of tea. The guides have a little lounge downstairs where you can rest for a moment, and the tea things are right there."

"Fine, fine," I said, anxious to get away. I couldn't concentrate on anything except the pounding in my temples and the thoughts filling my brain.

"Here, give me your arm, my dear," Mrs. Cribbs said. She led me to a small room tucked in between two of the wings in the servants' and employees' section of the ground floor. The room was tiny and furnished in someone else's leftovers, but it was private. Its saving grace was the huge window set in the back wall, giving a view between the two wings toward the back gardens.

I found a soft chair and almost fell into it. In a moment Mrs. Cribbs was at my elbow with a cup of hot tea.

"Now you're sure you'll be all right," she said in a last consoling gesture.

"I'll be fine, Mrs. Cribbs. You go on and get back to your work. I know you don't have time to sit with me."

"Actually, I do have to run. My next group is due to start." She looked nervously toward the door.

"Then hurry," I said, trying to reassure her. "And don't worry about me. I'll sit here a minute and then go look for my husband."

She gave me a warm smile as she reached for the door handle. "Please come and say good-bye before you leave Cavenly for home. It's been such a pleasure having you here."

"We will, Mrs. Cribbs. We couldn't forget to say good-bye to you."

At these words she was out the door, and I heard her footsteps hurrying down the corridor.

I let out a long sigh and sank back deeply into the softness of the chair. My hands began trembling again now that pretense was no longer necessary. I set my cup down on the table to keep from spilling its contents.

I closed my eyes and pressed my fingers to my temples. So this was the past I'd forgotten! How could it all be true? How could facts so fantastic be reality?

I turned to stare out the window, my eyes seeing nothing but the turmoil within me—so many pictures, so many memories that had evaded me so completely until that moment of seeing his portrait.

I remembered the moment of discovering him in my car as if it were yesterday. I remembered seeing his startled figure in a blue jacket just like the one he wore in the portrait, and I remembered my own fear and disbelief that he could be there. Then later, showing him all the wonders of the modern world, living with him and learning to know him better as each day went by. I remembered the painful months that followed—falling in love with him, and then the waiting and wondering, never knowing if he cared, or even if he'd be with me another day. I remembered the night when our love had finally blossomed, the days following—filled with unmatchable happiness—leading us through the cold winter when we needed nothing but each other for warmth and comfort. I remembered, too, the dark shadow of uncertainty that hung over our heads, that held the threat he would be taken from me and returned to his own time. And then our plans to seek the truth by coming to his former home to search through the records—and what a former home it was! Yes, I remembered it all, right down to the final moment when the car had crashed in London.

I felt drunk with the rebirth of all my memories—drunk and sick at the thought of how I'd been behaving toward him in the weeks of my amnesia. I'd denied him, I'd abused him. I'd rejected him and turned his love away, when all the while he'd tried to be kind and considerate and overlook the denials I'd constantly thrown in his face.

What a burden he'd been struggling beneath these last weeks, between his anxiety to discover his final destiny and what it would mean to his future, and his anxiety over a wife who refused to return his love and made each task more difficult.

My God, to think I'd almost thrown it all away! I could have lost him irretrievably through my selfish and inconsiderate behavior, and only now did I realize just how much he meant to me. I loved him...beyond any thought of ever losing him. It wasn't only my memories telling me this. It had been there all along in my darkness. The warm feelings I had while standing next to him, working silently beside him, which I had ignored. The emptiness when he wasn't in the room. My rebellion, my denial of my need for him, yet my weakness when he touched me. I'd fallen in love with him for the second time in my life, and this time I wasn't going to let anything stand between us.

I had to tell him—now, before it was too late to get back to the happiness we once knew. Tell him of my love. Tell him about the portrait and Mrs. Cribb's story. Tell him that, from all the evidence I'd just heard, there was no record of his returning to his own world after his disappearance in 1812.

Had he discovered in his searchings through Cavenly's archives the positive proof?

I ran on feet that had suddenly sprung wings to the muniment room. I pushed open the heavy doors. The room was empty. He was gone, probably in search of me. I ran back down the hall, out the side door into the garden. I saw him walking at the far end, beams of sunlight glinting on his dark hair.

I hurried down the steps, across the pebbled walk. Hearing my rapid footsteps as I approached from behind, he turned, just in time to spread wide his arms and catch me as I threw myself against him. An expression of pleased surprise crossed his face as his strong arms closed around me.

For a long moment I couldn't say a word. Neither did he. He held me close and let the other people wandering about the garden think what they would.

When finally I drew back a little from his arms and lifted my head to look up at him, he placed a gentle finger across my lips, telling me to hush, to wait.

"Christopher..." I began breathlessly.

"I know," he answered quietly. "I already know what you are going to say, and I have much to tell you, too. There is a quiet little spot where I want to take you before either of us says a word. Come."

He took my hand to lead me from the garden, across the side lawn into the shadows under the trees in the distance. I followed him in silence as we walked far from the house, over the velvet lawn, through the mossy stillness of a strand of woodland, then out again into the sunshine of a small meadow with a stream gurgling at its edge. We followed the stream to a natural clearing where the grass grew deep about our ankles.

Pulling me down into the grass beside the roots of an old

tree, he rested his arm easily around my shoulders. All was still except for the singing of the birds, the whisper of the wind, and the soft trickling of the brook. It reminded me of another meadow where we'd once sat, but that meadow had been on the other side of the ocean, and we'd been strangers then. "This was my own secret place when I was a boy," he said. "Even when I was a grown man, I would come here just to be alone with my thoughts. It has not changed in all those years...I thought it would be a good place for our reunion. It will be a reunion, Jessica?"

I nodded.

"I thought so." He leaned back against the trunk of the great tree and drew my head onto his shoulder.

"At first when I decided to bring you here today, I thought it would only be to tell you about our past...the truth you have been trying to pry from me all these days...the truth with an ending I did not know how you would accept. You see, I discovered yesterday afternoon that I was not going back. I could not tell you then, but I wanted to share my joy with you in whatever way I could. When I left the muniments room to look for you, I heard the piano, and when I went to the music room, I saw you there playing just like you used to do. If you had remembered that much, I had a feeling you would be remembering the rest soon." He took my hand and lightly caressed my fingers. "Have you remembered it all, Jessica? Our meeting, the love and happiness we knew?"

"Yes. Everything."

"And that remembrance was what sent you running into my arms in the garden."

"It is more than that." I twisted my head to look into his questioning eyes. "Christopher, I love you."

The eyes that watched me grew infinitely more tender at my words and glowed with a deeper happiness.

"I've been falling in love with you all over again these last weeks, only I was too blind and stubborn to recognize it. I tried to pretend it was something else. When my memory returned, I suddenly realized that I loved you already." I wrapped my arms tightly about his waist. "Oh, Christopher, what have I done to you?"

"Nothing, my love, that we cannot make up for in all the happy years we have ahead of us. We are together now. Do you realize that, Jessica? We can look forward to a future just like everyone else. We can make our plans, have our children. And someday we shall be able to look back without regret at all the wonderful years and what we went through to make them a reality."

We sat in peace, joined together by our love and the understanding we now shared. The waiting was over. The battles were won.

His lips moved against my hair. "Are you happy, my wife?"

"Yes...I'm happy. I'd forgotten how wonderful it feels to be in love."

"I had not. But now that I have you back and can feel your arms holding me the way I wanted them to do, the waiting was worth it. Tell me what happened to make you remember."

"After I went out to the garden this morning, Mrs. Cribbs came to find me. She wanted to show me something in the house, but she wouldn't tell me what it was. She wanted me to see. She took me up to the gallery. Your portrait was hanging there. You looked exactly like you did that day you popped up in my car, and all of a sudden everything started coming back. She told me the man in the portrait was the ninth earl, yet it was you. And then she told me the story. She'd read about it in some very old letters her grandmother had given her. She didn't know the story wasn't in the archives. I couldn't believe what I was remembering at first. I thought I was going mad with all the pictures and flashbacks I was seeing. But by the time she came to the end of the story and told me that the ninth earl's fate was still a mystery, I knew everything I was remembering was the truth...And that I could let myself love you because I knew now I wasn't going to lose you.

"I was shaking so badly, I could barely stand up. She took me down to the guides' lounge and gave me tea. I told her I was faint because I was pregnant. I didn't know what else to tell her. I don't know how long I sat there, but when it was all clear in my mind, I came to find you..."

"And you have found me."

"Christopher," I whispered, "how could you have endured being here all these days? It was one thing when I thought you were just a poor relation—but, my God, you were the earl! The master of this whole place. You owned it, you ran it. And then to come back to be treated the way you've been, as though you were a common tourist. No wonder Wadsworth thought you looked familiar—he'd probably seen your portrait, too."

His voice was deep when he answered. "I would be a liar if I said it has not bothered me being here the way things are. There were days when I wanted to scream the truth of who I was from the housetops. But I came to my sanity. It was a long time ago, Jessica, that I was lord and master here—I cannot confuse the two worlds. Cavenly is no longer mine, nor the title, nor the wealth. I have just as rich a future to look forward to, and that is all I care to think about at the moment."

"I never realized how much you had to lose when you came to my world," I said sadly.

He cupped my chin in his hand and brought my face up to his. "Just think of what I would lose if I had to go back."

The breeze gently rustled through the trees, the scent of flowers and new-mown hay lay heavy in the air, and the sunlight filtered through the overhanging branches to lay in puddles upon us. We'd found each other again. From this moment on, no wedge of time would drive us apart.

TWENTY-NINE

We finished up quickly at Cavenly, closing the doors of the muniment room behind us for the last time as we left with our precious knowledge.

The bit of evidence Christopher had finally discovered to substantiate his belief that he'd never returned to pick up the threads of his nineteenth century life was a personal journal written by his cousin James Algernon Dunlap, the traitor who had succeeded him. Though his cousin had methodically destroyed every other bit of information concerning Christopher's life from a period shortly before his disappearance through several years thereafter, some quirk in the man must have stayed his hand when it came to disposing of his own written account.

Christopher found the journal accidentally in the bottom of a cupboard in the muniment room. It had been hidden inside a metal box, hinges and lock now rusted, under a pile of unimportant documents. It had been only normal curiosity that had prompted him to pry open the box, and he hardly believed what he was seeing when he lifted out the fragile journal and inspected the yellowed pages. In precise terms James described his part in the foiled assassination plot, the fearful hours and days he spent following the capture of his accomplices, the sigh of relief he breathed upon hearing of the unexpected disappearance of his cousin, Christopher, the man who, he suspected, held very damning evidence against him. James told of the search that had taken place in the nine months following his cousin's disappearance, his own silent prayers that Christopher would never be found, or if he was, that his body would be lifeless. Finally the tension eased as the authorities showed signs of giving up the attempt and ceding the title and estates to James.

There was no mention of James's trying to shift the blame for his own treasonous actions onto his cousin's shoulders. No mention of his having attempted to smear Christopher's name. His posture instead seemed to be one of protective silence during the whole affair. The only action he did take, and that was done only after he was safely the possessor of his cousin's title and holdings for several months, was to destroy all of Christopher's written notes and any piece of material contained within the

walls of Cavenly relating to the last two years of Christopher's
occupancy.

James was no fool. He'd known for many years the low
esteem in which his cousin had held him. The written
memorandums and letters he'd found verified this. So he'd made
a personal effort during the following years to see that none of
the newspaper articles or accounts regarding his cousin's
unexplained disappearance were held within the house. In fact,
the only record of those troubled years was his own journal,
and that he was careful to keep hidden away from prying eyes.

For some time James was afraid what his journal revealed—
afraid that the monstrous head of his own perfidy would poke
above the ground, and in the event that horrible time ever came,
he wanted to be prepared. His plan was to point a finger of
accusation toward his cousin, to let it be believed that the man
had not disappeared mysteriously at all, but had made a timely
exit from the scene when the situation got too dangerous. This
was the story he had planned to tell, and since none of it could
be proved or disproved, his own part in the plot would not be
questioned.

But, as the years passed, his fears were nearly put to rest.
No ninth earl ever came forward to reclaim James' land, refute
his right to them, or bring the old scandal out of hiding. The old
man's mind wanted to be eased, but always in his private
moments, the fear and haunted feeling lingered. The crimes
he'd once planned became his personal ghost...and perhaps it
was a benevolent ghost, because his efforts to live above the
mark and make up for his earlier sins made him in the end a
provident and equitable lord.

There was more to it than just this knowledge, of course,
before we could write "The End" to this chapter in our lives.
We spent a few hours touring the rooms of Christopher's old
home so that I could see it with new eyes. It didn't seem to
pain my husband anymore to walk through the corridors and
apartments that held so many memories from the past, thinking
of the part he'd once played within the walls of Cavenly. I saw
the estate as though through the eyes of its might-have-been
mistress. Pictured it in its happier moments as Christopher filled
in for me the whole story of his life there.

We took a walk in the parkland arm in arm. We went up to
the gallery to see the portrait that had been the key to banishing
the fog in my mind, no longer caring if Mr. Wadsworth's eyes

were watching us. Christopher remembered the painting. It had been done shortly before his disappearance, and he assured me that he had, indeed, been wearing the same jacket that now hung in our closet at home.

Christopher had one more parting gesture to make before we left Cavenly behind for our humble home. In his own bold hand, he wrote an account of what, in truth, had happened to him, the Ninth Earl of Westerham, on that fateful day in May 1812. He told how he'd been carried away by forces he didn't understand to another century and another country, and how he tried to make a life for himself in this new world, never knowing if his stay would continue for the rest of his life or end with the setting sun. He described how the uncertainty of not knowing had driven him back to his home a hundred and sixty years after his leaving it to search through the family archives for some kind of proof or evidence. How he'd found what he'd sought, and now knew for a fact that he, the ninth earl, would not be coming back. He signed it, "Westerham, Christopher Robert Julian George Dunlap, Ninth Earl," a signature that could easily be authenticated should anyone attempt to check his story. He left his account tucked into the last pages of the family journal of births and deaths, where, we hoped, some future member of the family or an historian would find it, read it, and wonder.

For the supercilious Mr. Wadsworth, we left a patently insincere thank-you note, signed, "Jessica and Christopher R.J.G. Dunlap."

And, in saying our good-byes to Mrs. Cribbs, we handed her an envelope containing a recent full-face photo of Christopher, another of the two of us, and a third of the portrait of Christopher in the upstairs gallery. With the photos, we enclosed a personal note:

"Thank you for your friendliness and helpfulness during our visit to Cavenly and for the information you gave us about the Ninth Earl's disappearance. We are forever grateful. Study the resemblance in these photos and ponder the possibilities— but do keep your thoughts to yourself, unless you'd care to invent a new ghost for Cavenly. Perhaps you could bring the portrait of Christopher, the Ninth Earl, down from the gallery into one of the toured rooms, and regale the public with the stories of his mysterious disappearance. Such a plan could enhance your tourist revenues at Cavenly. Put the information in your old letters into the family archives for all future generations to see, keeping copies for yourself—and, under no circumstance trust Wadsworth. He has unscrupulous motives of his own and should be fired. Alert the current Earl and suggest that he have Wadsworth's account records checked by an outside source. We suspect the man is skimming profits. Commend the current Earl on his overall wise maintenance of this historic home, but tell him he needs to get in new breeding stock. The Thoroughbreds and hunters currently in his paddocks are too light-boned, and are perhaps too inbred to popular stallions. They'll injure easily and won't have sufficient stamina to win big prizes on the jump course, or have long racing lives. The Ninth Earl's stock was far more hardy and durable. Perhaps the best person to talk to is the on-estate manager—have him or her put a flea in the Earl's ear.

"Finally, we wish you well, and ask that you keep this correspondence of ours confidential. Save it, but don't make it public until you are ready to pass on your memoirs to the next generation. Again, we wish you well,

"The Earl and his 20th century Countess."

Obviously, Christopher had written all of the message about keeping an eye on his former estate, but I'd added my ideas, too. In particular, I was the one who suggested moving the portrait and building a mysterious myth around it, which Christopher only agreed to when he saw how such a myth would add to the coffers of his former estate and keep it solvent for years longer. In the back of his mind, I think he felt like he was still running the estate.

We left England on a Sunday evening, just a little over a year after his first, unconventional departure from his native soil. In our minds the future was secure. We had nothing to anticipate but the birth of our first child and good years ahead. When we reached home, we'd begin looking for that old colonial house in the country we both wanted. We could be firmly within its walls by the time our child was born, live out our days there, raise our family, and build together. Christopher would have his horses. I would help, and we would have our peace.

THIRTY

Today is Christmas morning. I wake to see my husband lying beside me, still asleep. So much has happened since our return to Connecticut. We have our house in the country, with its acres of land and two horses to start our stables. I lie contentedly under the covers of our four-poster, a replica of the one in his room at Cavenly, though a trifle smaller.

My husband is waking, his eyelids flicker. He rolls to his side to face me as his eyes open. He smiles sleepily. "I love you," he whispers.

And I love him, with a love that grows deeper and more meaningful as each day passes. I've learned to appreciate what I have and not take one moment for granted.

Our son, born almost a month ago, lies sleeping peacefully in the small room adjoining ours. Christopher had had his wish fulfilled to see our child born—perhaps more explicitly than he'd expected when he was at my side watching our son gasp his first breaths of life. As the baby's outraged cries had echoed in the air of the delivery room, I thought my husband would burst from the seams with pride and joy. Christopher Robert J. G. Dunlap, Jr. slumbers on in his room, unaware of the joy he has brought his parents...parents who thought at one time they might be worlds apart by the time of his birth. My little tenth earl, as I like to call him teasingly, is a beautiful baby who looks, even in his unformed baby features, exactly like his father. His father prefers to think our son resembles me. We could split hairs on this issue, but it really doesn't matter, just as long as we are all together.

We'll have a busy day today. It's off to Dana and Jim's, where the proud godparents can indulge their longings to pamper and spoil our little son. For now, Christopher and I can enjoy a few minutes of quiet togetherness before little Christopher's hunger pangs rouse him for his morning meal.

"Merry Christmas, my love." I turn to look at his waiting face.

"And Merry Christmas to you." He smiles in warm invitation, reaching out his arms.

"Not so close! Remember we still have one in the cradle."

Laughing, he pulls me against him anyway. "Why did my father never tell me of the horrors of post-pregnancy? Here is your luscious body back in its proper, seductive state, and nothing to be done about it."

"Think of what you have to look forward to."

"That is precisely what I am thinking, only I doubt I have the patience." He draws me down under the covers beside him until my head is nestled on his shoulder.

I bury my lips in his hairy chest. "Still love me, Christopher?"

"That much should be obvious." His eyes gleam down to mine and his lips move closer, but before our mouths have time to touch, the wailings begin in the next room, and steadily grow stronger. "Our son..."

"Hungry as usual. Shall I bring him in here?"

"Yes. Let us all spend our Christmas morning in here."

I rise and wrap my robe around me as our child's cries increase. He's wet, of course, soaked through and in need of a change. I put him in clean diapers and a warm gown, kissing both his chubby cheeks lovingly, then bring him in to see his daddy.

Christopher is sitting on the edge of the bed in his robe, his dark hair tousled his eyes bright with happiness. He spreads out his arms, welcoming. "Ah, let me wish my fine son a Merry Christmas, too." He is smiling.

I walk toward him, our child cradled in my arms, my answering smile radiant with the love within me for my husband and my son.

Christopher starts to rise, his arms still outstretched, when suddenly his smiling face begins to fade. His image is one moment bright, the next shadowy, wavering in the morning light. I blink my eyes once, twice. It makes no difference. He is still a blur before me, growing more vague, more obscure.

The smile on his lips is disappearing, being supplanted by alarm. He calls to me, but his voice seems to be coming from miles in the distance. I hear the echoed, "Jessica, come quickly! Take my hand!"

Holding the baby, I rush forward, my feet feeling leaden, reaching out with one arm for Christopher. His face and body are growing hazier and hazier...dim...mere outlines. I search for his hand. It's only inches away. I can barely see him. Where are his fingers? Oh, God, let me find them! I feel them...feel their warmth and strength as they close tightly about my hand. His eyes stare at me, brilliant, blue, unwavering, beautiful....

Then there is nothing.

EPILOGUE IN THE FORM
OF AN AUTHOR'S NOTE

Life is rarely fair, but a reader of this book needs to think optimistically, as I have done, about where "Then there was nothing" can lead.

Don't fear, I've written a sequel to this book. Don't cry and throw the book across the room, as previous readers have told me they've done. Just wait for the strange twists of the sequel, *Love Once Again,* coming from ImaJinn Books next month.

Jo Ann Simon

LaVergne, TN USA
16 December 2010
209002LV00001B/118/A

10